THE SHADOW GAME

A TEAM WALKER NOVEL

RODGER CARLYLE

This is a work of fiction. The names, characters, entities, and events are products of the author's imagination and bear no relation to any living person or are used fictitiously.

The Library of Congress Control Number: 2023912772

Published in the United States by Verity Books, an imprint of Comsult, LLC, Anchorage, Alaska. Inquiries may be directed to comsultalaska@gmail.com.

First published in 2023.

ISBN 978-1-960268-07-5 (paperback)
ISBN 978-1-960268-06-8 (e-book)

Cover design and formatting: Damonza

Books by Rodger Carlyle

THE TEAM WALKER SERIES

The Eel And The Angel

The Shadow Game

THE CHAD GRITT SERIES

Enemy Patriots

The Opposite Of Trust

Two Civil Wars

NONFICTION

Awake

Still Common Sense

Preface

The two Land Rovers in front of him began to slow. Thankful that he'd finally caught up to them Ahmed flashed his lights one more time and released his foot from the accelerator. Something streaked down from the sky followed by a second streak.

Instantly, the two vehicles in front of him disintegrated, their doors, windows and hoods flying through the air. Before he could touch the brakes, the blast flipped his Mercedes into the air and then it cartwheeled. Ahmed was still conscious when everything finally came to rest. He reached for his cellphone, or at least he tried, but neither arm would respond to his efforts. Then, everything around him went dark.

Chapter 1

FARID'S LIFE WAS only possible because of the kind of money his professor father and later his widowed mother could have never afforded. Until graduation day, all he knew about the uncle who provided him with a privileged lifestyle was that his mother had begged Farid to follow the uncle's wishes. Topping the list was to study and succeed in school, followed by learning how politics worked in Europe and in the United States, ignoring the trauma of his early life in Isfahan and Beirut, preparing for a successful international business career, and recognizing the debt to those who funded his life and be prepared to pay it back.

The smile on his mother's face as they left the ceremony made what admittedly was not a difficult existence even more worthwhile. As they slid into the limo next to his uncle, she lifted his right hand and kissed all of his fingers, reciting a prayer in Farsi. She rarely spoke in Farsi, although she made sure that her son learned the language as well as Arabic and the English he used every day. He mastered French while attending exclusive preparatory schools.

The brutal humidity of an unusually scorching English day made the limo's air conditioning welcome.

His uncle smiled as the driver worked his way through the crowded streets to the private airport where a Euro copter waited to deliver them across the English Channel. There would be no record of the flight. The pilots would hug the ocean on the return to France, but nothing seemed out of line to the young man.

The uncle had trusted and encouraged Farid's intellect. Farid's lack of personal discipline came with the British education. It was a risk, but one that his uncle prayed Farid could control.

"Tell me of the job offer?" offered Karim. He smiled at Leila, his sister-in-law.

"WILTON Limited is a global freight company, with twenty-some offices around the world. They started in marine shipping but when a new investment group took control a year ago, WILTON became interested in aviation. I'll be the primary assistant to the operational vice-president," answered Farid, wiping beads of sweat from his forehead. "They see great growth potential in the Middle East. They also do contract work for governments." Farid opened the tiny refrigerator across from his seat and considered opening a bottle of champagne, but instead grabbed a bottled water. He guessed that his acquired taste for alcohol wouldn't go over well with his uncle.

"And they accepted that I would not be able to start work for a month," he added. They have staff from all over the world, all with different customs. They didn't bat an eye when I told them that it was expected that I reconnect with my family before rushing out into the world. They really want me, someone who speaks multiple languages fluently, with an Oxford MBA.

"Would you be based here in England?" asked Karim.

"Maybe. Their main offices are here, but the majority of their business operations are in America. I will be expected to travel a lot. That will not make Sarah very happy."

"I am sure that she isn't happy today," said Farid's mother. "I'm sure that she planned on celebrating your success with you. It is a bit unfair to sweep you out of London the very day that you graduate."

"I told her weeks ago that you planned to bring family and old friends together for a short celebration in Paris," replied Farid. "Sarah is spending the next five days with her parents. Her grandfather owns a summer home right on the coast in Wales. It's a nice get away from the family business in the states."

"And she accepted being left out of our celebration?" asked Karim.

"She was okay with it," answered Farid. "She isn't much on traditional Moslem celebrations. Not enough champagne."

Karim felt his mother squeeze his hand and watched as she wiped a tear from the corner of her eye. "We will discuss the celebration on the helicopter."

From Biggin Hill Airport to Karim's estate north of Paris was less than two hours. They were barely off the ground when Karim opened the MacBook he carried and tapped a few commands. As the first photograph opened, he handed the computer to Leila.

"I have some photographs to show you, my son. They will be difficult, but it is important that you see them."

The image was of two Land Rovers, reduced to scrap and a third car, a Mercedes upside down on a narrow highway. The Land Rovers were torn and twisted almost beyond recognition. The glass was blown out of the Mercedes, its doors forced open. There was blood everywhere. Leila pressed a key on the computer. The next picture was of a man with twisted limbs on a stretcher being loaded into an ambulance. Leila's hands froze over the keyboard. Farid's uncle reached across and tapped another key on the laptop.

The next image was of four torn bodies and smashed heads held together by fabric.

"The one on the left in the rear was your father," said Leila.

The next picture was of a small funeral celebration at a location just outside of Beirut where Farid had spent a dozen years of his life. An early life filled with fears and distrust fueled by conflict between the Shia and Suni power brokers in Lebanon, Israeli threats and conflict involving the handful of Christians who somehow remained. Farid recognized the Suni Mullah from his early days in the mosque, the same man who had pressed his mother to leave the country and accept the invitation of her brother-in-law in Paris.

The following photo was of a much larger funeral and the next picture an even larger one. Farid didn't recognize the location of either.

"Save your questions my son," said Leila. "They will all be answered by tonight. You will meet those who can enlighten you, men from across the Middle East."

Farid had expected a large group to greet the helicopter. Instead, one graying man dressed all in black waited in a four-person golf cart. It was the same man who often accompanied his uncle on his trips to England. The man nodded to Karim and Farid as he helped Leila into the cart. He said nothing, as expected, since in the half-dozen times Farid had been around Ahmed, they had exchanged maybe a dozen words.

The five-minute cart ride from the helicopter to the home seemed to go on forever. In the last few years, Farid seldom heard about his father. He had been the love of his mother's life and his uncle's closest brother. He knew that his father had died in a terrorist attack only a few years before. Never had anyone shared the photographs he'd just seen or been willing to discuss the death. Why now on a day of celebration?

Ahmed hurried Farid, his mother and Karim past the butler and the two maids waiting near the door, almost racing to reach the library. Throwing open the doors to the cavernous room he repeated "Our day is finally come," first in English, then Farsi and finally in Arabic. He quietly closed the door and waited as the others moved into the room.

Instead of the large family gathering Farid expected, three men, all about sixty, wearing suits rose from heavy leather chairs. Karim slowed, shaking hands with each as he introduced his nephew.

"Reza here is the primary banker of the group you are being introduced to. He was born in Liverpool." The man was small and almost bald, his suit tailored but crumpled. Reza held a pair of bottle thick glasses in his left hand.

"Salman is the primary strategist of our movement.

His father is an advisor to the Saudi crown family." This man was the opposite of Reza; tall and lean like a leopard, he wore a nondescript brown suit that might have come right off the rack at Harrods.

"Mohamed is the liaison with our Iranian partners. Like your mother, father, and uncles, he was one of the Suni who left Iran when the Shah fell." Mohamed's smile gave away crooked teeth above a simple blue tie that clashed with his tan cotton suit.

Farid greeted each with a different response. The European greeting was followed by the traditional Salam Alaikum Arabic greeting and then simply Salam, standard in Iran.

"English would be easiest for your conversation," offered his mother to Farid. "All of us have waited years for this moment. You will make us all proud. Now, please excuse me." Ahmed held the door for her as she rushed from the room.

"And I am the leader of this small group," announced Ahmed. "I am the eldest brother of your father and of Karim. I am the man on the stretcher in the photos you studied on your trip across the English Channel. I am also the one man alive who sits at the left hand of the leaders of many groups committed to raising the influence of true believers in the world. I am close to even those who I disagree with, believing in that old Arab proverb, *The enemy of my enemy is my friend*. Your father hated that saying. He dreamed of a Middle East united by the words of the Prophet, with friends across the world.

Karim watched his nephew carefully, sensing shock on the young man's face. "We are not hypocrites, Farid. We are modern men, living in a modern world. We do not begrudge the Europeans their culture in their lands or the Asians the life they have always known in their countries. We move comfortably in those worlds. What we seek is the same for people in the Middle East. Your father mistakenly believed that the Suni and Shia were seeking the same thing. Many of the leaders of Jihad were lunatics. He gave his life supporting the Iranians in their efforts to convince the Americans to go home and to embrace the other Moslem sects. They betrayed him just like they betrayed our family years before. Many remain unwilling to give up their ancient dream of making the Shia faith the only true faith of the believers."

Farid stood stone still trying to take it all in. He had not prepared for anything except a celebration. The others remained still until he dropped into one of the leather chairs next to the massive fireplace.

Karim took the chair next to him. "Your father was the intellect in the family. He was the student and the pragmatic optimist who dedicated his life to you and your mother, but also to recreating the glory of the Middle East, one stolen by outsiders and sabotaged by a centuries old conflict that has no meaning in the modern word. While I worked at making money, your father was committed to changing the world. He was a university professor. Ahmed had been an officer in the Iranian army under the Shah. He was committed to your father's vision and as the eldest brother, to trying to help your father in spite of his propensity to trust everyone he met."

"Tell me of my father's death. Tell me of the other funerals."

"Your father was asked by the leader of what became known as the ISIS Caliphate, to come to Iraq. Your father, born in the holiest city in Iran like your mother, the so-called Emir believed that he could bridge the gap between the Caliphate and the Iranian militias that were fighting beside the Americans to destroy the Islamic State. Your father always believed that the schism between the branches of Islam was silly, a centuries-old spat over who rightfully inherited the leadership of Mohamed's movement. He believed that both could unite realizing that the word was the only thing that was important. He believed that the western powers were exploiting the ancient disagreement to slowly take wealth from the land and warp the minds of the faithful."

Karim continued, "the first funeral picture was the one in Lebanon, the one you attended. The second was held in Syria on the one day when the ISIS fighters and Iranian militia members put down their arms to celebrate the new martyrs. The last was in Tehran where your father was eulogized along with the Revolutionary Guard Corps members and militia members killed by the American air strikes. The Iranian regime paid tribute to his death even as they worked tirelessly to destroy his message.

Karim slid his chair closer to his nephew. "I am sorry that I never introduced you to Ahmed, your other uncle. We believed that keeping you focused on your studies was more important than challenging you to launch yourself into a rightful reprisal for the traitorous death of your father. Ahmed is still focused on righting that wrong on the movement and our family. We were afraid that he would share too much and set you off on a personal jihad before you were ready. But now you are here, prepared and positioned to help us make this all right."

Farid ran through the math in his mind. Much of what he was hearing was old history to a man of twenty-four.

The seriousness of the moment clicked into his brain as he realized how patiently those present waited. If he'd been a perfect student, he would have finished his education in three years, not five.

"And, young man, you will perhaps put an end to both the Shia-Suni conflict and the dominance of the Americans in our lands," said Salman lighting a small thin cigar. "There should be no one country representing the faithful. Each should select their own leaders, with only one pre-condition: faith must be central to the culture of the nations. Some may adopt democratic forms of government while others may remain comfortable with monarchy. But for that to happen, the extremes of the Iranian government and its power must be destroyed, and the Americans and other western powers must realize that medaling in the affairs of our lands is more costly than it is worth. We should be free to evolve as we see fit. Our family dedicated years to that vision. Only seven years ago, your father gave his life to it."

Farid watched as the small balding man from Liverpool used a cane to rise. "On equal terms, we will engage with the world. We can be a power for peace across the globe. But our window is closing. With the enormous mineral wealth of our region, we should be the financial center of the world. The world needs our oil and gas, but the damned Russians have spent two decades convincing the West that fossil fuels are bad instead of working with us to reduce their impact on the environment. If we do not act soon, reliance on our one great advantage will be diminished to the point where we become unimportant."

"And why have the Russians done what they have done?" asked Farid.

"Because the idiot leading the country has not figured out that we are in the twenty-first century, not the 1700s. He is obsessed with destroying the west, especially the U.S., and one of his strategies is to use propaganda to get them to weaken themselves. He encourages them to abandon fossil fuels even as he knows that it is impossible for perhaps another century. He still believes that territory is power. Putin is sitting on the richest mineral wealth in the world with a small, educated population and cannot see how powerful his country could be in 100 years if they just develop it. Instead, he seeks power only from conquest like some ancient warlord. His fiasco in Ukraine set Russia back decades. The good news is he has extended the window for our plans by accident. Russian petroleum deliveries are way down, and in the West, their own weakened oil industry is incapable of supplying the needs. Our region alone is keeping the world's economy operating."

Farid's initial shock was wearing off. "I understand the responsibility of a son to avenge a father's murder. I am my father's son. But you still haven't told me of my father's actual death."

Ahmed leaned back in his chair and closed his eyes before speaking. "The caliphate was crumbling, unable to overcome the power of the Americans, the Russians helping a dictator in Syria and the weak Iraqi army supported by Iranian controlled militias. Your father was touring each Shia militia, one at a time in hopes of getting them to stop killing fellow Muslims. He wasn't part of the caliphate, just an advisor. I was traveling with him, to coordinate security. The militias, upon orders from Tehran were ratcheting up attacks on the Americans which would have been okay except that at the same time they were working with the same Americans to destroy the Islamic State fighters once and for all. Most of your father's meetings degenerated into diatribes against the Americans. To those militias controlled by Iran, the only enemy worse were the fighters united under Suni banners, especially the ISIS black flag."

Ahmed stood and strode purposefully over to a bookcase, removing a large binder. He opened it and handed it to Farid. "Read the article under the green tab."

It took Farid a minute to read a New York Times article on an American strike to kill the leader of the leader of Iran's Revolutionary Guard Corps. The Americans had used a missile equipped drone to kill the man they blamed for planning most of the attacks on Americans across Iraq and Syria.

"I read about the attack on General Soleimani. Frankly, I think the world is better off without him," offered Farid.

"Later in the article, you will read about other strikes the same day. The Americans went after the leadership of several of the Iranian backed militias. They knew that there was a conference planned for that day and attacked several of the militia leaders while they traveled."

"I think I knew about that too," offered Farid.

"What you didn't know was that one militia leader was late leaving. He was delayed by a meeting with your father; a very heated meeting, one where your father was accused of actually helping kill militia members and of siding with the Americans." Ahmed seemed to wipe away a tear.

"As they wrapped up, a messenger whispered into the ear of the Shia leader. I believe he told the leader about attacks on other militias. The leader excused himself for a few minutes, I believe to phone Iran for advice. He looked rattled when he returned but offered to help us.

Instead of traveling himself he called your father into his office and told him that if he hurried, he might be able to catch the last couple of hours of a militia executive meeting where he could plead his case. He offered his car and driver as well as bodyguards to escort him to the meeting. He sent your father out knowing that any convoy from the compound might be a target. Instead of hitting the militia leader the Americans killed your father."

"But they didn't kill you," said Farid, his face twisted.

"I left the building to give your father privacy in his discussions. Outside I heard rumors of the attacks and walked across the compound to the militia's intelligence headquarters. Returning, I heard your father had rushed out, trying to save something from a disastrous day. We always traveled with our phones shut off to avoid being tracked, so my only hope was to catch up. I commandeered a Mercedes at gunpoint and raced after them. The Land Rovers were coasting to a stop when the missiles hit. I wasn't targeted, just too close to avoid the destruction."

Karim handed his older brother a clean handkerchief from his lapel pocket as he watched him fight off the tears forming in his eyes. "Farid, both the Americans and the Iranians are responsible for your father's death. Both are in the way of the lands we want to return to our people. We have a plan to target both, to right this wrong. And if we are successful, we may just land the one blow that makes our world whole again. We were once a land of poetry, music, astronomy, and mathematics; much of the world's culture came from us. Even an enemy was safe if he had been invited into our home."

Farid's incredulous look showed what he was thinking. "How do we do this?"

"To begin with we will take advantage of the fact that the Iranians and Americans do not like or trust each other." He motioned toward Salman. "Some years ago, Salman outlined a complicated plan, and we began preparing. We discovered one flaw, a hole. You are the one who must fill in the missing piece of the puzzle."

"I don't hate the Americans or the French or the English," offered Farid. "The Americans should pay for the death of my father, but even the Russians could not confront them."

"Nor do we," answered Reza. "We just want them to leave our lands so that the culture has time to really take root with the people. The teachings of our faith need to be stripped of the false interpretations. We need time to resurrect the civilization that once made the Middle East the center of culture and learning. In the future, the Western world is a logical partner."

"But your father's vision of bringing the Iranian dictatorship into the plan was always a pipedream," added Ahmed. "As long as they hate everybody who is different, the world remains divided and very dangerous. They now embrace the bloody Russians. No rational nation embraces them. The Iranian regime are hypocrites and defile the teachings of the prophet. There will be blood spilled to destroy them and to push the Westerners out of the Middle East. You will be part of a small army that will dip swords into the blood of thousands. But it will all come quickly, and that blood will nourish a reawakened people."

"We have spent years preparing you for one tiny part,

Farid. We will avenge your father together. We know we can count on you," added Karim.

Farid leaned back in his chair, again dabbing sweat from his brow in the cool room.

Chapter 2

THE CIA HEADQUARTERS at Langley, Virginia was always a hub of activity, literally a building full of worker bees all doing their part to keep America safe. Unlike a beehive with one queen, the building was divided into sections, each responsible for one piece of gathering information from the world, especially from unfriendly sources, and figuring out what it meant. Then they would figure out what to do about it. The screaming frenzy of only a year before, a frenzy created by the one thing that everyone hated more than anything else, was over. The group had been blindsided by a unique technology, a hybrid machine built by China that was almost undetectable. The agency knew something was out there but had no idea that any such technology could exist. People in the building hated a vacuum, a total unknown. It scared the hell out of them.

But that crisis had ended. Both sides backed away learning a bit more about the other and a lot more about themselves. That compromise left the agency free to go back to the study of more normal problems, like terrorism and nuclear proliferation and cyber warfare.

Director Mathew Chang began his morning briefing with his trained focus even though in his heart he was already teeing up the ball for his first golf game in a month. That morning's written brief included a report on Iranian efforts to bridge the last hurdles toward building a nuclear weapon as well as a report on the turmoil in Russia as their president battled to retain power, his credibility and judgement damaged by his blunder and quagmire in Ukraine. The final part was on three nations rumored to be developing nuclear weapons. Two of them were friends, but friends that had grown concerned about American willingness to help protect them. The third; well, it appeared to CIA analysts to be a case of a third world country angling for a big payoff not to develop a weapon. Just another day in the office for Chang. Nothing in the paper to interrupt an afternoon of golf.

He turned to the first briefer; Pete Wilson who headed the department focused on technology. "Pete, how long have we been discussing the Iranian nuclear risk?"

"Mat," started Wilson, "this has been part of our briefing for years. Every month the risk increases as the Iranians get closer to perfecting their design and enriching uranium to weapons grade. Today's threat remains as it has been for months, dangerous but not imminent." Wilson referred to his notes. "If they really want a bomb, they can produce one in weeks. Some of my people believe they already have enough enriched uranium. Such a weapon would be a threat primarily to regional adversaries since they have no viable delivery vehicle to threaten the continental U.S. We have not been able to clarify whether the new love affair between Russia and Iran includes Russian support for Iranian nuclear passions. On paper it would appear to be minimal as Iran also has interest in the conflicts between the Moscow regime and Russia's Islamic regions." Pete went on to discuss three other issues and was relieved when Chang didn't ask for more on anything.

Only months before it had been Pete's group that took a few minutes to interview an analyst from the Navy's Farragut Technical Analysis Center, a man who had patiently pieced together dozens of tiny threads that pointed to the Chinese Government's EEL project. His meticulous puzzle building had convinced Pete that the Chinese had fielded a virtually undetectable system to spy on America in its most protected places. Pete, unlike other intelligence leaders believed Lieutenant Chad Gritt, (the latest in a long line of Chad Gritts). Part of Pete's confidence in the young man came from a computer profile about the Gritt family over two centuries. But that was last year's problem.

"By now the Iranians must have some inkling of our ANGEL technology," added Wilson as he began to wrap up. "They know that we have something that stopped the Chinese with their advanced air delivery capability. They backed down. The Iranians must be back to square one."

Jana Taylor, the Director of Operations followed Wilson's report. With so many operations taking place around the world, she focused only on those dealing with immediate threats or longer term issues that might be catastrophic. With Wilson, she'd helped convince Chang that the Chinese espionage threat demanded immediate action. With that threat under control, nothing on her list was immediate or catastrophic. She knew that Chang needed a break, so she kept her presentation short.

"We continue to be focused on the threat of international terrorism, especially Islamic threats," she concluded. "ISIS and the remnants of that movement remain dangerous, but much of their command structure is gone, and we've managed to infiltrate the two remaining groups. Neither seems to be plotting anything except how to survive with most of the world trying to stamp them out. There remain groups from both Islamic houses who wish us harm."

The briefing was over in an hour.

Chang was pleased to see Chad Gritt's 1960 Corvette parked near where his limo dropped him and his golf clubs at the clubhouse. His game today would include only Gritt, and two bodyguards, both of whom knew when to disappear when he signaled them. For the third time in two months, he would try to coax the young officer into working for the agency.

Chang always puzzled himself as he struggled with his shy demeanor. Somehow a shy man fit perfectly into the job of running the world's premier intelligence agency. All four men had managed to drive their balls into the fairway of the fifth hole before Mat's conversation strayed from golf. "Are you settling back into the routine of research yet?" he asked Chad.

"Kind of. I guess I'm a lot like Thadius Walker, who lost his medical after flying for the Navy and turned back to education. Study bored him to death." Gritt smiled thinking about Walker, the aging spy who had mentored him through the China crisis. He could visualize the man and his dog sitting on a dock on Montana's Flathead Lake.

"I didn't know that about Thad when I asked him to

head up the team that put the EEL and Angel crisis with China to bed. Did he ever go to law school?"

"No, and I don't for a minute believe that you don't know his history, right down to what color socks he wore playing little league baseball," replied Chad with a laugh. "My point is that I'm not Walker, and I am not about to allow the adrenalin letdown from that operation ruin my Navy career."

Mat signaled for the two bodyguards to give him and Gritt a little privacy. He waited until each picked up their balls rather than play them. "You know Walker's career in the Navy ended differently than he had hoped. He ended up in the Marines but could never point a gun at another human being. That's the only reason he became one of us."

"We had enough time together for me to learn most of his story, the part that he will talk about and that is unclassified."

"Did you know that he worked for us while still in the Marine Corps?"

Chad didn't respond as he focused on playing a four iron. He ran his ball up within twenty yards of the green. Pleased with the shot, he gave himself permission to needle one of the most powerful men in the American government. "Director, you are about a subtle as the crowd at the Army-Navy game after Navy kicks Army's ass."

Chang laughed. "I just want you to remember that you don't have to give up anything permanently to come work for us."

"I'm on a project right now that is pretty damned important, Director. Knowing that our ANGEL technology makes it pretty hard to deliver a nuclear attack from the air, the Navy has me running what-if scenarios on underwater and surface weapon delivery possibilities."

Chang wasn't about to give up. He was Korean American and a master of the long game. He'd delivered the message that he wanted Chad to hear, so he changed the topic.

"Have you kept in touch with that Air Force Major you worked with in the Aleutian Islands; the woman who impressed the entire pentagon when her base police force battled those elite Chinese commandoes punch for punch?"

Gritt realized that Chang knew the answer, or he wouldn't have asked. Still, it bothered him that the Director of the CIA was interested in his relationship with Olga Tvorshik. His interest in the beautiful red head was no longer a military one. "Yup," was all he said, and then added, "it's a little tough to do anything but FaceTime when she's six thousand miles away."

The men finished their game and headed to the clubhouse for a beer as the two bodyguards moved ahead to assess any risk. Chad watched as four other men in Chang's security detail compressed their perimeter. He wondered if there were already additional security people in the bar. The lack of privacy was one of the things that really worried him about becoming part of the agency, but he wouldn't have the problems the guy at the top had.

"There is a Senatorial inquiry planned on the EEL and ANGEL incident," offered Chang as he sipped his beer. "That Major will be called upon to testify."

"I hadn't heard about any congressional hearings," replied Gritt, wiping a bit of beer foam from his lips.

"There won't be any publicity about this one, no

public report, and no grandstanding even though there are a couple of senators on the committee who are publicity hounds."

Chad knew that Chang probably had already sent a briefing paper to the committee members and his staff would be working closely with their staff to set it all up. His own security clearance was high enough that it was only a matter of time until he would hear about the hearing. He'd be called to testify. But he also knew that Chang wouldn't have brought it up without a reason.

"You can't communicate this to anyone," added Chang, "not even to Major Tvorshik, but she will need to be here for the hearing one month from today." Chang finished his beer and signaled that he was ready to leave. "You might consider stealing a little time from your job in that time period, you know, to see if you two can connect in person as well as over a digital connection."

Chang rose and extended a hand to Chad. I just wanted to give you a little heads up, Lieutenant." Chang started toward the door and then turned. "Sometimes we should play a round where we keep score."

Gritt had heard that while Chang was almost a scratch golfer, he never kept score. He hated making people uncomfortable when he won, and he really hated to lose.

Chapter 3

TRAVEL WOULD HAVE been easier on his uncle's Gulfstream, but it would also have made Farid's travel the subject of gossip and probably even the intelligence services of several countries. Even in France, which for decades had been home to his family, the French kept an eye on them, worried about political activity that might put France in danger or interfere with the notorious French custom to overlook politics and international commitments to make a buck.

In 1979, when the family fled Iran and the mobs welcoming the Ayatollah, they moved north along highways in a convoy of twelve trucks and more than thirty cars and limousines. Advance teams of heavily armed men, many employees of family owned businesses cleared the way for their trip. Tens of millions of dollars in antiques, art, jewelry, and other possessions filled the trucks. The eight heavy Mercedes limos that transported the family also carried millions in gold bars quietly withdrawn from bank vaults over the previous weeks of turmoil in Tehran. Other cars carried the families of their guards. Great additional wealth awaited the family in Swiss and French banks.

All in the convoy were on their way to a new life, but more than a dozen of the extended family had already died as the revolutionaries swept away most of those who served the Shah.

Cash payments to Kurdish groups in the north, people already terrified by the rise of militant Shia private armies, gave the family additional protection before crossing the border into Turkey. Friendly Suni businessmen made their trip across Turkey almost a vacation. The elite of Turkey's Suni business community entertained the immediate family in Ankara before a chartered Boeing flew them to Paris. The rest of the convoy was loaded on a ferry for the long trip across the Mediterranean to France.

The family transferred many of their business holdings in Iran to trusted lieutenants, most of whom remained loyal. There were no records of wealth moving from those business interests to the family in France. Instead, the lieutenants lived wealthy lives as the new owners, which included numerous trips abroad where they deposited cash in bank accounts from Greece to Germany. That money was in untraceable accounts held by interlocking corporations and shell companies. After four decades the total cash available had mushroomed.

Further declared investments in Europe created a cash flow that afforded an extravagant lifestyle including several private aircraft and homes across Europe. But private jets were easy to track and from the day the family decided that they had an obligation to right the wrongs that were limiting the advancement of the people in their homeland, strict care was taken to separate the successful lives of the family from the invisible organization they were building. What had been a subtle movement for years became a war after the betrayal and death of Farid's father.

There was no one there to meet Farid at the airport in Tbilisi, Georgia. He grabbed a cab to the Sheraton Grand Hotel. His room on the third floor was nicer than his flat in London, but rather utilitarian compared to his uncle's estate. After a short rest, he wandered down to the lobby and inquired about local museums. Armed with a tourist map and a recommendation he headed out, walking. He was only two blocks from the hotel when a cab with the number 16 emblazoned on the roof pulled to the curb in front of him.

"Do you need a ride?" called the driver. "You look like you are lost."

The passwords he had been told to wait for, "you look like you are lost," led Farid into the back seat of the old Renault. Ten minutes later the cab pulled into the interior courtyard of an old Soviet style building. A sign on the building read, INSTITUTE FOR BLACK SEA HISTORY. Farid followed the driver's counsel, through the main door and up two flights of stairs where Salman was waiting. He could hear conversations coming from what he assumed were classrooms on the way.

"I myself, only arrived here last night," offered the man who his uncle had introduced as the strategist, Salman. "Farid, please follow me."

Farid followed the man through a double door at the end of the hall, and then through a second metal security door. Finally, Salman opened the door to an enclosed room where five men waited. "This secure room was once used by the Russian GRU intelligence services when

Georgia was part of the Soviet Union," offered Salman. "There is no guarantee that the American or British could not listen in on us here, but the Georgian government has nothing that could compromise us."

Farid took a seat in the windowless room and waited for Salman to speak.

"Tell me, Farid, just what your uncles told you about our operations."

Farid prayed that his nervousness wasn't showing, but the knot in his stomach was almost crippling. "They explained that we intend to foment a war between Iran and the U.S. The goal is to create real fear in the Americans, a fear that will lead them to destroy the regime in Iran. The hope is that agitation against the regime will lead to an Islamic government that embraces all believers. The regime has been weakened by years of protest by the people."

Farid closely watched the man across from him. "The last thing the Americans want is to get bogged down in another protracted Middle East war. Our plan destroys those who guard the regime. Then we will help create a stable government quickly and avoid the propensity of Americans to remake every place they occupy into a little American democracy."

Salman nodded. "All of that is accurate. Your walk around the grounds of Karim's estate was successful. I hope you understand that the organization's leaders can only talk in generalities in any place where they may be compromised. That is part of our security protocol. With the exception of this building and two others, even general conversations only occur outside and far from places where listening devices are useful."

Farid really needed a cup of coffee, or even better a drink. He settled on something less obtrusive. "Would you have a bottle of water available?"

Salman motioned at one of the men. All conversation stopped until he closed the secure door behind him and handed Farid a Perrier. Farid emptied almost half of the bottle before speaking. "It is a very aggressive and dangerous plan, and I have many questions."

Salman just nodded. "Your uncles were to encourage your questions."

"How do we raise such fear in a nation with the world's most formidable military? If we provoke the Americans, what will keep them from turning most of Iran into a parking lot? If we stage attacks on either country, how do we ensure that they believe that it is their enemy hitting them and not some third party? If the Americans weaken the regime in Tehran, how can we know that it will not be replaced by someone from the Revolutionary Guard or another Shia hardliner? Assuming we are talking about armed attacks on both nations, how do we get weapons that can terrify a government into their country, especially into the U.S. where I'm sure they have a tight security ring?" Farid paused. He would have more questions, but these were the ones he had practiced on the Air France flight from Paris. He waited for Salman's answer.

"Allow me to introduce these men. ONE here is coordinating the technicians who are developing the weapons we will use. TWO is responsible for identifying the targets in the U.S. THREE is doing the same for targets in Iran as well as figuring out how to make any attack look like American retaliation. FOUR is responsible for ensuring that there are information leaks from each side that implicate the other and that ratchet up the tensions. FIVE controls security."

ONE, TWO THREE, FOUR, FIVE, Farid didn't know if this was normal security or if there was some question about him. He decided that it didn't really matter.

Salman opened a leather briefcase in front of him and extracted a blank pad and a box of pencils. "I find that I remember things better if I write them down," he said as he slid the pad across the table to Farid. "Feel free to take notes but understand that those notes and the pad will not leave this room and will be destroyed when you leave in three days." He stood and turned toward a map on a stand in the corner of the room.

"My introductions referring to these men by number is part of the security plan," said Salman. "We will be brief this afternoon since we want to leave you time to visit the museum long enough to discuss it if anyone asks. Now to your questions in the order that you asked. First, how will we raise fear in America to the point where they react but not overreact?" He pointed towards the four men seated across the table.

"We want to be prepared to strike two or three American targets," offered TWO. He was the only one in the room who looked European, and he spoke with an American accent.

"We will be using extremely low yield atomic weapons, one kilo or less," added ONE.

"We will use the weapons that the American people fear most," said Salman. "The detonations will be small, and we will attack remote sites where casualties will be in the hundreds, not the kind of strike that requires a massive nuclear counter strike."

"We have available plans to strike Iran," said THREE.

"After the first strike in America, we will make sure the Americans blame Iran, and after a strike on Iran, that the Iranians believe that the American hit them," said FOUR. We have studied the disinformation campaigns of the Chinese and Russians and recognize that we will have to prepare each side through slow and meticulous false intelligence leaks, social media, and lead mass media into investigations where we control the narrative. With you now ready to do your part, the clock will start. We will begin our information war this month."

"You said three or four American targets," said Farid. "Why more than one?"

"The strikes on American soil will be mass casualty events, but not like destroying a city. The Americans would never strike back with nuclear weapons to a small attack, but they will hit back hard with conventional weapons," added FOUR. "We must manage what each side thinks the other is doing and escalate slowly in a manner that their intelligence analysts will believe."

"We are prepared to use nuclear weapons?" said Farid, his voice shaking. "Do we even have such weapons at our disposal?

Salman reseated himself and smiled. "When the Soviet Union broke up, we were in a position to make a small group of struggling former Soviet officers rich by their standards. We purchased four tactical nuclear weapons. We weren't sure what we would do with them, but they were cheap. They are also small, weighing only about fifty kilos. And yes, we are prepared to use them. Hopefully, we will only have to escalate once or twice, at most three detonations before the Americans unleash the kind of non-nuclear strike that decapitates Iran. If we do this right, less than five thousand Americans will die and about the same in Iran. The Americans aren't about to target the general public in Iran. They will want the Iranian public ready to seize the opportunity they create by decimating the leadership. The Americans aren't ready for another twenty-year war like in Afghanistan."

"And the Americans will not risk the backlash of the world that comes from an overreaction such as a massive nuclear strike," said THREE.

Farid sat quietly. Salman waited for his response, and when it became clear that none was forthcoming, he continued. "Now down to the other questions you asked. I'll start with how do we control what happens to leadership in Iran?

THREE slid a pad across the table to Farid. "Here are the targets we intend to attack in Iran. You will note that we begin with a small attack on the harbors where the Revolutionary Guard keep their small fleet of attack boats. We will make the attack look like a raid of the American SEALs. Next, we will escalate to destroy an intelligence center. The third attack will be on the administrative centers of the Revolutionary Guards, with the goal of taking out their leadership. We will leak information that they, with the permission of the government, are responsible for the attacks in America. When the U.S. strikes back, they will focus on government leadership and the Guard itself. Most of the hard liners will be gone."

"For years we have been cultivating contacts in the Iranian Air Force, Navy and Army," added Salman. "Before the revolution they were led by three brothers, Suni but also Bahia. All three were executed. Their crime was being Bahia and they were killed in spite of their refusal to use the military to stop the revolution. Many in the military are deeply concerned with the direction of the nation. We do not think they will be targeted and after the shooting stops, they will not intervene to stop a popular government from taking charge. As long as Iran remains in Iranian hands, they will support the government."

"The right people will take charge, even after a popular election where our financing should help. The first thing that will happen is that Iran will withdraw financing for the Shia militias and terrorist organizations around the Middle East. They will not want to provoke the Americans again. I will personally make sure that any leadership that emerges will be friendly to our cause, offered FIVE. "We have learned already that dead opponents or traitors are little trouble. Even those who worked with us learned their fate when we even considered that they might betray us. Once there is a nuclear blast, no other nation will want any part of this conflict."

Farid noted others watching FIVE, the head of security. He wasn't sure if it was a threat or warning to him, but the message could not have been clearer.

"Now, about the last question you asked," started Salman. "You are right about the difficulty of getting even small nuclear weapons into the United States. We have tested their detection performance several times by shipping containers with limited nuclear radiation into the country and every single one was identified. Some held medical devices and supplies, others, electronics, even a load of stuff the Americans use in their homes so that their cats can crap in a box. All were inspected."

"Which gets us to your role in the plan," he continued.

"Over the last three years, we have quietly acquired a holding in WILTON Limited, your new employer. You will become our insider on all things shipping and within a year, we would like to have your advice on how we get the nuclear devices past American security. If the plan works as we hope, you may end up a hero by helping the Americans find the last device, maybe even two, but that depends on how many it takes to jar them into action."

Farid sat motionless, afraid to speak. Finally, he offered, "How many of us are involved in this plan?"

"You do not need to know that," replied FIVE. "The question you must answer is how many more will we have to add in order to succeed."

"You all understand that I know nothing about the shipping industry, I am for all intents and purposes an apprentice."

"You are critical to the plan," said Salman. "We have waited years for you to be in this position. We know you will avenge your father's death. We have worked to put you into the perfect job for your part of the mission. You will have a highly skilled organization, a successful corporation to teach you what you need to know. We will be available for counsel." Salman paused before adding, "and if your relationship with Sarah matures, you might find her father helpful. After all, he is in the medical supply business, and he ships all over the world. Some of what he ships is even radioactive."

Sarah becoming part of the conversation shook Farid, but it also made clear that the group's intelligence network was thorough.

Salman reached into his briefcase and slid a folder over to Farid. He opened it revealing enlarged copies of the photographs from Karim's laptop. The color photos of his father's death were even more graphic than on the Mac.

"You did not need to do that," said Farid. "I am part of the family." He hoped that his face made those in the room more comfortable with that statement than he actually felt.

Farid spent only eight hours over the next two days with Salman and his group. Every question was answered as accurately as possible without compromising the plan. His visits to the museum on the first day was complimented by a visit to an art gallery on the second.

Salman handed Farid a small laptop. "The materials in the first file are the same as we offer to visiting scholars and tourists who visit our institute. Feel free to discuss anything in that folder. The institute is the perfect cover for our work."

FIVE then slid into the chair next to Farid to explain how to use the secretly encrypted files on the computer to communicate. "You will have access to ten people. Every conversation will disappear in three minutes from the time you terminate. Files, like the ones you requested on what techniques we have already tested to breach American shipping security can be forwarded. For those files you will want to talk to TWO. He will forward the file. It will disappear as you scan each page. If you need to talk face to face, just ask. I will set it up and notify both parties."

Chapter 4

FARID CAUGHT THE evening flight on Air France to Paris, connecting to London. It had been weeks since his graduation, a period so crammed with learning that he needed some time off. Besides, his short phone calls with Sarah were creating an almost uncontrollable need that only she could satisfy. He expected her to be waiting for him when he arrived at his flat in a residential hotel, but one look in the refrigerator indicated that no one had been in the apartment since he'd left with his mother and uncle.

He tried her phone, but the call went straight to voicemail and when she hadn't responded in an hour, Farid wandered down to the lobby. He didn't recognize the lobby host who had just come on duty.

"I was just wondering if my girlfriend has come by looking for me while I was gone?" he said.

"Do I look like your social director?" responded the overweight blond. Then she laughed. "I'm Margaret, and

I've only been working this shift for a week, but if you will describe her, I'll try to help."

"She's tall, about five foot nine inches, with long brown hair and blue-grey eyes. She normally dresses in jeans and a frilly blouse this time of year. Men notice her," he added, "and she would probably have been wearing a floppy straw hat that keeps the sun out of her eyes."

Margaret smiled. "That woman was here a couple of hours ago. She said she needed to do some shopping."

The trip from Tbilisi had been exhausting, so armed with the information on Sarah, Farid retreated to his flat. He threw his jacket over a chair, tugged off his shoes and flopped down on the bed. He was asleep in seconds.

"Hey mister, I brought you a graduation present."

He struggled to wipe the exhaustion from his mind as he opened his eyes. That condition disappeared quickly as he took in Sarah standing at the end of the bed in a peach colored negligee that only accentuated the curves of her body.

"You, sir, are wearing far too many clothes for the present I brought you," she added.

Farid motioned her to the side of the bed. Sitting up, he placed a finger of his right hand on her cheek and then ran the finger slowly down her body, pressing his face against her breasts and stomach in order to reach her toes. "And you, lady, are a present that is more interesting when wrapped. Farid began pulling off his shirt and stood to unzip his pants. As he undressed, Sarah slipped past him and under the covers.

"You must be exhausted after your trip. You can tell me about it later," she said. "But for now, I have just the right pill to put you to sleep."

They awoke five hours later. Farid watched intently as the wealthy twenty-three-year-old student who had fully occupied his mind for a year slid from the bed and headed toward the shower. It troubled him that the mission he'd spent two weeks studying for, with all its earth-shaking ramifications, slipped into his head as he watched. The enormity of what he was part of, and what was expected of him caused him to gasp for air.

"Come dry my back," came a call from the bathroom. "Then you should scrub a little of your trip off too." Farid slid from the bed. "My father is in town to help me move. We're going to have dinner with him."

"Did you say move?" asked Farid as he slowly ran a towel down Sarah's back.

She turned, pressing her body against his. "Farid, we discussed this. I graduated a year ago and only stayed in London because you are here." Sarah pushed away and looked into his eyes until he moved.

Farid stepped into the shower. "I thought you going back to the states was just something you were contemplating," he said, adjusting the water temperature from the scalding water Sarah preferred.

"I'm ready to do something more," she replied. "Like you, I've been living off from family money for most of my life. I need to feel that I am doing something important, something that might change the world." She waited a full minute before heading back to the bedroom and the clothes she kept in his closet. She paused, studying what had accumulated over the last year, searching for something appropriate for the evening.

"You finally finished up," she called. "I know about the job offer, but is that all you want in your life? Don't you ever have the urge to take on the world, you know, right its wrongs?"

Farid followed her, drying his hair. Until two weeks ago, the only thing on his mind was a good paying job that would afford the life he had become accustomed to and trying to figure out if Sarah was the person to share that life with. He could come up with no response to her question and was relieved when didn't persist.

"Do you know where you are going to live?" he asked as they rode the elevator. Farid had been unusually quiet the previous half hour, and she was happy he finally asked.

"Connecticut, with my parents while I look for something of my own. My degree included a lot of study in the micro-economics field. Maybe I'd like to find work helping people start and fund small businesses, you know people from backgrounds where owning a company might be a ticket to a better life." She paused as they stepped into the lift. "Maybe work with inner city people or with Native Americans from one of the reservations. There's a lot of need in both."

'Change the world,' ran through Farid's mind as they slid into the backseat of a cab.

Farid had met Bill Thomas three times before. He seemed to approve of Sarah's relationship. He also knew a little about Iran, Farid's birthplace, and Lebanon where he'd lived before moving to boarding school in France. They'd never discussed Farid's family other than Bill's discrete inquiry into where the money that allowed an elite education and lifestyle came from.

Bill was waiting at the door of the small inn on the Thames. "Congratulations young man," he offered, as the waiter seated them at a corner table with a view of the river. He handed Farid a small package, wrapped in red foil and a blue ribbon. "A little something appropriate for a graduate on his way to an elite career."

They waited for their drinks to arrive before Sarah pointed to the package. Again, Farid seemed to be just starring out the window. "Open the damned box, Farid," she said.

Inside was a Rolex watch and as Farid removed it from the box, he noticed an engraving on the back.

"My father put both his and my phone numbers on the watch," she offered. "If you ever need help from either of us, we wanted you to have the numbers."

"I think I have your number pretty well committed to memory," replied Farid.

"That's the number of my phone here in England. In the states I have a different number."

Farid turned to Bill. "Thank you for the beautiful gift and the gift of friendship. I will try never to use your private number but feel honored that you offered it." Farid took Sarah's hand. "You have already made the most special gift a man could ask for, Bill."

"I appreciate Sarah's choices. But I'm kind of old fashioned. When you decide that you might want to spend the rest of your life with my daughter, I'll expect you to follow the old English tradition and ask me first for permission. It would be best in person, so that you could see the joy on my face when I answered, but with a career in transportation coming you might be anywhere in the world, I thought the phone number might come in handy."

The evening gave Farid a reprieve from the intensity of the of mission his mother and uncles started him on. It had almost slipped his mind when Bill observed, "international business of any kind is complicated today," especially shipping. Our firm moves hundreds of shipments across the U.S. and the world every month. The security alone requires us to hire specialists. I don't have to tell someone with your background about terrorism and how complicated it has made the world. I swear, especially in the U.S. and Israel and even here in England it seems that every government is scared to death. Every shipment takes longer, and the paperwork and inspections add a lot of expense."

"It's all necessary," said Sarah. "It's not just terrorism. Drugs and counterfeit merchandise are big business for the crooks in the world. I had two classes on the perils of international commerce and how even honest companies can get hurt."

"You know, I'd never even thought of shipping problems until I saw a movie about twenty-five years ago," said Bill. It was made from a Tom Clancy novel. I don't remember the name, but it rattled a lot of governments because it showed how easy it was for international terrorists to use commercial shipping to attack a country."

Farid's education in shipping was just beginning. Up until the offer from WILTON, he'd figured he would end up in one of the family's businesses, maybe cosmetics or specialized food, maybe even real estate. "It's probably a lot more difficult for the bad guys today," he said. "Twenty-five years is a long time. It's something I'm going to have to learn about."

Three days later he drove Sarah to the airport for her flight. It was really difficult for both of them, and Farid was embarrassed when she wiped tears from his face.

"Farid, you have been a little off, not your normal self. Is something wrong?"

"I've got a lot on my mind."

"You start your new job tomorrow," she said. "I know you will be tied up, but even if you can only get away for a few days, it would make me very happy." She paused a minute to dab at her own eyes. "Your company has offices across the states. Maybe they will send you as part of your training."

"Your father said people used to accompany travelers right to the gates of their flights," replied Farid. "Not anymore, not with today's security issues." He seldom took his BMW out of the garage where he stored it, traffic in London was just too difficult. But a last hour alone with Sarah made it an easy decision. "I'm not coming in with you," he said. You'd just disappear once you passed the ticket counter anyway." They shared a hug and kiss after he placed the four suitcases that somehow fit into the car onto the curb. Then Sarah was gone.

Farid drove back to London, deep in thought. It had been five days since he'd returned from Georgia. He needed to check in. With the new job starting, he'd been too busy.

Back in the apartment, he was instantly lonely. On a whim, he looked up the movie that Bill had referenced. He downloaded it onto his personal computer. THE SUM OF ALL FEARS included the shipment of a nuclear bomb into the U.S. Farid watched it and was awed by how easy it had been to ship the bomb. That was fiction and it took place decades ago. What his meeting with Salman made clear was that it would be a lot more difficult today and figuring out how to overcome that was all on him.

Chapter 5

UP UNTIL THE first day at WILTON, Farid had never worked for a living. He'd read about kids working at McDonalds or delivering papers, and some of the people in his classes talked about their parents pressing them to work as janitors or warehousemen, even couriers so that they could learn about family business. He wasn't quite sure what to expect. The first four hours were spent walking around with the V.P. of logistics, Dorsey McKenzie. Dorsey was continually checking his phone for messages and somehow Farid wasn't surprised when an alarm sounded, sending both of them rushing toward a conference room on the eighth floor of the WILTON building.

Inside, three of the people he'd met earlier were working their way around a table with an assortment of lunch item while a man and a woman, both in suits were already working their way through salads. "What I want you to do is take thorough notes on this meeting," said Dorsey as he handed Farid an empty plate. "Our guests are from one of our best customers, a firm that uses our marine services to move product from factories in Viet Nam and Thailand to the states and Europe. Every year we invite them to London for a little R&R to show our appreciation. They've agreed to discuss what they are doing in air freight. They know we are neophytes in the business compared to the company they use now but consolidating their shipping with one firm might be more efficient."

Farid frantically took notes for the next two hours. It was better than any class he might take. He finished with a clear understanding of the differences that determined whether low cost containers on ships would fit the customer needs or higher priced air freight was justified. His classes at King's Business School had included discussion of 'just in time inventory management' but listening to the customers discussion really helped clarify the concept.

The customer had moved much of their electronic component manufacturing away from Chinese medaling over the previous five years. New partners were operating factories in places where direct costs were slightly higher, but where less government interference in the ability to hire, manage, and deliver made it easier to meet market needs.

Dorsey handed Farid off to his secretary after the meeting, setting a follow-up for four-thirty. The woman helped Farid get settled into a tiny glass walled office across the hall from her desk. "Mr. Wilton really likes Dorsey," she offered as she began typing on a computer on Farid's new desk. "He's originally from New Zealand but spent twenty years working for a company in the states. He's a little brisk and sometimes gets frustrated with the slow pace here. Faster, better, more efficient, that's his moto.

On things he really understands, he's really hands on. He is constantly asking about how we can do things better."

She stopped typing, rose, and motioned Farid into the chair. "You're all set up now; you just need to enter your own security codes. That will give you access to everyday correspondence including the internal messaging system. For any files or correspondence marked LEVEL I, you need to use the retina scanner. I just used mine to open the file so that the system will record yours." She pointed toward a tiny camera mounted on the display. "It will read and record up to twelve inches from the camera."

Farid leaned toward the camera and was rewarded seconds later with a welcome aboard posting on the monitor.

"Dorsey will want to see your notes from the meeting by tonight." The woman leaned past Farid and typed in a couple of keystrokes. A menu popped up. "Just click on meeting notes. The system will walk you through everything."

She headed toward the door, stopping for a moment. "Like I said, Dorsey is really hands- on. He's counting on you to be his hands for the air freight thing. That's all new to him. Just do what he asks, keep him informed, and volunteer any ideas you have, but be prepared for him to disagree. How you handle when he disagrees with you or shuts down an idea will determine how successful you are here.

Farid watched as she seated herself at her own desk. "Good Luck," she called.

It was almost five before the intercom on Farid's phone startled him. "Farid' let's spend some time discussing today's meeting...in my office."

"Tell me the three most important things we should

have gotten out of today's meeting" said Dorsey, before Farid could even sit.

He paused, staring out the floor to ceiling windows behind his boss's desk. Before answering he glanced at the pad he'd used in the meeting, just snippets that allowed him to type in compete notes on the computer. "First, air freight is all about keeping the customers happy." Farid paused, thankful that he'd typed in complete notes earlier. "Second, only a small portion of what they build should go on air freight. Most general consumables can use less expensive surface transport."

Farid watched his new boss, looking for any indication of how he was doing. Dorsey gave no signals at all. "Third, faster, better customer service for the components that need to move by air still must fit into their budget. They will do business with the lowest cost provider that can meet their criteria. It's all about keeping their core customers happy."

Dorsey rewarded his new assistant with a huge smile. "You were recommended by one of the investors and Seymour Wilton himself asked me to give you a shot. Whoever talked to Seymour said you were smart and a quick study, and apparently, they were right. You hit all three that I jotted down."

"Thank you, sir."

"When you discuss business with anyone other than Martha, I'd appreciate you using Mr. McKenzie, just so that we telegraph the chain of command," answered Dorsey. "But among the three of us and when we are alone, I'm Dorsey. Now let me offer a few more things you will need to understand."

Farid began to relax. He slipped a pen from his pocket and prepared to take more notes.

"First, the big guys in the air freight field are focused on the big markets. We will play hell even getting landing rights for a WILTON plane in any of the major cities in China. But in the smaller markets like today's customer operates, their service is not nearly as good." Dorsey watched as Farid stopped writing after only a few words.

"Second, the same is true of major markets in the U.S. and in Europe. The big guys are well entrenched."

"Third, they have built the kind of scheduled service for their major customers so that they can fill their airplanes. They can keep them full flight after flight. That means that they can buy expensive new planes from people like Boeing and make them pay. We are a start up in this field and we need to really control our capital expenses."

Dorsey reached into the bottom drawer of his desk and produced a bottle of Knob Creek whiskey. "I developed a taste for American bourbon while I lived there. Do you drink?"

"I was raised not to," replied Farid, "but five years in London changed all that, so yes, sir, I enjoy a drink from time to time."

Dorsey poured an inch of Knob into each of two glasses and slid one across his desk. "Let me tell you why Mr. Wilton brought me into the firm."

Farid picked up the glass and sipped a bit. He had no experience with bourbon, but he figured that didn't matter when his boss offered a drink.

"I am really good at making secondary markets pay. You can build megaships to service huge markets. The guy who figured out container shipping was from the states. He built a very expensive ship purely for container shipping and it took a long time to make it pay. Today some companies, including WILTON, build ships eight times that size, but they won't pay in smaller markets even though you can get a little higher tariff. I helped the company buy up older ships with a lot of life remaining and convert them to containers. We work on their power plants to reduce operating expense. We automate as much as we can to reduce labor expense. But mostly we do not have huge initial capital costs and we keep them full on every trip because of their size in smaller markets."

Dorsey finished his drink and watched Farid's face as he got half of his drink down. "That's what I need your help on, Farid," he said. "I want to know how to get serious about the air freight business by repurposing aircraft the same way we do ships." He paused while Farid finished his drink. "Beyond learning our core business, that will be your baby. I want you to understand marine shipping. But more, I want you to help me understand how to get into air shipping without the capital it would take to buy a whole new fleet." He paused again before adding, "and just so you know, you've just passed one of my tests. One of the best definitions of a successful person is someone who will learn to do from habit what others might do from choice. You don't have to ever develop a taste for bourbon, but when necessary, smile and join whoever offers it."

Chapter 6

LEARNING ABOUT AIR freight was easier than Farid had imagined. It turns out that being the researcher for Dorsey McKenzie at WILTON opened a lot of doors, and behind many of those doors were people anxious to sell planes, handling technology, and consulting and management systems to a company with WILTON's balance sheet.

And finding Boeing 767 medium size passenger aircraft sitting idle, just waiting for a new owner was also easier than Farid thought it might be. Ten minutes on the computer introduced Farid to the three companies that dominated the market for converting passenger jets to freighters. One was in Israel, and the other two in the U.S.

Farid's preliminary report for Dorsey was due in ninety days, and at the end of sixty, his laptop included solid research on every part of moving freight by air except the regulatory requirements and security issues. That was next on the list.

Farid leaned back against yet another stack of pillows

on an oversized bed in one more hotel room. Maxwell Stephens, the CEO of a small airfreight company headquartered in the Bahamas had been a referral from one of the aircraft brokers. His research on Max Stephens turned up almost nothing about the man or his company and Farid was feeling totally unprepared for the meeting. Equally troubling was a warning from Salman on the last day of his visit. "There are a lot of intelligence organizations with undercover agents whose only job is to look for traces of organizations like ours. Their national fears are critical to our plan, but you must be very careful not to give anyone a reason to begin tracking you and what you are doing."

Farid recognized Maxwell Stephens by the light blue blazer he was wearing. He walked up to the table and extended his hand. "I'm Farid," he said, "and unless I am mistaken, you are Maxwell."

"I am the man you are looking for," offered the short, pudgy, greying man with a full beard. "I was expecting you to be a bit older," he continued.

Farid slid into booth across from Stephens. "Does my age bother you Mr. Stephens?"

"I was hoping to be meeting with someone who can make decisions."

"And I am looking for someone who can help me flesh in the regulatory and security aspects of my company jumping into the freight business."

Stephens picked up his coffee, eyeing Farid across the table. "Call me Max," he said. "I am probably the right guy to help you with all that, I just spent the last two years making my way through that minefield myself. It took a lot longer than my partners and I thought it would.

To be honest, I'd never start that process from scratch again." Max sipped from his cup before setting it down with a thump. "If I had it to do over, I'd buy a small company with all the paperwork and expand it. We just spent months hemorrhaging operating capital trying to get into the air."

Farid finally smiled. "Would you be someone who could guide us through that kind of transaction?"

"You're a smart kid," replied Max. "Before I helped found Bahama Air Freight, what we call BAM, all I did was security consulting for big carriers. Stopping smuggling is critical to maintaining hard to get operating agreements. With the air freight business booming during the COVID shutdown, I approached a couple of big money guys I knew and pitched them on jumping into the business. We did it all wrong. We never realized that to land significant contracts, you needed to be certified in the European Union, the U.S., Japan or one of the Commonwealth countries. At least from some major government that the American government trusts. Our application for American FAA operating certification took us more than a year. In the interim, the two planes we own barely pay for the fuel we use operating primarily in South America. It seems every landing in the U.S., using our Caribbean operating credentials, just gets our shipments and our planes hung up while the Americans look for drugs."

"My girlfriend took some classes on how western countries defend against trafficking. Her dad runs a big pharmaceutical company that ships radioactive materials, and he mentioned that getting shipments cleared can be a bitch."

"Both true," replied Max. "Going into the U.S., there

are protocols for clearing shipments. The big guys with really tight corporate security are still subject to random drug searches. There are just too damned many planes going into the U.S. to tear them all apart looking for drug stashes, so unless there is a tip of some kind, they usually leave the aircraft alone." Max smiled at Farid. "I'm hungry, so if it's all right with you, lets order some breakfast."

"What about the radioactive stuff Sarah's dad was talking about?" asked Farid after the waitress disappeared with their orders.

"Different types of fissionable and radioactive material give out varying degrees of detectable radiation. There are systems in place to detect even minute radioactivity operating in most of the targeted shipping ports. The government later added foreign airports installing detection tools. The number or airports equipped with those testing systems has been expanded constantly.

Back in 2003, the government set up what they called the Megaports Initiative for marine shipping. Today a carrier must disclose any radioactive component in a shipment. They still spot check other shipments. It doesn't make sense, but the materials that might be used in a dirty bomb, are actually easier to detect than fissionable material. Most of the inspection is on the foreign end, but arriving shipments are subject to inspection." Max waited a moment as the waitress refilled their coffee cups.

"Part of what you need to launch a successful company will be not only the actual operating certificates, but formal written plans for training personnel, maintenance, and security. It would be a lot faster for WILTON to buy an operating company with all of that in place."

"I am speculating here," replied Farid, "but if I were

to ask if BAM is for sale, you might answer yes? That's why you were so anxious to meet."

Stephens tugged his ugly blue striped tie loose just as breakfast arrived. "My partners want out. They are tired of feeding this hungry horse. So, yes, we are looking for a buyer, but all we really have to sell is a couple of freighters, four pilots, and a pile of paperwork that will cost you a bundle to replicate." He took a few minutes to inhale some minced ham with scrambled eggs while Farid picked at some fruit and yogurt.

"I'm not the guy who can do a deal," answered Farid, "but I work directly for him."

Farid finished his yogurt, pushing the plate to the edge of the table. "Tell me more about what you were doing before you and your partners founded BAM."

"Aviation security is mostly about research. You want to know everything you can find out about every vendor and customer. You need to have solid plans in place to vet every employee." Max signaled to the waitress for more coffee. "For example, you're obviously from the Middle East. With a name like Farid, anyone hiring you for direct operational involvement would be advised to go through your background with a fine-tooth comb. I'm not implying anything other than the obvious. Even though the region has settled down a lot in the last ten years, almost all terrorism in the world is rooted in Middle East conflicts."

"And you would be the guy a company might call on to vet me?"

"No, I spent twenty years with the Defense Department and then five more with Homeland Security. At Homeland my job was developing intelligence protocols for how to look for the bad guys. I'm not much on actually doing the vetting."

"Well, the good news for my employer is that I'm an office guy." He finished his coffee. "It would be really helpful if we could accommodate a couple of passengers on some of the flights we are planning. We have some high-tech customers who would like to send techs with shipments to provide installation and training. The big guys can't do that."

"From a business perspective, I can see how that might help cement relationships, but from a practical perspective it would add complications to shipments since any passengers would be subject to customs clearance."

Farid opened his laptop and typed for a minute before turning back to Max. "I just sent an email to my boss, asking when he might be available for a meeting with both of us. I suspect that it might take a few minutes to get an answer."

"You know that I will do everything I can to make this work out," said Max.

Farid almost felt sorry for the desperation in the voice of the man across the table. "In the interim, just out of curiosity, you mentioned earlier that it is easier to detect materials for a dirty bomb than an actual nuclear device. How can that be possible?"

"All nuclear materials give off gamma rays which produce electrons. Nonexplosive isotopes are used in medical and testing applications. They could be really dangerous in a dirty bomb. There are a half dozen technologies that can detect them. Fissile isotopes, like uranium 235 or plutonium emit almost no gamma rays. There are new highly sophisticated technologies that can be used to trick such material into detectable emissions, but they are expensive and not readily available. There are even technologies that can tell you where any nuclear material was manufactured. That would help track down an entity trying to slip nuclear materials into the U.S."

He paused for a moment studying Farid. "Most explosive devices would be shielded with lead to protect those handling them. The best defense against a nuclear explosive is intelligence and maybe a mobile Xray device that can scan a container and detect the shielding."

"Is security against this type of smuggling part of what you have developed for BAM?"

Max laughed. "Not really, what the carriers need to focus on are their customers and staff. Their primary responsibility is to recognize risks and then get the government involved."

Farid's laptop pinged. He had to reenter a security code to read Dorsey's reply. "Could you gather the documentation for what you have to sell, and be in London by next Tuesday?"

"I'd be willing to actually bring most of the documentation on my computer for the meeting," replied Max. "We can show your boss what kind of a paperwork jungle you are up against."

"I'll confirm it with Dorsey," replied Farid. He slid from the seat as Stephens handed a credit card to the waitress. "I appreciate your candor and help on this. I work for the kind of company that was built believing nothing is impossible, it might just take a little longer."

Stephens extended his hand. "One thing about putting this in your hands, Farid, is that you aren't burdened by a deep knowledge of how everyone else does it."

Farid retreated to the elevator. Two thoughts ran through his mind. First, he needed to get Maxwell Stephens name to Salman and FIVE to make sure he wasn't a sleeper agent. Second, there was something about Stephens' discussion of the nuclear detection technology that was bothering him. He slid off his watch and turned it inside out and called Sarah's phone number. He had the entire weekend available, and he wasn't about to waste it alone.

Chapter 7

"HAVE YOU FIRMED up your career plans?" asked Farid.

"No," replied Sarah with a laugh. "I have resumes out to a number of places, with a focus on Native American communities. I don't want to anyone to see me as another East Coast liberal coming to save them."

"I can imagine the reluctance of someone with a public-school education looking at your British degree," replied Farid as he fumbled through his pocket for cash to pay the cab driver.

"The elites from the tribes are all Ivy League grads, the majority went to Dartmouth, but there are plenty of Yale and Harvard grads," replied Sarah.

"Then why are so many of the people poor?"

"That's what I want to be involved with." Sarah shifted the overnight bag next to her as the cab turned toward Grand Central Station. "Most of the tribes cherish their traditional culture. They are still hunters, and shepherds and farmers. I suspect that finding a way to really succeed financially means giving up your traditional culture." She leaned over and put her head on Farid's shoulder before adding, "but if there is a way, I'd like to be part of finding it." Farid offered no response. "Are you okay?" she asked. After she asked a second time he just smiled and nodded his head.

Farid opened the door and set Sarah's bag on the curb. He turned as she lunged herself toward him, wrapping her arms and one leg around his body. Her kiss lasted most of a minute and as she unwound her body from his she was giggling. "You coming across the pond was a wonderful surprise. Next time a little more notice would be appreciated, but the surprise was nice."

"I don't know when I'll be back," said Farid. "I'm making real progress on the project. I'll work more travel into the weeks ahead, maybe even a trip to the Bahamas."

"It's a little hot down there this time of year," replied Sarah. She turned her face partially away from Farid, her neck turning a bit red. "But that just means we can wear less clothing. I love you."

He reached out and pulled Sarah close again. "Yeah, me too. Now I've got to run, I don't want to miss my plane."

Farid watched Sarah until she disappeared into the terminal. With continuous trains running north to Connecticut, it didn't really matter what time it was. But his flight to London was departing in two hours. "I need to be at JFK, terminal one in less than an hour," he said to the cabbie as he closed the door. "I'll tip you exactly what the meter says if you can get me there."

Three hours later, Farid reclined his business class seat and opened his laptop. He spent the next hour reviewing the notes from his meeting with Stephens and updating a report that was already on Dorsey's desk. The idea of quietly absorbing Stephens' BAM airline made a lot of sense. Farid began outlining his ideas for additional due diligence.

After he'd covered every contingency that he could come up with and satisfied that he'd identified most of the items Dorsey would ask for, he closed his company laptop. Something was troubling him from his meeting with Stephens. There was nothing obvious, but Farid had the gut feeling that it tied in with something else he had learned.

Perhaps it was time to check in with his uncle. Maybe a meeting with Salman, maybe even a couple of his experts would help him figure it out. He took out his personal computer and began composing an email.

"Uncle Karim, I apologize for not keeping in touch. But my new job involves a lot of strategy. I thought that I had only one task, but the job has evolved into at least five. If you can spare the time in the next couple of weeks, I'd like to make a trip over the channel to meet. You're the business expert in the family, and I could use your advice. Farid."

He hit save. He'd send the note from the terminal in London where it would be almost impossible to track. The simple code, requesting the strategist be involved and if possible, ONE the technician working on the weapon and FIVE, Salman's head of security also be there was so simple that anyone who might be looking at his correspondence would never find anything wrong.

Farid ordered a Scotch. Whatever was bothering him was making him nervous and he didn't want the middle-aged man who spoke with a Scottish brogue sitting next to him taking notice. There was something Stephens had said and in the back of his head, it tied in with something Farid had learned about the mission. But he knew almost nothing about actually shipping a weapon into the U.S. His only knowledge came from a short briefing on his trip to meet Salman and the movie he'd watched after Sarah left London.

He scowled through his laptop and clicked on the movie. Maybe if he watched it a second time, something would click. He finished his second Scotch and ordered a third as the part of the movie where the bomb was delivered into the U.S. and then transported to some sports stadium ran. The explosion had obviously killed thousands and he felt lucky that the plan he was involved in included minimal casualties. He had just started his third drink when it hit him. One of Stephens' off the cuff comments and the movie aligned.

He wasn't sure whether he was distraught or relieved. Salman's plan would never work. What was clear was that his email to his uncle and a meeting was critical.

Chapter 8

CHAD GRITT, WORKING with a dozen other analysts finished a draft report on the six most plausible scenarios for using surface transportation to smuggle a dirty bomb into the U.S. The report was thorough and well-reasoned and in Gritt's opinion totally inadequate. Where a year ago, as a junior Navy analyst with a scientific background his would have been just one more signature on the cover page, after the EEL and ANGEL crisis with China his was the most important signature. With pressure from the head of the CIA, the Navy had promoted him to Lieutenant Commander and made him the head of the unit researching transport of nuclear threats.

The most plausible possibility was some enemy putting together the materials for a dirty bomb and hiding it in a truck that would cross the border from Mexico. Countering that was the extraordinary web of technology at border crossings from Mexico. Every crossing had nuclear detections systems that had been refined over the years and now were capable of sensing almost any form of radiation. Security included Xray machines that could see into vehicles. Usually what they were looking for were either smuggled migrants or drugs, but any heavy lead shielding around a nuclear shipment would show up like a bear in a kindergarten classroom.

The use of commercial shipping was the second most plausible scenario, but again here American ports were filled with detection technology. Maybe the third possibility, a foreign power loading a submarine with a nuclear device and slipping close to the American coast before a high-speed run to where the device would be detonated was possible. But the Chinese EEL incident had taught the American Military a lot about detection of even the quietest submarines and the country was already deploying yet another ring of detection monitors. The next three options were all similar with defensive measures already available in the arsenal. That was the problem with the report. It did a great job of analyzing what was known.

Before signing off the report, Gritt walked it into the Admiral who commanded the Farragut Technical center.

"How can I help you Mr. Gritt?' asked the admiral.

"Our draft report is complete," answered Chad. "But it's way too technical. I know that sounds nuts when our entire mission here is technical analysis, but the report is missing a review by someone with a totally different perspective."

"I signed off on one of your wild hunches before and caught hell for it." The admiral paused before adding, "and it was the right decision."

"I know that sir, but that one had some hard data to justify you sending the report over to the CIA. This report has nothing of the kind. It's just a gut feeling that were trying to fit the risk into something we are comfortable with."

"Do you want to run it by your friends over at the agency?"

"Yes, sir, I'd like to run it by Pete Wilson, head of their technology group. But even more, I'd like to discuss it with the guy who mentored me through the China crisis. With Wilson's blessing, I'd like to get Thadius Walker's ideas on what we might be missing."

"Let me think this through," offered the admiral. "Late summer, amazing weather, and perfect stream conditions for some fly fishing and you want to go visit Walker who just happens to live in Montana."

"I wasn't thinking about fishing, honestly Sir," replied Gritt.

"Relax, I'm just letting you know that I wish it was my idea. If the folks at the agency think it's a good idea and they authorize your buddy Walker to take a look, I'm in. You'll have to fly commercial, probably out of uniform, and see if you can get this Wilson guy to pay for it. I never got to say thank you for what you did in the last crisis, so take a couple of extra days to get away from this place and recharge."

Five days later, Chad walked out of the Missoula terminal. There waiting in a spotless GMC pickup was Walker and in the back seat a Gordon Setter who almost never left Walker's side. "Throw your bag in the back," directed Thadius. "I'm happy you took my advice and threw in a rod case. When do you need to head back?" he asked as Gritt slid into the passenger's seat.

"I've got three days," replied Chad, turning to rub the

ears of the dog that had pushed his head between the seats resting his chin on Gritt's shoulder. "I'm happy to see you too, Winchester," offered Chad. "I assume that you read our report," he added turning back to Walker.

"I had a bitch of a time getting it to download. Agency data security was beefed up, but I finally got it. I read it."

As Walker slid into the traffic and headed for his lake house on Flathead Lake, he began to laugh.

"That's all I get. You read it," said Gritt.

"Relax. And congratulations on your promotion, Chad. Yeah, I read it. It is a great summary of the obvious. But let's discuss this over a beer down by the lake."

Late that afternoon, his bag stowed on the narrow bunk in Walkers spare bedroom, Chad grabbed the onion bag of Moose Drool Beer that Walker handed him. He watched Winchester race down toward the dock on the lake below the small bungalow. Chad followed the aging spy who used his cane to support a bad leg as they crunched down the gravel trail to the lake. Above their heads six camp robbers squawked after finishing a little kibble from the dog dish.

"There is a metal hook on the rope around that cleat," said Walker pointing at the same cleat that held a line keeping Walkers pristine old wooden rowboat from floating away. "Pull out a couple of beers and then slip the hook through the mesh of the bag and drop it off the dock."

"Isn't the water a little warm to keep beer cold this time of year?" asked Chad as he lowered four more beers into the water.

"Only a young inexperienced kid would drink a dark heavy beer cold," replied Walker. "Kind of like a good

English ale, it should be a bit chilled but not cold. Half the flavor comes through the nose." He used a Leatherman to pop the cap off from two bottles and handed one to Gritt.

Walker took a drink of his beer and then set the bottle on the dock as he slipped off his shoes and socks to dangle his feet in the water. "I can summarize my comments on your report in three short sentences. First it is a thorough analysis of how to detect a maritime or surface delivery of nuclear material. Second, it almost ignores all other possibilities, such as air delivery. Third, if the bad guys had money to burn, they could probably get nuclear material into the country no matter what sensors or inspections we set up."

That's not very encouraging," replied Gritt. He took a moment to savor the strong sweet flavor of a beer he had never tried before. Thadius was right, it wouldn't have been nearly as flavorful if it was really cold. He smiled at his mentor. Working with Walker over the last few months had taught him that the man was always focused on the holes in a plan.

"Kind of like why you lock your car," replied Gritt. "It keeps the amateurs and honest people out, but it won't stop a determined pro."

"Exactly," said Walker. "Ninety-nine percent of those who might try to get such a weapon into the country will fail because we implement the ideas in your report. We will use tomorrow morning to kick around the other one percent. In the interim, we can discuss what those goofballs in Congress really need to hear when you testify at that hearing next week."

"You know about that?" said Gritt.

"Director Chang asked if I thought I could add

anything to the hearing. I assured him that hours on a jet from here to Minneapolis and then on to DC was not going to happen. I also assured him that you and the team we assembled as well as the Air Force folks from that base in the Aleutians knew more than I did."

"You know more than I do about who will be testifying," replied Chad. "I assume our technical team will be there along with Colonel May and Major Tvorshik. They were critical to stopping the Chinese raid and protecting the real secrets of ARCTIC ANGEL.

"Any more than that will just confuse the senators. You guys know all the facts. Stick to them but when some hot shot senator with a good staff asks what we can do to avoid being blindsided with a threat like the EEL again, you will need an answer."

"I've given that a lot of thought, and I'm not sure that I have a good answer," said Chad.

Walker drained his beer and pointed at the rope to the bag of beer in the water. Chad lifted the bag, dropping the two empty bottles in and pulling out two full bottles. Walker opened them and handed one back to his young guest.

"All the techno geeks and their magic gadgets and computer programs in the world cannot detect the one percent. Hell, they didn't detect the EEL project that probably cost one of our adversaries ten percent of their total budget to develop. There is no substitute for agents with their eyes and ears open. One tiny fragment of a conversation or one shipment of something that shouldn't be needed where it is delivered is the key to our security. Then, like your work on the EEL threat, some smart kid will have to piece together the puzzle. That's the only way to prevent disaster. You need to tell that to the Senate. The CIA needs the money to go back to what it was best at."

Chad worked on his beer as he watched Walker's Gordon Setter rip from the shade of a tree near the dock as a squirrel chattered in the trees closer to the house. "I agree," he offered, "but I was only able to piece together the threat after the fact. The bad guys had already hurt us. They were snooping on our most sensitive secrets for months before we began to figure it out."

"And there is the rub," said Thadius, "unless we get really lucky and the other side makes a mistake that points directly at what they are up to, the best we will probably do is minimize the damage after we get hurt the first time."

Walker finished his second beer and started to rise. Gritt jumped to his feet to help the man with a bad leg to his feet.

"Let's go get some dinner," said Walker. "Just leave the last two beers in the water. They will be perfect for tomorrow evening's conversation."

"You don't see anything we might do to avoid getting hurt in the first place," offered Gritt as they started to walk up the trail. "I mean in my report; we are dealing with a nuclear threat."

Walker called his dog as they walked. In seconds, the dog took the perfect place for a trained hunting dog, at Walkers left leg. "How do we stop that?"

"If we have the right people and enough of them, and they are trained, someone might just hear something. It's been my experience that almost nobody wants a real crisis or a war. With enough assets, over enough years, someone on our side will get a tip or see something from an old contact that gives us the first clue. The bad guys always leave a crumb or two, but they are only important if someone is experienced enough not to just brush them onto the floor."

"We will stop on the way to dinner and get you a fishing license," added Walker.

The next morning, Walker rousted Chad from his bunk early.

"Where are we headed?" asked Gritt as he watched Walker throw his fly rod case and tackle bag into the back of the truck and slip his laptop into the console between the seats. For the first time in weeks, it felt good to Gritt to be dressed in a T-shirt, shorts and a pair of tennis shoes.

"Pan trout for dinner tonight," replied Walker. "I'm going to drop you at the upper end of a stream I used to fish all the time when I was younger. You can almost jump across it in most places. It runs under an old logging road up in the mountains and then wanders well away from the road for several miles. Once you get away from where the road warriors stop to fish it is incredible fishing. I can't handle the rough terrain anymore, but you can. I'll bet it is as good as it ever was and you're going to check it out for me. A couple of twelve-inch trout out to be just about right for tonight. I'll coax some little ones out of the pool next to where I pick you up."

An hour later, Walker watched Gritt string up his small fly rod, "Go with Chad," said Walker to his dog. A moment later the man and dog started down the stream. "I'll pick you up where the stream re-crosses the road," yelled Thadius. It's about three hours if the fishing is good."

When they had disappeared, he started the truck and headed down to a beautiful small glen next to where the road and stream came back together. Taking his computer, he crossed to a place where he could watch for Chad and Winchester. He sat and leaned back against a huge pine tree. In minutes he was sorting through pages of notes he'd kept from years of operations, carefully selecting examples of the types of fragments that he and Gritt had discussed the night before. They would go into a short summary that he hoped might make it into Gritt's report. That summary would focus on good old-fashioned spy craft as the best defense against a catastrophic attack. The quiet pool in front of him showed the dimples of feeding small trout and an hour working dry flies would be his reward for a couple of hours of intense work.

When Walker dropped Chad off for his trip back to the East Coast, a folded hard copy of that summary was tucked into Chad's zip up lapel pocket. The message, 'don't let what you already know or are looking at, stop you from digging for what you don't know,' was cemented into Chad's head.

Chapter 9

"THAT STEPHENS GUY is a walking 'how to' manual for what we are trying to do."

It was Thursday, after six when Dorsey and Farid shared a drink.

"We should hire a private investigation firm to vet the guy," said Farid. "I want to take a look at his company as well. Before we leap off a cliff with them, we need to know just how much he is playing us."

"Are you always so skeptical?" asked Dorsey. "I'm not saying you aren't right, but sometimes a really good deal drops into your lap. If this is legit, it could take a year off from our plans."

"I guess that I've had a couple of really good things turn out to be more complicated than I thought they would be," answered Farid. "Anyway, you didn't hire me to throw things up against the wall, hoping that some of it would stick. Finding a way to really go through this guy and his company will make us feel really good about getting in bed with them or save us a lot of grief."

"You're right. Go talk to legal tomorrow and see who they recommend."

"If it is all right with you, Dorsey, I'd also like to pop over to France for the weekend to visit with my uncle. Over the last twenty years he's acquired more than a dozen companies. I'm not working around you; everything we are working on will be your decision and of course, Mr. Wilton's. But coaching on what to look for will better prepare me for asking the right questions."

"Good idea. It can't hurt to have another set of experienced eyes advising you. In the interim," said Dorsey, I'm glad you had some time with your girl last weekend. If this gets really rolling you won't have much time for the next few months."

Farid left the building before phoning his uncle to confirm the email he'd received before work that evening. It read, "Let me know if I can help with strategy. I'm available on Saturday if you want to talk. I've found that dealing with one thing at a time helps me make good decisions." Strategy was code for Salman, and one meant just what is said. Salman and ONE would be available at his uncles on Saturday.

FIVE, the head of security wouldn't be available, but WILTON was going to pay for an investigation of Stephens which was what he was going to ask FIVE to do. It was good idea to dig a little deeper into Max Stephens, to make sure he wasn't a security plant. But if the meeting with his uncle and Salman and ONE went as he thought it would, it probably wouldn't matter.

The drink with Dorsey elevated Farid's exhaustion from a week of intense business, cramming everything possible into his weekend with Sarah and travel. He stopped at his favorite Fish and Chips place for a takeout dinner where he also picked up a copy of *THE TIMES*. Farid tossed his shoes into the corner and tugged off his tie as he settled onto the old couch in his apartment. He folded the bag from the restaurant flat on the table and spread his dinner out. He followed up a mouthful of vinegar fish with a swig of bottled water and opened the paper. The first story was an exclusive. A *TIMES* reporter was reporting that the government of Iran had hard proof that the United States had somehow planted listening devices at the headquarters of the Revolutionary Guard. Worse, the Iranian intelligence services reportedly had detected an effort to hack the communications network that tied Iranian coastal defense installations together. "The only reason any country would try such a thing would be to disable the coastal defense missile systems in preparation for an attack," the reporter's anonymous source had added. The article went on to explain that the paper had not been able to independently confirm the report, but that the reporter had great confidence in his source.

Even though he had been working on his part in the plan for months, his suspicion that the story was part of the plan planted by THREE shook Farid. Up until that moment the entire plot had been something that he felt would never happen. His time with Sarah had been real. His connection to Maxwell Stephens was real. Building an airfreight division for WILTON was real. It hit him like a hammer as he realized the plot to start a war was real. He crawled into bed an hour later, thoughts that might possibly derail his uncle's plan running through his head. Much needed sleep eluded him.

Those same feelings left his stomach rumbling as he

started a long walk through his uncle's estate with Karim, Salman and ONE. He had arrived early after taking a Friday midday flight from London. "Tell me, Salman, where did you get the idea for your plan to trigger a war between the Americans and Iran?" he asked. "I ask because it is the same plot, I watched in an American movie from years ago."

Salman began to laugh. "I am guilty of plagiarism. I too watched that movie when it first came out. I was at a meeting in New York and that movie was the hot topic on the news shows. The way the scheming Russian plotters bought an old Israeli atomic bomb from some Egyptian herders who found it at a jet crash in the desert and then smuggled it into the United States became the root of our plan. When the Soviet Union collapsed, the opportunity presented itself to buy Soviet suitcase RA-115 weapons. We'd originally planned to use them in Iran. I'm pleased that somehow you also viewed that movie. You saw how one nuclear explosion sent the Americans to the brink of war."

Farid stopped in the middle of a field where Karim's prized Arabian horses grazed a quarter mile away. "Uncle, Salman, in that movie, *The Sum Of All Fears*, the Americans do not go to war."

"You are correct, Farid. With only one explosion they chose diplomacy. The Russians themselves hunted down the plotters and killed them. That is why we must be prepared to use two or three bombs."

Farid turned to his uncle and ONE, "Have either of you ever seen this movie?

Both answered no. "But," interjected Karim, "I've known so many Americans and they all are so convinced of their exceptionalism and the power of their military to protect them, that Salman's plan seems almost foolproof."

Farid shook his head. "Uncle, Salman, the reason the Americans did not strike back is that they have technology that allows them to analyze the residue from a nuclear explosion and identify exactly where the nuclear material was refined. In the movie they realized that the material came from one of their own reactors and was stolen or given to the Israelis. They knew it wasn't from Russia."

He paused while the three men with him struggled with what he had just told them before adding, "If we explode a bomb made with Russian uranium in the United States, they will know within hours that it was not from Iran."

"I heard nothing like that while watching that movie," offered Salman.

"It was not spoken when the discovery was made. The report of the origins of the nuclear material came in on a computer screen," replied Farid. "It was there in print. In my research for our project, I am working with a former American intelligence officer who confirmed that the Americans have extraordinary analytical tools. It is part of why it is so difficult to smuggle a bomb into the country."

Salman looked defeated as he seated himself on a stump, his face in his hands. "I speak fluent English," he said, "but I do not read it."

Farid began to relax. Maybe this plan was impossible. He felt both sadness because it was his duty to avenge the death of his father and comfort that a war that might kill tens of thousands might be impossible.

"I want to see that myself," offered Karim. "I would like to see how the Americans figured out that they should not attack the Russians."

"I have the movie recorded on my laptop," said Farid. "When we get back to the house, I can show it to all of you."

"You must wait until tomorrow," replied Karim. "I want to bring the others who have worked for years here to view it. But before they do, I want FIVE to bring his security team to the house to assure that there is no way that the French or any other government can listen in to our conversation."

The same men who had been at his Uncle's house the day of his graduation assembled in the same den at midnight on Saturday. FIVE and two other men had swept the room for listening devices. They disconnected every data port in the house along with the telephone lines. Special mesh screens were taped up over the windows. Farid had fully charged his laptop since the circuit breakers that bought electricity into the house would be turned off until the meeting ended.

Two hours later the mood was one of defeat. Years of planning and a well-financed and strategized plan seemed a shamble. Salman's plan assumed that the Americans would deploy sensors to detect nuclear materials entering the country, but no one understood that for decades the Americans had the ability to identify the origins of that material. As the movie ended, Mohamed motioned for ONE to join him at a corner table. They conferred for five minutes before turning to the rest of the men.

"I am the liaison between our group and the Iranian military," said Mohamed. "An Iranian general told me several years ago that their scientists have actually built small atomic devices. They are not really bombs in that they would have to be triggered by an electrical signal from a control center. They were going to use them to test the refining process they were building but never detonated them because the Americans had installed sensors in neighboring countries that would detect the explosions. The fissionable material is probably junk compared to what the Russians built, but since we only want to create small explosions, they might still work for our plan."

"That is well and good," offered Karim, but we only have the Russian bombs."

"ONE here thinks he would be able to modify the Iranian material to work with the outer workings of the Russian RA-115 bombs. He has already modified the devices so that they can be detonated either by a timer or a cell phone signal."

"But we do not have the Iranian material," said Farid.

"Then I must find a way to steal the fissionable materials. I will find a way to get the actual specifications of the Iranian's material. ONE believes that the major difference will be the diameter of the ball of enriched uranium. He thinks it will be a relatively simple task to modify the shell of explosive material that is used to compress uranium of a different size."

"I do not understand this shell," said Farid.

"To detonate fissionable material, you surround the material with a traditional high explosive shell. By detonating the entire shell simultaneously, you compress the fissionable material which initiates the nuclear explosion," said ONE. "This is an oversimplification, but basically how a bomb works."

"Can you really engineer such a theft?" asked Reza. "We have plenty of cash to entice someone to steal the material, but I doubt that the Revolutionary Guard who protect such state secrets in Iran can be bribed. Even if we can find someone to steal it, they must have a system in place to keep an eye on such a valuable secret. The minute they find it missing, they will sound the alarm. That will destroy the effort that FOUR is making to ramp up the rhetoric and press from both sides."

"That is why you are our banker," offered Karim. "You have the most detailed mind. You have used that intellect to protect our plan for decades." Karim turned toward Mohamed. "Reza is right," he said.

"Then instead of stealing the Iranian material, we will have to exchange it for the Russian material that we no longer have a use for," said Mohamed. "I have two highly placed contacts that have offered their help to bring down the regime. Both lost sons who died protesting the regime."

"So, we just continue with our plan and assume that somehow this exchange will work out," said Farid, his anger and distrust barely under control.

"That is exactly what we do," offered Ahmed speaking for the first time. "Your part is to figure out how to get the bombs into the U.S. This is no more a challenge than a dozen we have overcome before." He turned to his brother. "Karim, you will be the communicator. Mohamed will keep you informed, and you will find a way to keep the rest of current. Nothing has changed."

The short commuter flight the next day had no beverage service, which meant that Farid's first stop after dropping his bag in his apartment was a local pub. He'd left his uncles home angry and frustrated. While he had never allowed himself to think openly about it, the idea of starting a war to avenge his father shook him to the core.

He was halfway through his second Irish whiskey when it finally hit him. He was trapped.

He also couldn't shake one observation that FIVE had uttered. One of the technicians working with ONE, building a bomb, had been overheard talking to his Iranian mother, now living in Belgium. His brother had returned to Iran after he graduated from college and was now an officer in the guard. FIVE's sentence stuck in Farid's mind like glue. "That man will never utter another word."

Chapter 10

THE HEARING IN Washington DC took place behind closed doors surrounded by tight security. The EEL and ANGEL incident took up the first morning, with six of the American participants outlining their part in protecting the nation and keeping an armed incident from becoming a war. Seven senators listened without interruption, a function of how intense the story was and also of the closed hearing where there was no press to grandstand in front of.

The afternoon session was taken over by top brass from the Navy, Air Force, and the CIA. All of them were challenged by the select committee for what had obviously been a failure of intelligence as well as huge holes in defending against the Chinese. The Air Force had inadequate security at the secret Aleutian Island base. The security personnel there had performed extraordinarily. But that didn't change the fact that a small Chinese commando team had penetrated a top-secret American facility.

The Navy had to admit that their part, a plan to deploy

a SEAL team to the facility, went completely to hell. The CIA admitted that until a young Navy officer sent them a hypothetical analysis, they had no inkling of the Chinese technical achievements.

As negative as the afternoon went, all three agencies finished the day heaped with praise for their overall performance. More importantly the airing of dirty laundry set the stage for the next day's session where the technical report that Gritt's team had developed was to be presented. The addition of Thadius Walker's notes would be a great starting point to argue for more budget to somehow detect the unknown.

Major Olga Tvorshik was waiting at the curb outside her hotel when Chad Gritt rolled up in his vintage 1960 Corvette. Olga and Chad managed a long-distance connection after the EEL and ANGEL event. The attraction between the two was immediate, but improbable with six thousand miles between their duty stations.

Gritt started to exit the car, his old-time manners pounded into him by his mother demanding he open the door for his date. Before he could swing his legs from the seat, Olga dropped into the bucket seat of the vintage American sports car and slammed the door. Dropping an oversized handbag behind the seat, she tugged at her short black skirt as she settled into the seat. Her emerald silk blouse perfectly complimented her auburn hair. She slipped a pair of sunglasses from the top of her head onto her nose as Gritt sat watching.

"I'm sure I'm not the first pretty girl in this car," she said. Olga put her hand over his, which was gripping the gear shift lever between them. "You can drive this beautiful old antique, can't you? I'm starved."

"I'm sorry," mumbled Gritt as the throaty engine rumbled to life. "I mean, I knew that you were beautiful, but wow."

It took ninety minutes on I-95 to reach Baltimore and Gritt's favorite restaurant, Phillips Seafood. Both watched the parking attendant's joy as he slipped into the seat of the vintage Corvette. Five minutes later they were seated at a window table overlooking Baltimore's inner harbor. Across the bay, the biggest American flag that Olga had ever seen floated over a Fort made famous during the American Revolutionary War.

"I've read about this place," said Olga as a bottle of champagne arrived at the table. "My mother brought me and my little brother to the states. She met an American while working for the German company Siemens in Moscow. They too had a distance relationship for a couple of years before my stepdad asked her to marry him. I missed my first six years of American education including the basic American history taught here."

"This city was central to the war against the British," replied Chad as he sipped champagne. "I wondered about your background. It's not often that I meet an American officer with a Russian name."

"My dad drank himself to death after the collapse of the Soviet Union. He was like a lot of Russian men; lost with a dead-end job with only one real benefit and that was that they didn't care if he was drunk or not. He was as mean as any man I have ever known. Anyway, coming to this country was a great opportunity for us. And I love my stepfather."

They finished an appetizer of award-winning crab cakes. While waiting for their lobsters Gritt asked, "tell me about becoming a citizen and then how a woman who spent her development years turning every man's head ended up in the Air Force."

"My stepdad was a former Air Force pilot. He was working for Siemens on some aviation radio project in Europe which included Russia. He insisted on his new family becoming citizens and I think one of his friends was a Senator in Arizona where we lived. Anyway, I ended up with an appointment to the Air Force Academy." Olga finished her wine and waited as Gritt poured her a second glass. Dinner was just arriving when she added, "you're right about attracting attention, it's been part of my life from the time I was twelve. One thing I liked about the academy was that every man there was respectful. That hasn't always been my experience. Attention is fun, but only from the right person and in the right situation."

Gritt's face turned red. "Olga, I've been attracted to you since you escorted me and my team across an airport in the middle of a Typhoon. Writers have commented on it for centuries, passion is heightened in times of crisis, and that's how we met."

The conversation that evening covered every subject, from their time together and the small contingent each led battling the Chinese to American football and Olga's relatives still in Russia. The conversation eventually evolved into more personal subjects including a joint passion for wild places.

It was after ten before Gritt handed the parking attendant a twenty dollar tip. He took a minute to put the top up on the car before the couple started back for the nation's capital.

"I'm not much of a car person," offered Olga as they

turned onto the highway, "but I know this is a classic and it is fun. There is only one thing I don't like about it. I'd like to be sitting closer to you." Olga slipped her arm through Gritt's which hovered over the shift lever and pressed her cheek against his shoulder. They rode that way, talking when necessary for an hour. "Perhaps you would not think terribly of me if I asked to see where you live."

Gritt's townhouse in Georgetown was small compared to the neighboring homes, but Olga realized that it must mean that Gritt had some means beyond the pay of a junior officer. She really didn't care. Since she had watched the jet lift off from the Aleutian Island runway carrying Gritt and his team from the island, she couldn't get him out of her mind.

"Where is the bathroom?" she asked as they dropped their coats over the back of the couch. Gritt pointed down the hall. Carrying her large handbag, Olga disappeared into the first door on the right.

Five minutes later she appeared again, this time dressed only in a sheer lime green gown that flowed around her naked ankles. "Now, where is the bedroom?" she asked. "Oh, and you better set your alarm for early enough to get me back to my hotel to change into my uniform. The senators would probably not think well of me if I arrived dressed like this," she added with a giggle.

"That may be the case," replied Gritt as he followed Olga, his eyes locked on her back as she walked, "but I guarantee you would have their attention. Even that female senator from South Dakota would have to think, wow, before she threw her mandatory fit."

Gritt handed Olga a glass of orange juice as she fussed

in front of the mirror in the early morning light. "You know that today we will be getting into what I have been working on—how we keep the country safe from a limited atomic attack."

"I guessed that was coming," replied Olga as she added a little lipstick. "That wasn't part of my pre-trip briefing file, but it makes sense now that much of the world knows how we can defend the country from traditional aerial attack."

As Gritt closed the door behind them and began walking Olga to a waiting cab, he added, "I'd like you really focusing on our report today. Thad Walker and I both agree that we are covering the known bases really well, but that isn't where we might get hurt. He believes that our best defense is someone hearing or observing something. It won't appear critical, but it will lead to figuring out what is important. I'd appreciate your thoughts after the session. You know, one more 'out of the box' mind on what we don't know."

Gritt gave Olga a quick kiss on the cheek as she slipped into the cab. With parking at the capital so difficult, his car would remain in the garage and he would walk. He couldn't remember when he looked forward to a walk like he did this morning.

Chapter 11

THE DRIVE SOUTH from Tehran to the beautiful city of Natanz would have taken the better part of four hours. Instead, Mohamed and Ashraf boarded an Army helicopter. A general in the Iranian Army, Ashraf knew flying was a way to avoid the scrutiny of Revolutionary Guard checkpoints protecting the top-secret underground base only thirty miles away. Iran, like Nazi Germany in the 1930s and 1940s, has two militaries: The Iranian Army to protect the nation and its citizens, and the Revolutionary Guard, to protect the religious leadership and their government led by the Grand Ayatollah.

The traditional military had evolved from that established by the late Shah of Iran, deposed decades ago. The Revolutionary Guard Corps had evolved from the loose-knit supporters of the revolution. It was the best equipped, best funded and most powerful entity in the country and the government made sure that the Guard had a finger in every government policy. Their financial power extended to control over much of Iran's industry, especially in defense industries and technology. They accumulated business interests around the world.

Mohamed was part of the underground network outside the country that helped the Guard invest in targeted business interests, especially in locations where they wanted to keep an eye on foreign government efforts to 'study' Iran. It occurred to Mohamed for the hundredth time in the last twenty years just how ironic it was that he was actually helping the group that he, Ahmed, Karim and the others had sworn to destroy. But that help and years as a trusted outsider working to bridge the differences between the Guard and the Army were the only reasons that he was flying to Iran's most secret base. The base was officially run by the army, but like most things the traditional military did, the Guard was always hovering and watching to ensure that the effort supported the policies of the government.

Many nations including Iraq worked to quietly suppress the Guard; a fact well understood by the Guard's leadership. Because of that, when the Guard wanted specific technology from around the world, they pressed the Army to negotiate, to acquire what was needed. With most of the Middle East praying for the army to eventually assert its power against a hated regime, they often got what they wanted. Ashraf was officially on such a mission, reaching out to Mohamed to find components for a new missile guidance system when he traveled to Iraq.

Mohamed understood his old friends growing angry over the direction that Iran was headed. It grated on him that an Army General had the equivalent of a Guard captain constantly looking over his shoulder. That frustration turned to fury when his son had been executed for supporting anti-government protests. That son, the child of an impossible love affair that Ashraf kept hidden for decades, a relationship with a Kurdish woman he'd met while in college in France before the revolution, was Ashraf's only child. He loved his wife, the daughter of a politically valuable associate, but their inability to have children together had slowly turned the marriage into one of mutual respect and support. The woman he called Daria was the passion of his life, even as her hair turned gray. Old friends helped the two remain close even after Daria moved back to France. His son's return to his Iranian roots frightened both mother and father. But the boy was his father's son, even if he didn't know it, and he was determined to be part of fundamental change in Iran. Now he was just part of Iranian soil.

The entry to the facility, code named EAGLE, was through a fairly small institute whose stated purpose was preparing young men to serve in government. The facility operated like a boarding school, with busses moving workers disguised as students and administrators between EAGLE and Natanz. Those present were sworn to secrecy, much the same as Americans who worked at Area 51. Below a 20,000 square foot concrete building, surrounded by gardens and fountains, a secret facility carved into a hill lay covered by a quarter mile of earth.

Even Ashraf didn't know all of the security measures and he was the Army's most senior administrator at the facility. What he did know was that Mohamed had spent weeks working out, strengthening his body, to carry the small briefcase as if it were not lined with lead.

The guard at the building entrance examined

Mohamed's papers and even though Ashraf was known, he scanned his badge and then directed him to a fingerprint scanner before they were allowed to enter. They stepped through the door, each clinging to their briefcases, as a young army lieutenant carried their luggage behind. Inside the feeling changed. Ashraf was greeted by a half-dozen people as they made their way to the elevator and eventually to Ashraf's apartment in the top corner of the four-story building. Inside the apartment, Ashraf pointed toward the guest room. Mohamed returned to the living room rubbing his arm and shoulder, pleased that his sixty-something year old body had managed to carry the one-hundred-pound case.

Ashraf had briefed his old friend the night before. He suspected that his apartment might have hidden listening devices. The Guard trusted nobody completely, perhaps not even each other. He'd surveyed the apartment more than once, determining where hidden cameras might be hidden and determining areas where visual surveillance would be impossible. But listening devices might be hidden in the concrete itself. Until that moment, he'd had no reason to worry about surveillance, but like so much of the Guard's activity, it grated on him that they might be watching.

"We will not be able to spend any time with the staff for a couple of days," offered Ashraf. Most of them are with their families for Nowruz. My closest staff have volunteered to give up the New Year's holiday since we were coming. It's too bad that you couldn't arrange a different date to look at how the technology you sourced in Turkey is being used."

"Living in France, Nowruz is just a secular holiday

to me and my family," said Mohamed. "Among those in Iraq some will celebrate it with religious zeal. I want to be back in a couple of days. I just appreciate you and your wife giving up the spring celebration to make this trip." He motioned for Ashraf to come closer before whispering, "I know that a couple of my sources will want assurances that what they helped us buy is not being used by the Guard. Your idea of setting up a static display that I can photograph, one that shows how the components are being used purely for scientific purposes, is all I need." The two men nodded at each other.

While Mohamed was speaking, Ashraf walked into the hall between the bedrooms where he scribbled frantically on a pad from his briefcase. He held it up as Mohamed joined him. "Thank you for being so careful," he said. "We will take the tram down below. I've set up the display there only fifty meters from the vault where the enriched uranium balls are stored."

Mohamed smiled and nodded before stepping into his room to unpack his small overnight bag. At the bottom was an identical pad and a pen. He quickly scrawled, "I assume you overcame the problem of getting into the vault or we wouldn't be here." He handed the pad to his friend.

It took Ashraf a few minutes to answer. "The Army captain who controls access to the different parts of the facility is the nephew of the other General we discussed. He would probably volunteer to help us, but I will not ask. I will just send him on an errand while I cover his position. While my friend's son was not executed, he died from gunshots at the same rally my son attended. The guard didn't care who got hurt. He was just observing, and the Guard has taken pains to explain how sorry they are. You would never know it from my friend's public statements, but if he could single handedly kill all of the top Guard officers, he would."

"How long until dinner?" asked Mohamed aloud. "I'm a border-line diabetic and I need to eat regularly."

"We will eat in an hour." Ashraf walked over to a window overlooking the gardens. He opened it and then set a metal garbage can on the glass table next to the window. He plucked a pack of Marlboro's from his coat and handed one to Mohamed and then place one between his lips. He lit his and handed his lighter to his friend, motioning for him to light up. At the same time, he ripped the pages he'd been writing on from his pad and then those on Mohamed's pad and wadded them up and dropped them into the waste basket. Both men puffed the cigarettes for a minute before dropping them into the trash can. Ashraf lit the edge of the pages and watched the pages ignite, burning to cinders in seconds along with most of the cigarettes. "Damn, I did it again. I should quit this nasty smoking habit. This isn't the first time I've absentmindedly tossed a butt into the trash. We have to be really careful with fire here," he said aloud. "Any emergency services call leads to a pile of paperwork."

A moment later he closed the door behind them and locked it leaving the window open.

"No one is to enter my apartment," he said to the lieutenant in the next room with the door open. "My friend here has several documents with him that are nobody's business except his and the Guard unit that he is sourcing materials for."

With the lieutenant's acknowledgement, Ashraf pushed the button for the elevator.

At nine o'clock the next morning the two men stood outside a nondescript steel door with no lock or door handle apparent. The items you seek are in six small metal cabinets just to the right of the door," said Ashraf. He handed Mohamed a tiny flashlight. "You will need this," he added before turning toward the guards control desk two corridors over. "You will know when I unlock the door."

Five minutes later, the door clicked loudly and popped as it was opened from the security desk. Mohamed plucked a penlight from his pocket and directed the beam to a metal box that looked like a small chest freezer. Opening the top, he gripped the bars on either side of a lead cover. Inside was a small orb of enriched uranium. Mohamed slipped on a pair of cotton gloves before adding a heavy pair of lead infused rubber ones hanging next to the line of chests. It took him only a minute to remove the orb from his briefcase and exchange it for the one in the cabinet. He repeated the exercise twice more. It seemed surreal that such a tiny glob of metal could kill thousands. Re-sealing the large cabinets, he turned toward the door. Outside in the hallway, he could hear voices. He held the door almost closed as they passed. Then, he stepped into the hall just as more voices could be heard. Again, he retreated into the vault as at least two people held a conversation no more than ten meters away. He checked his watch, knowing that Ashraf had only allowed for ten minutes for the exchange to be completed. The task he sent the watch officer on, wouldn't take much longer than that.

He checked his watch continuously as the deadline and then several more minutes passed. The vault was Iran's most carefully guarded secret and if anyone found him inside, both he and Ashraf would be dead. Finally, the voices disappeared, and he stepped out, pushing the door closed until a heavy click indicated that the three deadbolts were engaged.

Mohamed carried the briefcase to the guard's control desk. There he found Ashraf, smiling and joking with the security officer. Ashraf remained in the guard's chair while the young officer, also laughing, leaned on a counter that shielded him from seeing the display consoles. Mohamed watched his friend wipe drops of sweat from his forehead as he rose and motioned for the security officer to retake his seat.

"The corridors here are really a maze," said Ashraf, looking at Mohamed. "I'll bet you got lost on your way to the bathroom."

Mohamed forced a big smile. "Since I turned sixty, I need to find a restroom way too often."

Normally the activities in the complex made any listening devices useless. But on the first morning of the Nowruz holiday the place was almost empty. "You're sure that nobody will notice the differences in the nuclear material?" whispered Mohamed. "The orbs may be slightly different."

"The director of the weapons program is not here today. He's an old man with no political agenda," replied Ashraf. "He is as pure a scientist as I've ever met, not the kind of guy that goes looking for trouble. Nader somehow talked his way into American universities right after the revolution before anyone in the U.S. ever considered Iran a military threat. Nobody really knows how a good student from a poor family, working as a border guard managed to get an American educational visa, but we are happy to have him. His doctorate is from some place in Michigan, and it didn't include much in the way of management education. It would never occur to him to check on the orbs. To him, this project is just one great scientific challenge. If you could look into his brain, you might see a man wondering how anyone could work on such weapons; but he is a brilliant engineer."

An hour before, the men had photographed and made a recording of the mockup of a scientific experiment designed to look like a balloon payload destined to monitor atmospherics. They had talked openly about how the experiment might someday allow Iran to trigger more wet weather to help the country become more food independent. Ashraf made sure that the commentary emphasized how the Army had accepted the challenge of the research and how they were working with two universities. They'd timed their trip to the weapons research center, to allow their visit to be complete before most of the skeleton staff on duty for the holiday finished a special breakfast that Ashraf had ordered.

Ashraf and Mohamed thanked the young Army captain at the security station as they waited for the ride back to the surface. The ride up on the number three tram took six minutes. Ten minutes later they were again in the apartment where each placed their briefcases in their bedrooms. Mohamed wandered out to the living area, scribbling on his pad.

"Is there no record of my entry and exit from the vault?"

Mohamed read the message and laughed. Then he wrote back. "There is so much coming and going to the facility that tracking would be almost impossible. So, we track tram access and only track each room by when the lights are turned on or off. The security console showed the vault door open. I didn't dare allow the guard back into his seat. What in the hell took so long?"

"Four or five people stopped to talk in the hall. I couldn't leave," scribbled Mohamed.

Moments later, Ashraf dropped a lit cigarette onto the pages from both tablets and lifted his waste basket to the open window for the two minutes it took for the pages to become ashes.

The men spent the rest of the day enjoying the New Year holiday with the staff, all of whom were amazed that the general had chosen to spend the day with them instead of at his home.

They were on the helicopter back to Tehran early the next morning. From where the young army pilots landed, Ashraf's car whisked his friend to the private jet parked only ten minutes away. In less than two hours from leaving EAGLE, Mohamed was on his way to Tbilisi where he would hand his briefcase to ONE before continuing on to France.

Before takeoff he took a minute to send the following message from his encrypted tablet. "I hope you all had a great Nowruz celebration. I spent mine with an old friend who made it really special." The coded message would be passed on to those who needed to know.

Chapter 12

FARID WAS HAVING an especially good morning. The investigation of Max Stephens indicated that the man's tenure as a security analyst ended when he got into a jurisdictional dispute with the leadership of Homeland Security. He'd walked away determined to help airlines avoid endless hours of federal oversight which he believed was all fluff, just busywork designed to check the boxes; what the industry called 'the illusion of safety.' In a letter to the Director, he'd emphasized that the only real security would come from traditional intelligence work to find threats before they materialized. It was almost impossible to monitor the huge number of aircraft entering U.S. airspace every day.

Farid committed to meet the man in the Bahamas the following Monday. He and Stephens were going to do an inspection of the jets that WILTON just committed to purchase. They were already modified for freight, but part of the business plan that was coming together called for the installation of a first-class passenger cabin for up to four passengers.

The business effort was coming together. Just as important to Farid, it had been four weeks since the meeting at his uncle's. Mohamed had assured the group that if there was any way to overcome the nuclear origin issue, he, Salman, and ONE would notify everyone within a month. He knew that there was no way that his family would walk away from his father's death without exacting some revenge, but it looked like starting a war would not be the way.

He picked up his phone, which he'd silenced for the meeting and called Sarah, sending her a message. "Hey girl, its spring in the Caribbean, you know, warm without being scorching, gentle breezes, lots of lobster and chilled wine. I'm flying to Nassau tomorrow, care to join me?"

He finished the message just as a new message popped up on his phone. He read a note from his uncle suggesting that he look at some photos that he'd just sent to Farid's personal tablet. The note finished with, "all good stuff, better viewed on a larger screen than your phone."

A chill went down Farid's spine. He'd hoped the message would be angry or frustrated, meaning the war was off. But the tone of the message told him what he was about to find when he got home and opened the message. The pictures sent to his regular account would just be cover for an encrypted message; a message he'd convinced himself would never come.

His phone beeped entering the elevator to his apartment. It was a reply from Sarah, giving him planned flights to the Bahamas and asking him to confirm that they worked with his schedule. He unlocked his apartment door, struggling to feel the joy he should feel. Kicking off his shoes he dropped onto the couch and opened his tablet. In the open messaging were six posts advertising products, travel, and men's pharmaceuticals. More than twenty additional Facebook posts covered subjects from politics to new book launches. He found one from Karim and clicked on it. What popped up were several pictures taken on the day he graduated.

Reluctantly he entered a complex series of codes and then leaned close to the camera for a retinal scan. A moment later, Mohamed's message opened, along with a second from ONE indicating that he was comfortable that the "Materials recently acquired" would help in the development of the project he was working on.

Farid poured himself a Scotch and wandered into his bedroom, almost in a daze. He knew that the only way to stop what he was beginning to think of as madness would be a direct conversation with his mother and uncle. He also knew that the family might just be so far into the plot that they would be honor bound to silence him. He sat on his bed next to an open suitcase and sipped the drink. His western life and education were colliding with the traditional values and honor code of his family. He finished his drink and wandered out to the living room and poured another. He wanted this to end, but the only idea he could come up with was to reveal the plot to the authorities, which meant prison for everyone involved. He was also knowledgeable enough to realize that there would be some involved who he didn't know about and revealing the plot meant he would be a walking dead man.

He switched to a new screen on his tablet and stumbled through flights to Nassau, selecting one that got him there only an hour before Sarah's planned arrival. He booked the flight and then a hotel on the beach. Things were easy when money was no object. In the end, nothing had changed since he'd made his commitment the day he graduated. It was best to get this over with. He sent Sarah a note with his arrival information.

"See you then, Mr. tall and dark. Love, Sarah," popped up on his phone.

He began to pack for a five-day trip with the woman he loved. When this was all over, he decided, spending the rest of his life with her might heal the guilt he was feeling. And for now, three nights of bliss, three mornings of sleeping late, three days on the beach and exotic dinners would take the edge off.

Farid ordered take-out before setting his alarm for early the next morning.

Farid waited in baggage claim for Sarah. She was the second person from her flight headed toward the luggage carrousel. He watched a smirk emerge on her face and then waited impatiently as she stopped to study every sign and poster as she crept toward him.

"I wouldn't want you to think I'm too anxious," she whispered as she pulled his head down and kissed him on the cheek. Stepping back, she launched herself into his arms, wrapping her arms and legs around him as she smothered his face with kisses. The people around them were all smiling.

After sailing through customs, Farid and Sarah were in a cab on their way to the hotel.

"Your text really surprised me," said Sarah, scrunched

so close to Farid's side that he couldn't raise his right arm. "Your timing couldn't have been better. In a couple of weeks, I'm off to a new job in the middle of the country, to a place that will make it a lot harder to meet you without a very long trip." Sarah checked to see if the cab driver was watching before she moved over a couple of inches and pulled Farid's hand forward and slipped it onto her thigh just behind her knee. "That's all you get until we are in our room," she whispered.

❧

"I would really like a swim before we dress for dinner," offered Sarah as she rolled off from Farid, her body glistening. Then, instead of some fancy place, I'd like to find a local diner where they specialize on conch soup. It's been a favorite since the first time my parents brought me here."

"How many times have you been here?" asked Farid.

"In Nassau, maybe three times, but growing up, we vacationed in the Bahamas and down in the Virgin Islands almost every winter." Sarah stood naked as she dug through her suitcase for a next to nothing string bikini. "I hope you don't mind me showing off a little,' she said as she dropped the suit onto the bed. "I've been working out every day. And I remember my mother looking at me one day as she pulled on a one-piece swimsuit. 'The time comes too soon when you no longer feel comfortable flaunting what God gave you,' she said. I'm not going to waste any of those years."

"I'm okay with it," said Farid as he rolled out of bed. "Maybe we should take a quick shower," he added, "I'm kind of sweaty," he paused, "but I am not complaining."

"Everybody is sweaty here in the afternoon," said Sarah with a laugh, "but if you want to, I'll meet you on the beach." She watched the man tug a surf style swimsuit from his luggage.

Dinner that night was in a small restaurant with six tables. They were the only tourists there, but the locals that filled the place knew what they were doing. Almost everyone was eating a huge bowl of soup or a salad with seafood. There was no chilled wine, but plenty of cold beer.

"You were right," said Farid as they wrapped up their meal. "This was exactly what I needed tonight."

She was glad he was loosening up, he'd been especially quiet up until that moment. "I've always liked to try local foods," replied Sarah. "I'm going somewhere that has a completely different cuisine for my new job. I'm looking forward to it, but I'll bet it is heavy with beef, and I don't eat a lot of red meat anymore."

"Tell me about the job."

"I'm moving to North Dakota. I'll be working for a non-profit that is leveraging private funding and grant money to help local Indian tribes build their economy. My office will be in Minot, but I'll be traveling and meeting with tribal economic development groups from all over the state."

"I have no idea of where that is."

"West of Chicago, in the northern Midwest. They have an airport. But if you want to fly anywhere you have to connect through one of the major airports in the center of the country. I've never been there, but I'm told it is extraordinarily beautiful country. There are a lot of ranches and big farms. A lot of the local economy is military, but that doesn't necessarily help the local people on their reservations. It's my dream job, that is if I can't go to Africa and do the same thing."

"So that just means that I will have to give you more than a day's notice when I'm in the country." Farid paused. He watched a young couple with a little girl get up from their table and head for the door. "It's probably not the kind of place where I can make a living."

Sarah reached across the table and covered his hand with hers. "That's okay. If and when we decide we are forever, I don't plan on working. My mom gave up her career when my folks got married. They spent the first few years just traveling. She did volunteer work while my dad built the business. When kids came along, she was completely devoted to them. I've always thought that I might follow her lead."

"I like that," said Farid. "I'm beginning to think that's where we are headed."

"You make me happy," she said. "The last couple of times we've been together, you seemed a little distracted." She paused a moment before adding, "I thought that was my job."

Farid almost forgot about his uncle's messages as he watched Sarah race through the doors of the airport. Sarah had moved up her flight when she learned that Farid had a nine o'clock meeting. He'd almost forgotten the message, but it was there in his mind as he gave the cab driver a new address which turned out to be only a five-minute drive away, just on the other end of the airport.

Time to be the executive that gets WILTON into the air freight business. But the mission had changed a little. The retribution for his father's betrayal that landed Farid at WILTON had morphed. Now, Farid needed to find a way to support the attacks planned by ONE at locations targeted by TWO without destroying the company he worked for and without leaving a trace that could lead to him. His thoughts turned to joy of the little girl and her father the night before. He'd never thought much about having children, but they were having a lot of fun. The cab pulled up to where Maxwell Stephens waited outside a small office. Behind the building rose the tails of two jets emblazoned with the airlines name, BAM.

Stephens introduced Farid to a graying man in a pair or worn jeans and a blue Carhartt T-shirt. "Perkins here, is a retired aeronautical engineer. He moved down here about ten years ago after a long career with Douglas Aircraft. Anyway, I told him about your idea of adding a little passenger space to our Boeing 767s and he offered to take a look with us."

Farid shook the man's hand then all three made their way through BAM's tiny office. Farid made note that there was no warehouse or hanger facility. They stopped at the bottom of the roll-up stairs, studying the plane. "You can't see it from the outside," started Perkins, "but the structural changes that convert a passenger jet to a freighter also take away most of the internal attachment and bracing for adding modifications." They climbed the stairs and opened the door, "just a big barn in here," said Perkins.

"I'd think the right place to add four luxury seats and a small galley would be near the cockpit where you could share the toilet and where the passengers could communicate easily with the flight crew," said Stephens.

"Makes sense, said Perkins, and if we do it right, it won't significantly reduce the freight capacity. But it will affect the weight and balance of the plane. The freight loading center of gravity will move aft, so we will need to consider that."

Farid just stood there, not understanding much of what was being discussed.

"The new owners envision a different business model," said Stephens. They have contacts to work with defense contractors and the governments. That may put the aircraft into locations where there are threats most carriers don't worry about. We might add a little weight forward by adding some electro-magnetic shielding to the radios and operational computers."

"Can one of you explain what we are talking about?" asked Farid.

"Almost every part of a modern airplane is controlled by computers. Those and the radio and navigation equipment are all vulnerable to electrical interference from lightning or other natural generators of electrical interference. They are also vulnerable to attacks by weapons that generate an electrical pulse, including a nuclear weapon," offered Stephens.

"Most of the components have significant shielding built into them," added the engineer, "but we could add some additional lead shielding. It would decrease the risk and might actually improve the plane's balance characteristics. Since most of the critical components are housed in the same area, it should be pretty easy."

Farid finally began to grasp what they were talking about. He'd never considered what carrying a nuclear weapon might do in an aircraft. He logged the conversation away for a future discussion with ONE and Salman as the three men continued their survey of the planes.

Chapter 13

THE U.S. CAPITAL was strangely quiet, like it was resting as the hearing got under way. It took less than three hours of questions and testimony for Gritt and others to realize that the senators were happy with how the EEL and ANGEL conflict turned out and even more pleased that they could quit worrying about a surprise nuclear strike on the homeland. No surprise bomber attacks, no cruise missile strikes, no traditional or hyper-sonic attack would penetrate the new defense system once the last five ANGELS were operational.

In the interim, the nations that posed a threat were as quiet as they had been for decades. Their strategic investment in nuclear strike capability was turning out to be just money poured into old fashioned outhouses. America's nuclear deterrent faced no such restriction and would not for whatever time it took for the other side to field powerful defensive systems. The other players were being very quiet. As a courtesy to those who had been involved in the North Pacific crisis, the chairman of the Intelligence

Committee continued with the schedule, but a sense of security after years of worry over the threat of a surprise attack permeated the room.

By noon on the last day, Gritt was becoming concerned. The report he'd spent months on, making clear that the real risk was what the nation didn't anticipate, was being received with a huge yawn. The traditional military hawks now believed the top Pentagon brass who were quietly pressing for money to complete the ANGEL umbrella and the expansion of special forces to support allies facing local threats. The progressives were already chomping at the bit to dismantle much of the strike capacity of the Army, Air Force, Space Force and Navy. A senator from California summed up their take on what they had heard with, "imagine what we can do with the money we save on our traditional military. Eliminating poverty is within our grasp."

As Gritt waited for Olga to finish dressing for Director Chang's invitation-only dinner party, he found a private corner of his house to make a quick call to Thad Walker at Flathead Lake.

After a brief update on fishing, where Gritt could only be envious of Walker answering his phone while rowing his wooden boat on a glorious evening on a flat calm lake, Gritt finally asked, "are you following the hearings?"

The chuckle from his mentor was unexpected. "Yup, kind of like what happens after every war ends. The military shifts their emphasis to protect their budgets. The liberals declare our universal safety and launch policy campaigns to shift spending. The intelligence community whose job is to anticipate risks and study snippets of potential problems is ignored. Our allies anticipate more help dealing with their threats but wonder if America will slip into one of our periods of isolation. The press will make headlines of the little they are allowed to really know, usually trumpeting something about our children, grandchildren, grandparents, and friends now being safe. Democracy is safe. Kumbaya, let's all get together and love one another."

"Are you always such a cynic?" asked Gritt. "There was no war, and that's what we were sent there to prevent. The leadership is taking a victory lap and ignoring our report."

"After Viet Nam, my whole career has been focused on keeping small conflicts small," replied Thad. "I've walked out of a dozen meetings and hearings feeling just like you do now. If I'd known just how much joy there was in slowly rowing a boat on a crystal-clear lake years ago, I'd probably have thrown in the towel. But I didn't and neither will you. We both know that there are threats out there, some we don't even know about. Nobody ever thanked me for never letting down my guard, but if it helps you stay focused, let me be the one to thank you. I don't want anything interrupting my focus on bird hunting this fall while I can still walk a little."

Olga found Gritt sitting near the downstairs window, his feet propped up on what she suspected was a very expensive antique table. She waited as Gritt finished his conversation. "Who was that?"

"Thad Walker, and he just gave me a pep talk on doing my job."

"We both walked away from the hearing worried."

Gritt picked up his travel vest and zipped his wallet into one of the pockets. He held the door for Olga and watched her descend the steps toward the street where Gritt parked his car. Her movement was slow, graceful, kind of like a stream current swirling in a long gentle pool. He had every reason to shake off his conversation with Walker as he closed the Corvette door on an eighty-degree evening in DC. But he couldn't. He slipped the key into the ignition.

"Walker says it's always like this after a conflict. He said it was up to us to never let down our guard. He knows that there still are threats and it's up to people like us to keep our eyes and ears open."

"And he knows we will," replied Olga as the car pulled away from the curb. "But it's somebody else's job for tonight." She was silent until Gritt pulled onto the entrance ramp to a highway. "Tonight, we are going to enjoy the wind in our hair, at least until one of the people you work with at the agency starts to talk shop." She loosened her seatbelt and pulled herself up to where the top of her head was slightly above the windshield. She fluffed her medium length auburn hair with both hands. Turning her head slowly from side to side, she let the wind undo her earlier effort to style her hair. Then she kissed her left forefinger and tapped Gritt on the cheek.

Both Olga and Chad were surprised when Chang's dinner party turned out to be a simple get to know each other better event. Pete Wilson the agency's director of technology, a small wiry man with black horn-rimmed glasses and a receding hairline was there with his wife, a stunning woman a few years older than him, who worked as a substance abuse counselor for the Veteran's Administration. Jana Taylor who headed operations, was there with her girlfriend, a doctor. Director Chang's wife,

Nancy was from a wealthy California family. Previously, she was with Boeing's international sales division, but following Chang's appointment and their move to the East Coast, her full attention now turned to the couple's twin daughters and sixteen-year-old son. The kids were all staying with friends for the night, a complicated event with the security that surrounded the Chang family. Dinner that night was a fusion of Chang's favorite Korean dishes and his wife's light California fare, prepared by Nancy Chang herself.

As the host worked his way around the table pouring each of his guests a glass of a late harvest dessert wine, Pete Wilson turned to Chad. "I know the boss said no work tonight, but I just wanted to pass on that we would still like you to consider moving over to the agency."

Jana began to laugh. "You are like a broken record sometimes, Pete. Chad here is exactly where he needs to be right now, using his engineering skills in a military think-tank where he has access to DARPA and every other technical group in the government."

Pete just smiled before he added, "for now then, just keep in touch. Your hair-brained, off the wall ideas are exactly the thing we need to stay sharp." He paused a moment. "The Director and I were discussing the paper you developed on future threats, and Thad Walker's notes. We agree with everything in them."

"The Director introduced me to Thad," replied Gritt. "When I first met him, he told me that we are always playing catchup. That for some reason, it seemed, like we never take a threat seriously until it bites us in the ass."

"Mostly true," replied Chang as he reseated himself. "But not entirely. We never took the threat of nuclear war lightly. It took us seven decades to come up with a good defense. Up until that time, our answer was making the cost of any attack so overwhelming that nobody would try it. We're still focused on biological and chemical warfare threats. The damned COVID thing a few years ago taught us how even a mistake by country can cause major damage." He sipped his wine before adding, "but in general, Thad you're right, and that doesn't make any of us feel very good. The key is to try our best to anticipate who might harm us and work from there."

Nancy Chang held up her hand. "A toast to a well-executed mission, whatever you all did together that justified a senatorial hearing." She lifted her glass. "And for Commander Gritt here, and Major Tvorshik, who are at least twenty years younger than anyone else in the room, and who live thousands of miles apart, a toast to being together. Now let's wrap this up so they can spend some time together before the Major heads back to her duty station."

The young couple were on their way home, the purr of the mufflers on a classic Chevy V-8 the only sound as Olga flew her flattened hand in the air above the windshield. "My C.O. has been making some noise about me moving out of the Aleutians. He mentioned security here in DC, but I told him I'd rather stay engaged in actual Air Force security for now."

"I'd like to have you somewhere closer," replied Chad.

"My boss mentioned that the Air Force is getting a lot of feedback from the intelligence community because of what happened in our little adventure out there. I think I'll have a couple of options in the next month, but I'm not anxious to leave the Aleutians until a replacement arrives and I can pass on my experience. That job is like no other in the military." She paused as she studied the dashboard in front of her, pointing at the old-fashioned AM radio. "How about some music?" she said as she pushed the power button.

"Great, if you can find some," replied Gritt as he pulled onto the highway back to DC. "Most AM stations are now just sports, talk or news."

The radio came to life just as the news reported, "... and the Iranians are threatening a major retaliation for what they claim was an American commando attack on a Revolutionary Guard base where they operate most of their light maritime patrol craft. They said at least twenty boats were destroyed by a surprise American commando attack."

Olga began scrolling through AM stations, finally finding one that barely came in, playing Mexican music. The announcers spoke only in Spanish. "This will have to do for now," she said.

But both were still thinking about the news they'd just heard.

Chapter 14

KARIM AND SALMAN huddled at the kitchen table in Farid's London flat. Salman had been briefed only days before by ONE. He had no way to test the uranium balls from Iran, to actually determine if they met the 90% purity most scientists believed was necessary to create a nuclear weapon. But based on Mohamed's briefing, drawn from his visit to EAGLE, he felt comfortable that the Iranian scientists would have never milled the material into explosive devices if they didn't believe they would detonate. In the early days, the Iranians worked directly with scientists from Pakistan who were contracted to help the Persian Gulf country become a nuclear power. Those same scientists had helped North Korea become a member of the nuclear club. The world now knew that they were building weapons that posed a real risk.

Farid mostly listened as Salman and his uncle explained progress in every area of the plan. They were especially happy with the progress that FOUR was making. He, working with some of Mohamed's contacts had orchestrated the attack on the Revolutionary Guard Navy base. They had killed two watchmen and then dropped timed explosive devices into twenty armed speedboats before retreating without being detected. Before leaving they dropped a swim fin and a weight belt off from a dock well away from the exploding boats. Both were American manufacture and similar to what American Navy SEALs used.

Karim carried copies of London newspapers reporting the disruption in the U.S. Capital caused by a phone call that programmers working out of the Tbilisi facility had routed through a telephone exchange in Tehran. The article reported that American intelligence agencies were working hard to trace the exact location of the calls and that the Americans had confronted Iranian authorities at the United Nations.

Farid had prepared a report on his progress, including the acquisition of BAM by WILTON and his visit to the Bahamas. He wrapped up with a discussion of his visit. Perhaps the discussion of possible interference to a plane's operations from a nuclear weapon might again derail the project. The more progress they made, the more he regretted being involved.

"This engineer that I met in the Bahamas tells me that there is something called Electro Magnetic Interference and that can cause major problems with the flight controls and radios and anything else on an aircraft," he said. "He also suggested that you might be able to reduce the risk if you added more lead shielding to critical systems." He paused, waiting for any response from the others. They remained silent.

"The guy specifically spoke about interference caused by nuclear weapons," he added.

Both Salman and Karim laughed. "The learning curve is steep," said Karim. "You are right to question every possible flaw in our plan, Farid. But think about it; American, British, French, Chinese and Russian planes have been carrying nuclear weapons for decades."

"ONE explained it to us years ago. The actual explosion of a nuclear device sends out a pulse of energy. It can disrupt anything electrical, especially any device that can be programmed. We are counting on that to ramp up the impact of a small detonation. We don't want to kill a lot of Americans, but if the explosion destroys a thousand computers, or takes down the local communications network, or impacts factories or even aircraft in the area, well, that works in our favor."

Farid remained silent. He wasn't sure if his colleagues were laughing at him or chastising his lack of knowledge. His silence, he realized, might also be disappointment. The plan was moving forward.

"Do not be so somber, Farid," said Salman. "What you just discussed may just solve a problem that ONE has wrestled with for years. If the aircraft modifications are made and additional lead shielding is installed, and a small area the size of one of our suitcase bombs is left empty, that is where we will hide the weapon. Any detection devices at an airport will be useless if the weapon is surrounded by shielding." He paused, then added, "thank you for being so thorough. The only thing left is to figure out a justification for such a hiding spot."

"I will discuss it with the pilots on the family plane when we return," said Karim. "They were read into our plan years ago. One of them will have a good idea. I'll share their insights next week."

"Just how many people know about our plan?" asked Farid.

"It is a small and very loyal group," replied Salman. "You do not need to worry about that. You are the only new member in the last five years. There will be no leaks. Anyone who became a concern was permanently replaced."

"What we will need from you as quickly as you can provide it, will be a timeline for when WILTON's new planes will be finished and operational. We are already working on some actual freight contracts that will allow deliveries to locations selected by TWO." Karim picked up his suit coat from the chair near the window. "Now, I am starving. Where are you taking these two old men for dinner Farid?"

Over dinner, Karim revealed that the group had purchased a small liquor and wine distribution company. The acquisition was done through shell companies registered in Europe. Existing management in each company was retained.

"According to the attorneys we hired to make the acquisition, the new company's management team had never heard of our unique business philosophy of 'hit them where they aren't' but weren't about to turn down new development capital to expand into a list of cities we provided," explained Karim. "We gave them enough capital to lease facilities in ten smaller cities around the U.S. Three of those cities are close to targets identified by TWO."

"Explain hit them where they aren't," said Farid being careful with his language to avoid giving any clue that what they were discussing was anything other than a business conversation.

"Simple, since the new companies are small it will be

easier to build up market share where they don't have to go head to head with huge competitors. Once we gain dominance in smaller cities we can expand into the larger markets, but with strong cashflow and organizations behind us, The business interest is a bonus added to our plan."

Farid was surprised by the depth of the planning. But it made sense. WILTON's growth plan was similar, especially for the new aviation unit.

"We would like to help you out in your new career," said Salman. "If we can use your company's new aviation unit to move freight, we will."

"But keep your pencil sharp when you give us pricing," added Karim. "We aren't so loyal to family that we will waste money."

The cab driver dropped Farid at his building before taking Karim and Salman to their private jet. It had surprised Farid that they used the jet for a short hop from Paris, when the helicopter would have been faster. It turned out that the two were not returning to Paris, but they hadn't discussed the destination with Farid.

The following evening, Farid received a text from Karim, letting him know that he was sending some photos. Farid was still in the office, working out the final details of the acquisition of BAM aviation. It was after ten when he finally got home and opened his laptop to find a picture of the two men and Mohamed at an outside table in Turkey overlooking a busy waterway. He wasn't surprised by the location or by the message received after he opened the secure messaging system.

"With the plan to add seats to the WILTON air freighters, it only makes sense to include a location for any specialized computer or communications equipment

a client may need. Recommend a shielded space of about 100 centimeters wide by 90 centimeters deep by at least 60 centimeters high. Recommend that inside include a floor that allows equipment to be secured. You will not need to include any holes through the shielding for electrical or antenna cables as the client will need to specify where they are needed and pay for any installation. The space will need a shielded door that can be locked from the outside." –Karim

Karim converted the metric measurements to inches and composed a memo to Perkins who was now on retainer to WILTON with a recommendation that he add such a space to his plan for converting the two planes. The goal was to have the conversion complete as quickly as possible. That was consistent with Dorsey's direction that Farid brief the company sales department to begin looking for customers and freight loads.

Farid mixed himself a drink and picked up the phone. "Sarah, it's me, just checking in."

"Thanks, my love, but I can't really talk right now. I'm going through security for a trip to Minot. I'll be apartment hunting. My dad refuses to buy a place there until he is convinced that I'll be staying."

"That makes sense to me," replied Farid. "Anyway, I was just thinking about you and wanted to hear your voice."

"Love you too. Give me a couple of days. I'll call you on Saturday mid-morning if I can keep the time zones straight. Gotta go. Bye."

Chapter 15

ONE HAD BEEN reworking the suitcase bombs since Mohamed returned from Iran. The orbs of enriched uranium from EAGLE were slightly smaller than the Russian uranium they replaced. The shell around the orb was made of nine pieces of explosive material all wired to detonate simultaneously. The tiny gap caused by the smaller orb would make it impossible to get the concise and uniform compression needed to reach the critical state that would cause a nuclear reaction.

"Have you solved the problem yet?" asked Salman.

ONE held up one of the silver-grey orbs. Then he lifted a second that was now a brilliant white. "The second orb is now encased with a uniform coating. It makes the diameter identical to the original," replied ONE. From everything I can find, the coating will allow a uniform compression. The material has about the same hardness as the uranium underneath it, and there should be no chemical or mechanical interference with the explosive material.

There are no 'how to' manuals for what we are attempting, but I see no obvious problem with the solution."

"So, it will work," said Salman?

"My friend, we have been working on this for more than a decade now. But the plan changed when we had to replace the known Russian material with the unknown from Iran. If the uranium that Mohamed brought from the EAGLE base in Iran is properly enriched, then it should work." He paused as he placed each orb back into a lead container. "I have handled the materials enough that I have exceeded the recommended exposure on my monitor tag. This must be done as perfectly as possible, and I trust only myself to accomplish the task." He paused again, "but we will not know for sure that this material will go boom or explode with enough energy to cause the damage we seek until we test it."

Salman put his arm across ONE's shoulders. "We did not ask you to sacrifice your life to achieve our goals my friend."

"I do not think we have reached that point yet," replied ONE, "but if it is so, then it will have been for a good cause."

"Can we not share the burden with any of your people?"

"Now that I have figured out how to do the coating, I intend to allow others with less exposure do the other two orbs."

"And you know," said Salman, "that it will be impossible to test the device any way except to see if it explodes at the first target. We will choose where to place the bomb after TWO drives through the area. We want the greatest emotional impact with a minimum loss of life. There are so many security cameras that a nuclear explosion at night will be impossible to miss."

"I pray that you are right about the damage. If I thought we could bring down the regime that is destroying my homeland using the devices with their original Russian uranium by attacking the government and Revolutionary Guard directly I would prefer that, but with only four devices it is impossible."

"They are too deeply entrenched after all these years, they are so sure that they are doing the work of Allah that they will not go away until they are destroyed," said Salman. "Only the Americans have that kind of power."

ONE smiled for the first time that day. "We will not need our own cameras to watch that. Wherever the American military goes, the world watches. The media will be covering it like it was some big circus. Our new country will show the world that a successful nation does not need that kind of deprived thinking. Perhaps we can lead the world in destroying such weapons."

"Farid sent word that the planes will be ready to transport the first bomb in a couple of months. Will you be ready?" asked Salman.

"The first will be ready," replied ONE. "Now that I have perfected the coating, the others can be finished, but we will prepare one at a time. The finished orb must be as precise as possible."

"That is good, my friend. TWO has chosen five targets, but we will only strike three. The first is in a fairly urban area with only civilian targets. If that does not provoke the Americans, we will select another. Some have American military close by." Salman turned toward the door. "I will be meeting with TWO in the next couple of days, before he travels to America. We will confirm our timeline after he returns."

"If the plan fails, we will use the fourth bomb with the Russian material to blow up the Territorial Guard Headquarters, hopefully while the political leadership is visiting," said Salman. "I doubt that one explosion will lead to regime change, but we will have done our best."

One smiled at his mentor and boss. "I assume TWO will travel under a new identity. He already looks like an American, went to school there and speaks English with an American accent, so with an American name and passport he should be able to travel freely."

Only Salman knew that TWO was an American. "We have taken the identity from an American who died while volunteering in Ukraine. Nobody was ever notified of his death. Our humanitarian efforts in Ukraine, including paying to repatriate or bury foreign fighters was set up to find just such a person."

"So, TWO will travel with a new identity?"

Salman paused a moment. "He already is. I am even working on a third identity, just in case. TWO doesn't know it yet, but he will also be the courier who accompanies the bombs and places them at the target sights. He will be in and out of America a lot. It is time this becomes more than an intellectual exercise for him."

Chapter 16

THE STRAIT OF Hormuz was glassy calm. The American Destroyer *Walter* moved quickly past naval ships stationed at the entrance and began its transit to the Northwest. The ship had completed the passage ten times in the last three months, the last time just over three weeks ago. The ship's new instrument array, quickly installed at the Diego Garcia Naval Base, included additional monitors that would record electronic signals emanating from the Iranian coast which at one point would be only fifteen miles away. The communications network that tied together the Iranian coastal defense network was mostly fiber-optic cable, impossible to read. Where it was converted to electronic communications, verbal or machine language, the new sensors could intercept the transmissions, maybe.

The retrofit, scheduled for the *Walter's* next home port visit, was accelerated and moved to the Indian Ocean base as tensions rose with Iran. The Americans knew that they weren't responsible for the attack on the Revolutionary

Guard base as Iran was claiming and stated that in every possible venue. But satellite photographs taken the next day confirmed that someone attacked the base.

The *Walter's* job was to transit the narrow waterway, passing just north of Oman's Khasab peninsula. Almost every system not necessary to operate the ship was shut down to reduce electronic interference to the new sensors, all now pointed north. Normally the ship's captain would make the run at higher speed to limit the time close to Iranian defenses, and the ships radar operators would be on high alert for any risk from the air or one of the Iranian ports. But tonight, they were fishing for every possible signal between Iranian strong points and for any indication of heightened attack redlines. In every crisis, the Iranian authorities threatened to close the straits, where any disruption in oil tanker traffic could cripple the world's economy.

The run just east of the major Iranian port of Bander Abbas began just after ten at night. While it was impossible to coordinate with the Iranians, the American Navy had quietly arranged with every other nation with ports in the region to halt shipping for the ten hours that the *Walter* would be transiting. The straight was frighteningly empty on the dark night. Extra lookouts scanned every direction with binoculars in an attempt to replace a level of security now missing with the sensors including both radars shut down.

"God how I hate to rely on human eyes and handheld radios," offered the Captain to everyone on the bridge. "That Iranian Naval gunboat coming out of Bander Abas worried me," he continued, "but it turned the other direction. At least it was regular navy, not a Guard vessel."

"That was more than two hours ago," offered another

officer who would normally have been patrolling the ships Combat Information Center below the bridge. "We are at full combat readiness, and only the throw of a couple of switches away from engaging anything that challenges us."

I get it," replied the Captain, "but at eight knots, we will remain in the Iranian shore battery kill zone for five more hours." His comments did nothing to calm the nerves of the six other men on the bridge. Most American naval vessels were named after famous people or military heroes. The *Walter* was named after some anonymous former CIA operator; and now she was herself a spy ship.

"So far nothing on the monitors indicates a threat," replied the CIC officer. "The Saudi's have six small wooden boats just floating along the demarcation line. They are all carrying radios dialed into our frequencies. If they see anything, they will call."

"I know the mission profile," spat the captain. "I don't even mind the job. We follow orders, but we are vulnerable as hell."

Two hours later, in the distance the lights of a large ship were called in by one of the lookouts. "Ensign, get a night light profile book out to that lookout and tell me what is coming at us. Hell, we're so shut down that we aren't even getting information from that ship's transponder." The most junior officer on the bridge rifled through a set of manuals, selected one, and burst out the door from the bridge.

The CIC officer fought off a smile as his own binoculars offered the rough outline of an oil tanker, probably just leaving one of the Iranian offshore oil loading platforms only twenty miles away. A minute later, he double clicked the transmit key on the handheld radio on his belt. "Sir," he said tapping his earpiece, "lookouts confirm an Iranian tanker, but it's still too far away to confirm her identity." He paused as he studied the old-fashioned paper chart on a table behind him. "I can faintly see the lights of what I think is a loading platform behind that ship."

Three hours later, safely in a friendly port, the same CIC officer supervised five enlisted people as they pulled digital and hard copies of the data gathered from their instruments and packaged them in small, lined metal briefcases. They would be analyzed at the Farragut center in the states within hours.

"I assume that your people saw nothing that we should be really concerned about," offered the Captain. The CIC officer was finally making his way to the officer mess after handing the cases off to an air force officer and aide waiting on the dock.

"No Sir, nothing out of the norm. And the air force major who will accompany the data all the way to the states, indicates nothing new in their aerial recon runs today."

"Our orders keep us on this side of the Straight for a week, and then we do this again, after the techies and spooks in Navy Intelligence look at the data." He paused over his coffee before adding, "it was just our luck that we were the closest ship to Diego that could accommodate the new sensors. We are going to do this again."

"Probably several more times," said the CIC officer. "I'm off to get some rack time."

***

Chad Gritt hadn't planned on a drive out to the CIA headquarters when he headed for work that day. A small army of analysts at the Farragut Technical Analysis Center had poured through the data collected in the Strait of Hormuz. Gritt himself had been on the phone with his counterparts in Naval Intelligence. Neither group found anything earth-shaking in the information. So, the call from the Agency telling him that they were sending a car to pick him up a little before ten that morning was a surprise.

On the ride to the CIA's rural headquarters Gritt took a few minutes to reread the report on the data and then a short memorandum he'd authored to the head of the Farragut center. He was just finishing the reading when his phone buzzed with a text.

"*You're the first to know. Relocating to the real world. Replacement already on the island, so should be rotating in about thirty days. I have some leave coming. How about you? Love Olga.*"

Gritt thought about the two documents he'd just studied to prepare for his meeting with Jana Taylor. *No real news and no good news* flashed through his mind.

A guide met Gritt at a secure door well away from the reception area of the massive facility. In ten minutes, he was seated in a small conference room with a fresh cup of coffee and there he waited for another ten minutes before the Operations Director of the Agency burst into the room, flanked by two of her staff.

"Lieutenant Commander Gritt, this is Marjorie Smyth from our Iran desk, and Ray Callaway, who monitors military hardware movement in the Persian Gulf. Marjorie and Ray, you have never worked with Gritt before, but he's kind of become our liaison with the tech geeks at the Navy."

Gritt shook hands with all three. "Please call me

Chad," he started and then turned to Jana. "You summoned me, so you start first."

"Let's start with the data that you got from that destroyer who we dangled out as bait in the Strait of Hormuz."

"I doubt that the crew of the *Walter* would appreciate you referring to them as bait," replied Gritt. "Anyway, here is a complete copy of the data and the report from the Farragut team. Basically, it's baseline data since we were looking for signaling that we had never recorded or analyzed before. We see nothing pressing in what we collected."

Jana pointed at Marjorie. The trim fiftyish woman with salt and pepper hair cut short and wearing a bright yellow pant suit opened a file in front of her. "Our collective intelligence tells us that the Revolutionary Guard is furious over the attack on their base, but that the religious leadership that calls all the shots wants to tone this down." She paused, and Gritt could tell there was a big BUT coming.

"The problem is that the Guard who were created as a private army for the Mullahs running Iran have grown a bit too big for their britches. We have electronic intelligence as well as some limited HUMINT that the Guard leadership is quietly plotting a tit for tat revenge. A couple of analysts on Marjorie's staff believe that a small attack against America, probably in the region would be overlooked by the Regime." She turned to Ray and nodded.

Ray tugged at his bright red tie, a color that clashed with his Peach colored ill-fitting blazer. He brushed his long blond hair out of his eyes and hesitated before starting. "You guys in the Navy know a lot better than me about the military strength of the Iranians, especially the weapons deployed by the Guards small boat militias and the Iranian Navy. With that said, apparently the Guard has been aggressively looking for components for a new missile guidance system. Our contacts in Turkey and Iraq have been very helpful on this. We thought it was all about one of their Intercontinental Ballistic Missile programs, but some of the data from Marjorie's people indicate that they may be modifying some of their mid-range missiles for coastal defense. They have a half dozen systems already deployed now, but this would be an enhanced version, designed to overcome our electronic countermeasures. Enhanced guidance would be necessary if they were modifying missiles to fly erratic patterns on the way to a target. A multi-missile launch using erratic flight paths would make it difficult to intercept everything thrown against a target, especially if it was a single vessel."

Marjorie picked up the conversation. "The chatter we are monitoring indicates that they are working on a combined system capability designed to overwhelm our navy's defenses. If that is the case, they may be targeting one of our carriers, especially one that is transiting the Strait. They know we would hit them back hard, but they might be willing to take the hit. They don't think the U.S. would use nuclear weapons to retaliate and they seem to think they can deal with anything else." She referred back to her notes. "We also have communications intercepts indicating they knew the *Walter* had turned off their electronic defenses."

"Anything else that you can give Chad? Anything really specific that he can home in on?" asked Jana. Both Marjorie and Ray shook their heads. "Alright, stay near your phones in case we need more and feel free to take any calls from the Lieutenant Commander in the future." She waited until both were gone.

"Now let me tell you how I look at all this," she continued. "This all seems a little bit too packaged to me. I can't imagine the guard defying the Religious leadership openly. But tensions are high, and you needed to hear these reports. The top brass in the Navy will take this seriously coming from you, and your people on the tech side might be able to come up with even more ways of monitoring any expanded threat. We didn't hit that Guard base, and the Navy didn't, and we are assured by the Saudi's and the Israeli's that they didn't. But someone did and the folks at the Guard are just fanatical enough to do something stupid."

"Like I tried to point out at the hearing a month ago, the greatest threat to us right now is probably something or someone we don't know about. We know about the Iranians, and I will pass the word that they may be fraying at the seams. With internal problems among their own people they are already stressed. I'll ask our people if they can come up with any other ways of monitoring the Guard's marine units, the Iranian Navy, and the coastal defenses. Maybe we can look at the sensor array on the *Walter* and tweak it to look for something more."

Gritt paused as he watched Jana fold up the briefing folder in front of her. "I agree with you, something might not be as it seems." He slid both the folders he'd brought across the table as he leaned his chair back. "That bomb threat at the hearings came from a telephone exchange in Iran. It may be a warning." Jana led him to the door where his facility guide waited. "I'll keep in touch," he said.

Chapter 17

General Ashraf's wife rushed his phone to the courtyard where the general sat watching two hummingbirds at a feeder. Watching them was his favorite way of meditating. When handing him the phone she noted a worried look on his face, a look she'd seen more and more over the last year. The phone quit ringing before the general could answer. He waited for a message signal and then clicked on the message button.

It was his friend Reza. Ashraf hit return and Reza's number began to ring.

"She is moving," said Reza, without even a salutation.

Ashraf knew that Reza was referring to the American ship *Walter*. Reza was regular army and as troubled about the direction Iran was moving as he was. It had been Reza's nephew who had helped Ashraf and Mohamed switch out the uranium orbs.

"Are we in a position to interrupt her trip?" asked Ashraf.

"There are some men who are as worried as we are,"

replied Reza. "They are only an hour away and have offered to help."

"We should encourage them," replied Ashraf.

"I will call my old friend." And with that Reza was gone.

Ashraf ended the call and then called Mohamed's number. "Salam, my old friend. I wanted you to know that some friends have offered to help that woman we discussed the other day. I know nothing more, but they indicated she may need help tonight."

"Many thanks for letting me know," replied Mohamed. "As Confucius said, the longest journey begins with the first step. Your friends will be much appreciated."

ぐ

Hours later, two men dressed in Revolutionary Guard Uniforms braked their Toyota truck next to a small promontory overlooking the Strait of Hormuz. One of the men unlocked the gate surrounding a small block house then both made their way across the parking lot behind the building. The one dressed as an officer tapped on the door and a moment later a young guard lieutenant opened it.

"We are visiting each of the Zafar missile batteries in this segment tonight," said the officer. "We are to observe you and your two men prepare to engage an American ship right up to when you would actually fire the missiles. When we are finished with your site, we should still have time to visit two more sites tonight."

The officer handed the junior officer a letter assuring the man that the inspection was part of an enhanced readiness. "With the heightened tensions we must all be ready to defend the government and people without any delays. Just as important, we must ensure that nobody lets their passions get away from them. We do not want any accidental war before we are ready to destroy our enemy."

Moments later, an operator in the corner called out a warning. "Sir, we have a slow-moving ship just entering our protection zone. She is not emitting any radar signals, but our optical enhancement indicates she is an American destroyer." The man paused before adding, "I think it may be the same ship that passed a week ago gathering intelligence."

"Great timing," said the officer, "we can get this over in a few minutes and then we will be on our way."

"What exactly would you like to see, Sir?" said the site commander.

"Order your team to prepare to intercept and destroy that target. We will observe right up to the point of actually launching the missiles, and then you may stand down."

"Are we to prepare to launch all four missiles?"

"Prepare to launch two, per protocol. But be prepared to launch the other two within two minutes. In a real situation, you would receive specific orders to launch and the other three batteries in your unit would all be launching at the same time. That would be eight missiles launched and eight in reserve." The officer slid into a chair as his aide leaned against the wall near the operators. "You may start now."

The room erupted into well-organized motion.

~

Aboard the *Walter*, the routine was identical to the transit one week before. Eight pairs of eyes were glued to binoculars as the ship reached the narrowest part of the strait.

"I don't know why," offered the captain, "but I'm even more nervous tonight than last week."

"Last week went quite smoothly," replied the same officer who would normally be in the combat information center. "We made small adjustments to the new equipment as ordered. The manuals transmitted by Farragut tell me this test is designed to watch for increased electronic activity at each defensive location along the Iranian coast as we traverse. That will be compared to the baseline we got last week. I guess we will keep doing this until something changes, and I assume that will mean something to someone."

"Now there is a first-class explanation of a bullshit mission," offered the captain. He turned to the Lieutenant JG who had just spoken. "That's not a critique of you Jones, just a simple statement of how little this makes sense to me. At least we are already at battle stations."

The captain turned to a young ensign at the rear of the bridge. "Mr. Roberts, the bad guys on the northern shore are certainly looking at us and wondering just what in the hell we are doing creeping along with no emissions. Can you take a quick look and tell me how they are armed?"

The ensign tapped on the keys of a computer in front of him and waited a moment to study a map that popped up. "Right now, Sir, we are crossing an RG missile battery with four launch sites all equipped with ZAFAR anti-ship cruise missiles. They have a range of about 25 miles at a speed of about four hundred miles an hour. One or two hits would probably not sink us, but they could cause a lot of damage."

"That's enough, Roberts, I know what the capabilities

of the ZAFAR are. They could sure slow us down while the other side rolled out some heavier ordinance."

The captain refilled his coffee cup and plopped himself into his chair.

"The techs below report nothing unusual," said the CIC officer. There appears to be no increase in chatter as we transit. With our own active radar off, we are monitoring incoming radar more closely. The ZAFAR uses its own active targeting radar to track its targets. If one of them lights up, we will know."

"I get it Mr. Jones," said the captain, but if that happens and we are only fifteen miles from the launch point the damned thing will be here in two ..."

His speech was interrupted by a warning bell and light above their heads. A moment later one of the enlisted men at a console looked up. "We have a radar lock-on, Sir." The panic in his voice showed.

"Damn, not tonight," replied the captain. "Those bastards love to tease us with radar locks that disappear in seconds, just to harass us."

"Do you want to light us up, Sir?" came a call from the back of the bridge.

"If we do, it will wipe out any data coming into the sensors," said Jones.

The captain hesitated, but for only a few seconds. "Fuck the data, let's see what's out there."

Everyone was in motion at once. What was advertised as instant on, didn't really mean instant as it took more than thirty seconds for the radars to search the ocean and then get their signal to the consoles.

"CIC reports a ZAFAR missile lock," came from the back of the bridge. Almost simultaneously those on the bridge could hear the buzz of the anti-missile gatling gun just below the bridge as it began to pour out hundreds of shells. That sound was drowned out by the blast of one missile detonating against the hull well back of the tower.

"Damage report get me a damage report," ordered the captain, not as calm as he had ever been. "I fucking knew this was bullshit."

"Damage control says it will take a few minutes. We have two sections not reporting."

The captain slid up behind a console operator who monitored a radar information feed from the Combat Information Center. "Anything else in the air out there?" The clock showed just under two minutes had elapsed since the initial alarm.

"That damned missile was in the air just seconds before we detected it," said the captain.

"My read, Sir, "offered Lieutenant JG Jones, "is the same. It was already in so close that the radar on the close in defense systems could not track it before it hit."

Before the captain could respond, a warning of a second missile shook everyone. This time their own radar began tracking it and within seconds the missile disintegrated as it was shredded by the same gun battery that had missed the first.

Power on the bridge began to flutter as the ship's propulsion system failed.

"I have hard coordinates for where both of those missiles came from," advised Jones. "Do you want to return fire? It seems it was just one battery."

The captain, hesitated. Seconds later, most of the power failed. "One battery, only one out of four launched against us. Every site has multiple missiles. Any other threats out there?"

"Nothing, Sir. We're struggling to keep the systems powered up, but it's a quiet as I've ever seen it."

"Get damage control on getting us emergency power," snapped the captain to the young ensign at the back of the bridge. We're almost stopped, a sitting duck. Get CIC power first, and then make sure our close in air-defense weapons are operational." The ship began to list to starboard.

"Check with the sensor operators. Is there any chatter between the four known ZAFAR sites?"

It took more than a minute for CIC to report back. "It took a while to get enough power to the new sensor consoles to get a reading. Nothing, Sir. No chatter at all and all the emissions from the site that launched have disappeared."

The first damage assessment came in. "We're hurt, sir. The missile hit almost on top of a berthing area. Thank God we were already at combat stations. We appear to have two fatalities and two wounded, but it could have been a lot worse. The engine room reports part of the above deck crashed onto the main electrical panel. They have lost propulsion power and primary generating capabilities. They extinguished a small fire and have backup generators online. It will take a while to reroute that power."

The young officer was holding up well, thought the captain.

"Sir, we have emergency power to the bridge, the anti-air defenses and our main gun battery. There is no way we can launch missiles." The ensign continued to scribble on an old-fashioned pad as he listened.

"Get me the admiral," ordered the captain, just as a small explosion shook the ship. "Get a distress call out and ask for air support and surface help. We're going to need a tow."

A call to the fleet commander took almost three minutes to connect, the noise of a cocktail party at the admiral's residence in the background as he answered. It took only a minute to brief the man on what had happened.

"This does not add up," commented the captain. "If the Iranians wanted to sink us, they would have launched a dozen missiles at once.

"I agree," replied the admiral. "This is not the start of a war, but someone is sure as hell sending us a message. Hold on a minute; I have another call."

It took less than a minute for the admiral to come back on the line. "You will have some air cover in less than ten minutes and there will be three ships on the way to help within a half hour.

"Sir," started the captain, "do you want us to take out the Iranian Guard battery that fired on us? The main gun is operational."

"Can you make the computer connection to load targeting data?"

"We can send the data down on a laptop. We've taken on about a seven-degree list, but we can elevate the gun. The target is only 18,000 meters away."

"Then wipe those bastards off the face of the earth," replied the admiral.

Within three minutes, the first of two guided shells from the Mark 45-gun turret was on its way.

ණ

There was a minute of stunned silence. "What in the hell are you doing?" screamed the site commander. "You just launched a missile at an American ship." He turned, just as the man in the officer's uniform pressed a pistol against his forehead and pulled the trigger. The shot sent blood and brains across the room where the commander's aide pressed a second button, launching the second missile. As he stepped away from the console, he pulled a pistol from his holster and calmly shot both console operators while his boss killed the fourth man as he tried to escape through the door.

As the two men dressed in Revolutionary Guard uniforms closed the door to the missile battery and took a moment to orient themselves. They'd turned off everything, even the lights after they made sure the four men were dead. They hadn't bothered to gather up the spent cartridge brass from their PV-9 Zoal pistols. They had been extremely careful when loading them. There would be no fingerprints or any DNA that could be traced back to them, and the Zoal was widely carried by the police, Guard and even the regular military. Besides, the plan assumed that the Americans would turn the site to dust in minutes.

The launch of the second missile had been planned, and the two-minute interval from the detonation of the first missile assured it would be destroyed. The men wanted the Americans to shoot it down, to see they were wounded but not helpless. Making sure the Americans could pinpoint the launch location was critical.

As they drove away, the man in the officer's uniform

pulled out his phone and called Reza's number. When Reza answered, he simply said, "that woman has been helped," and hung up. They were over a mile away when two detonations so close together they seemed one, shook the ground behind them.

Chapter 18

MATHEW CHANG SAT at his desk, stunned at the brazen attack on the American destroyer, now being towed to a secure port in Saudi Arabia. The latest casualty figures indicated that there were four dead and another seven wounded, many of the casualties from the engine room where a secondary explosion, that nobody had yet explained, occurred minutes after the Iranian Zafar missile struck the destroyer.

Jana Taylor sat in Chang's office, the same two people who briefed Chad Gritt at her side. "No, she said, "there is not a single indicator that the Iranians were about to fire on an American ship."

"What about their response to that same ship pulverizing the Guard battery that fired the two missiles?"

Jana looked over at the head of the Iranian desk, Marjorie. "This afternoon, you will hear screaming at the United Nations. Inside the country there is a war of words going on, with the Guard covering their ass by arguing the Americans fired first and the Army saying that if that had happened there wouldn't have been any missiles to launch."

"I have to brief the president in a couple of hours. "Is there any indication of an immediate Iranian retaliation for what they are calling American aggression?"

"None Sir, replied Marjorie, "but they are discussing alternatives. The one that seems to be winning out is the closure of the Strait to all marine traffic."

"That would hurt them as much as us," said Chang. "If it were to last more than a few days, it could really hit the world economy, especially with most of the world refusing to buy Russian oil."

"What does the Navy say about keeping the Strait open?" asked Jana.

"If the Iranians are determined to close it, the only solution would be the use of massive firepower to take out the Iranian missile sites that threaten shipping. The Navy would also have to destroy the entire Iranian Navy and the Revolutionary Guard Maritime units. In other words, they would have to start a major war."

Chang turned to Jana. "So, what do your folks think the next Iranian move will be?"

"It would be pure speculation, Sir."

"All right, then speculate away."

"My guess is that they will use their small patrol boats to harass every ship that passes

through the Strait. They might even use small arms against a tanker or two or maybe a freighter just to send a message that they can close the passage any time they want."

Chad Gritt got home a little after eleven that night. His people had specifically been tasked with updating the nuclear attack risk assessment following the attack on the *Walter*. Nothing had changed, but that in itself worried Gritt. There was no explanation for the surprise attack on an American war ship. His conversations with Jana Taylor at midday confirmed his personal views. There was nothing to be gained for the Iranian regime.

He opened the bag that held two double cheeseburgers and some onion rings and grabbed a couple of paper towels. He opened a Pepsi, turning on the small kitchen computer he usually used to look up recipes, favoring those that used only one pot and yielded enough food for a second or third meal of leftovers. He fingered the keyboard until he brought up a 24-hour news streaming service and then he unwrapped a burger. Famished, he began devouring the burger just as a segment showing the president's speech from earlier that afternoon came on.

"And, just so the Iranian authorities do not mistake this conversation, let me emphasize this once again. "The Iranian's launched an unprovoked attack on an American warship in international waters. That attack killed and wounded almost a dozen American service people. In order to prevent an additional attack on that ship, she was authorized to destroy the Iranian missile battery launched two ZAFAR missiles against it."

The president paused as he referred to his notes. "The United States reserves the right, under international law, to take further actions. These will not be a knee-jerk response, but a reasoned one with the specific purpose of assuring the safety of American warships in the region, and also the unrestricted passage of commerce. If the Iranian authorities launch any other attacks like what they did to the *Walter*, then that response will be immediate."

The president took no questions and signed off with the traditional *God Bless America.*

As Gritt finished his second burger, he finally tugged the phone that he'd ignored all day from his jacket. He went to his messages, scrolling until one from Olga popped up.

"Hi, checking in. I can't make heads or tails out of that attack off from Oman last night. Do you have a read on it? You won't be able to call me for a couple of days. I'll be on an Air Force hop into McCord Air Force Base, and then I'm going down to Arizona to see my family for a few days. I'll call. Love, Olga."

Chapter 19

A SMALL FEAST WAS laid out on the folding table a couple of hundred meters from Karim's palatial home. Two servants served strong black coffee to Karim, Salman, and Mohamed. The men shared small talk until the two maids retreated to the golf cart and started back to the house. Four guards slowly moved through the small glen to the north, making sure that the meeting was not being observed or listened to.

"It is moving really fast now," said Mohamed. "I talked to Ashraf this morning. The general said that the EAGLE facility is crawling with Guard officers since the attack in the straits a week ago. They come and go, but they have really stepped up security."

"Was the missile launch his idea or Reza's?" asked Karim.

"I think it was Reza's. He commands regular army units along the Strait of Hormuz. But it really doesn't matter who planned the attack. It was brilliant and perfectly executed. Within the country, it heightened the divide between the army and guard, and it sure as hell ramped up the tensions between Iran and the U.S."

Salman sipped his coffee as he listened. A strategy that he'd perfected for years was finally being executed. "Is there any chance that the authorities in Iran can trace the missile attack back to us?"

"Not much," replied Mohamed. "The Americans did just what we hoped. They hit that tiny site with two high-explosive shells. Any evidence was probably blown to pieces and what little was left burned when the fuel for the backup generator spread across the site and ignited."

"So, what's next?" asked Karim as he tugged a strand of grapes from a large bowl and popped one into his mouth. Remnants of a lunch that the men were too nervous to eat sat untouched.

"The Americans say they can trace the attack on their ship directly to the Revolutionary Guard Corps. The guards are bound by their sense of duty to do something stupid to further inflame the Americans. We will wait for that before we strike again in Iran," finished Mohamed.

"Are we ready to position one of the bombs in America," asked Salman. "I haven't spoken to Farid in a couple of weeks."

"WILTON begins flying their new freighters this week. The modifications recommended by ONE were made, so once the bomb is aboard, it should be undetectable. We need WILTON to fly a few missions for others before we charter a flight," offered Karim.

"I'll have TWO standing by. Our new American company is ready for us to fly a load of Georgian wines and brandies to the states. The load will go into our primary target city first," offered Salman.

"TWO will accompany the shipment from Tbilisi. He will work with our new employees in North Carolina to price the shipment which will give him an excuse to stay in the area for several days. The plane will hold there for two days before departing. WILTON has no facilities at that airport, so the customer is responsible for unloading. TWO will live on board. It's his job to move the package and make sure that the cell phone trigger is armed and has enough battery power to detonate when we are ready."

"Will TWO depart with the plane?" asked Mohamed.

"No, he will survey the area for a day or two to assure that the target warrants one of our precious weapons. Then he will fly to New York before making his way back to Tabilisi."

"So, TWO has selected North Carolina as the first target. I don't even know where that is," replied Karim. I know the liquor company has a large warehouse and store there but nothing more."

"The airport is in a fairly remote but urban area. At night it will be almost deserted, but it is close enough to major urban areas that a detonation will scare the hell out of the authorities," said Mohamed.

Ashraf was surprised, and not pleasantly when he was summoned from his home in Tehran by a Revolutionary Guard officer that he'd never met. He'd been at EAGLE for nine days without a break and was just sitting down for a dinner with his wife.

"Do not be concerned," said the officer to Ashraf's wife. This will be a very short meeting. I will have the general back in two hours."

The two left before Ashraf's wife created an uproar. The Guard was rude and dangerous.

Thirty minutes later, Ashraf was ushered into the Guard's massive headquarters building where he was whisked into an executive elevator to the top floor conference room. Somehow, he was not surprised to find the commander of the Guard waiting there.

"General, thank you for coming with no notice," started the commander. "I wanted to personally introduce you to my senior aide. Ashraf, this is Hussein. Technically, you are of equal rank, but since the issue we will discuss involves EAGLE where you command, I wanted to pull a little rank when I told you that Hussein will be joining you at EAGLE next week. I have given him some very specific instructions and told him that he is to work through you as needed."

The Guard was sending observers to EAGLE, but never before someone with the equivalent rank of general. "Can I know his mission?" asked Ashraf.

"Of course," replied the commander. "With the tensions between our nation and the Americans so high, and since my own intelligence group has not been able to tell me why, I want to know how long it would take to produce enough tactical nuclear weapons to assure that the Americans leave us alone."

"I understand the term tactical weapons," replied Ashraf, "but our research has been focused on preparing for deployment of warheads capable of severely damaging our enemies, especially Israel, and responding to any attack that threatens our homeland. Our work is all on strategic warheads.

"All true, but a small warhead that can be fired from

artillery or attached to a small rocket, a warhead that could destroy an American aircraft carrier with a single strike will push the Americans back from any stupid attack. We would, of course, need to be prepared to demonstrate such a weapon. Hussein's job is to determine just how we might do that."

Good to their word, Ashraf was home in ninety minutes. On the surface, nothing had changed, but somehow, he felt that his summons was a test. He waited as his wife poured him a glass of iced sweet tea before removing a cover from his dinner.

"Ashraf, you do not look all together well," offered his wife. "What was that sudden meeting with the Guard all about?"

"I'm not quite sure that I really know," he replied. "It was really nothing. The actual commander of the Guard is sending one of his senior officers to EAGLE with me next week."

"You said the Guard has already added personnel to the facility. Is this something different?"

"I don't think so. The commander took pains to make sure that I understood that the man was to work through me." Ashraf could say little more, and his wife would not expect him to. He began to pick at the small plate of cold meat with beans in a cucumber yogurt sauce. He loved dinner in the courtyard, especially on an evening when the temperature would still bring a slight shine to his wife's face. "I will not let anything interrupt our two days together," he said.

"That is good my husband. I fear that the conflict between our government and the Americans will make it difficult to find time together. You will do your duty and I will do mine."

Ashraf watched her smile, knowing that she would do everything she could to make him comfortable, to help him relax when they were together. This woman was not his first love, but years together had allowed both to love and support each other. He wished he could disclose more to her. He knew her beliefs were identical to his. She was from a traditional upper-class family and worried all the time about the country's direction. When the time came, he already had a plan to move her to their summer retreat in the mountains.

At seven in the morning, Ashraf arrived at the airport where his helicopter was waiting. Hussein slid from the backseat of a black limousine as he parked his own Toyota. "I see you are one of those general officers who does not take advantage of the perks of your status," he said.

"I prefer a simple life in a simple country," replied Ashraf. "One needs only their family and faith to be fulfilled." He tossed his bag and briefcase onto the floor of the Russian made transport and then pointed for Hussein to climb aboard.

"Simple life," said Hussein just as the pilot pressed the starter for the engine. "You and your family enjoy a place in Paris, and I am told, a mountain retreat where you go sometimes to fish." It took only a minute for the engines to warm up on a hot morning. The liftoff in a helicopter always made Ashraf's stomach a bit queasy.

"Perks from marrying well, General. My wife's family owns one of the largest construction companies in the country. Her grandfather founded it when the country began its oil boom. Prior to that he had worked as an engineer for a French petroleum firm."

"That gave you quite an advantage," said Hussein. "I am the son of a farming family. My father grew up as a goat herder, a man who's only education was in the mosque. He spent some time in prison under the Shah, for protesting that pig's reforms. After the revolution, I had my chance at an education. Like you, my entire career has been in the service."

The rest of the trip was quiet, as was the short car ride from the landing pad to the EAGLE Institute. As they made their way across the lobby, Hussein finally spoke. "I want you to guide me through the lower facility and introduce me to the critical staff. And then I will need a small private space to interview each of them."

The tone of the conversation, thought Ashraf, flies in the face of the assurances from the Guard commandant that Hussein was to work through him. He smiled inside. Within months men like this would no longer be commanding anyone to do anything. Now was not the time to challenge him.

An hour later, the two men shared a tram for the long descent into the bowels of the top-secret laboratory. Again, there was little conversation. As they reached the first floor of the underground facility, Hussein handed Ashraf a list. "Here are the men I want to meet today, in the order that I would like to meet them."

Ashraf took the note and unfolded it. The first name was Nader, the chief scientist who Ashraf had discussed with Mohamed only weeks before. After Nader, the list was in good order for a man who wanted to understand how and when Iran could field a small nuclear weapon.

The list didn't bother him. By the time that any decision to build such a weapon and then actually bring it into being, the Guard would be no more.

Ashraf motioned for one of the runners to find Nader and bring him to where Hussein and he would be walking through the laboratory. It took more than fifteen minutes for the runner to reappear, an out of breath greying scientist in a worn tweed coat at his heels.

"Nader, my old friend, this is Hussein. He is a general officer with the Revolutionary Guard, and he wants to talk to you and several others about a matter of national security. It will take us another hour to finish our tour so could you meet us in the small conference room in about ninety minutes?"

Nader just nodded and headed back to whatever he was working on.

"You address your staff like they are friends, not subordinates," observed Hussein.

"That is because they are. If you press these high-strung scientists like some recruit soldier, they close up like a clam."

"I'll remember that when I talk to them. Thank you," said Hussein.

Hussein finished his initial interviews with six men that evening. Over a private dinner he confided with Ashraf, "your staff seems very competent. I have given them all day tomorrow to commit a preliminary plan to writing. I will meet with them again the next morning and then I will be out of your hair."

"Do you and your superiors have a specific timeline for when you might want to test such a weapon?"

"No, but sooner would be better than later," answered

Hussein. "We will test this weapon on a target that does not directly challenge the Americans. They must see the risk, so it will take place when the Americans have one of their precious carriers in the Persian Gulf. We will trap it there. They must be convinced that we can destroy it and the thousands of sailors aboard anytime we want."

"I understand," offered Ashraf, "and I assume that once the decision is made to actually manufacture such weapons, that all of the work my people are already working on will be suspended until you get what you want."

"That is a good assumption," replied Hussein as he poured himself more tea. "But it cannot be stalled for long. If this confrontation escalates, Iran must have the ability to strike the Americans hard, and to destroy their friends in Israel."

The next morning, Nader was waiting for Ashraf in his laboratory office. "There is no possibility of converting any of our current research into the weapons that your Hussein wants."

"I understand," replied Ashraf. "Perhaps what he wants is impossible in the short run."

"That man knows about the enriched uranium that the Pakistani's helped us refine," said Nader. None of us really know if it is fissionable. It may not be suitable for a bomb. It is the only material that might meet Hussein's needs. I thought a couple of you in the army and four of my scientists were the only people who knew it existed."

"Since the revolution, the Guard has been favored by our leadership. I always assume that they know almost everything." Ashraf paused, a chill running down his spine. The Russian material now in the vault most certainly had been refined to the 90% necessary for a reaction. "You and your staff must proceed as the Guard has ordered. I will see if there is any way to make sure it is not used to start a war."

An hour later Ashraf was passing by the vault as Nader was closing the door. The worried look on his face was the same as in their earlier conversation, maybe even a bit more strained.

Ashraf had no idea what Hussein did the rest of the day. He borrowed an institute car and left the facility early in the morning. He was back before dinner but ate alone and ignored Ashraf until offering a small gesture. "You should plan on sitting in while your staff presents their plan in the morning." He didn't wait for an answer.

The meeting began with Nader calling on the five other staffers who had worked late into the night. He held up a small file. By name he asked each the same question. "Is this your best effort at meeting the task Hussein assigned to us?" Each answered yes and was then excused to go back to their work.

One page at a time, Nader presented their work to Hussein. Each page had a drawing with notes. "The design for a missile warhead will be easier than for artillery," he stated. "The detonator must explode the bomb in proximity to the target, since creating one that might survive actual contact will be very difficult." He waited for Hussein's comments and continued when the man said nothing.

"The apparatus for creating the explosion is identical to that already designed for larger devices. All we will have to do is scale it down. Regarding attachment to an actual missile, we have worked extensively with the groups building our rockets. We have designs for two long range vehicles. You will need to approach them for a recommendation on modifying an existing missile as it would take a couple of years to create a new one. Once they identify the delivery vehicle, we can work with them to scale the actual device."

Hussein was taking notes on his laptop as fast as his fingers could move. "So, the challenges you see are almost all in scaling a weapon for a missile that we already possess?"

"That is essentially correct," replied Nader. "When I was working on my doctorate in America, almost every class I took indicated that nuclear fission and fusion are both relatively simple but getting the scale right is critical. Assuming the six orbs of material in our vault is enriched to the point that it will detonate, creating what you want is simple mathematics."

"So, my next task is to talk to the companies building our missiles?"

"That would be my recommendation, and once you have a recommendation, we will need to get with them to design the interface," replied Nader. "If you will take a look at your list, the next two men will be the ones to design the interface. My report includes their direct telephone numbers here at EAGLE." Nader presented the last page and then slipped the pages back into the folder.

"What is your estimate of the time necessary to create a working weapon?" asked Hussein.

"Without any rocket interface problems, we should be able to scale an existing design down and build a prototype in two or three months. But before we can do anything, we need to get our two best interface engineers together with the designers of the designated delivery system. If you can get that done in the next two weeks, such a weapon is possible in three months."

Hussein stood up, placing both hands on the table in front of him as he leaned across the table. "I will get the delivery people started," he said. "But I am not going to be the one who puts this all together. That will be your job. Once it is assigned to your team, it will be totally your responsibility. Is that clear?"

Nader just stared at the man. "You may go back to your regular work now," said Ashraf.

After Nader left, Ashraf matched Hussein's posture, his hands turning white on the table across from Hussein. "I warned you the first day you were here," he started, "that you must treat these scientists with respect. You will only slow their work and assure they begin making mistakes if you speak to any of them like that."

He didn't wait for a response before adding, "you have your report, and my helicopter is waiting to fly you back to Tehran. Since none of this should ever be discussed over a telephone, I await your call telling me when you will be back to move your project forward." Ashraf opened the door and waited for his guest to follow him to the tram.

It took a couple of hours to get Hussein on his way and for Ashraf to make his way back to the office. He wasn't there for more than a minute when Nader walked in and closed the door. "General, I have not taken any time off for more than a year. And if this project really gets approval, I will be stuck here for months longer."

"Nader, do not let that pompous ass upset you."

"I admit, he does upset me, and this sudden shift in focus upsets me. What this man proposes is a pin prick to the face of an enemy that could turn Iran into a parking lot of glass. But what I am really trying to say is that I need a short break. I need a clear head if I am to deliver on this new project."

Ashraf took a full minute before responding, "You are probably right. We will need to wait until we have a timeline on the new project. You are right to take the time now because when the project really gets started, I suspect that I will not have the authority to approve it." He smiled at the graying scientist. "Where will you go?"

"My old friend, I am an amateur archaeologist, and my favorite beach setting is on the coast of Turkey. I can roam around ancient ruins and museums in the morning and evening and just sit on the beach watching the surf in the afternoon. I think I would like to go back there."

"For how long?"

"At least a week, but even better, maybe ten days or two weeks."

"Good idea. Spend a weekend with your wife and then take a week. Have a good time, and while you are gone, I will try to exert a little control on this new project," added Ashraf.

Chapter 20

The ships in front of The Liberian flagged tanker were creeping through the Strait. The first two were on their way to loading platforms on the Iranian side. The ship directly in front and the Liberian ship were moving toward Saudi ports. In the world's most patrolled waterway, everything seemed normal, but following the short skirmish only days before, the ship's captain knew that was an illusion. And the slow pace meant that before his ship reached the narrows, it would be dark.

The captain, a Brit with a crew mostly from the Philippines, had been piloting ships in and out of the Persian Gulf for two decades, and as the ship slowed to a crawl, he couldn't remember a single passage when tensions in the region hadn't brought the hair up on the back of his neck. He especially hated night passages.

"There are two small Iranian craft pulling alongside the ship in front of us," reported a lookout.

The captain smiled through his nerves. "Is there any indication of weapons being deployed?"

"No ,Sir, and the two boats are already turning away."

"I want all eyes on those boats and the three holding parallel to us," ordered the captain. He turned to the radio operator standing by only a few feet away. "If there is any indication of an attack, you know what to do."

Below the bridge, and unseen, two more Revolutionary Guard boats slid up to the side of the empty Liberian tanker, and moments later, turned away.

The normal transit time of four hours stretched until just before sunrise. But with no reports of attacks to any ship, the captain was more than pleased as two harbor tugs helped push the ship up against an Aramco loading platform. The ship they'd been following was tied to another platform a hundred meters away. In the distance, Iranian and American patrol aircraft passed each other, their navigation lights barely visible.

The captain's orders, "prepare for onloading," were disrupted by two dull thuds, not really explosions, that sent a shiver through the ship. He looked up from his computer just as two waterspouts erupted next to the tanker in front of him. There was a terrible screeching sound. Part of the platform loading the other ship begin to crumple into the water. His eyes were pulled back to the side of his own ship where a sheet of flame shot into the sky. On the platform burning crude oil sprayed everything and everybody.

On the wing of the bridge closest to the Saudi oil platform, one of the ship's lookouts screamed as he threw his burning body through the open bridge door. Another man on the bridge foamed the flaming man with a fire extinguisher while the captain slammed his hand down on the ship's fire alarm.

⁂

Two men from the Navy waited in Jana Taylor's office. One was from Intelligence and the other was Chad Gritt. They waited a few minutes before Taylor and Pete Johnson, the CIA head of technology rushed into the office. "Our people in Saudi Arabia tell us that the explosives that caused that mess on the two tankers were probably magnetic mines."

"Our sources give us the same story," replied the Naval Intelligence officer. "Thank God that the automatic shut off valves on the platforms kicked in instantly or the fire could have destroyed both the platforms and the ships. As it is, Saudi Intelligence was able to interview officers from both ships and the loading supervisors who survived the fire. One captain reported observing Iranian patrol boats alongside the ship in front of him. They quickly moved away."

"Our best guess is that the Iranians somehow placed mines on the hulls of both ships and detonated them using timers or some kind of remote devices when they began to load," added Gritt. "The technology is really simple and by attaching the explosives and then moving away, there is no hard evidence of the Iranian Guard's responsibility."

Jana finally sat in her chair while Pete remained standing. "The reason we were late was that a new report just came in. It appears that less than twelve hours after the explosions at the Saudi terminal, someone blew up the Revolutionary Guard's Maritime office in Bushire. The Iranians are screaming that it was an American stealth bomber attack."

"Was it?" asked Gritt. "We were briefed only minutes before we drove out here. It wasn't the Navy, we're still trying to figure out a proportionate response. Our people were still talking to the Liberians and Saudis."

Pete Johnson just shook his head. "We talked to the Air Force, and the Saudi's and they claim they are still doing the same, trying to figure out a proper response. We already have satellite photos of the building and unless the bomb penetrated all four floors before detonating, this was some kind of explosive device that was planted below the main offices. The building is still standing but the center is collapsed. My tech geeks can't figure out how any explosive deployed from the outside could cause that type of damage. It looks more like a bomb hidden in a basement or a huge truck bomb that penetrated the first floor before exploding."

"I'm not sure that matters anymore, the real question is what are the Iranians going to do next," said Jana. "This is the second direct attack on the Guard, and they will strike back."

Chapter 21

WILTON AIR FLIGHT 6 touched down at the Piedmont Triad Airport just outside of Greensboro North Carolina just before five in the afternoon. As arranged, U.S. Customs met the plane and checked the manifest, reserving the right to do an actual inspection of the cargo as it was unloaded. Beyond the two pilots they checked the credentials of the only passenger, Robert Thompson, of New York, and an employee of the holding company that owned the liquor distributor receiving wines and liquors from eastern Europe. All three were American citizens.

"Mr. Thompson," started the regional manager of Exotic Beverages, Inc., "we are not going to have the staff to unload until tomorrow. Can I take you to dinner somewhere?"

"Call me Bob," replied Thompson. "No, maybe tomorrow night after we finish an inventory. I've been to Greensboro a couple of times in the last year and promised some friends who helped me research our investment in your firm that I would see them the next time I was in town."

The manager took out his phone. "Let me get a picture of you to give to the crew so they know who is in charge." Pocketing the phone, he asked, "how about breakfast then at your hotel?" asked the manager.

"WILTON's jets are equipped with a small apartment for people traveling with their shipments. I plan on staying on the plane tonight, that is if you can help me get whatever credentials I will need from airport security. I'll be off the airport for a few hours and then need to get back through one of the gates. But breakfast tomorrow sounds great.

One of the pilots, standing only feet away pulled out his cell phone scanned it for information for a minute and then began dialing. He handed the phone to Bob after a short conversation. "The woman on the phone is Linda at the Airport security office. She said she will wait there to issue you a temporary security badge if you can make it to her office before six.

Bob turned to the manager. "How about a ride, and then do your guys have a car that I can borrow for the evening? I will leave it parked next to the airplane."

TWO smiled at how easy it was to get a temporary security badge that gave him access to the parking apron where the WILTON jet was parked. Bob Thompson had given up his life fighting in Ukraine a few years earlier, but now he was back in the U.S. TWO parked the Ford pickup he'd borrowed at the foot of the access stairs that were still set against the side of the plane. A security guard in a small electric Chevy coup stopped next to him. "You that Thompson guy that Linda called me about?"

Bob slipped his badge from his shirt and handed it to the guard. "I'm just picking up my briefcase and then I'll be out of here until later this evening."

The guard scribbled a number on his card and handed it to Bob. "The gate you are using has a bad habit of rejecting entry codes sometimes. Here is my cell, if you have a problem, call me. I'll be on duty until midnight." A moment later the guard was gone, and Bob was inside the plane where he used the small electric screwdriver in his bag to remove the cover panel to the communications cupboard. He used a key to unlock the lock to the shelf that held the lead lined case and removed it. Then he pocketed the lock before reattaching the cabinet cover. He added the screwdriver to his pocket and then carefully lifted the heavy case.

TWO was on his way to a storage facility that he'd rented the last time he was in Greensboro. It was less than two miles away, in an industrial area with only a few apartment buildings nearby.

He used the code he'd been assigned when he rented the unit to get through the security gate and drove directly to the end storage unit in the back row of the complex. He rolled up the door and placed the suitcase bomb on a shelf that someone had previously added to the unit. Using the light on his phone, he inserted a bit in the screwdriver and began drilling a small hole through the outside wall next to the ceiling. Minutes later he had a small solar charger on the roof connected to a cell phone strapped to the bomb. In twenty minutes, Bob was on his way to find dinner. ONE's testing of the bomb's cellphone detonator had identified a single weakness: if the cell phone battery failed, there was no way to detonate the device. The solar charger fixed that problem. Bob had been designated as the one to set off the blast, and he intended to be somewhere in Greensboro when he called the phone number and entered the detonation code.

He pulled into a restaurant with a Middle Eastern name, excited that he would be the only member of the group who would actually witness the explosion. He'd waited a long time for this moment. As he ate, he studied his list of additional cities. The East Coast American city would be the first target. He still needed one in the Midwest and one in the West, although Salman's plan assumed only two atomic detonations would be needed to spur the Americans into action. The third was insurance.

Chapter 22

THE UNEASE IN Farid's stomach turned to turmoil as he read the secure post from Karim.

'Your aunt just bought her first handbag,' was code for one bomb in place. He didn't know which city was targeted. It probably didn't matter, but he'd ask TWO what the target is when he met him in New York next week.

He and Dorsey were wrapping up an airfreight convention in Las Vegas as the message came in. "You don't look so good," offered Dorsey as the two met for a drink after the final presentation.

"I've just been burning the candle on both ends," replied Farid.

"Close enough," said his boss. "You have a meeting at the end of the week with a representative of the liquor company we're supporting," he added. "Why don't you take a couple of days in between and go visit your girl. Where did you say she was moving?"

Farid slipped his phone from his pocket and scrolled through messages. "Minot, North Dakota," he replied.

Dorsey pointed at the door. "Probably only a thousand miles from Las Vegas. I doubt that there are any direct flights, but it shouldn't take more than six hours if you want to visit."

Farid was up before Dorsey could finish the sentence. "Thanks, he said as he headed for his room. "I'll call you from New York after I meet with that guy who's importing European liquor. He plans on two more shipments in the next month."

"Get out of here," replied Dorsey. "See you back in London."

Farid reached Sarah on the first try. "I'll have to call you with my flight arrival times and flight number."

"I have a big, rented house," she said, "and my dad bought me a Ford Bronco to get around. "I'm meeting with some tribal people in the west of the state right now, but I plan on heading home this evening. So just call me when you get this firmed up."

A flight to Minneapolis and then another to Minot took Farid five hours. Not having any idea what a Ford Bronco looked like, he carried his bag from the airport and began walking down a line of cars looking for something 'big, boxy and kind of truck like.'

He walked only a few seconds before he noticed Sarah, dressed in jeans and a plaid shirt sitting on the hood of her Bronco. She was talking to someone in a uniform but waived over the woman's head as she noticed Farid. He looked around, feeling completely out of place in a suit and tie. The only divergence from cowboy central were some military uniforms.

"Yeah, I can see why you would want to pick him up," said the woman airport security person as Farid approached. "He is kind of cute." As she turned to go, she added, "Next time just park over in short term parking. You can wait in baggage claim."

Sarah jumped off the hood and gave Farid a quick kiss on the cheek. "I need to move the car," she said.

"That's it," replied Farid, "after weeks, all I get is a kiss on the cheek?" He slid into the passenger seat.

"This place is the definition of conservative," said Sarah. "If you can wait twenty minutes, I will show you how I really feel." She paused a minute. "Are you hungry? I haven't eaten since this morning. Maybe you will have to wait a couple of hours."

"I'm starved," he answered.

"There is a cute little bar and grill only a mile from my house," said Sarah. "If you can wait for dessert, we can stop there on the way home."

"If I have to wait for dessert, I will, but I feel really out of place in my suit. Maybe I should change before dinner."

"Not a chance, lover-boy. I intend to show you off," said Sarah. "I live north of town. We will be there in fifteen minutes."

There were four empty beer bottles on the table along with two plates with left over French fries and the remnants of two oversized burgers. Farid was working on his third beer as Sarah observed, "I've never seen you drink two beers in a row, let alone three."

"I followed your lead on the drinks," replied Farid. "Honestly, the last couple of months have been really high-test for me."

"I can tell. You are not your normal boisterous self," she said. "Is something wrong?"

Farid, chugged half his beer before answering, "nothing you should worry about." He took another swig before adding, "for the next three days, everything will be as perfect as possible."

&

Farid was thumbing through messages on his phone as Sarah slid a plate of poached eggs on toast with grilled tomato across the counter. "I haven't cooked a European breakfast since I came home," she said. "After last night, I can't believe that you have anything on your mind but me," she added.

He put down his phone. "Don't take it personally. Beyond the new career, I'm still dealing with some family stuff. "You know about that. Responsibilities."

She pushed a second plate across the counter, and then slid onto a stool next to Farid. "Is it anything I might help with?"

"No," he answered as he picked up a knife and fork. "It will be over soon."

For the next two days, Sarah commanded Farid's attention. They balanced time alone with a tour of the Minot area. "There is a big Air Force base only a few miles north of here," said Sarah, responding to Farid's question about the community. "That's a big deal here. But most of the community grew up around cattle ranching."

Farid continued his gaze out the window of the Bronco. "This place just goes on forever," he observed. "No mountains."

"You're right," said Sarah, "but where I do most of

my work, in the western part of the state, there are forests and mountainous areas. The people indigenous to the area had a good life, mostly hunting and gathering what they needed. Some of the conflicts with the early whites are still remembered. Today, the challenge is to build a modern economy without losing their culture."

He turned to Sarah, "you really like this and what you are doing, don't you?"

"Yup, cowboy," she replied. "I'm a city girl from birth, but I don't miss crowded streets and buildings so big they block out the sun. I don't even miss fancy restaurants."

"From what I've seen, it wouldn't matter. I mean, burgers, ribs, steaks, all served with potatoes. It would take me a while to adjust."

"Don't get too fancy for your new jeans," replied Sarah giving Farid a sharp punch in the shoulder. "You've always loved a good burger."

They stopped in a tiny town where two roads came together for lunch. You could order almost anything as long as it included beef or chicken. Over fried chicken sandwiches, with the mandatory French fries, the two talked mostly about Sarah's work. Finally, Farid asked a question that had been lurking in the back of his mind. "What don't you like about this place?"

"Well, I haven't been here for a winter, and I'm told it gets quite cold with a lot of blowing snow. In fact, I hadn't thought about it, but I could do without the wind. It blows here most of the time. If you put a pie out to cool, folks twenty miles away could tell you what flavor it is."

The evening before Farid's flight, the two picked up American style Chinese food for dinner and shared it in front of a fire in a huge rock fireplace that dominated the center of Sarah's rented home. "Do you have any idea when you might be able to come back?" she asked.

"Not really," Farid replied. "I'm going to spend a couple of days in New York on the way home, but for now, I'm still based in London." He drained his beer.

"I'll get you another," offered Sarah as she jumped up from the huge leather couch. A moment later she called from the kitchen, "I'm out. It will only take ten minutes to pick up some more."

Farid heard the door slam and watched as the Bronco turned out onto the quiet country road. In three days, he'd become comfortable with the area around the house, made up mostly of other houses, and a few small warehouses and companies that catered primarily to the military. A mile away were some apartments and some large, fenced complexes where people stored things, and in the outside were yard boats and motor homes. Why would anyone need to rent storage for any reason in a place where the land was mostly empty? He couldn't figure it out. The little country store and gas station where Sarah was headed was just past a small school.

For the first time in days, Farid dug his laptop from his briefcase. When Sarah returned, he was just sitting in front of the dying fire staring at the screen. "Something wrong?' she asked as she carried two more cold beers into the living room.

Farid closed the computer and worked up a smile. "Nothing really, it's just that the guy I'm meeting with in New York is bringing one of his colleagues with him. Farid' shrugged off a shiver. He had no idea why Salman would be traveling to New York to meet with TWO.

The two lovers were only minutes from the Minot

Airport when Sarah's cell rang. She talked for only a couple of minutes before turning her full attention back to Farid. "I'm a little worried about you," she said as she started into the airport. "Sometimes you're here, but a lot of the time, you seem like you are somewhere else. Are you going to tell me what's worrying you?"

Farid smiled. "Well, for starters, I'm not even on the plane yet and you are setting up a meeting with someone else at your house."

"Don't be a bore," she answered. "That call was from a woman who is moving here. She was looking for a place to live with some privacy. I posted that I was looking for a roommate and she called."

As they pulled to a stop at the terminal, he asked, "I know what brought you here. But what could possibly bring another single woman to this place?"

"She said she is transferring here in the Air Force. She's an officer." Sarah leaned across the seat and wrapped her arms around Farid. "I love you. You know that, right?"

"And I love you," he replied. As they wrapped their arms around one another, Sarah slowly twisted in his arms, her breasts caressing Farid's chest. It usually drove him crazy.

As Farid slid his suitcase and briefcase from the back seat she added, "two people in love should feel comfortable sharing, especially if something is bothering one of them."

"Sarah, it will be okay. We've discussed how different my traditional culture is from yours. I'm just working out how the two fit together." He reached across the seat and grabbed her hand and kissed her fingers one at a time. "I'll call from New York. I love you." Moments later he was through the doors and inside the terminal. It occurred to Sarah, that this was the first time she had ever sent him on his way. She cherished his kiss but couldn't shake off the last moments before he disappeared. Farid's face was expressionless.

Chapter 23

GRITT WAS IN his office when his phone rang. He was so deep in thought about what was going on in the Persian Gulf that he almost ignored it, but seeing Olga's name pop up changed his mind.

"Well, this is a surprise. I didn't think I'd hear from you until next weekend," he added after hello.

"I'm going to be in DC for a week. I wanted to make sure that you aren't traveling," said Olga.

"If you are coming all this way just to see me, then I would be a complete cad if I wasn't here."

"I can see the smirk on your face from here. I have several days of briefings for my new assignment. But I have my nights free."

"For now, I have no travel plans," he replied.

"But," she said, "I'm sure that you are up to your cute little ass in whatever is brewing in the Middle East. I kind of thought you might be going over there."

"No, for now, it's just paperwork and meetings and analysis. When are you coming in?"

"I'm leaving Phoenix tomorrow with a stop for a day in North Dakota. I plan on being there on Friday night."

"What in the hell is taking you to North Dakota?"

"My new assignment is deputy to the head of security at Minot Air Force Base. I'll be in DC for some briefings on extra security issues surrounding a base with nuclear weapons."

Gritt paused a moment. He leaned over to a second computer on his desk and typed in Minot North Dakota before commenting, "there's no ocean there, so no Navy. Are you sure there is really an Air Force Base?"

"Don't be one of those 'other military smart asses, love.' It's the only truly multi-role air base in the system. For someone in security, it is one of the most important assignments in the states."

"So, you are stopping there just to make sure it really exists," joked Chad.

"No, I qualify for base housing, but I'm single so I thought it made sense to leave the housing for some family. Besides, after being stationed in the wilds of Alaska, I've kind of gotten used to a lot of privacy. I'm meeting a woman there who has a big house. The pictures look great, and I don't want to lose the place if it's what I think it is. The woman says she spends a lot of time traveling around the area, so I'll have the place to myself a lot of the time."

"Just text me your final arrival information, and I'll make sure that there will be someone there to pick you up," replied Chad.

"You won't be there?"

"I plan on it, but this hornets' nest in the Gulf is rattling a lot of cages and everything new seems to gin up a meeting that I can't get out of." He looked again at the screen of the Air Force Base in Minot before adding, "if you could see the smile on my face, you would know that only a direct order or a pending war will keep me from the airport when you arrive."

"Okay," replied Olga. "I'll be traveling in uniform, but between now and then, I want you to imagine what I will be wearing under it after days of lingerie shopping here in Scottsdale."

Chad's work required intense focus which was difficult for the rest of the day.

Chapter 24

AHMADI NADER'S FLIGHT from Khomeini Airport to Istanbul was uneventful. He'd almost canceled the trip after spending a night with his wife. She seemed to be growing weaker by the day. With his promise to spend a couple more days at home after his travels, she gave him her blessing.

His departure, however, was delayed for an hour which wouldn't have bothered him except for five minutes of questioning at a security checkpoint. He was traveling on his own money with his own passport, but it seemed that his name had set off some kind of alarm bells in security.

He waited until arriving to rent a car, mostly out of concern about his travel security. Any good intelligence operation might flag his travel; the Turks, or the Americans, the Revolutionary Guard, or worst of all the Israeli's. Only the Guard would know his actual position as head of design for the Iranian Atomic Weapons development program. For twenty years he'd scrupulously protected his private life and avoided any publicity. But the others would know of his doctorate from the University of Michigan and anyone living in Iran with an advanced education in atomic physics would be of interest.

Nader stopped at a store specializing in communications for immigrants and bought a prepaid cell phone. Next, he found a small hotel in Izmir, only a mile away from the facility that had actually brought him to Turkey. He asked the front desk clerk if there was any place close where he might get a traditional American style dinner, explaining that he had gone to the university in the states. Armed with a recommendation he walked the fifteen minutes to *The Real Texas Steakhouse*. Inside he found just what he was looking for, an American style menu and a dozen tables busy that Friday evening with American servicemen enjoying a night out.

Nader was seated at a small table only a few feet from one table of what he suspected were junior officers from the Izmir Air Station. But the table that drew his attention was occupied by a middle-aged man with a military haircut dining with what was probably his wife, a trim, conservatively dressed red head who spoke English with a drawl. She was drinking one of the excellent local red wines, while the man drank Scotch.

Nader ordered barbeque ribs, a baked potato and salad. His cover might have been perfect if he'd ordered an American beer, but somehow even in his nine years in the states, he'd never touched alcohol. Instead, the waitress brought him a tall sweetened iced tea. As he slowly ate dinner, he scribbled on a notepad and watched the couple laugh and talk about the half-dozen places they'd lived. Nader recognized three of the places. All were cities with American military bases.

A half hour later, the man at the table stood and headed toward the restroom. Nader looked around and noticed a man who had followed him into the restaurant watching him intently. Nader slid his chair back and followed the American to the men's room.

"Excuse me, sir, but I couldn't help but overhear your conversation," started Nader. "Are you from the Air Station?"

The man turned toward Nadar, moving into a slightly defensive posture.

"My name is Nader, and thirty years ago I was a student in the States for almost ten years. It's nice to hear the language spoken with an American accent again."

The man smiled and extended his hand. "Name's Brian Wilson, Lieutenant Colonel Brian Wilson, and my wife's name is Susan."

Nader suddenly turned very still as he surveyed the bathroom for any other patrons. "Brian, he whispered, I need to give you a note. I need for you to get it to your commanding officer who needs to make sure it reaches your embassy without any chance of the content being divulged." Nader paused, listening, thinking someone was about to enter. When the door didn't open, he continued, handing the note to the startled officer. "I'm Iranian, and your intelligence people, especially the man this is addressed to will know who I am. Please believe me when I say, that note may stop a war." Nader smiled, then turned to the urinal just as the door opened and the man observing him earlier brushed past Wilson. Nader zipped up his fly and headed back to his table.

Nader, with the most dangerous part of his trip over, decided a Texas dinner should be eaten American style.

He picked up a large rib-bone and began gnawing on it, quietly noting that his new friend, Brian showed no sign of anything changing as he and Susan ordered desert.

Two hours later, after a short walk, Nader was back in his hotel where he managed a reasonable night's sleep on a mattress that felt a lot like sleeping on a pile of bamboo. *It's okay*, he thought, *tomorrow night will be better, the beds at the Kemer Resort are always better even than my own.* That night he had a dream of his wife, Ariana, and his last trip outside with her. She really loved the Kemer and tolerated his day trips to ancient sites as long as every other day was spent at the beach or the pool. It would have been better if she was with him, but that was impossible, maybe forever.

Nader skipped breakfast the next morning and was on his way to Antalya before eight. Arriving before his room was ready would be a waste of time, so he would indulge his passion with two stops at archeological sites. The beach would be there whenever he arrived.

As Nader began his drive, Lieutenant Colonel Brian Wilson was winging his way to Ankara in a C-12 Heron. Use of the small Beechcraft built transport plane would cut hours off from any other form of transportation. The small American contingent at Izmir didn't have their own intelligence officer. The base was part of the mission of the huge American, British, Turkish Air Base in Adana. The intelligence office at Incirlik Air Base was headed by an 04 officer, a colonel, and after a secure video chat with the man early that morning, it was clear that even he had no idea what to do with Nader's note. It had been addressed to a CIA operative who didn't show up on any directory, which was not surprising. What had been a bit of a surprise, was the 04's short conversation with the head of intelligence at the American embassy, who also claimed to know nothing of a Thadius Walker. The decision was made to hand carry the note to the embassy in Ankara where the content and how it came to be in Wilson's hands might be important in figuring out what to do. Nader's comment on stopping a war had everyone's attention.

It was a crystal-clear late summer day on Flathead Lake when Walker's phone rang. Thadius was out in his old rowboat, his Gordon Setter sitting in the stern watching every stroke as the graying former spook worked his way down a rocky shoreline. Walker considered rowing the best exercise in the world and he and the dog both hated the handful of days each year when weather kept them from their twice-a-day rows.

Somehow Thadius wasn't surprised when the caller display came up empty or even when the voice on the other end asked him to wait for Mathew Chang, head of the CIA. That changed as Chang came on the line.

"Thad were trying to track down someone who handed an Air Force officer in Turkey a note," started Chang. "It is addressed to you and appears to be from a man named Ahmadi Nader. The Air Force report claimed this Nader guy says he is trying to stop a war." There was a long pause before Chang continued. "The only Ahmadi Nader we know of is a former exchange student who studied nuclear engineering here in the states. There is some speculation that he is way up in the Iranian government's efforts to procure nuclear weapons, although we have virtually nothing that would confirm that."

Walker stopped rowing. "Mat, I know Nader. I helped him get a student visa, He helped me stay alive and out of an Iranian prison about the time you were born. Read me the note exactly as it was written."

Few gave Mathew Chang direct orders, but Walker's temperament was about as no-nonsense as anyone Chang had ever worked with and years of professional contact had taught him that Walker's intuition was to be trusted.

To: Thadius Walker via the American CIA

Thad, I do not know how to contact you directly, so I am trying the only secure means I can think of. I need to meet with you personally. I believe what we need to discuss is critical to the national security of the U.S. and Iran. I will be at the Kemer Resort in Antalya, Turkey for seven days. Remember the old Studebaker truck my friend. Ahmadi Nader.

Chang stopped reading, and then added, "I am reading from the actual hand scrawled note that this Nader guy gave to an American officer in the men's room of a restaurant in Izuir, Turkey."

"Mat, can you get me transport to Turkey?"

"So, you really know this Ahmadi Nader and you think this is serious?" Chang began tapping keys on his computer. "What in the hell does an old Studebaker truck have to do with this?

"Mat, Nader is one of the most serious men I have ever known. We stay in contact, but only occasionally, when it works for him. The last time I heard from him was in a letter posted in Turkey about seven years ago. It was one of the saddest letters I've ever received, full of grief over his wife's reoccurring cancer. And the truck, I was smuggling some people out of Iran right after the Iranian Revolution. Nader was a low-level border guard who caught us hiding in an old soda company truck. Turns out he wasn't much of a fan of the Shah but even less of the new regime."

"You think he is really trying to stop a war?"

"Nader never told me what he does for a living. But with his education, the regime would be nuts not to have him up to his ass in their nuclear program. But I know Nader, and while he loves Iran, he spent enough time in the states to understand that America could step on his homeland and never feel it under the sole our boot. If he reached out, he is dead serious."

"Thad, how fast can you arrange for someone to watch Winchester and your place?"Give me a full day."

"There will be a private jet waiting for you at the Missoula airport at nine in the morning, the day after tomorrow. I want us to meet here in DC before continuing on to Turkey. What else do you need?"

"Get me a room at that resort, and I will need someone to travel with me. My memory and reflexes aren't what they used to be, so I'd like someone with a second set of trained eyes to drive and watch my back. It would help if it's someone already familiar with what's going on in the Persian Gulf."

Chang paused for a full minute. "I can send one of Jana's operatives."

"Mat, this is no time for on the job training, especially since whoever goes will need a separate room and from the time we arrive, cannot appear to have any connection to me."

"How about we ask the Navy for Gritt? Your guys make a solid team."

"Perfect, but you will have to sell him hard. I hear that his girlfriend is coming to visit and leaving her alone in DC just to save the world is probably not on his radar," replied Thad.

"How in the hell could you know that?" asked Mat. "I've got a couple of people keeping track of him, hoping to convince him to join us, and they just heard about Major Tvorshik's new posting and her trip to DC yesterday."

Walker began to laugh. "Mat, even after decades of this, I myself don't know how I find out things, but I do and that's why you still call an old man who walks with a cane."

"As I recall that cane come complete with a .410 shotgun shell embedded in the handle and a one-shot solid teak barrel that looks just like a walking stick below."

"If you manage the situation correctly, one shot is usually all you need," replied Walker.

❧

Chad sat up in bed as Olga slipped from the covers and headed for the kitchen. "You remember to make the coffee last night?" she asked.

"My God, you are just stunning," he answered. "From the back, you look like one of those twenty thousand dollars a day fashion models."

"But you still think my front is the best side of me?" she answered with a smirk. "Did you or did you not remember to start the coffee?"

"You can smell it from here," he answered.

Olga reappeared a minute later carrying two cups. "Yup," started Chad, "front's pretty damned good too."

She handed him a black coffee as she balanced her own while slipping back under the sheet. "Drink your coffee."

Both sipped scalding coffee for a minute before Olga asked, "we have today and tomorrow before I start my training. We can just stay in bed or, I thought you might have a surprise in mind."

"I was planning on taking you back to that seafood restaurant in Baltimore for dinner tonight, and tomorrow we could just wander around Washington. You and I have never had the chance to do the tourist thing. Just us with no shop talk."

Olga placed her cup on the nightstand and snuggled up next to Chad, folding an arm over his chest. "I really missed you Mr. Gritt. Both of those things sound really nice."

"At least we are reducing the distance between our duty stations to a more manageable five- or six-hour trip," he replied. "I was kind of hoping you would be transferred to DC."

"I was offered a staff job here," she said, "but after my adventures in Alaska it sounded really boring. The job will probably keep me in North Dakota for three years. I'll still only be thirty-five, you will be thirty-two. I think I'll be ready to settle down about then." She picked up her cup and spent a minute savoring her coffee. "I'll also only be seven years away from having my twenty in." She watched Gritt's face intently, trying to figure out how he was taking the conversation.

"I hadn't done the math," he replied, "but my heart says it seems about right."

"Put down your coffee, Lieutenant Commander Gritt. We have nowhere to go until this evening."

Late that afternoon, Chad watched Olga unpack a pair of jeans and a stunning yellow blouse. She laid both on the bed next to a lacey bra and panty set that must have cost her a fortune.

Watching him watch her she commented, "I warned you about what I would be wearing under my uniform when I called."

"You know that my job requires me to focus on tiny details, even those you can't yet see. I'm good at that." He watched as Olga headed for the shower.

She emerged from the bathroom moments later, vigorously toweling her hair. Chad sat in bed; his back propped up on pillows and finishing up a conversation on his phone. He was scowling.

"Who was that?" she asked.

"My boss. I am being loaned to the CIA." He looked up at the woman he loved, a woman that he'd only spent days with over the last several months. He watched her smile fade. "I'm joining Thadius Walker on a whirlwind trip to Turkey. It must be something big and urgent."

Olga sat down on the edge of the bed but said nothing.

"We still have tonight," he continued, "but I'm supposed to be at a briefing at six tomorrow evening. Thad will be coming through on a Gulfstream. We may be on our way right after that, or maybe the next morning. I'm packing for five days at some fancy Turkish resort on the beach."

He looked over as a tear formed in the corner of

Olga's eye. "I love the idea of the beachfront resort on the Mediterranean, but I wish it was us."

Olga forced a smile. "If they are hauling Thad all the way from Montana, it must be critical."

"I am told that it is," he offered. And then a smile crossed his face. "It may only be a day or two in Turkey. You can stay here while I'm gone. I should be back before you need to report."

"Do you really trust me in your place with you gone?" she asked. "You might find it completely redecorated when you return."

"The place could use a woman's touch. Let's get dressed and take our time driving to dinner. I have a couple of places I love to show you."

Chapter 25

"HAS MR. BOB THOMPSON checked in yet?" asked Farid. The clerk at the Sheraton New York Times Square checked her computer terminal.

"He has, sir, would you like me to leave him a message?"

"I'm meeting him here," replied Farid, "but my flight was late." Farid handed the woman his British passport and a credit card. "Perhaps he left me a message."

The woman finished checking Farid in, and then scowled down looking for any message. "He certainly did, sir. He and his colleague just phoned from a marina. They have arranged a private harbor tour with dinner." The woman smiled up at him. "It is a beautiful fall day. I am envious." She scribbled a note on a pad and handed it to Farid. It included only an address and a time. "You are to meet them."

Farid picked up his bag and briefcase, suddenly feeling out of place for the second time in just a few days. The Wrangler jeans Sarah had bought him, and cotton plaid shirt seemed a little casual for a private dinner cruise. He stared down at his new hiking boots.

"You might be a little underdressed," observed the clerk.

"Bob's home is in New York, and his friend has homes in Tbilisi, Georgia and in Paris. I suspect you're right. I've never seen his friend in anything other than a suit and tie." Farid tipped the woman ten dollars and headed for the elevator.

That afternoon, a cab dropped him at a boat landing along the East River. At the bottom of the ramp a small motor yacht was tied to a float as two people signed back and forth as they handed coolers to an aging tall man dressed in a captain's uniform. The captain looked up and yelled, "you Farid?"

Farid nodded. Moments later he stepped onto the deck. "Your friends are on the upper deck behind the bridge," offered the captain. "It's not often I get international businessmen who want to talk privately about shipping caviar and truffles. I'll be up as soon as I help your caterers get set up and then we will get under way."

Farid found the men sipping coffee at the rail, overlooking the new World Trade Center. He extended his hand to TWO.

"You know my friend Max," offered Bob, referring to Salman.

Farid shook Max's hand. TWO was now Bob, and Salman was Max, and he was still Farid. The security seemed over the top on a boat with only three other people who would be isolated from the men except for at a dinner that was being laid out on the lower deck.

"Get used to referring to me as Bob and refer to Salman as Max if anyone is near."

"While they are setting up, it would be a good time to get a little work done," offered Bob.

Farid took a seat and the others pulled deck chairs close to his, a small table between them. "The first delivery went as planned," said Farid. There was a little bit of question in his voice.

Bob nodded. "Exactly as planned. After our conversations here, I'm on my way back to Tbilisi to set up the second delivery. It's going to Nevada. Air shipping a heavy load of wine all the way from Georgia just doesn't make sense, so the load will be exotic foods, mostly truffles, caviar, and cheeses. Exotic Beverages distributor in Nevada will be hosting two presentations to promote the products along with samples of our wines. One will be in Reno and the other in Las Vegas. I was in Reno last month."

"Bob's special sample case will be staying in the Reno area," offered Salman.

"Where did the first shipment go?" asked Farid.

"Our new company has distribution in a half dozen cities," replied Max. "The first shipment went to Greensboro, North Carolina."

"We'll be underway in a couple of minutes, called the Captain as he entered the bridge. Below, dock hands loosened the lines and then tossed them over the rail as the rubble of two diesel engines coming to life drowned out the sound of city traffic. The boat backed away from the dock and turned upriver. "I'll be calling out the landmarks as we travel," came from a loudspeaker on a bulkhead near where the men sat.

"I noticed the caterer and waitress signing as I came down the ramp," said Farid.

"When I booked the boat, I asked the boat owner for a recommendation. He suggested a non-profit that trains people with handicaps. I don't know if the two down below can hear or not, but it made the captain who is also the owner happy. The caterer is his son, who gave up on taking over the father's business when the Coast Guard challenged his medical. He's a trained deck hand so, one less set of ears on the boat."

Salman smiled. Farid had only seen him smile a couple of times before. "One more layer of security," he said.

"So, the first shipment went to North Carolina and the second is going to Nevada," said Farid. "Have you identified the third... market?"

"Salman has refined the strategy," replied Bob. "The first city, Greensboro has been first on our list for two years." He looked around, checking the position of the three people on board before continuing. "We always saw the second market as just another smaller community."

Salman picked up the conversation in hushed tones. "If the first delivery does not spur the Americans into action, we decided that the second needs to ramp up the risk to America. Reno is a joint civilian and military airport. Even a small detonation there will poke their military right in the eye."

"I have your second flight from Tbilisi scheduled for twelve days from now."

"That works," replied Bob. "There are some new developments in Iran that require us to push up the timetable. We don't want to leave time for the Americans to overthink this. But at the same time, after the first blast, we anticipate that the borders here will tighten, so we want to prepare all three targets before the first explosion."

"Probably a good idea," replied Farid. "I just pray that one will be enough."

Salman leaned back in his chair. "You are not getting cold feet, are you? You seemed very uncomfortable with what you were learning in Tbilisi."

"No, I'm fine. My uncle and mother made my responsibilities clear. Remember that I grew up mostly in the west and I haven't had a decade of preparation to prepare my mind for all of this. "This is a hard thing we are doing."

"Any comments on the first two targets?" asked Bob.

Farid was struggling to turn TWO into Bob. With nobody in ear shot and the sound of diesel engines and one of the world's noisiest cities only a few hundred yards away, this seemed excessive, but he was the new guy. "No, Bob, both seem exactly right. What are your plans for number three?"

"I haven't picked the target yet. If two locations don't trigger the response we are looking for, the third will have to ramp up the threat. And wherever we choose, I will need to make the decision quickly. We want to bring both devices into the states on the next plane. Any security analyst will tell you that a single act is almost impossible to detect, but two increases the chance of someone figuring out what is happening dramatically. A third act signifies a pattern and a good research team will eventually define the pattern. It's just a matter of time and manpower."

"Bob is right, we need to limit the WILTON flights. We will already have planes landing close to the first two events, so the third must exclude air transport," said Salman.

"And per the plan, if two catastrophes do not trigger the Americans, the third must present a real risk to the country," added Bob.

"I'm thinking that I may end up moving to the states," said Farid. "Obviously not right away, so leaving no crumbs pointing at WILTON and me, makes sense."

Salam leaned across the small table. "We assumed that you would be joining us in your birthplace after this is finished."

Farid could feel Salman's discomfort, maybe even anger. "I haven't lived there since I was a small child. And I can't imagine Sarah giving up her career to follow me there." He turned to Bob. "You were born here. Are you going to be part of the new Iran?"

"No," answered Bob bluntly. "My part is driven purely by anger. My father was American, and my mother was Iranian. When she went back to visit her parents, the Guard arrested her for speaking out. My father disappeared a year later, on a trip to find her. The American State Department did nothing to help. They weren't big shot industrialists or athletes. I haven't heard from either of them in almost ten years."

Farid started to speak. "Let it go," ordered Bob. "In the new Iran a European educated businessman would be welcome, but of course his American wife would probably have to convert if she was to fit in. But I have no roots there and I kind of like Tbilisi."

"We ask nothing of you except for what you are already doing," added Salman. "You have fixed the logistical gap in our plan and in less time than we ever dreamed possible."

"But," added Bob, "those in Iran after this is finished

will be heroes. Those of us living elsewhere will still be at great risk if anything about this plan is ever revealed. You will have to keep your mouth shut for the rest of your life."

In the background the captains voice came over the nearby speaker occasionally as he pointed out landmarks, but none of the three even heard him. To Farid, the whole meeting, the whole plan was not something he would have chosen. But his education was a gift of his uncle and his mother had been waiting to avenge the death of her husband. He understood his role in his head but wondered if he would ever get his head and heart together after it was all finished.

He watched the body language of his two colleagues, recognizing that both of them were actually joyous that their plan was so close to fruition. He also noticed that both had leaned back a bit in their chairs. In a negotiations class at the university, he'd learned that usually meant that the person on the other side was uncomfortable.

The waitress dressed in black pants and shirt with a red tie bounded onto the upper deck. She held up a small sign that simply read, YOUR DINNER IS SERVED.

As the three men rose, Farid stopped. "I will do my part. I will avenge the betrayal and death of my father." He turned to Bob. "And like you, I realize that any disclosure of what we are doing will cost me everything."

He led the others down the stairs as the boat rounded the end of Manhattan Island.

Dinner that night was what an American caterer believed were lamb kabobs.

Chapter 26

GRITT SAT IN the back of Chang's limo as he, Chang and Jana Taylor watched the Grumman Gulfstream taxi from the runway at Andrews Air Force Base. They remained seated as the two pilots and the male steward departed the plane and disappeared into the waiting area. Chang tapped his driver on the shoulder. The lavishly equipped black Chevy Suburban, pulled to the bottom of the air stairs and the three slid from the back, all wearing stocking caps pulled low and sunglasses. A moment later they were inside where they found Thad Walker already seated at a small conference table.

Chang watched Thad reach for his cane. "Don't get up," ordered Chang. He stood across from the old pro and extended his hand. "Nice to see you again, my friend. You know Chad well, and you remember director Taylor."

Thad smiled at each as he shook hands. "What more do you have on this Nader thing?" he asked.

"Nothing more on Nader," replied Jana, "but the Washington Post is reporting that they have a letter that was somehow spirited out of Tehran. It appears to them to be authentic, and it supposedly discusses some major strike at America for destroying their maritime facility. The Post is claiming they got it from a critical source that they have worked with for years and so far, have refused to give us a copy."

"I won't divulge how we will get it, but I expect to have a copy by tonight," said Chang.

"Iran is a beautiful country," replied Thad, "but the politics there have been a shithole since the '60s. I'm told that the internal politics are just as messy."

"I thought you had finally retired, you know rowing your boat and training your dog for pheasant hunting," commented Chang with a laugh.

"You know better than that," offered Thad, "or you wouldn't call me about once a year when you need an old head on a new problem."

"Don't blame us," said Chang. "The last crisis was all because Gritt here couldn't ignore an impossible line of unrelated things that turned out to be a major problem."

"How you been?" asked Thad as he turned to Gritt. "When we get this all figured out, you and the director need to set aside some time to go do a little fall fishing and some bird hunting with me. I like Chang being there. With his security detail around we move by helicopter. We can cover a lot more country in the couple of days he gives me each year."

"I'm in," said Chad. "How long a drive is it from Flathead Lake to North Dakota?"

"An easy day," replied Thad. "Mostly open highway with little traffic after the tourists get their motorhomes off the road for the season. How is Olga?"

"Just great, happy to be a bit closer. She's staying at my place in Georgetown, and if we wrap this up fast enough, maybe we will get a couple more days together before she leaves."

"Okay, enough of this," said Jana. "The three of us were chatting while we waited. Give us a bit more on this Nader guy."

"Mostly you know what I know," said Thad. "He was just a twenty-year-old kid. He could have arrested me and the two people I was moving when he caught us climbing out of the back of an old truck as we were trying to cross the border into Turkey. Instead, he helped us hide for a day. His dad was a teacher and he'd been fascinated by America since his father gave him his first English language book. His first year of classes at the university had gone to shit after the seizure of the American embassy. He was really worried about the turmoil in Iran killing his chances for an education. His passion was the potential of nuclear energy to replace oil and what that would mean to his country's economy."

"And you kept in touch with him?" asked Chad.

"Kind of like you, kid, he had something that I really liked. When Reagan was elected and the embassy crisis ended, I helped him get a student visa. The agency helped. It was a pretty small gesture for saving my life. We saw each other off and on the whole nine years he was in the states. Hell, we were almost the same age."

"What little we could find on him, indicates he was a good student," said Jana.

"More like brilliant. Even then, he hated standing out. He'd call me from time to time when he felt pressure in class. I know the guy would deliberately blow questions on tests just so he wouldn't get the top scores. He even dumbed down his final theses. His advisor chewed him out, knowing it could have been better."

"And his politics?" asked Chang.

"Kind of an intellectual patriot. His dad was hassled after the new regime consolidated power for his views about a modern Iran. But in the few conversations we've managed since he went back, that all ended when they realized how much they needed Ahmadi's education. His joy in life is his wife, who's successfully battled cancer for years. They have no children."

"You think he really has access to information that could help avoid a war?" asked Gritt.

"I doubt that he has hard proof, but you remind me of him, Chad. "He's the kind of guy that can extrapolate one or two clues into a plan. With the tensions between the countries so high right now, he's risking his life just to reach out."

The conversation continued for another hour, with Gritt covering the Navy's technical and intelligence on recent Persian Gulf events and Jana explaining what the intelligence community was hearing. "The thing is," added Chang, "with the recent unrest in Iran, the only advantage of stirring up a conflict with the U.S. would be to deflect from internal issues. But those would not include really damaging attacks on the Revolutionary Guard infrastructure."

"So, you're telling me that the U.S. had nothing to do with the attack on their small boats, the destruction of a missile site or the Maritime building," replied Thad.

"The ship, the *Walter* did destroy the missile launch site that hit them," said Chad. The entire engagement took less than five minutes. The ship was on a special mission to monitor electronic emissions from the Iranian coastal facilities and nothing in the data they had collected indicated any preparation for an attack. It just materialized out of the blue. Not a single additional site even went to a ready status until after the *Walter* shelled that site."

"The U.S. had nothing to do with the attack on the small boats or the building. In fact, Pete Wilson's technical group seems to think the building was destroyed by a bomb hidden on the first floor or in a basement."

"So, let me summarize," said Walker. "We are getting blamed for some piss-ant strikes that don't change the balance in the region one bit. The bad guys are, for some reason actually poking us with a stick, but like so often in the past, are really being bombastic. None of this is helping the regime unless it somehow unites the badly divided nation. But there isn't really any direct advantage to the Revolutionary Guard."

"From a Navy standpoint, mostly correct," said Chad. "But unlike in the past, when the guard stirred up a hornet's nest, the army and navy are sitting this one out."

"We know there are real differences between the official military and the guard," said Chang. "But there may be some logic to the guard stirring the pot. The regime isn't tottering, but it is under domestic pressure and the guard's position as the dominant force in the economy and as the protector of the regime is probably threatened. We are their only real enemy, so if they are going to sell the regime and the public that they are still critical to the nation, they may need a show of force and there isn't another target out there that makes sense."

"Who actually runs their nuclear program?" asked Thad.

"We are fairly confident that it's the Army, but the Guard has their fingers in everything," said Jana.

Thad turned to Gritt. "So, my old friend may be seeing things from both the Army and the Guard. We need to track him down and quickly before this gets any hotter."

Chang's cell rang. "Your replacement pilots are here as is your new steward and some food. Chad, you need to grab your stuff out of the car."

"I'd like to give Olga a call, to let her know that we're leaving."

"Let me take care of that," said Chang. "I'll have Nancy call her and invite her to dine with us this evening. She'll get the message."

Chad bounded down the stairs to where Chang's driver waited with a briefcase and bag. He waited as the director and Jana came down. Each shook his hand as they passed. He followed the two new crewmembers back up the stairs and watched from the door as the limo disappeared and a fuel truck approached. The co-pilot did a walk around then bounded up the stairs.

Chad slid into the seat next to Walker. "Nice to see you again, Thad. Do you want to brief me on what you need from me now, or after your nap?"

"You just can't let an old man rest in peace? You know that I normally take an afternoon nap. After dinner we'll have plenty of time to strategize."

The steward closed the door as the pilots started the engines. "Can I get you anything before takeoff?" asked the burly steward. "Besides a pillow and a blanket," he added as Walker tipped his chair back and closed his eyes.

Chapter 27

THE GULFSTREAM LANDED in the dark and taxied to a secluded spot at the Izmir airfield. A cab met the plane and whisked the men through the streets to a very nice boutique hotel only minutes away where each tugged worn wallets from their pockets to pay for rooms reserved under their new names. Thad was now Theodore Walker, of Missoula Montana, his place of residence an apartment in a small building he actually owned. Chad's new ID identified him as Chadwick Von Gritt of Rockville Maryland. He had previously lived at the address on his passport before he bought his place in Georgetown. The cab driver accepted an American twenty-dollar bill before pulling away. He'd known where they were going without ever asking, and never spoke a word.

The men were shown to adjoining rooms overlooking a small garden. They didn't have time to unpack before there was a tap on Thad's door. He welcomed Lieutenant Colonel Brian Wilson and two other men and then opened the door between the suites to let Chad join them.

"You must be Wilson," said Thad. "And you have the look of a non-descript embassy head of station," he offered to a small portly man with thinning hair. "That makes you part of a security detail," he offered to the third man who wore a light blue blazer that covered up the weapon on his belt.

"Guilty, guilty and guilty," replied Wilson pointing at the other two men. "Caleb here is the one I met with at the embassy the day after I met your friend Nader.

"Paul is my regular traveling companion," offered Caleb. "By now you know more about all of this than I do, so I guess my job is to make sure you have everything you need and to let you know that while you are here, Paul and I will be only a short drive away."

"Chad here is a Navy scientist who's helped out the agency with thorny problems in the past," said Thad. "He will be shadowing me. I can't think of why he would need a weapon, but it might make him feel better if he was armed.

"You're young for a Lt. Commander," said Paul, handing Gritt a Glock 9mm pistol and holster from a bag and two extra clips of ammunition. "The weapon is registered to the U.S. embassy security office here in Turkey, so it is traceable, but it would take someone about three days to learn anything except for the fact that it is in Turkey legally."

"Please sit," offered Thad. "We'll stand a while after ten hours in the air." He waited until his guests occupied the small couch and the chair at the desk. "Brian," he started, "did you notice if anyone was following Nader?"

Wilson pulled out his phone and opened a section with photos. "I got this picture of your guy leaving the restaurant. I had to take it from about a hundred feet away where I was parked, and it was dusk. Scroll to the next picture," he added as he handed the phone to Thad. "About a minute or so after Nader left, this guy left the restaurant before he could have finished his dinner. He watched your man walking toward his hotel before he jumped into a dark blue Fiat coup and followed."

Thad handed the phone to Gritt. "Those really help. I wasn't sure that I would recognize Nader. It's been years since I last saw him. The other guy looks like some young officer assigned to make sure that Nader isn't abducted."

"Or under the circumstances, maybe his job is to see if Ahmadi meets anyone interesting," offered Gritt, handing the phone back to Wilson. He caught a subtle shake of the head from Thad.

"I knew Nader decades ago while he was in the states as a student. He's a quiet, very private kind of guy, so I've got to take his note seriously, although he has always been a bit of a conspiracy nut. It probably comes from living in a police state." He wandered over to a counter where he opened a bottle of sparkling water and downed half of it.

"What are our travel plans?" asked Gritt.

Caleb handed Gritt a set of keys. "You are driving a rental. There is a map and notes on the hotel in the glove box. We've arranged for a limo to pick up Thad at ten tomorrow morning and drive him to the hotel where you both have rooms on the second floor. We tried to contemplate how to facilitate a chance meeting between Thad and his friend, and the best we could come up with was to book all three of you on a half day archeological tour the day after tomorrow. One of you will have to find a way to get word of it to Nader. After that you are on your own."

Paul handed an iPhone to each of the men. "The phone number is on the back and its preloaded with thirty numbers, all in the states. Look for Paul, Caleb, and Brian as first names. One tap will get one of us. When you're ready to leave, call Caleb or me and we will send a limo for Thad. We'll make time for a quick debrief and ensure that the flight crew is standing by to get you on your way home."

"Do you expect any trouble?" asked Gritt.

"No, but Iran has a fairly large and active security presence in Turkey and from what I can glean from what you aren't telling me, this Nader guy is pretty important to them."

Thad just smiled. "We got some sleep on the flight, but we haven't eaten in hours. Any chance of some food?"

"Sorry," replied Brian, "there is nothing open at this time of night. Get some rest. I'll see what I can do about making sure the limo driver has a lunch for Thad here. Chad, you're on your own. If you get out of here early, you should have plenty of time to stop for breakfast and still get to the hotel in Antalya before Thad."

Paul handed each of the men new passports that matched their new wallets. Gritt took a moment to count the Turkish lira in the wallet.

Chad looked over at Brian, a little bewilderment on his face. "I know you had no time to prepare for this," said Brian, "so I made sure there is a good travel guide in the rental. It's written for Americans. The sales sticker on the back is from a Maryland bookstore."

"I'd like to hear more about what we are all doing here," said Caleb. "You know, just a hint of what this is really all about, whatever you can tell me when you return."

"I'll pass on what I can," said Thad. "Now go home and get some sleep. Chad and I have a little planning to do and then we'll grab a nap."

Paul made a quick cell call to confirm security before the three let themselves out.

"Here, copy the information for the archeological tour. If you find Nader before I get there, see if you can slip him a copy. Even if someone is tracking Nader, they couldn't object to two archeological buffs talking on a tour."

"Got it. And I'm just a technology analyst with an American think tank who's fascinated by ancient knowledge. The identities are really solid."

⁂

Chad would never have recognized Nader without the help of Brian's photo. Gritt had slipped on a pair of swim trunks and a Georgetown University sweatshirt and headed to the pool within minutes of checking in. Nader was in a lounge chair under a big umbrella near the corner of the pool. He was dressed in tan slacks and a bright red shirt. Gritt threw the sweatshirt and a small beach bag on a chair before diving into the pool on the muggy afternoon. He surfaced in the middle of the pool and took a full minute to turn slowly studying everyone in the area. The second man Brian had photographed was on the other side of the pool, sipping a drink and reading.

Gritt began swimming laps, finally finishing directly in front of Nader. He waited until the scientist looked up before commenting. "Almost as good as when I was a kid and my dad used to take the family up to a lake in the old Studebaker."

Nader didn't bat an eye; he just nodded and went back

to studying something on his laptop. Gritt climbed out of the pool and wandered back to his chair where he took out a book. An hour later, Nader rose and began gathering up his things. Across the pool the watcher closed his book and rose, moving in front of Nader, heading for the lobby. Nader paused in front of Gritt, "you must be American." He extended his hand. Chad cradled the note in his palm as the two men shook hands. "I went to school in the states. I miss those cool clear lakes myself." Nader continued toward the lobby before the watcher could turn around.

Chad watched him slip the note into his pocket.

Gritt was a little sunburned when Thad finally wandered down to the pool. Chad nodded at his old mentor as the man walked past. Later that evening, Walker called the number of Chad's agency supplied phone.

"Look around in the morning and see if you can find some place to rent a rowboat for a few hours," he said and then hung up.

Gritt slid into the second seat next to Thad. Both were waiting when the Toyota minivan arrived for the tour. Two young women who Gritt guessed were university students from Europe were the next to board. A minute later Nader walked from the air-conditioned lobby.

The watcher followed Nader, obviously out of breath and looking confused. Nader shook hands with the tour driver as he approached the van.

"Here, I'll move back a row and let you older gentlemen share the second seat."

"That was very considerate of you," offered Thad. "I don't move around as well as I did when I was younger." He held up his cane for Chad to see.

Watcher grabbed the tour guide's arm as he started for the driver's seat. The two exchanged conversation for a couple of minutes before watcher pulled out his wallet and handed the guide several bills. "It is fortunate that there was still one seat available," said the watcher in clipped English as he boarded the bus, taking the seat next to Gritt. "I have always wanted to visit the Xanthos Site."

"I myself have never been there," said Thad. "I've visited the British museum and always marveled at the originality of the Lycian civilization. I'm anxious to finally visit the site." He turned to his seat partner. "Us old history students seem fascinated by that civilization."

Nader smiled as the van began to move. "You are right. I've been to the site twice before." He turned to face Thad. "The Lycians developed an attitude about their freedoms, always risking death rather than surrendering to any of the many armies that challenged them."

In the back seat, one of the women was translating their conversation into what Chad thought might be Italian.

"I'm Chadwick Von Gritt," said Chad to watcher sitting next to him. "I spend my life analyzing new technology. One of my old professors once told me that almost every technology in use today is just an old one redesigned to do something faster or better. The poet Homer wrote about Lycian's. I'm especially interested in the technology of their soldiers who fought in the Trojan war."

"You too are American?" said watcher.

"Yup," replied Chad. "I actually won this trip at an archeological conference in New York almost a year ago. I've only got a couple of days before I move on."

"I once lived in Iran," offered the watcher. "I now

live in Istanbul. This is just quick trip for me." He paused before adding, "both Iran and Turkey are very old."

"And you two ladies?" offered Chad, doing his American tourist thing. "Do I hear Italian from the back seat?"

Neither responded to the young American dressed in lime green pants and a colorful flowered shirt. His ballcap featured Einstein's famous E=Mc2.

For the drive, Chad did everything he could to attract attention. It would be the last thing a security person or intelligence officer would do.

In the ancient city of Xanthos, the tour guide did his best to keep the six people together.

The city built on two hills overlooking a fertile plain was expansive, with ruins stacked on ruins. The two women paired off as they walked and listened, as did the two older men. Chad and watcher unintentionally became a pair. As they walked, Nader added to the guide's narrative, demonstrating an amazing knowledge of the site and the civilization. Gritt bombarded his walking partner with questions. Over the next couple of hours, Nader and Thad had the opportunity to spend a few minutes together away from the ears of watcher and the noisy American who never stopped talking. It was clear that watcher was very uncomfortable when Nader was not in sight.

Even Nader couldn't help but learn from the guide, a retired archeological professor, and took several opportunities to engage in deep conversations. The guide herded the six people back toward the van a little before five. "I hope you all enjoyed your tour." The man handed each of them a card. "I would be happy to arrange private tours to other sites," he said before starting the van.

"I studied in America," said Nader as they pulled

away. "I have never been in the place you live." He was facing the man who had introduced himself as Theodore Walker. "How long is the trip to get here from Montana?"

"More than a day," replied Thad. "My body does not like all that sitting. At home I try to row my old boat out on a beautiful clear lake every day. I love the water and the quiet of a boat without a motor. It is a wonderful way to get away for a few minutes and it's great exercise."

"When I was young, I too liked to row. I lived in your Michigan. There are many lakes there." Nader turned to face Thad. "You are right about the quiet. Often, even if you have others with you, an hour or two may pass without a word. There is not enough of that in today's world."

The rest of the drive was silent, except for Chad, who kept up a banter with watcher, who finally introduced himself as Bazhad. Chad recognized at least five different languages in the lobby as the group said their goodbyes and went their different directions.

Gritt and Walker made it a point to eat at different times. Chad wandered all over the resort, at one point passing the restaurant where Nader was having dinner. Bazhad was quietly watching him from the far side of the room.

Later he found Thad seated in a beach chair along the shoreline after dark. He took a seat next to him. "I tipped the man from the small marina just up the beach to deliver a boat to you at eleven tomorrow morning. He will pull it up right here and will wait until a man with a cane arrives. He will walk back; it is only about a fifteen-minute walk. When you are done with the boat, just row it to the marina."

"I'm going for a night swim in the ocean, and then hope to get some sleep," he added.

"I asked Nader to meet me at the beach tomorrow after breakfast. I told him that I had a plan to buy us a few minutes alone," said Thad. "It is going to drive that Bazhad guy nuts."

"I'll do my best to distract him," offered Gritt, as he pulled his shirt off and dropped it in his chair. It had been years since he'd taken a long swim in the ocean. The water was divine. It gave him an idea for a getaway with Olga.

Chad was seated on the terrace overlooking the beach as the small rowing skiff pulled up. He watched Walker gather up his things and slip off his shoes. Further down the beach, Chad noticed Nader doing the same thing before starting a slow walk to where Walker and the man who brought the boat stood talking. Well behind Nader, Bazhad almost leaped from a beach chair and followed.

"My new friend," said Nader as he approached Thad. "You have found a boat."

"I arranged it early this morning," answered Thad. "The water is beautiful. Would you like to join me? I've rented it for two hours. I would be happy to share the rowing."

"I would not impose on you," replied Nader.

"Nonsense," offered Thad. "You sit and think while I row and then we will change seats."

A moment later the boatman helped both older men into the skiff and pushed it out. Bazhad could do nothing but watch, trying not to standout as he stood hands on his hips.

"Those two old geezers could end up best friends," offered Chad as he walked up to Bazhad. "I'm going to go get some lunch. Would you like to join me?"

"I doubt that they will become vast friends," said Bazhad. He turned away, ignoring the lunch offer.

"I'm told that the restaurant has several excellent lamb dishes," said Chad, following Bazhad. "We don't eat much lamb in Maryland, but I'll bet you're an expert. Maybe you can give me some advice."

ꟷ

"Nader's story is enough to bring the hair up on the back of my neck," said Thad. He was sitting on his bed, talking to Chad on his encrypted cell phone. "We will discuss it on the trip home. I'll give both Brian Wilson and that Caleb guy enough to make them feel good about helping us.

"Can you give me a thumbnail on what brought us halfway around the world?" asked Gritt.

"Wait until we are airborne," replied Walker. "And when we get back to the states, plan on being available for a little brainstorming with the agency people." Walker could sense Gritt's unease over being left out. "You will be heading back to Izmir tomorrow afternoon. We will have no contact tomorrow and I'll be staying another day. You're an easy target if the other side wants to know if we have been talking to Nader, and you can't divulge anything you don't know."

"What about you?" asked Chad. "You're going to be here alone and then travel back with only a driver."

"I just talked to Caleb," replied Thad. "I'm about to have a mild heart attack, and the embassy will have an ambulance here to transport me to a medivac flight from Izmir. One of the medics will be that Paul guy. I'll give him enough to keep Brian and Caleb happy. In the interim, I will try to only make casual contact with Nader, although we may owe him a lot."

An ambulance pulled up to the side of the Gulfstream at a little after eleven two days later. Two paramedics helped Thad from the gurney. While one helped Thad climb the stairs, the other carried the oxygen tank connected to Thad's facemask. At the top of the stairs, Chad, dressed in a medical smock and mask took Thad's bags and briefcase from one of the medics and pretended to carry on an intense conversation about the patient, gesturing and pointing.

Inside the plane, all of the window shades were pulled down as Walker stripped off the mask and walked toward the steward in the back of the plane. "Any chance of a Jack Daniels on the rocks before we get airborne?" asked Thad.

Chapter 28

THERE WERE SIX people from the agency waiting for Walker and Gritt the next day. Jana had two of her people with her. With Pete Wilson was the man who tracked military hardware in the Middle East, and the last person introduced herself as a direct contact to Director Chang.

"We had about ninety minutes together," said Thad. "Nader was taking a terrible risk meeting with me, but I think we did a great job of giving him some cover." He took a minute to open his laptop. "I assume each of you have the written report we transmitted from the plane."

All five nodded. Walker had spent enough years with the agency to know that all of them had been on call from the moment the mission started, and that he and Gritt probably got more sleep the night before than they had.

"I condensed Nader's comments into three summary paragraphs. First, years ago, the Pakistani scientists who helped the Iranians get into the atomic energy business actually helped their students refine a small amount of local uranium ore. For the final refinement the entire group flew to Pakistan where they helped concentrate the U-235 content in the ore to at least 80% purity. The Iranians have six small balls of weapons grade uranium. They originally planned on testing a bomb or two but backed away when the U.S. and our allies made it clear that they would never allow an Iran with atomic weapons."

Pete Wilson looked up from his computer. "Bottom line is, they have a supply of weapons grade material." He waited for Thad to confirm it before continuing. "Did your contact give you an exact quantity? I mean small balls doesn't tell us much."

"No, but my second paragraph might give you what you need to figure it out. Nader's group has been taken over by a General of the Revolutionary Guard who is demanding that they produce a small warhead capable of destroying an American aircraft carrier. He wants at least two weapons, one that they can use to demonstrate they are now a nuclear power and a second that will be available to attack a carrier, either artillery delivered or more likely mounted on one of the existing Iranian rockets. Nader basically said the planned weapon would be what we define as a tactical warhead."

"If they have the ability to create six weapons, why would the Guard limit them?" asked Jana.

"Nader asked General Hussein that very question," said Thad. "He didn't get a straight answer, but he thinks that the Guard realizes that they are still about a year away from the ability to start building up a nuclear arsenal and their goal is to deter any American action, not provoke a war. The U.S. has sworn to keep Iran from nuclear arms, but if they already have them, that horse is out of the barn. He also believes that they will be ordered to accelerate their secret development program."

Thad waited for a follow up question and when he didn't get one, he continued. "Third, after the new orders came down, Nader himself took a few minutes to open the vault where the weapons grade uranium is stored. Each of the uranium balls or whatever you people call them are in a small separate lead lined case. What he found rattled him. To him, three of the balls had been replaced with similar orbs. He later checked again. Three of the orbs were slightly larger than the others. He weighed them to confirm it. He also believes that the replacements showed a more refined final processing finish. He has no way, without running up a dozen red flags to prove it. If he spoke out, he would be unable to travel. But someone now has Iranian weapons grade uranium, and he suspects that the replacement material came from Britain, France, China, Pakistan, India, Russia or even the U.S."

"Something was wrong, for sure," said Gritt. "Thad's old friend was being shadowed by some guy who called himself Bazad. I got close enough to him to confirm that he was not armed when we were around, so his logical mission was to watch over Nader and report on him."

One of Jana's analysts pointed at Gritt. "When the Soviet Union collapsed, there were reports that the Soviet's lost at least 85 or as many as 215 small RA-115 portable nuclear devices. The RA-115 estimated total weight was in the thirty kilogram range, maybe sixty pounds. I've seen explosive yield estimates of from three to fifteen kilos, but most analysts think the lower number is more plausible. If the reports are true, then it's possible that someone has possession of several of these weapons."

Pete Wilson tugged his ill-fitting tie loose before interrupting. "That's a hell of a discrepancy, from who knows what to fifteen kilos of power. Depending on where you detonated such a bomb, a three kilo weapon might decimate a couple of city blocks, maybe kill a few thousand while a fifteen kilo weapon could take out a small city." He paused while he tapped away on his computer. "For a sixty-pound bomb, my guess is the yield would be below those estimates. Uranium is twice as heavy as lead, so in order to accommodate batteries, electronics and the material necessary to start a reaction, the uranium core would be really small."

"Okay," said Chad, "but why would someone dismantle what is probably a well-designed and potent weapon, and take out the explosive material, and what advantage would they gain by replacing it with material of unknown, and probably inferior fissionable uranium?"

Pete Wilson stood and walked over to a window. "Are we getting ahead of ourselves here? Is the evidence of the Russians actually building suitcase weapons credible? And if it is, are there really missing nukes?"

Jana shifted in her seat. "In May of 1997, General Lebed, former Secretary of the Russian Security council told an American congressional delegation that they were building such weapons. He reported missing weapons. The Russian government denied his claims. A former Russian environmental advisor, a guy named Yabolov, claimed to have interviewed the scientists and engineers who built the weapons. He said each of them deployed in a city could kill 100,000 people." She watched Wilson plop back into his chair. "We've been looking for confirmation on these missing bombs for twenty-five years, and only have anecdotal evidence they ever existed, but we still consider the risk as highly possible."

Walker looked directly at Jana. "Don't nuclear weapons require constant updates? Wouldn't they be so out of date by now that they no longer work?"

"Actually, if they remained connected to some electrical power source they could last indefinitely. Perhaps you would have to replace old battery packs from time to time, but there is no reason why a quarter-century old weapon isn't lethal."

Ray Callaway, who earlier had briefed Gritt on weapons movement in the Middle East leaned back in his chair staring at the ceiling.

"You have something, Ray?" asked Pete.

"We have this backward," said Ray. "Whoever has a handful of these RA-115 bombs may be planning to use them. Hell, for all we know, the missing bombs may still be in the Russian arsenal, but in the chaos over the collapse of the Soviet Union, it's almost probable that some disappeared. They know that the U.S. has the ability to analyze any nuclear explosion and that we have the world's most complete library on the origins of fissionable material. I think someone doesn't care if the bang is big or little, what they care about is that we don't blame it on the Russians."

"So," started Jana, "the Russians have bribed someone in Iran to swap out the nuclear cores. They certainly are still looking for some way to punish America for helping the Ukrainians, but a nuclear attack seems over the top."

Jana's other analyst leaned across the table. "I spend fifty hours a week studying Iran," she started. "The place is a ticking bomb. First, because of internal unrest.

Second, because of how the Revolutionary Guard bullies everyone else in the name of the Supreme Leader. And finally, because of the growing tensions between the traditional military and the guard." She paused as she pulled up some material on her computer. "We have credible reports that the Guards hard crackdown on the Iranian demonstrations actually led to the arrest and even death of family members of senior military leaders."

"And this is important, how?" asked Jana.

"Just brainstorming here." continued Marjorie. "What if the Army or Navy or Air Force in Iran is about to strike the Guard? What if the Guard's new focus on quickly building a weapon to challenge the U.S. is screwing up the plan? The traditional military knows they are no match for the U.S. They may just want to change the government, but if we blast most of Iran into the stratosphere, there is nothing left to save."

"I'm not a geopolitical geek like you guys," started Chad, "but I am a pretty good engineer. Three things stand out. Most importantly, I can't even imagine any country's military using nuclear weapons to attack an adversary in their own lands. Beyond that, the idea of internal Iranian conflict makes a lot of sense. Nader knew he was being followed. He knew if he waited, he would never have been granted a 'vacation.' From our discussion on the plane, he was more worried about the missing Iranian material than how to use the replacement material to build the bomb ordered up by the Guard. The guy doesn't want a war. He knows that a nuclear strike by the U.S. could simply end the country's existence."

Marjorie smiled at the young Naval officer. "That tracks with our earlier meeting. None of the Iranian provocations against us make political sense at a time when they have so many internal problems. We know that the retaliatory strikes that Iran is blaming on us, didn't come from us. Maybe someone internally or externally, but with Iranian ties is determined to start a shooting war."

"Shit," mumbled the woman who was in the meeting only to brief the director. "I can't imagine the U.S. not kicking the hell out of Iran if we could prove that the Iranians launched even a small nuclear strike on this country."

Jana began to laugh, which seemed completely out of place. "And Peggy, that is why the director and all the rest of us put up with you. You are blunt and always to the point which keeps the director pointed in the right direction."

"We need to really cast a wide net," offered Thad. "There are a number of possible scenarios on this. I've chased rabbits down the wrong hole more than once, but two things are really clear. Someone has a plan to use a nuclear bomb and we are the most likely target and whoever that is, wants us to know that the bomb came from Iran."

"So that's where we start," said Jana. "Pete and I will put out heads together for the rest of the day. Peggy's style will guarantee that Mat will be listening when we brief him. I suspect that by tomorrow the same effort that we used in the EEL and ANGEL crisis will be in order. I just hope that we have time to figure this out before someone really hurts us."

~

Gritt and Walker arrived at Andrews Air Force Base, where they were met by a driver arranged by the agency to deliver them to Thad's hotel near CIA headquarters, and Chad to his place in Georgetown.

"Do you really question that we are looking for an outside threat?" asked Chad.

"No," answered Thad, "and that is what is driving me crazy. The damned plot is too complex and the time it would take to put it all together, well, it would take years. Yet nobody has ever picked up even an inkling. The more logical answer is that somehow this is a continuation of the Guard versus the U.S. that goes back to we took out a head of the Revolutionary Guard Quds Force for killing Americans."

"Maybe," said Gritt, "it's both. I'm not quite sure what I mean by that, but I think your right, this is all tied together."

"I suspect that you will be summoned back to Maryland tomorrow," offered Walker as he stepped out of the car. "Enjoy your evening with Olga, I suspect that we are about to be locked away somewhere until we figure this out."

Chapter 29

THE WILTON AIR 767 freighter touched down in Reno, Nevada just before three on Thursday. The pilot had called ahead to arrange a temporary airport ramp permit for Bob Thompson. Thompson waited for the two pilots to leave the plane before he called the number of the Exotic Beverages Reno agent. "You can begin pulling the inventory as soon as you can arrange it," he said to the voice on the other end of the phone. "I've got some running around to do, so call me when you're ready to get started."

"Damn, I'm sorry Mr. Thompson. "I have you arriving tomorrow. "

"Tomorrow works. I probably screwed that up in my email to you. I still get the time changes confused. The WILTON plane isn't scheduled out of Reno until tomorrow afternoon. Anyway, I'm going to the airport manager's office for a few minutes and then I'll pick up a rental."

"Do you need a ride?" asked the agent.

"No, I'll catch a ride with the pilots over to the terminal. They have a hotel shuttle coming."

Less than an hour later, Bob was back at the plane, where he quietly carried his personal luggage for a week's travel along with two lead lined cases to the Chevy Traverse he'd rented. He took a few minutes to register at a nearby hotel and then used his phone for directions to an address across town. Pulling out of the airport he was a little disappointed to see only Air Force National Guard C-47 Chinook helicopters parked at the military ramp across from the terminal. Perhaps it had been a fluke, but the last time he was in Reno, there had also been a couple of heavy transport planes on the ramp. Making the area around the airport a target was as much to sting the American military as it was to cause civilian chaos. It really didn't matter. There was no time to change targets now.

SIRI guided him the address located in a suburb of small ranch houses only a few miles from the casino district. He pulled up and parked next to a small tan house. In front was a Ram truck with a bed of complex locking storage and doors. Before he could get out of the car, a burly man walked out on the concrete porch. The man was dressed in a Budweiser T-shirt and a pair of worn jeans. He was leaning on a crutch.

"You Bob Thompson?" said the man with a slight accent. "I saved the truck for you, just like you asked. I was kind of surprised that someone from New York was looking for a good work truck. I only had it listed on Craig's List for a few days."

"And you're Mike," answered Bob. "I'm the regional manager of a small construction company and we just got a job down by Las Vegas. We needed another work truck, so when I saw your ad, I figured it wouldn't hurt to call since I needed to be in Reno anyways."

Bob began a slow walk around the truck, not really knowing what he was looking at. "The key is we're going to be on and off the job for several months as we wait for others to do their part. We need something that we can park at the job site, to lock up our supplies and tools."

"I been using the truck for two years. Bought it used for about the same reason. I used to do plumbing until I had an accident. My back just won't let me do that work anymore. I need to sell the truck. Never figured I'd end up working for one of the casinos, but that's where I'm headed."

"Can I take it for a drive?" asked Bob.

Mike tossed a heavy set of keys to him. "The one with the rubber cap is for the doors, and ignition. The others are for all the compartments. The two Master Lock keys are for the heavy steel doors right behind the cab. I put heavy locks on them in addition to the regular ones after someone tried to jimmy the doors open at a job site. Those two cabinets will hold a pile of tools."

Bob started the truck and then backed out of the driveway, turning toward the freeway. The truck seemed to run well. He stropped a block from Mike's and opened each of the six storage compartments. The two with double locks were big enough to accommodate the special cases in the back of his rental.

He was back in fifteen minutes. "Can you still drive?" he asked Mike.

"Yup, I just can't crawl around under houses or work up in ceilings and an hour on my back working on a sink just kills me."

Bob took out his wallet and counted out six thousand dollars in cash. "That what we agreed to?" he asked.

"Yup, it's a fair price. The truck's got some miles on it, but it's in great shape."

Bob handed half the cash to Mike. "I'll need the title signed over. Just sign the release that you sold it, my boss didn't tell me how he is going to record the title. There's another couple of hundred in it if I can get you to drive the truck to the hotel where I'm staying. I can bring you right back."

"Got nothing better to do, and I can use the two hundred. Just give me a minute to get the title and my coat."

Bob handed Mike a card from the hotel and the truck keys. "Meet you there."

He was almost to the hotel when his phone rang. The crew would be there to unload the plane at eight the next morning. That worked perfectly. He had one more stop after taking delivery of his new truck. It was at a storage unit almost identical to the one in Greensboro, but this one was only yards away from the airport; just two blocks from the Air National Guard building.

He waited until after dark to transfer one of the two bombs to a locked cabinet in the new truck, parked as far away from security cameras mounted on the buildings as he could get.

He then drove the rental and second bomb to the storage facility he'd rented two months before. As in Greensboro, it was an end unit. In thirty minutes, he had the bomb in place and a small solar panel mounted inside a small skylight that eliminated any need for electric lights inside the unit. Finished, he headed back to the hotel.

He spent the next two hours munching on bar food and drinking beer while feeding quarters into a slot machine.

With the plane unloaded and the local agent fully in control of setting up the two shows, Bob returned his rental and took the airport shuttle back to the hotel. An hour later he turned east on Interstate 50.

He figured it would take two days to reach the next target, but once there all he would have to do is set up a small solar panel right on the truck and park it. He'd never been to the small city chosen for the third attack, but it fit the criteria of slowly escalating the crisis. He'd park the truck then catch an Uber to the local airport. In three days, he'd be back in Greensboro awaiting the go ahead to start the ball rolling. He smiled as he thought about how innocuous that statement was compared to the mayhem he was about to unleash.

Chapter 30

SARAH COULDN'T QUITE figure out why Farid was calling her daily. He seemed depressed, yet their conversations were all about work except for a new emphasis on his mother and experiences growing up in Lebanon and then France. Perhaps he was just nervous over their discussion the night before he'd flown to New York. For the first time he'd talked openly about them spending the rest of their lives together.

"Farid," she said as she cradled the phone in a hallway where she'd slipped out of a meeting, "like I said yesterday, I can't give you any advice on how to tell your mother and uncle that you may be walking away from the job. I know that they pulled strings to get you into that WILTON company, so yeah, they may be disappointed. And I don't know if there is anything you might want to do here. But we won't be broke. We have my trust fund."

"There is nothing bad about WILTON," he said. "It's just that you seem to have found your calling. I'm not so sure that I wouldn't be happier away from a big city.

First Beirut, then Paris, then London and with my current company, the only options in the states are New York or Los Angeles. Neither of those places work for what you love to do."

"Look, my love, you said you might be able to come visit in the next couple of weeks. We can talk about it then. For now, you have to let me get back to my job. Call me tomorrow night."

Perhaps he was just lonely. She certainly was. Olga, her new roommate was scheduled to be in Minot the day she got back from her business trip. Having another woman to talk to would help. She'd need to make it clear that Farid would be staying with them from time to time. She remembered how excited Olga was to be on her way to see her boyfriend. She'd understand.

Walker was wrong. Gritt had not been summoned back to Agency headquarters in Maryland the next day. Chad gave Olga a kiss as each headed their separate ways the next morning. They had one more evening together before she left for her new posting. Walker on the other hand found himself on the phone explaining to the young woman who was watching over his lake house and more importantly his dog, that he might be delayed a few more days. Mathew Chang was assembling a research team to try to qualify and quantify the potential threat that Nader's conversations represented.

"Tell me about your training," said Chad as he and Olga fussed in the kitchen.

Somewhere she had found an Eastern Europe grocery

and was in the process of making pelmeni, small ravioli type pastry envelopes stuffed with spices, meat and potato cooked in a rich broth. She'd even purchased two red crockery pots to serve it in. "I'm making you a Russian dinner, one I haven't had in years, and you want to talk shop," she said.

"You just told me that those little pots would be in the oven for an hour."

"In Russia, that would be just enough time to open a fine bottle of Vodka and drink a toast to the chef."

"I'll get that bottle from the freezer and open it," replied Chad. "I just thought you might want to talk about your new job."

Olga waited for Chad to open the bottle of the best Vodka she could find in DC and pour two small glasses. He carried both glasses and the bottle into the living room then typed a request into a laptop that connected to his stereo system. "I hope you don't mind, but this dinner goes best with a little traditional Russian music."

The two settled onto the couch. On the coffee-table a small platter of fatty sausage, cheese and dark bread waited to compliment the frozen liquid fire that Chad had poured. "I do want to talk about it," she said. "There isn't a damned thing that I can do to protect the base from an air attack. That's not what the training is all about. What we worry most about is some kind of terrorist attack. It might come from anti-nuclear activists or a foreign group who has it in for the U.S. The nuclear arsenal is quite isolated and shielded by hardened facilities and there are armed patrols around them 24/7. There are always bombers pre-loaded with nuclear weapons on standby. They are heavily guarded. We also have enhanced security all the way around the base perimeter.

She stopped to sip her vodka and waited for Gritt to sample his. "Do not ever drink Vodka without some fatty food and bread," she admonished. "Without something to help your body burn off the alcohol it goes straight into your blood stream and to your head."

Chad placed a small piece of sausage on some bread and devoured it. "Am I doing this right?"

Olga laughed. "Perfect." She took another sip of her Vodka before continuing. "We pay a lot more attention to national intelligence briefings than most military installations where the focus is on theft and dumb pranks from young service members. The arsenal there is a deterrence to foreign actors. Any security breach that allowed someone access to the weapons wouldn't lead to a nuclear detonation, the fail safes are solid, but it could lead to fallout contamination. That could shut down the base and kill or at least sicken everyone that it reached. Our instructors challenged us to develop our own regional intelligence."

"Thad Walker always says that most major threats are defeated by someone hearing some tiny snippet that worries them, usually from a contact they've worked with in the past or someone who tips you off with a clue that even they don't know is important."

"It was nice to see you working with Walker again," said Olga. She slipped some cheese into her mouth before she refilled the small glasses she'd purchased just for that evening.

"I can't really get into what we were working on," said Chad. "It's still considered a top security matter, and maybe it isn't even really important, but if it is, we are going to be buried in what-ifs and possible scenarios for a while. We're working on the same kind of thing you will be paying attention to, but our focus is global."

Olga ran her hand across Chad' cheek. "Are we talking Armageddon here. If we are, let's just skip dinner and go straight to bed."

Chad smiled. "I am not skipping a dinner that you have been talking about since last night. And no, this is not an Armageddon scenario, but it could be damned painful." He paused a moment. "That's if it is really anything at all, but I'm up for not wasting any of our together time."

⁂

Karim, Salman, Mohamed, Reza and Farid all opened their secure laptops the next morning to a simple message. "Our aunt wasn't happy with the new purse; she went ahead and purchased a second and just today a third. If approved, I'll help her get rid of the first one the day after tomorrow."

Mohamed called and left a message for General Ashraf. "Please tell those you are working with that I expect to acquire the materials we need to finish that project for the Guard in the next couple of days."

That night, eight people around the world celebrated. Farid left work early and called an Uber to take him home only three hours later, at the insistence of a bartender.

⁂

Olga walked out of the terminal at the Minot airport and looked around for Sarah's Bronco. She carried only the bag she'd taken to DC. The personal things she'd shipped from Arizona should be waiting for her on base, maybe even the four boxes she'd shipped from Alaska. *You know girl, you're over thirty and everything you own except for your substantial bank account can be shipped in a handful of boxes. Maybe you've finally found that reason to settle down that has evaded you for her entire life.* In the distance she could see the Bronco just turning into the airport.

Olga and Sarah barely left the airport before Sarah shifted the 'hi, how are you' conversation to something more serious. "How was your visit with your boyfriend?"

"Especially nice, at least for the time we had together. He had to make a sudden trip the day after I arrived and only got back for the last couple of nights."

"You know we live in a huge house," continued Sarah.

"I saw it, remember," said Olga. "We two can rattle around in there when we are both in town without ever getting in each other's way. Are you getting cold feet about a roommate?"

"No, but I wanted to let you know that my boyfriend may be coming to spend some time with me in the next couple of weeks." She glanced over to watch Olga's response and was pleased to see her smile. "You'll like him. He's originally from Iran but grew up in Lebanon and later in Paris. We went to school together in London. He still lives there and is an executive at a big deal transportation company. He's a bit rattled right now; not really sure he wants to spend his life in a big city. I suggested he come visit me here. He spent a few days with me just a couple of weeks ago and I think he liked the wide-open prairies."

"If you two want extra privacy while he is here, I can move onto the base for a few days, into the bachelor officers' quarters," replied Olga.

"I don't think that will be necessary. But it is a very nice offer. We can plan for me to be on one of my trips if your friend comes to see you."

Olga liked the younger woman. She'd not really had any specific expectations when she'd stopped in Minot to check on the house rental but was still surprised by a young European educated woman of means with a foreign boyfriend in a place like North Dakota.

"Chad, that's my boyfriend's name," said Olga, "was born and raised in Alaska and he now lives in DC. He's military, and committed to his job, but I think he might like this place too. He grew up hunting and fishing, and Washington DC isn't exactly known for its outdoor activities."

"I just wanted to clear it with you before he calls tonight. Lately he's been calling every day," said Sarah. "You hungry? There's a great little bar with good burgers and stuff on the way home."

Bob didn't even check into a hotel after his late arrival at the Greensboro airport. He used an Uber to visit the storage unit and arm the weapon, then hired a cab to take him directly to the Amtrak station. At 6 a.m. he boarded the #20 Crescent train from New Orleans, now headed to New York. The train was only ten miles north of the station when he dug out the burner phone he'd purchased in Reno. He called cell phone number connected to the bomb. The train slowed as the trees whipped and the coach shimmied. He'd expected a bigger flash and a louder boom, but the important thing was that the bomb had exploded. America and Iran were officially at war.

In Greensboro, emergency response vehicles were converging on a huge explosion. Something had incinerated everything for hundreds of yards in every direction. The local fire chief jarred from bed by the blast miles away was already on his home phone with local civil defense agencies trying to determine what in the area could possibly have been so explosive that windows shattered miles away. He'd tried his cell phone, but something had interrupted cell service. The local emergency management office had no idea of what might have caused such a blast. Local radio stations were off the air as were the emergency radio networks.

Whatever had blown up took down his ability to communicate with his people in the field. He dressed hurriedly and headed toward the scene. Thank God, he thought, that this happened in an industrial area before most people headed to work because as he approached the area, it looked like something had simply erased part of the city, including the airport.

There were flashing lights everywhere and, in every direction, buildings were burning. The chief's car was flagged down by two people in front of one of the last buildings standing. Both wore blood smattered white smocks and looked panicked.

As he rolled down the window of his Greensboro Fire Department vehicle, one of the people thrust a small plastic badge through his window.

"What am I looking at?" he asked.

"We work at a radiation oncology clinic. That's a radiation monitor. It's off the charts."

Chapter 31

"I SENT A HELICOPTER for you," said Walker. "Director Chang has put the two of us back on the payroll."

Gritt checked his watch. It was just seven. "Thad, I didn't get home until midnight. I was planning on a little extra sleep. My first meeting isn't until nine."

"You haven't heard?"

"Heard what? I turned off the alarm."

"My old friend Nader was right. There's been a small nuclear explosion in North Carolina."

Somehow Chad believed what he'd just heard. "Do I have time to shave and shower?"

"Be in at the elementary school playground just down the street in fifteen minutes. The president has locked down the city. Pack what you may need for several days." Walker hung up.

He was still walking to the school when an Air Force helicopter swung into the wind to land. "You Gritt?" asked a young woman as he jogged up to the open helicopter doors."

He nodded and handed her an overnight bag and his briefcase before climbing in and strapping his seat belt. He slipped on the headset she handed him. "Do you know where that bomb went off?" he asked.

"About three hundred miles south of here, in Greensboro."

"What in the fuck is worth blowing all to hell in Greensboro?" he muttered into the microphone.

The copilot leaned around to look at him. "If nothing else, some of the best ribs in the South." The man had a southern drawl and Gritt could see real fear in his face.

"You from that area?" asked Gritt as he struggled into the coat he'd carried from home.

Both the copilot and crew chief recoiled slightly as they recognized the man dressed in a maroon sweatshirt and jeans, with a day's growth of beard was a Navy lieutenant commander.

"About a hundred miles south of Greensboro, Sir," answered the Air Force lieutenant.

Walker met him at a helipad only seconds away from the CIA Langley headquarters. "This just got more complicated," said Walker. "I'm not sure that I buy a message on the explosion getting to news outlets across the world in less than two hours, but all of the stations are reporting a written statement from someone who claims to be the deputy commander of the Iranian Revolutionary Guard. He says the strike was in retaliation for the bombing of that Guard Maritime building and warns that the Guard is prepared to strike again if the Americans don't back off."

Gritt picked up his bag and briefcase as the two walked toward the huge building that was the nerve center of

American intelligence. "The message specifically says the Guard is prepared, not Iran is prepared?" asked Gritt.

"Am I not speaking clearly?" replied Walker.

"Sorry," said Chad. "I agree, it all seems a bit too canned." The two security guards that accompanied Walker to the landing pad held the door open for them as they entered. Both presented their ID to another man at a window just inside the door. "Or, the situation in Iran has reached a point where the Guard has lost its mind," he added.

"We will know more in a couple of hours," offered Walker as they waited for the elevator. "There are two teams on the ground in the blast zone as we speak. They should have hard data on the origins of the blast shortly; both on the orebody and if it's from a known processor, where it was refined. Most of the first responders have backed away until they can get into hazmat suits," added Walker. "A lot of them were exposed before they knew it was nuclear.

"As we discussed on the plane the other night, if the refinement came from Pakistan, we might not have much data. If it's from Iran, we will have to compare the signature to the data gathered by the International Atomic Energy Agency during the prior inspections."

"Like I said," replied Walker as the two walked into the conference room adjacent to the director's office, "this just got more complicated."

The room filled with analysts and only moments later, the door to the director's office opened and Jana Taylor and Pete Wilson followed Director Mat Chang into the room.

"Emergency services from the North Carolina governor's office is reporting more than eleven hundred wounded. With one local hospital badly damaged and another possibly contaminated the National Guard is moving patients to wherever they can find beds. Nobody could have survived in the immediate blast zone, but it's mostly industrial, so the death toll could be a low," said Chang. "The good news is that the blast was small for a nuclear device and there was little wind, so there should not be much extended radiation fallout."

"I just told the director," started Jana, "we have nothing more on the threat than he was briefed on just a few days ago. My people have been scrubbing every bit of information we can find; pushing every source we know about, and we still have nothing more than what Walker and Gritt brought back from Turkey."

"I'm sure the president isn't going to be satisfied with that assessment when I brief him this afternoon," offered Chang. "We've been friends for years. He isn't a hothead, but he does believe in an eye for an eye."

"Mat," started Thad Walker, "I suggested the other day, that we cast a wide net here. There isn't an analyst in this room that can't follow the breadcrumbs we already know about. I'll bet my retirement that they all point to the Iranian Revolutionary Guard. But this reeks of a disinformation campaign to me."

"Thad, you haven't cashed a retirement check in years," replied Chang. "I understand your concerns, but someone just blew up part of an American city with a nuclear device. There are going to be a lot of powerful people looking for payback."

Chad was standing behind where Walker was sitting. "Thadius and I discussed this for hours on our way back from Turkey, Sir. This Nader guy might be the top scientist working on Iranian nuclear weapons, yet he risked his life to warn us about missing fissionable material. He was really worried about someone triggering an American nuclear attack that would decimate his home."

"And someone might just have done exactly that," offered Chang.

"Mat, there may be at least two more devices out there," said Jana. "And the Iranians admit they are working on air launched devices powerful enough to destroy an American aircraft carrier. According to this Nader guy they have the ability to build five more weapons without much trouble. It might be a lot easier to blast Iran back into the dark ages than to figure this all out. We need to try to keep a lid on this until we can really minimize the risk from any retaliation. Whoever is doing this may have already distributed the bombs. If they see the imminent destruction of the entire country, they have no reason not to use them."

Walker tugged a pipe out of a pocket and began packing it with tobacco, even knowing that it was a non-smoking facility. He ignored Chang's look of disapproval. He struck a match and puffed the pipe a few times to get the peach brandy scented tobacco burning. Finally, he spoke. "The war on terror has been going on for three decades. But it really ramped up after 9/11. We lost about 3,000 Americans that day and over the next two decades twice that many more. Today we may have lost less than a thousand. If that bomb had gone off in Miami or New York or here in DC, we would have already taken ten times that number of dead. Whoever is responsible for this tapped us, they didn't slap us. We need to figure out why. If we are going to really punish someone it should be those who actually hit us."

One of Pete Wilson's people stood in the back of the room glaring.

"Monte, you have something to add?" asked Pete.

"No matter which fringe group or militia or army did this, they are all part of a problem we and much of the world have had with Iran for almost a half century. No one would blame us, after today, if we used the old Marine Corps solution. Kill them all and let Allah sort it out."

"Monte, you're offering a solid permanent solution to the Iran challenges," replied Pete, "but you are wrong about how the rest of the world would respond. Even our best friends couldn't help but look at America as the ultimate bully. We would never again sit down with an ally and really know if they were our friend or just afraid of us."

Chang invited Walker and Gritt into his office as the meeting broke up. "Thad," he started, "I'm going to counsel the president to show real patience right now. I'd like to take Chad with me to the meeting since after the EEL and ANGEL crisis he has solid credibility with the military, whom I suspect will not be suggesting patience. "I'll have him back here this evening. In the interim, I'd like you to begin constituting a new Team Walker. We need to figure this out before a second bomb goes boom. After that all bets are off."

Chang paused. "Right now, I'm recommending that every possible means of smuggling a bomb be inspected, even those with historic approval."

Chapter 32

FARID TAPPED ON Dorsey's closed door and waited as his boss finished up a phone call.

"Come," called Dorsey. He waited until Farid was seated across the table. "You heard that the American's have slapped extensive new restrictions and clearance policies on all marine and air transport into the country. I don't blame them after what just happened."

Farid said nothing.

"Both of our planes are here in Europe right now," continued Dorsey. "We have a ton of work already booked in the states, so we need to get at least one plane and crew back on American soil."

"So, what do you want, Sir?"

"I want you to jump seat back to the states on a plane and stick with it and the crew until they get full permission to work there. Work out of WILTON's maritime office in New York. They will be battling the same issues, so you can help each other."

Farid just stared.

"Hey, you okay?" asked Dorsey.

"Just a little shocked about that attack on America; it may have killed a thousand people and several thousand more may have been exposed to radiation. I talked to Sarah this morning; she's scared to death."

"Once you get our plane working, take a couple of days off and go see her. Just remember, we are still in a startup mode and the board could well shut down the entire aviation effort if we don't manage this. This crisis kind of feels like COVID all over."

"I'm not quite sure how to go about getting us cleared to fly into the states," said Farid.

Dorsey handed him a note. "That's the name and number of an old friend at the embassy here in London. He has an idea. I've made you an appointment for you this afternoon."

The timing worked out way better than either Dorsey or Farid had expected. With every cargo flight going into the states undergoing extensive scrutiny, the embassy arranged for an expedited inspection of the WILTON plane at McGuire Air Force Base in New Jersey. Instead of an empty load, they would be carrying a load of household goods for Air Force personnel rotating back into the states. The Air Force plane originally scheduled to make the trip was being re-positioned in case it was needed for conflict with Iran.

Before Farid could even take off his shoes that evening, his phone rang. "Farid," said his uncle, "Salman and I will be in London for a short chat the day after tomorrow. We will be at your apartment about seven."

"Uncle, make it tomorrow. I will be going to New York the next day. I may be there several weeks."

"That is very good news," replied Karim. "Your old friend Bob was mugged leaving a train station in New York. They took his wallet, and his cell phone and tablet were smashed. You need to take him replacements."

Karim and Salman arrived with Indian takeout. Both seemed as happy as Farid had ever seen, as they privately discussed what had just occurred in Greensboro. "It was a perfect target," said Salman. "Few casualties but a huge response from the American government. Their president has sworn to bring those responsible to justice. His advisors are already talking war."

"They are taking their time figuring out what to do," added Salman. "That means that the threat of an overwhelming nuclear strike on our homeland is probably off the table. Instead, they are building up air and naval forces in the region."

Karim laid his fork on his plate next to his Chicken Tika Masala. "As hoped, they are responding with careful planning. Hopefully one bomb will be enough."

"That bomb killed over 400 people, Uncle. Another thousand are hospitalized and many more have been exposed to radiation," replied Farid.

"We knew there would be casualties on both sides," offered Salman. "Hopefully the majority of any future casualties will be with the Guard. The Americans don't need to kill them all, just the leadership, but the Iranian people must believe the Guard is responsible."

"I pray that is the case," said Farid.

"Remember Farid, the original plan assumed it might take two explosions to force the Americans into action. The second will sting not only the public, but also their military. We hope that is not necessary, but it may be.

The Iranian government and the Guard have been all over the media denying they are responsible. We must allow a couple more weeks for the water to clear. We have a plan to infuriate both sides."

Farid stopped eating. His task now was to keep what he'd already consumed in his stomach. "You mentioned that the second explosion would ratchet up the pressure. Bob set the second bomb somewhere in the Reno area. I find no military bases in that part of Nevada," he said.

"There is a small national guard aviation base right at the Reno airport. The rest of the area around the airport is sparsely populated like Greensboro. That attack will be felt mostly by the military." Karim watched his nephews face and realized that he was deeply troubled. "But a second attack may not be needed."

"Is there a specific target for a third attack if one becomes necessary?" asked Farid.

"You will have to ask Bob," replied Salman. "The third weapon is in the Midwest. There are several potential targets. The weapon will not be armed until he chooses a target."

Karim handed Farid a package with expertly forged identification and new bank cards. "Get these to Bob. He needs to travel to do his job. Have him buy a new computer in the states and then contact FIVE using your secure device to download the appropriate software."

Salman handed Farid a handwritten note. "This is the phone number and address of Bob's apartment in Manhattan. Let us know after you two meet. We are counting on you."

"I will do my duty to the family and to avenge the death of my father, uncle. But I admit, being part of a war from a quarter century ago, especially with the weapons we possess is troubling. I struggle to keep my heart and my head together."

His uncle grasped his shoulder and squeezed. "It will be over soon."

The men weren't to the elevator before Farid poured himself a scotch. He retreated into the bedroom and laid down on the bed, trying to calm his nerves. He finished his second drink before calling Sarah.

"Jesus," answered Sarah, "do you know what time it is?"

"I just wanted to pass on that I will be relocating to the states, to New York tomorrow. I'll call as soon as I can figure out when I can come visit."

"Good. Message received. Good night," she replied.

~

The helicopter carrying Chang and Gritt landed next to Marine One on the lawn of the Whitehouse. Instead of escorting the men to the building, a secret service agent rushed them toward the Marine Corps helicopter and up the stairs.

"You can brief me on the way to Greensboro," said the president. "I want to see the damage for myself and to talk to the governor. We have no contingency plan for a nuclear attack in Podunk, North Carolina."

Only moments later the rotors began to turn for a two-hour trip. Chang's briefing was constantly interrupted by a communications person briefing the president, who handed Chang one of the notes. "The residue from the blast had the earmarks similar to those that the IAEA found in Iran, but not identical."

"Those findings will give me a little cover," offered the

president. "I meet with the joint chiefs tonight. I will not order an immediate strike on Iran and the report on origins will be part of my justification. But we will continue a buildup of air and naval power in the region." He looked at Chang and then at Gritt. "I know you two just warned us about this risk. I read the report on the origins of your warning. You damned well better figure out who we are going to crush for this while I still have the political power to control what we do."

The helicopter made a high-altitude pass over ground zero. The damage was total in an area about the size of six football fields with crumpled buildings extending for another hundred yards, the destruction slowly fading to just broken windows only a half mile away. Marine One landed next to ten huge green tents pegged out on a driveway next to a hospital.

A dozen local police assisted two secret service agents in establishing a loose security perimeter as the president and his entourage emerged. Outside the closest tent, dozens of blood-soaked body bags littered the ground.

They were greeted by North Carolina's governor and the mayor of Greensboro. "What do you want to see first, Mr. President?" asked the governor.

"I want to talk to the doctors. He pointed at the Secretary of Homeland Security. Mark needs to know exactly what they need right now. Whatever it is, can probably be sourced quickly. There are a half dozen military bases within hours of here."

Inside the closest tent, a combination of local doctors, nurses, and paramedics were rushing from table to table doing triage. Blood and clothing stripped from patients by the medics littered the floor. Some patients appeared comatose, although they looked uninjured. "The blast shocked the brains and nervous systems of a lot of victims," said a physician who was walking with them. He pointed toward others with broken and lost limbs. "The blast turned every building, every vehicle into a flying weapon." There were more than thirty patients crammed into that tent, and there were nine more tents. The president, a retired Army officer had seen war in Iraq, but nothing like this.

As they exited the tent, the exhausted doctor found a stool that someone carried from the adjoining hospital. "The worst is that almost every patient is badly burned. We need more supplies to treat burns. And we have nothing to deal with the internal radiation contamination. We need Potassium Iodide, Prussian Blue, and Diethylenetriamine pentaacetate and anything else you can supply us. Many of these patients will need to deal with Acute Radiation Syndrome. This can be done wherever they end up, but they will need medicines to speed up blood cell production. Even those of us treating them will probably need to deal with exposure."

The head of Homeland Security was furiously taking notes. "Most importantly, continued the doctor, "we need to get these people out of the area and into hospitals where they can be cared for correctly. We could use Navy Corpsmen and Army medics, trained in injuries."

The president turned to the governor. "Max, can you have one of your people get Mark here, to someplace where he can find a secure telephone line so he can get started on that list?"

He turned to the Homeland Security Secretary. "Mark,

see what you can get done in an hour. I want to be on the way back to DC by four this afternoon."

It took a few minutes to organize the trip. "While they are gone, Max, is there someplace we can talk privately? The guy in the sweatshirt is really a Navy Officer and I want him to brief you privately about what we already know. Just keep it completely under your hat. I mean just between us and you. By tomorrow CIA director Chang will have all hands-on deck to figure out just who hit us and what we're going to do about it."

"This is different than the challenge of the China problem," said Walker as he and Jana Taylor walked into a large conference room. "We need to build on the tiny amount we already know. A plot like this took years to put together, but your people suspected nothing, so were probably looking for a tiny highly motivated group with a lot of money behind them."

As they talked, technicians and staffers were already converting the room into a command center. "The first person I'd like to find is that retired Army colonel who helped us on the EEL and ANGEL problem. Bob Phillips probably knows more about nuclear arsenals and how to track down weapons inventories as anyone on earth," said Walker.

"He's good," replied Jana, "but we have people here who are probably more current."

"The string we need to pull isn't current. Hell, it's thirty years old by now. Phillips was the guy when the Soviet Union collapsed. He's the one who might still know someone who knows something. Put that Callaway guy on his team. He is a Middle East weapons expert."

"The boss made this Team Walker II," replied Jana.

"No territorial battles here," said Walker. "Let Phillips know about everyone who can help. Now, and this pains me to say, but I need a couple of the best data mining experts you can find. We're looking for a needle in a haystack; more likely a dozen haystacks. They will need unlimited access to the agency's super computers."

"I can have five or six people that fit that description here in an hour. Pick the ones you need," replied Jana. "We both believe human intelligence yields better and faster results, so we should meet daily to share what we learn."

"I'd also like to have Marjorie Smith on the team. She has spent years studying Iran. We will want to keep Gritt, and we need a couple of good old-fashioned detectives; you know the kind that don't let obvious facts get in the way of their intuition."

Thad, that's out of my wheelhouse," replied Jana.

"We'll get the director to call his counterpart at the FBI. I'm looking for one loud and boisterous one with a lot of recognition. You know the type; they have to win. The second, should be the opposite, someone who doesn't need to be number one, but hates to lose."

"What else?" asked Jana.

"We will probably need you or someone at the top of the agency food chain to interface with counterparts in foreign governments. This is not a homegrown plot, so we will need research help and maybe permission to kick some butt in someone else's sandbox. Oh, and we need at least one or two planes with crews. Once we begin moving, we can't wait for airlines."

"That's only nine people," observed Jana, "not very many people to cover so much ground quickly."

"Small, tight, it's enough," said Walker. "The rest of what we need is in this building."

Chapter 33

THE WILTON BOEING had been on the tarmac at the New Jersey Air Force Base for hours as military, customs and homeland agents slowly unloaded the plane.

"Is this normal?" asked Farid as he and the two pilots sat in a military hanger drinking coffee and watching.

"Not even close," replied one of the pilots. "I've never seen this kind of scrutiny before, and our flight originated on an American/British air base in England."

"God, can you imagine what flights from commercial locations are going through?" added the copilot. "The country's industry is based on 'just in time' delivery."

"Not right now," replied the pilot. "More like just when the government releases it."

Every container was scanned for radiation. The pilot's American credentials were double checked against an updated database. Farid's French passport had been confiscated by a security officer for two hours before being returned. "You seem okay," was delivered at the same time the passport was handed back. "Iranian heritage, French citizen, living in London, arriving on a freighter on the way to New York; you've got all the makings of one of those characters in a Humphrey Bogart movie," offered the Air Force lieutenant. "But immigration in DC says to let you in."

The man left and then returned only ten minutes later. "All of the stuff on the plane is cleared," he said. "We're under orders to do a thorough search of the plane itself. One of the guys detected a little radiation so I'd like one of you to accompany him. He needs to pull off an inspection cover."

The pilot tossed the coffee cup in the garbage as he followed the lieutenant. He was back in fifteen minutes. "You'd think the people on an Air Force base would know about the radiation from radios and electronics," he said. "I had to show him the plane's operating manual to explain why the modifications to the radio bay included extra shielding. He'd never seen a freighter with passenger accommodations for contract work before. The guy was all rattled until he called his own radio shop. Anyway, we're cleared to get the hell out of here."

"You guys head for home," said Farid as the three stood on the tarmac. "I'll call late tomorrow from New York to give you an updated schedule. Unless things have changed, a client will have a load for you in Pennsylvania in three days. Then its Phoenix and Seattle, and Biloxi. We're working out of the FBO in Hanover until we can go back to the base in the Bahamas."

"The pilot looked over his shoulder at the huge hanger. "Will the Fixed Base Operator be supplying people for loading and unloading, or do we need to contract for it?"

"The guy who owns this place says they will do it all. Get out of here," finished Farid.

An hour later, Farid was on a commuter flight to JFK in New York. After checking into a hotel only a block away from WILTON's offices he called the number that Karim had given him. "Bob, I've got a package from my uncle," he said after TWO finally picked up the phone. "I'm tied up most of the day, but we can meet tomorrow evening."

"Come by my place. We can talk first and then go grab some dinner," replied Bob.

Farid arrived at the expensive apartment building a little after seven. The security desk announced his arrival and then sent him to the sixteenth floor.

Like his uncle and Salam, Bob was at ease, almost jovial as he greeted Farid. "How was the trip? I hear that our decision to move the remaining two bombs before the first one went off was a good call."

Farid briefed Bob on what they had gone through to get into the country. "You couldn't have gotten those devices past security today, so yeah, it was a good call." Farid stripped six cards from his wallet. "Karim sent you replacements for the documents you lost. Here's a driver's license, a couple of credit cards, and a couple of additional cards that you obviously need." He fished an iPhone from his pocket. "Here, it's already programmed."

Farid stood near the windows overlooking the Statue of Liberty. "Can I get one of whatever you are drinking?" he asked pointing at a glass of tawny liquid.

"Fuck, man. I didn't think any of you Moslems drank. My bad." Bob pulled a bottle of Knob Creek Rye whiskey from the cupboard. "Ice?" he asked.

The two men settled into two chairs. “What about a new computer?” asked Bob.

“I was with Karim and Salman just a day ago,” started Farid. “They said to buy what you need and then contact FIVE for a download of new software. We will use my computer to get into the secure network.” Farid sat staring out the windows for a full minute. “I have to ask, what was it like to set off that bomb?”

“It was a rush,” said Bob. “When this is all done, I’m moving to Europe, and I hope I never see the U.S. again.”

“That wasn’t your plan the last time we talked,” said Farid.

“This place is turning into a shithole. When those two punks roughed me up and robbed me a block from Grand Central Station, it scared the hell out of me.” Bob walked over to a small table and pulled out a drawer. “I bought this from a friend of a friend.” He handed Farid a small Glock semi-automatic pistol. “It came with a belt holster, some ammunition and a travel case.”

“You can’t get on an airplane with that can you?” asked Farid.

“All you have to do is leave it unloaded and put it in a locking case in your luggage. When you check in you need to declare it. One of the cards you gave me is a forged permit to carry it in New York. Your uncle agreed it was a good idea for me to be able to protect myself.”

Farid thought about that statement for a long while. “I have to tell you,” said Farid, “I for one hope that we are all done blowing up cities. I hope that you never need to set off another one of those bombs.”

“I don’t know,” said Bob, “I still owe the U.S. a bit more for doing nothing about my parents. When Salam tracked me down and hired me to do my part in all of this, I told him that I carried a hell of a grudge. It's probably a lot like you feel for what they did to your father."

Farid picked up his drink and emptied it. TWO was hired. "How about one more before we get dinner?"

"I understand your family's need to change what is going on in Iran," said Bob as he handed Farid a second drink. "Your mom and uncles blame both countries for what they did, just like I do for my parents disappearing. They have a political agenda. Mine is just to right a wrong and your uncle made that even more attractive by making me a wealthy man. After the war starts, he doubles what he already paid me. Without me, this would be impossible."

"I helped get you to Reno," said Farid more than a little angry. "Is that a similar target to Greensboro? I mean big boom with limited casualties."

"Maybe even fewer casualties, but Salman and I agree that if one bomb doesn't work, we need to hurt the American military with the second. And if that still doesn't get a good old war started, the third will have to scare the hell out of them."

"Have you picked the target yet?"

"The third bomb is in a parked truck. I've looked at three possible targets, all within a day's drive. They are all in the Midwest; all include military facilities as Salam ordered."

Farid felt a bit of a shiver run through his body. "When you pick the third target, will you let me know?"

"You got it my friend," said Bob. "Let's get some dinner, I'm starving."

৵

Team Walker was up and running the next day. The Air Force flew Bob Phillips in from a vacation in Costa Rica. Ray Callaway, who'd been engaged with the problem since Walker and Gritt returned from Turkey, was briefing Bob.

A retired New York detective, and one of the most decorated policemen in the country, Callaway chose to drive himself from Long Island. His counterpart, New Orleans detective Nancy Omfir had always hated flying, but the president of the United States sending a private jet made it impossible to refuse. Both were huddled in the corner with Marjorie Smith and Gritt who outlined his theory that the attack was grounded in Iranian politics, including the actions of the Territorial Guard, but perhaps not directly tied to them.

Walker had spent enough time with new Montanans to accept, without question, Jill Pinky Swanson as the lead data tech, even as Jana coached him to use a nickname consistent with the color of her hair which changed depending on her stress levels. Her associate, Winston Wang was the exact opposite; a Chinese American so buttoned down you could see your reflection in the polish of his shoes.

"We're not involved in border security," started Walker. "Our job is to look at every possible way that the bad guys could have smuggled a bomb into the country and find that one weakness. From there, we need to identify the specific means, day, and source. We also need to begin searching for someone or some group, probably from outside the country, who's schedule, and travel make them probable suspects to set this all up."

"You know boss," replied Pinky, "there is no pattern in one of a kind."

"We've discussed that for days. So, we begin searching possible routes and means. The only hard lead we have is an informer's report that the nuclear material was stolen in Iran and replaced with material from some other source."

"Identifying where that replacement material came from might give us a lead on where this all started," said Wang.

Walker just smiled. He'd never considered that while he was meeting with Nader. But he had briefed Nader on a means to send and receive messages. Walker's first personal challenge was to see if it worked. If Nader wasn't really trying to help, if he was on the other side, Thad's only other personal contact in Iran would be dead in days.

"I'll start with tracking every port on the East Coast and specific shipments from those ports to the Greensboro area," said Pinky. She turned to Winston, "you start on air transport from outside the U.S. into North Carolina and the adjoining states. We will look at the last thirty days and expand from there if nothing pops up."

Later that day, Ray Phillips and Ray Callaway huddled around Walker's desk in the corner of the conference room. "My counterpart in the Russian army firmly believed in the existence of RA-115 portable nuclear devices and also what he called RA-115-01s devices designed to be submersible. Both were not controlled by the Russian military, but by Russian civilian intelligence, probably the KGB. The suitcase device was created to be moved to where it could threaten the western alliance, it was a blackmail weapon, not really designed to make much difference in a war. The submersible version, on the other hand was built to be a first strike type weapon. By planting a couple dozen of these weapons in western naval ports, before the shooting started, the Russians could level the maritime playing field."

"Did you actually track any such devices?" asked Callaway.

"None," answered Phillips. "But we weren't tasked with that as the Soviet Union crumbled. We were trying to account for the strategic weapons in all of the newly independent nations. The portable weapons were under the control of Soviet Intelligence and the majority of those guys were so enraged by the nation's demise that they refused to even talk to us."

"One of those pissed off spooks now runs the country," said Callaway.

"So that was it, there was no real effort to determine if the weapons actually existed, let alone where they went?" asked Walker.

"The army was about the only institution still intact when the Soviet Union was dissolved. Remember some of them sided with the intelligence people and actually tried to overthrow the government. But the majority of them saw their duty to preserve the integrity of Russia and they realized just how vulnerable the nation was at that moment. They didn't want to provoke anyone, especially the U.S. who was pouring millions in aid into the nation to stabilize it. My contacts thought the army probably forced the surrender of the 115 designated weapons and disposed of them."

Callaway opened a screen on his computer. "There were reports of 84 of these weapons disappearing were as late as 1997."

Phillips nodded. "Two of my Russian counterparts believed that there might have been a handful of RA-115's that disappeared. Both believe that the strategic targets they were originally designed for were no longer a threat, so the weapons were destroyed. Hell, it's been a more than a quarter century without a single credible sighting."

"The analysis of the materials in the Greensboro bomb appears to be a mix of Iranian and some other material. Based on what our source told us, probably from Pakistan," offered Thad. "But the device itself was used for almost the exact same purpose as the Russian suitcase bombs."

"So," said Phillips, looking up at Thad, "I read your briefing from the trip to Turkey. Your source says the stolen Iranian material was replaced. We need to know the origins of that replacement material."

Thad used his cane to help slide his chair back and stood. "That's the second time that has come up today. That Wang kid who is working data suggested the same thing. I'll be working on that starting tonight, but I don't expect immediate results if any. My contact is under close scrutiny and getting a message to him, let alone from him may be impossible."

"So, while you work that possibility," said Phillips, "we will try to track down any of my old Russian counterparts and see if they can help."

Callaway closed his laptop. He paused before adding, "would it build a fire under those old comrades if we let it slip that whoever blew up Greensboro may have used Russian bombs, tying the explosion to Russia?"

"I can see why you work for the agency," said Walker. "Let me clear it with the director, who might have to take the idea to the president, but that certainly would make helping us more palatable."

The agency arranged catering and sleeping quarters for Team Walker. Gritt finished his meal and headed back to the command center. Half of the team was still at their desks including Marjorie who stopped him as he walked by.

"It's only been a day, but the two cops and I keep coming back to the same incidents. Whatever triggered this effort, if not the Guard themselves, must be something that hurt someone or some group who are looking for payback. Over the last thirty years a lot of people have been imprisoned or simply disappeared at the hands of the Guard. But the real crisis periods, the kinds of events that might galvanize a multi-year effort like this came with the original revolution, the end of the embassy hostage crisis, the Iran-Iraq war, and when the repercussions when the U.S. took out Salamonie."

"Marjorie, I'm just an engineer and analyst who until a couple of weeks ago was tasked with figuring out how someone could attack this country even though a major air attack seemed out of the question. Someone figured out how to do just that before the entire American defense establishment could stop it. But something you and Jana said sticks in my mind. The agency has picked up on absolutely no chatter about such an attack and the Iranian revolution was almost a half-century ago. Me thinks, thou shalt start with the most recent incident and then backtrack. Most of those who were really hurt in the first few years after the Ayatollah came to power, are dead now."

ꟹ

Karim and Ahmed sat quietly on a bench near the fountains. "Do you worry about our nephew?" asked Ahmed. "I know most of what we are doing was my idea, but since the plan has been moving forward, I have tried to stay out of the way. I haven't talked to Farid in months."

"He is of a different generation, brother. He was raised as a modern European Moslem. He had no idea of our plan until the day he graduated from college. His mother did not know what the plan was, only that the loss of her husband would be avenged. Farid was not prepared for jihad or even a tough fight, but he has done his part already."

Ahmed smiled. "He is the son you never had."

"And probably much like the son you lost when your boy and wife disappeared," answered Karim.

"Then you do not worry about Farid betraying the effort?" said Ahmed.

"When I saw him in London, he assured me that he understood and willingly would fulfill his duty."

"You know brother, I would abandon the plan if completing it would hurt Farid," said Ahmed.

"There is no need of that, brother. But it is time to give Salman approval for the next step. Since the Americans have only ratcheted up their dialog and moved forces into the region, it is time to ratchet up the pressure on the other side."

"I will tell Salman and Mohamed that it is time for the next strike on the Guard." Ahmed began typing on his laptop. "For an old man who only learned to type a few years ago, the phone would be faster. But I understand the risks. FIVE has pounded security into me from the day he joined us."

Eleven men dressed in Guard uniforms arrived at the Fateh missile battery along the Iran Iraq border just before midnight. In seconds, the six guards protecting the site were dead, all killed instantly by snipers shooting silenced weapons with night scopes. Minutes later, four of the men surrounded the small sleeping quarters of the Revolutionary Guard missile unit. They planted a dozen explosive charges before following four others to the missile command center.

Inside the command center, the snipers killed the duty crew, while four of the attackers took their place at consoles and began typing on the keyboards that controlled four intermediate range missiles. Outside, the grinding noise of launch vehicles started as the missiles were turned away from the targeted American bases in Iraq and Syria toward Tehran. Precise coordinates were entered into each missile's navigation system.

The attackers were at the site less than ten minutes when the missiles were launched one at a time toward a precise target in Iran's capital. Moments later, the explosives planted at the sleeping quarters turned the building into toothpicks.

As six of the attackers drove away, four of those still on the ground planted helmets, scoped rifles, and explosive packs around the area. All of the items were from the American military, abandoned in Afghanistan and purchased from the Taliban. Their commander called a number and spoke only six words into his cell when his call was answered. Their job done, the five army reservists piled into a second vehicle and raced from the site.

The dust from explosions at the former American embassy compound in Tehran hadn't yet settled when the attackers arrived at safe houses. They quickly shed their Guard uniforms and tossed them into preset fires. Dressed in civilian clothing they split up into different cars for a leisurely drive home.

Soon after, a carefully forged document patterned after American Army documents found in Afghanistan, was leaked to the press. The document outlined a plan for U.S. Special Forces to seize an Iranian missile site and use it to destroy the old embassy compound in Tehran.

The justification part of the document, in clear American military English noted that the compound was now the brain center of the Revolutionary Guards Quds Force, the arm of the guard responsible for supporting terrorist and unconventional warfare across the region. The Quds Force had been responsible for direct attacks and coordinating terrorist attacks against American targets in the region for decades.

In Tehran, the four missiles totally destroyed two buildings and killed more than a hundred men, including part of the leadership of the paramilitary unit. All of them had been summoned by email and phone to an emergency meeting only an hour before.

In Tblisi, Mohamed praised the two men who had routed the AI generated calls to the Quds Force leadership through several sites to avoid them being detected. The same men had distributed the forged American document. Next to him, THREE and FOUR beamed. The attack on the Iranian Guard had succeeded and the disinformation campaign was under way. Even if the Revolutionary

Guard did nothing, the world would believe that the next attack in the United States would be launched by them.

Nader hadn't been home for two weeks. The pressing schedule of turning enriched uranium into weapons that could be used against the American Navy had kept him working sixteen hours a day since his return from Turkey. His surprise visit home was courtesy of General Ashraf who recognized that his most knowledgeable scientist was exhausted. It helped that Ashraf personally was in no hurry to finish the job ordered by the Guard.

Nader's wife met him at the door, wrapping her arms around him as she had done for decades. "Will you stay long?" she asked. He wrapped an arm around her as he felt her knees wobble. Her face was flushed and pale.

"Only three days. Please forgive me if I sleep at least half the time. I am exhausted."

"Go into your office then, and I will fix you a cup of tea. I will have dinner ready in an hour." The woman beamed at her husband. "If I had known you were coming, I would have prepared a special dinner."

"I am home with you. That is special enough."

In his office, Nader found a package. It was from the Kmer Resort in Turkey. Inside was an identical cell phone to that he carried. Thad Walker had taken pictures of his phone and then used some kind of device to copy the programming and memory. He knew that when he opened the phone there would be one new name and number. He also knew that when the phone arrived, he was to give that person a call as soon as possible.

Walker advised him to only use that number only

when he was away from the house and any other place that might make monitoring the call easy.

His wife arrived with the tea. "I didn't know that you lost your phone?" she said.

"I didn't, but my old one was acting up in Turkey, so I bought a new one and had the seller transfer the information from my old one. It turns out, the only problem with the old phone was a charger that was acting up. So now I have two."

He'd planned on sleeping all of the next day, but Walker wouldn't have risked sending the phone if it wasn't critical. While at EAGLE, he'd been isolated from any news, but once back in Tehran, the nuclear attack on America was all that anyone talked about. He would need to go out for at least a few minutes. But that would be tomorrow's problem. For now, the only thing that mattered was his wife, dinner, and sleep.

He watched his wife's weak body slide into the bed next to him.

"Are you alright?" he asked.

"It is back again," was all she said.

Chapter 34

TEAM WALKER HAD been pouring through every lead for almost a week before Walker called them into a meeting. "It's time for you all to spend a couple of hours talking together. Let's see if any of the disjointed pieces fit together."

Pinky started. "The largest marine terminals in the country are on the West Coast. Along the Atlantic side there are five major terminals and with the advent of huge freighters, few others could even handle a modern ship. The problem is that there is no direct land link from any of them to the Greensboro area. Any shipment would move from a port to a distribution center and then be broken down for reshipment. Those reshipments would go to a regional distribution center, where they would be broken down again for local delivery. Anyone moving a bomb would have to trust that it could be handled four or five times."

"In New Orleans, my primary job was interrupting drug shipments into the area," said Nancy Omfir. "A shipment of drugs from Mexico might be worth as much as a million dollars. A bomb like the one in Greensboro would be priceless to whomever planned this. I can't imagine a cartel routing a shipment with that many chances for discovery or even to get lost."

"That is my gut feeling on this as well," said Pinky. So, I've shifted my focus to other marine possibilities, maybe a large commercial fishing boat, or a tour ship, even a private yacht. So far, nothing like that within a couple of hundred miles of Greensboro has popped up."

Winston Wang squirmed in his chair as all eyes focused on him. "I'm not good talking to groups," he started.

"Then just talk to me," said Thad. "We'll pretend the others aren't here."

"Okay," said Winston. "First the biggest air freight terminals in the country are," he paused to read from his laptop, "Memphis, Anchorage, Louisville, Miami, and Los Angeles. Anchorage, Miami, and Los Angeles are a long way from the target. None of the top twenty-five are close. Memphis is almost all Federal Express, and they have very tight security protocols. That leaves Louisville. But that is still five hundred miles away. Like in marine ports, freight coming into Louisville is handed off to forwarding companies, who hand it off to local distributors. Pinky and I talked. This looks complicated to us." Winston took a deep breath, proud that he had stayed focused. He looked around the room, nervous and then started to hyperventilate.

"Stay focused on me," said Thad.

"But if our target area is anything within a few hundred miles of Greensboro, there are dozens of airports that cater to small regional airlines and private planes.

I've contacted all of them and most are forwarding their landing logs for the last two months." Winston stopped as a couple of people shifted in the room, drawing his attention from Thad. Sweat broke out on his forehead. "The small private airports do not keep logs, but few of them handle international flights."

"Winston," said Pinky. "Just talk like we do all day long.

It took a full minute before he began to speak. "T... The one that is missing is Greensboro itself. The bomb was close enough to the airport to blow the glass out of the tower. It's still contaminated, and I haven't been able to get any data from there."

Let me get on the phone," said Chad. "I'll track down somebody to help pull that data. I'll be on a helicopter this afternoon."

Walker pointed at Bob Phillips. "I found a couple of my old Russian counterparts. My primary partner is in a retirement home in St. Petersburg. With the current problems, he can't get out of the country. But he suggested that I find a Sergey Kazamov. Somehow this Sergey ended up with enough money to be able to retire on one of the Greek Islands. I think I've tracked him down, but so far haven't been able to make contact. Jana has asked the Greek authorities to confirm where he is living, but as of now they haven't gotten back to us."

"Anything else promising?" asked Thad.

"Not really. The silence around these devices is deafening."

"Bob, if you get confirmation, I want you on a plane to Greece immediately. Work with the director's office to get Air Force transport," said Walker.

"Thad, I'm a little old for that kind of trip," said Phillips. "As it is, I'm breaking for a late morning and late afternoon nap. You're going to have to cut this mid-seventies body a little slack."

"Fine," answered Thad. "Make sure the transport is an executive jet, with a steward and sleeper seats." He turned to Ray Callaway. "Ray, you go with him. I'll have the director send one of his field agents experienced in Greece with both of you."

Finally, Thad turned to Marjorie and the two detectives. "You're on."

"The three of us are focusing on the open warfare between the U.S. and the Iranian militias in Iraq and Syria. All of that was directed by the Guard, specifically the Quds Force. If we are right, and this is being stirred up by some third party, there has to be a reason why someone just took out much of their leadership and blamed us."

"Whoever did it is pretty damned sophisticated," said Tony Gerano. "In the early days of battling New York organized crime, once you found a single string tied to the mob's records, it was relatively easy to unwind the camouflage they used to hide their money trail. Today, they have better communications security and encryption than the cops do. Jana's people tell us that the document that came out implicating the U.S. in the attack in Tehran was a masterful forgery. The routing, in a way to bar tracking, was top notch. Somehow someone got the leadership of Quds to that compound in the middle of the night, or at least breached their security to know they would be there in time to plan the attack on the missile base."

"Thad," continued Marjorie, "I'd love to see us

destroy the Revolutionary Guard once and for all, but we don't think they are behind this; at least not all of them."

"So, we are pouring through the actual conflict reports from the agency, the embassy and the military for that period," said Nancy. "So far, we have identified twenty-two direct clashes between the Iranians and the U.S. The one that stands out is the one on the day we killed Soleimani. There were actually six different attacks that day, and we only have hard data on one. In the rest, we used drones to kill the leadership of several Guard backed Iranian militias."

By the next morning the group of nine was down to six. Gritt was working with a Navy decontamination unit and an investigator from the FAA in Greensboro. Phillips and Callaway had been joined by a twelve-year veteran field agent on the Gulfstream to Karpathos where Greek intelligence was waiting to escort them to the seaside villa of Sergey Kazamov.

❧

After helping Bob program a new computer, Farid found himself buried with work at WILTON. The big carriers had been caught with much of their air fleets overseas. The WILTON jet had five days of work scheduled, with the first load from Hanover already on its way to Phoenix. Existing WILTON marine customers were bombarding him with inquiries, just trying to move components from one location to another to keep production flowing or projects moving.

He'd watched the news broadcasts about the attack in Tehran. He was no longer a critical part of the plan, but knew enough to recognize that the next step, a second attack on the U.S., was only days away. The news was also focused on a screaming match between the U.S. and Iran where each was accusing the other of falsifying reports and planting stories with the media. Cable news was filled with pictures and stories of the movement of American air assets and Naval forces into the Middle East. Talking heads were speculating on why the U.S. had moved the carrier task force normally patrolling the Persian Gulf out of the Straits where it joined two other carrier groups further from Iranian soil.

When he hadn't heard anything from Bob for four days, Farid tried to call him, but got no response. If he was on the way to the Reno area, the second nuclear attack on America was imminent. Farid sent Salman a message but again got no response. His internal tensions going through the roof, he tried Sarah. He left her three messages, with no call back.

Farid checked his watch. It was just after seven in the evening when he called his mother. "Farid, my son, you have not called me in two weeks," she said. "Karim has told me how proud he is of all of your good work."

"Mother," replied Farid, "how much do you know about what uncle Karim and Ahmed are doing?"

"Almost nothing," she said. "I asked not to be involved. I left our family's duty to a son who I knew would never disappoint me. Karim tells me that your total focus is now on your new job and that you are doing well."

So, his uncles were keeping a close eye on him, using their financial stake in WILTON to follow his career. He wasn't sure whether that was good or bad. "Mother, I will be here in the states for at least another month and then

I hope to be back in London. I will be over to see you as soon as I am back."

"I look forward to that my son. We do not talk often enough, but I knew that you would be busy for several months after the last time you were here."

The two cut off the call with their normal messages of love and blessings. Farid felt better, but only for a few minutes. He slipped his phone back into his suit coat and headed to his temporary office. He had just sent a new routing schedule to his pilots when his phone rang.

"Yo, Farid," came Sarah's voice, "what's so pressing that you try to call me three times in three hours? Tomorrow is Friday. You know I'm slammed when I'm traveling, but I'll be home tomorrow. We can talk then."

"Nothing really pressing, I just wanted to tell you that I plan on coming out there tomorrow. I don't have reservations yet, but I need a short break myself."

"Great love. If I'm not back to Minot when you get in, I'll have my new roommate pick you up. You'll really like her. She's smart and beautiful, but a little old for you."

❧

Nader's wife wasn't surprised to see him up early and heading out the door for a walk. In more than thirty years, she'd never seen him sleep more than nine hours. He'd managed ten before he quietly slipped out of the covers, dressed and left, thinking she was still sleeping.

Well away from the house, he scrolled through his new phone until he found a name he didn't recognize. He called it and when there was an answer, he simply said, "I am Nader."

"I will meet you at your favorite park near your house

in twenty minutes said a voice. I will be wearing blue slacks, a blue shirt, and carrying a blue backpack." The phone went dead.

❧

Nader was seated when the man started by, stopping in front of him. "I am Reza, an old friend of your friend Thad," said the man. He extended his hand toward Nader. "May I sit?"

Seated, he leaned back, casually stretching his legs out in front of him. "Our friend needs to talk to you." Reza handed a phone to Nader. It was already ringing.

"I am sure you know by now that your fears were warranted," said Thad Walker. "Someone is working very hard to start a war between your country and mine. They seem very determined to make sure we believe it is the Guard."

"I personally would not miss that group if it came to that," answered Nader.

"That could yet happen," said Walker. "The people I work with think this is all being pumped up just to get us to smash the Guard, but as we discussed in Turkey, there will be thousands more dead if America unleashes our military on a group whose leaders vow to fight to the death. In the attack on Greensboro, the death toll is now almost six hundred. If another bomb goes off, the American public is going to demand action."

"What more can I do to help stop this?" asked Nader.

"The man you just met is an airline pilot. We met years ago in Paris. He is a trusted friend, not a spy or warrior like you or me. We need a tiny sample of the material from the replacement balls we discussed in Turkey. Just a few scrapings, enough to track where it came from. Hopefully, that will help us find those responsible for all of this before it spins out of control."

"I go back to work the day after tomorrow. Once there, it will probably be a couple of more weeks before I get back out again," said Nader.

"My old friend, by then, I fear it will be too late," said Walker.

"Then I will have to come home immediately because I am sick," offered Nader. "All I need to do is skip my diabetes medicine a couple of days and it will not be a lie."

"Get us those shavings. Wrap them in some kind of lead wrap or something where they will not make either you or Reza ill. Reza can take it somewhere we can pick it up on his next flight."

Somehow Nader felt better than he had in weeks as his wife met him at the door. "You know my love that when I am home, you cook morning, noon, and night. But not today. We will start with breakfast out, and then go for a drive. While we are driving, you can tell me where I can take you to dinner tonight.

"Nader, I will pretend to sleep every morning you are home," said his wife. "But if it means going out, I will wake you up so you take a walk. It seems to do well for you." She kissed him as he stepped into the house. "I will need a short rest before dinner."

"I need to shower and dress more appropriately," he said, before adding, "I think it also does well for us. Maybe we can take a morning walk together."

"Nader, that is a nice idea, but probably not. "I am an old woman battling a disease and I wear out easily anymore. My energy is way down."

"What does your doctor say? Maybe you should go see him," replied Nader.

"Maybe, but not while you are here my love. But a drive sounds wonderful."

Chapter 35

IT WOULD HAVE been impossible to miss Sarah waiting at baggage claim. "You smell like a fireplace," he said as she reached up to kiss him."

"I spent the day at a client's new business. The Native Americans smoke their harvested meat to preserve it forever. Instead of just selling the cattle they raise to big processors, they are setting up a commercial processing plant to make and sell smoked meats. It's the kind of project I was trained to support. It means more jobs and profit from what they already do."

"I'm proud of what you are doing," said Farid as they walked toward the parked Bronco.

"How long are you staying?" she asked as they left the airport and turned north.

"If you can get some time off, I'd like to stay four or five days. We only have one plane in the country right now and it is scheduled for the next ten days. Then the pilots will need rest."

That night, as the two of them finished dinner, Sarah's

roommate bounded through the door. "Hi, I'm Olga." She extended her hand. "You must be Farid."

He stood and smiled. "Sarah said you were in the military. She didn't tell me you were an officer."

"I don't fly or anything," she replied. "I just do security work around the base."

She started to walk away, then turned. "I'm just home to change into some fatigues and then I've got to work late. There is a base wide security exercise this evening." She turned back toward Sarah and Farid. "Sarah tells me you were born in Iran and for much of your early life lived in the Middle East. What are your thoughts on what is happening over there?"

Farid paused, several different answers running through his head. "I think that Iran is really struggling. There are different factions in the country who have very different visions of the future."

"But why is Iran prodding the U.S? This country could turn their entire country into a glowing ember in less than a day."

Farid didn't answer.

"Farid isn't some expert on Iran or foreign relations," said Sarah. "He' just a manager for a startup division of a global transportation company."

"I didn't mean to press," said Olga. "It's my job to try to understand threats to this country. Farid is the first person from the region that I've ever met personally, and I was just hoping that he might have more insight than the briefings I've seen."

"My father died in one of the insane Middle East clashes," said Farid. "I just hope that whatever is going on is over soon and that not many more people get hurt."

Sarah helped Farid forget his troubles for the rest of the night. He awoke when Olga came in a little after midnight and again when he heard her leave about seven the next morning. He was sound asleep when Sarah bounced on the bed, juggling two cups of coffee.

"You were different last night," she said.

Farid took the offered cup. "What do you mean, different?"

"I don't know, more gentle. You held me differently."

"I'm just happy to be here. I love you."

"I love you too. I was a little worried before we went to bed," said Sarah. "After you and Olga talked you seemed really tight."

"She got me thinking about the danger in the world today. A lot of stuff looks like it doesn't make sense, but it probably does, at least to some people." He blew on his scalding coffee before taking a sip. "I'm just happy you are safe."

"That's an odd comment, Farid. But I'm happy you're safe too. Now, what do you want to do? I've cancelled my meetings for Monday and Tuesday, but I have to be at a meeting near the Montana border on Wednesday morning."

"I think I'd like to take a drive again. Maybe see some of that country where there are mountains," answered Farid.

"Anything special you'd like to see?"

"No," he answered. "Well, maybe just find a big rock and sit there with you watching a river run by."

"Wow, that's not like you, but it sounds romantic. If we get our butts out of bed and get going, we can spend the day. There's a place over on the Little Missouri River that I like."

Farid bounced out of bed and headed for the shower.

"We're meeting Olga at eight, so we have about ten hours to roam around," called Sarah. "I'll use the other shower so we can get going."

Sarah pulled the Bronco on to Highway 83 headed south. "We're going right through Minot and then south another hour before we turn west."

"You said we were meeting your roommate at eight?" said Farid as he watched the small city of Minot race by.

"She is taking us to dinner in town. When I called her, she said to tell you she was sorry about rushing out last night. She wants to get to know you."

The early morning helicopter ride got Nader back to EAGLE before nine on Monday. He dropped his bag in his apartment, slipped on a white coat, and headed for the laboratory.

"You look a little under the weather," offered his second in command, a lean young man with bifocals resting on a jutting nose.

"You forget that you are just forty-five and I am seventy, Ali. But your observation is correct, I haven't felt well since last night. Anyway, can you organize the team for a short meeting in an hour. In the interim, I need to do a quick check on a couple of things in the vault."

Nader was waiting in the lower conference room when the first people on his team arrived. As he took a seat, a sharp pain from his groin area told him he needed to shift the tiny lead foil packet in his pants to a different pocket. But that would have to wait while the team discussed their progress the previous week and tasks for the next few days. General Ashraf sat next to Nader taking notes as did the Guard's General Hussein.

"The scaling down of the triggers we have designed for the larger weapons is proving more difficult than we thought it would be," said Ali. The missile teams have identified two existing delivery systems and we plan on developing identical warheads to fit on each. For more powerful weapons, we were able to use the designs provided by the Pakistanis. But depending on how we run the numbers, getting the trigger just right is proving to be a challenge."

The group broke up an hour later, leaving Nader, Ashraf and Hussein alone.

"Someone knows how to do this," said Hussein. "That explosion in the United States must have come from a similar type of warhead."

"We'll get it," said Nader. "I measured the uranium cores again this morning. We have a preliminary design that would stimulate the reaction using twelve detonator attachment points. That is proving difficult because of the tiny size of the core. We would like to simplify the design because nano-second delays in any one stimulation could reduce the power of the weapon and multiple differences could lead to a sizzler instead of an explosion. We can simulate what we are looking for, but without an actual test detonation, we run the risk of failure.

Ashraf sat tapping his pencil on the table. "It might delay us a few weeks, but I may have a source that could get us specifications for a similar weapon built years ago by the Soviet Union. We have used that source for many components in the past."

"Reach out and see what you can find," ordered

Hussein. He turned to Nader. "Remember, when we feel we have a solid design, we intend to explode one device in a way to tell the world that we are now a nuclear power. The Americans would be crazy to attack us after they realize the kind of weapons we possess. They have never challenged the Chinese, or North Korea once they had nuclear arms. You can use that for your test."

"That would be helpful," said Nader. "But it must be done in a way that a failure will not be detected. Letting the enemy know we are strong is important, but so is making sure that he doesn't know we are close to perfecting a weapon but have failed."

He stood. Gentleman, I am not feeling very well. If you do not mind, I'm going to take a couple of aspirin and lean back in the chair in my office for a half-hour. I need to shake this off before I tackle the marathon schedule my staff just laid out."

It had been twenty-hours since Nader's last dose of insulin. He knew mild diabetic shock would kick in soon. He just prayed that he would be functional enough to demand being sent home to his own physician rather than to the campus clinic.

Ashraf went to check on him when he hadn't joined him for his scheduled Monday lunch. "How do you feel my old friend? You look terrible."

"It might be the flu, or a relapse from the COVID I had a year ago, "said Nader. "My wife was not feeling well when I left home this morning. Perhaps I should just go home for a few days and get better. I don't want to spread this to my staff."

Ashraf summoned one of the security people and together they headed to the tram. "I'm going to the surface with you," said Ashraf. "I'll get you on a flight home and make sure that you have a ride from the airport once you get back to Tehran."

"Thank you," offered Nader, now shaking with chills, sweat pouring from his face.

"Would it help your team, if we could actually get our hands on one of the Russian designed weapons?" he asked.

Nader's mind wasn't working as it should, but Ashraf's offer was clear enough that he simply nodded his head.

An hour later Nader was airborne. The crew chief riding with him accepted Nader's assurances that there was nothing he could do to help. Nader waited until the man turned to stare out the window before he carefully slipped the cover from the needle of an emergency vial of insulin and rammed it through his pants fabric into his leg. "Could we open a door?" he asked. "I am very hot."

As the crew chief finished securing the door, Nader flipped the used insulin vial out into space. He had calculated the dose so that he would feel better within an hour, but he knew he would need another dose at home to be conscious enough to finish his task by getting the tiny package of uranium filings to Reza, who would be traveling to Turkey the next day. He needed to get the package to Walker. There was something about the morning really troubling him, but his head was doing everything it could just to stay focused on his plan.

&

Dinner that night had gone from a planned semi-formal to a casual dining when an accident on the highway cost Sarah and Farid two hours on their way home. Instead of meeting Olga at the house, she met them at a steakhouse off from Highway 83, north of downtown Minot. "How was your day?" asked Olga. "You two walked into this place just beaming."

"We had a great day," replied Sarah. "The country out west of here is stunning. Farid wanted some place quiet to just talk, and we found the perfect place." She looked over at the man who was smiling. "We aren't ready to make it formal just yet, but we talked a lot about starting a family sometime soon."

"Wow," replied Olga. "Congratulations you two."

Over the next two hours, the three talked as if they had been friends for years. Olga tried to steer the conversation to something Farid said the night before, something that had sparked her curiosity. When asked about the death of his father, Farid pointed out that he was young and didn't really know much more than he had died in a military crash. It didn't make sense to him since his father was a university professor.

Farid was fascinated by Olga's transition from a child in Russia to American Air Force officer.

Olga found Sarah and Farid in the kitchen when she finally rolled out of bed on the one day, she had off that week. "I loved being with you two on such a special night," she said. "My boyfriend, Chad and I had a similar conversation while I was in DC. I mean we are both getting older, and we have both been married to our jobs for years. It's not enough."

"You two are like us," replied Sarah. "You are both really busy and you live a long way apart."

"I've used that excuse for a long time. I've almost been in love a couple of times, but this is the first time that made me put my career second." Olga wandered over to the coffee maker and started it rather than use the little pod machine Sarah used. "I'm used to plain old black military coffee. It fuels everything in the Air Force." She turned back to the others.

"What are you two up to today? I'll be gone for several hours. A couple of the guys I work with are taking me to a shooting range where I can learn how to shoot a shotgun. Chad grew up in Alaska hunting, and I'm trying to coax him to come out here for a few days. If it is connected to some pheasant hunting, I don't think he can turn me down."

"I'm going to introduce Farid to a couple of leaders of one of the tribes I work with. After that, we don't have any plans."

Farid watched the two women talking, thinking that he's never seen Sarah with the kind of friend that she and Olga had become. "I've spent my whole life in big cities," he said. "Sarah is showing me around North Dakota. I like what I do, getting a new air freight company off the ground, but I think I could learn to love it out here."

"How long will you be staying?" asked Olga.

"I plan on leaving Tuesday afternoon," said Farid.

"So, we will have more time to get to know each other," said Olga as she slipped a denim jacket on and picked up a tiny purse. I'll see you later."

She got back a little after five to find Sarah sitting on the porch, staring out at nothing.

"Something wrong?" asked Olga as she took a chair next to her friend.

"Farid got a call from someone. He got all freaked out and then really quiet. He went for a walk."

"It sounds like what might happen if you were an executive at a new company, especially in air freight. I hear they are really slammed right now."

"Maybe," said Sarah. "But he's been off for months. Something is really troubling him. I don't think it's the business. The man I spent two carefree years getting to know in London changed right after he graduated from college. We've never had secrets from one another, but whatever it is, he isn't ready to discuss it."

Sarah stood, staring out at the wide-open spaces interrupted only by the sounds of jets taking off from the nearby Air Force base. "Maybe it's something from his past. He's commented on his father's death several times in the last few months. He never spoke of it before; I learned of it from his mother."

~

It was an hour's drive from the airport to the waterfront villa of Sergey Kazamov. The driver was a special security officer of the Hellenic National Police. He knew nothing of the mission other than he was to take three Americans to a specific house, inform the occupants that they were there with the full authority of the Greek government and be prepared for any disagreement that spun out of control.

The officer moved out of the way after a brief conversation with Kazamov and Bob Phillips stepped forward. "Sergey, I think you were notified by a mutual friend that I was trying to reach you. This is my associate Ray Callaway and another of my colleagues, we'll just refer to him as Carl. May we come in?"

Kazamov motioned for them to follow. He led them to a patio overlooking the ocean. "Tanya," he said to a woman less than half his age, "will you excuse us for a few minutes? I need to speak to these men. I think they want to talk about old times and things that are best discussed in private."

The woman stood, smoothing out her short sundress and wrapped a silk shawl around her shoulders before retreating into the house. "I was told that a friend of a friend was interested in what might have happened to some old Soviet weapons that probably never existed," said Kazamov.

"Sergey," said Phillips, "they existed. The proof is that one was just used to blow up a city in the United States. He turned to Callaway.

"Ray, tell Sergey what was found."

"The residue from the explosion has been positively traced to the Soviet era production in Novouralsk. As you know, some Soviet insiders claim that as many as eighty-five RA-115 suitcase devices disappeared. All were, at one time, in possession of the Soviet Intelligence Services and not the military. One was just used, and we are very interested in tracing any others before someone uses a second and the United States is forced to retaliate."

"And how can I help?" asked Sergey. He motioned for them to sit.

"You, like me, spent several years tracing nuclear weapons that had been distributed to the former states of the Soviet Union," said Phillips. "Some in Russia believe that the disappearance of these weapons was facilitated by the very inspectors who were charged with finding them. They are very unhappy that one of the missing bombs was just used to kill Americans. There is enough stress between our two countries as it is. So, we agreed to share our findings. Anyone who helps us keep this from spinning into a major nuclear confrontation would certainly not be a person who was hiding their criminal involvement in the theft of the weapons in the first place."

Sergey smiled. "I do not believe anything you just said. But I do believe what your friend Ray said and will be happy to help, if I can."

"Tell us what you know about the missing devices," said Phillips.

"When the Soviet Union collapsed there were rumored to be devices like you describe. A handful, and by that, I mean perhaps twenty were in the hands of intelligence operators in states, like Romania, Bulgaria, and Czechoslovakia. Most of those places went through a fairly civil disillusion from Russia. The intelligence operators there packed up their stuff, and I mean all their stuff and moved to Russia. Some other places, like Hungary and Georgia were not so peaceful."

Kazamov leaned across the table. While I was in those two places, I found that most of the Soviet Intelligence operators had simply fled. In each location, local associates were left with what they had abandoned. I heard that some of those local associates were selling everything from encoding machines to actual cabinets of files to whoever would pay for them. If there were such things as the weapons you seek, those would be the places where I would look first."

"How was it that you were allowed to operate there, as a former Soviet official?" asked Callaway.

Kazamov began to laugh. "You must ask your colleague here who had the power when he visited former states of the Soviet Union. Was it the Russian or the one from the West; American or British or French? In my case, my counterpart was British. Unfortunately, he was killed in an accident less than a year after we finished our work."

"Is there anything else that you think we should know?" asked Ray.

"My friends, it has been decades since I was in that business." He paused before adding, "it was rumored that there were groups from the Middle East interested in these types of weapons. Most of them were from Arab groups who hated Israel. They were very vocal about their hatred. I suspect that the Israelis paid handsomely for help finding any such groups and eliminated the threat. But there may have been groups with no interest in Israel so the Israelis would have no interest in them. I would have no idea who they might be."

"So, you really have no idea who might be using such a weapon to stir up trouble between the U.S. and Russia?" said Callaway.

"If I did, I'm sure that people like yourselves would pay handsomely for the information, and as a retired civil servant I could use the money. I would love to have something to sell, but I don't."

"Nice place you have here," Sergey," said Phillips. "Enjoy your retirement."

"Allow me to show you out," said Sergey. He turned to Carl, who hadn't said a word. "For a period in my life I had a Carl who traveled with me. He sometimes got excited and intervened in some of my negotiations. I am pleased that you are not like him."

They were in the car on the way back to the airport when Phillips' phone rang. "We have to make a stop in Paris on the way home," he said after he hung up. "Thad says there was an important package from old friends just delivered there. He says it is about the size of a tiny envelope but needs to be handled carefully."

Chapter 36

TEAM WALKER'S MONDAY morning session was completely different from the one only four days before.

Bob Phillips opened his computer. "The tiny specs of material that your friend Nader sent, are of Russian origin. Whoever switched out the cores for Iranian uranium, had access to Russian materials enriched in the 1970s. It's pretty crude stuff, but similar to that we were developing in the 1960s." He looked over at Callaway.

"Which means it might well have come from one of the weapons that Kazamov alluded to. He suggested we focus on Hungary and Georgia. In both cases he suggested that Soviet intelligence operators might have abandoned KA-115's. Hungarian or Georgian in state associates could have become very wealthy selling them to Middle Eastern terrorists."

"Do you think he was directly involved in the sale of atomic materials?" asked Gritt.

"Possible, he is living a very nice lifestyle, but he

alluded to making a lot of money steering the Israeli government to possible nuclear threats coming from that period. The Mossad was very active about then, with rumored surgical strikes in several Arab countries."

"About the same time, the Israeli's were reportedly working with the South African government on weapons development. Our satellites detected more than one suspected nuclear detonation on a remote island off from the coast of South Africa. It has always been assumed that they were new weapons tests, but at least one could have been used as cover to destroy any weapons they seized in raids," said Phillips.

"Or they may have stripped the enhanced uranium from captured weapons and used it as part of their own nuclear development," observed Gritt. "Either way, Israel may have done away with at least some of the missing Russian nukes."

"Great work," observed Walker. "We need two things. First, we will need to see if we can retrace any missing weapons from Georgia. And second, we need to approach the Israeli's and see if they did in fact hunt down some missing Russian bombs."

"Why just Georgia?" asked Callaway.

"The conflict with the Russians leaving Hungary was all fueled by the fury over what Russia did during the Hungarian uprising. The new Hungarian government wasn't sure that The Soviet Union was gone for good, so they involved western intelligence services from the first days of independence to root out any Russian sleeper activity. Virtually all of the Hungarian members of the KGB either fled to Russia or were actually picked up and held, some for years. If there was any inkling of missing weapons in Hungary, someone would have picked up on it."

"How in the hell could you know that?" asked Chad.

"I've had a very interesting career," answered Walker. "I'll take a few minutes to go visit the director after we break up and ask him to call his counterpart in Israel. The Israelis have never openly discussed any involvement with nuclear materials, but the world knows they have an arsenal. With what happened in Greensboro, I think our closest ally in the Middle East will cooperate in our search."

He turned to Marjorie. "Can you spare either of your detectives to go kick over some rocks in Georgia?"

"Whatever needs to be done," replied Marjorie. "Nancy would probably be better for that task. It would also tie into some research we are already discussing."

She tapped a couple of keys on her computer. "The day the United States took out Quasem Soleimani, the head of Quds Force in Iraq, they also hit four other Iranian militia leaders. They were all part of Iran's Popular Mobilization Units, a collective of Iranian militias who were constantly attacking American targets in the region. What drew our attention was that the American military originally reported five more drone strikes. All were carried out while the militia leaders were traveling to a planned meeting with Soleimani. We used Predator drones armed with missiles to destroy their cars. But after-action documents only reported four militia leaders dead. We either missed with one missile or killed someone other than our target."

"How does that tie in with a trip to Georgia?" asked Walker.

"About the same time, the head of the Political Science

department at a university in Lebanon disappeared. There was a report that he was active in trying to calm the Suni-Shite divisions in the Middle East, which in Iraq and Syria had erupted into actual warfare between militia groups. It is believed that he was in the area on the day of the drone strikes."

"I still don't see the Georgia connection," said Walker.

"The same report indicated that he always traveled with a brother, who was also his bodyguard. That man was last reported to be living in Georgia, although our research indicates he has another brother who lives in Paris."

"Again, great work," offered Walker. He turned to Nancy Omfir. "While I am with the director, get with Jana and have her assign you a couple of people with ties to whatever assets she has in Georgia."

"Do I get any frequent flyer miles?" quipped Nancy. Laughter rippled through the room.

"We needed that," offered Walker.

He turned to Chad. "I got your message that we were able to download all of the records from the airport in Greensboro."

"We were back in one long day. I gave Pinky and Winston all the data files. They have been scrubbing them."

"You guys are not going to believe what they told us," said Pinky, staring at her laptop. "It didn't seem important until this morning's briefing. In the last two months, six cargo planes from overseas used call out customs support to clear entry through the Greensboro Airport. One of those originated in Georgia."

The silence in the room was replaced by everyone talking at once.

"Do we have the records of the pilots or anyone else on that plane?" asked Gritt.

"I have requested the actual records from Immigration and Customs," offered Winston. "In some cases, even remote clearances include facial recognition as part of clearing people into the country. Maybe we will get lucky. If we have an actual photograph of a suspect, we can probably track them down. At least we will have names."

"Even if we can't," offered Tony Gerano, "as sensitized as the country is right now, if we flood the media with a picture, someone will have seen them. The media and Congress are whipping the nation into a frenzy." He nodded at Marjorie. "I'd like to help young Winston here work that angle."

"I realize that there is no pattern here, said Gritt. "But my guts tell me that somehow that weapons came in by air. Every other means seem way too complicated."

"Agreed," said Walker.

"After we got back from Greensboro, I talked to the FAA administrator. I asked if there was a centralized point where landing logs from the nation's airports were kept. The answer is no, but he's working on trying to centralize a database of landing logs," said Gritt. "He's not sure how fast he can do it, and asked who was going to pay for it, but if they can pull it off, it would simplify Winston's work."

"You think there are more bombs?" asked Pinky.

Gritt looked around the room. "I think we all do."

ꟹ

CE flight 34 from Boise to Reno began to slow as the pilot dropped the flaps for landing. "Thank you all for flying

Casino Express tonight. It's just past midnight here but rest assured that the casinos will still be open when you get downtown. We will be on the ground soon." Three minutes later the crew lined up for a routine landing on the lighted runway.

A flash like a dozen suns surrounded the plane. In the cockpit, both pilots were instantly blinded which really made no difference. The electro-magnetic pulse shut down almost every electronic system and device in the plane. A shock wave slammed the fuselage before the plane rolled onto its back and dove toward the ground.

While the area around the airport was mostly empty at that time of night, the terminal was still open for one more late flight. Windows exploded, and entire walls were crushed as several Air Force helicopters were thrown across the runways and into the building. Waiting shuttle busses and taxis were tossed like toys as the blast wave swept across the field. The explosion shook houses and broke windows as far as three miles away. Within seconds, buildings ripped from their foundations, and torn gas lines provided fuel as fires ignited in every direction, pushed by a twenty mile an hour wind from the southwest.

TWO tucked his sunglasses into a shirt pocket and pulled his rented vintage Mustang back onto Highway 80, headed west. He liked to drive and was happy that he'd scheduled his trip through San Francisco instead of Sacramento. The extra hours in the car would give him plenty of time to cherish what had to be the total destruction of the Air Guard Base in Reno. He was careful not to use a cell phone or to try to make contact with his computer. He wanted to leave no digital footprints in the area. For the same reason, he'd driven a circuitous route to Reno, spending the night before in a small-town motel that was happy to take cash. He'd paid for fuel with cash. When he checked his rental in, the odometer would show more than twice as many miles as the trip from San Francisco to Reno, and the vintage car had no GPS tracking.

Within an hour, the FAA grounded all flights in the region, including SFO. TWO considered rescheduling his flight to Minneapolis and checking into a hotel, but with the turmoil resulting from shutting down air travel in a quarter of the country, a little nap made more sense. The monitor at the gate showed only 'delayed.' The airport television had only one story running: the destruction of the Reno airport and surrounding area and the fear of people in Sparks, Nevada when it became clear that the cause had been another nuclear blast, and that the prevailing winds were carrying dust, debris, and radiation over their city.

⁂

Farid had finally managed to drop off to sleep. He and Sarah were awakened by "OH MY GOD," ringing through the house, followed by the noise of Olga rushing around.

"What's going on?" called Sarah.

"Another blast," replied Olga. "This time in Reno. I'm sure it's on TV. I've got to go; the base is going into lockdown."

The door slammed and the sound of Olga's spinning tires slowly faded.

"Did you hear her?" asked Sarah.

"I did," answered Farid.

"I'm going to turn the television on," said Sarah.

"Go ahead. I'm staying here."

From the living room, Sarah called, "you need to see this. A landing plane crashed with at least two-hundred people on board. There are no estimates of people dead on the ground."

Farid didn't respond. He was trying hard not to throw up.

"Did you hear me?" called Sarah.

"Yes," was all he said.

An hour later she was still watching CNN News as Farid somehow managed to stumble from the bedroom. He was carrying his laptop in trembling hands. "I need to see if I can get a flight back to New York."

"My God, Farid, I'm scared to death, and you want to leave."

"Sarah, I don't want to go anywhere, but the FAA is screwing with every plane in the country. My one plane is stuck in Denver, and I don't know how long it will be there. I need to get back to where I can try to clean up what is going to be a huge mess."

His arms hung at his sides, one hand barely gripping the computer. His eyes were sunken, and he was struggling to control his shaking.

"You're in no shape to go anywhere, Farid."

"I have no choice," he said. "I need to be in a conference tomorrow, and I can't do it here."

"Farid, you have been rattled since you got that phone call. What's going on?" she asked.

He forced a smile. "I love you, Sarah. "I just told you. I hate what just happened. I pray that this is all over."

She sat staring at him for several minutes, before

walking over to her computer. She spent several minutes typing, "You can get a flight at ten this morning. You will have to connect in Minnesota, but it will get you to New York by five this evening."

"Make the reservation," he said. "And then come back to bed for a couple of hours before I have to go."

❧

The only member missing when Team Walker assembled at four in the morning was Nancy, who was already on a jet to Europe.

"I'm sure you all heard about the attack in Reno," said Gritt. "Thad's on the phone with the director who is on his way to the White House. I don't have much of an update. But here is what I do have. At about five minutes after midnight local time, a nuclear explosion on or directly adjacent to the airport in Reno, Nevada shredded the area, including an Air National Guard facility there. One plane on short final crashed, killing everyone on board. There are no hard numbers of other casualties, but the time of the attack likely limited those killed outright to a few hundred. The areas north of the blast, around Sparks, Nevada are all shut down with orders for everyone to shelter in place due to radiation contamination carried by strong winds."

He waited for everyone to take in what he was telling them. "It's been almost three weeks since the blast in Greensboro. We have intelligence that there are three bombs in play. We need to figure this out right now, before another city goes boom."

"Is the U.S. going to strike Iran?" asked Pinky.

"Not if the director can convince the president that this is a terrorist attack and not state sponsored."

"With Iran's history of state sponsored terrorism all over the world," said Marjorie, desperately trying to get a contact lens into a tired eye, "that is a pretty tall order."

"I suspect we have no more than a couple of days to either prove they did it or find solid evidence that they didn't," said Gritt. "Either way, we need to find that third bomb. Grab a nap when you can. From now on, were a 24/7 operation."

Chapter 37

FARID HEADED TOWARD his connecting flight on concourse G.

"Fancy meeting you here," said a voice from behind him.

Farid turned to see Bob, rushing to catch up. "You on the American flight to New York?"

"I am," replied Farid. "You too?"

"No, I've got a couple of days of work here, and then I'll be home."

Farid took the smaller man's arm and steered him to a quiet corner. "Have you seen the casualty counts for what happened in Reno?"

"No, but I did talk to Salam before I left San Francisco. He says that the European and Middle Eastern media are reporting nothing else. The Americans have to act."

"It's been almost a full day, and they haven't," said Farid.

"Give it some time," replied Bob. "I'm living proof

that when it comes to Iran, the Americans move very slowly. But if this doesn't do the trick, the next one will."

"I pray that will not be necessary."

"Both sides have it coming. I'm taking a couple of days to look at other targets, and to fix a problem that created trouble for me in Nevada," said Bob.

"What kind of problem?"

"When I armed the bomb in Reno, the battery pack was dead. I bought one of those portable jump starters and connected it before I left town. I'm going to do a little preventative maintenance on number three just in case."

"Where is number three?" asked Farid.

"Only I know," said Bob. "That was always FIVE's security plan. It's in a location where I can leave it close to where it is or move it to another location in less than a day."

"What we have already done has to work," said Farid. "The Americans have over a thousand dead."

"You only lost one parent to this conflict," said Bob, "I lost two, and my Iranian grandparents. Nothing is too brutal for what they have done."

Farid took a step back. "Are you part of the conference tomorrow night?" Bob's hate was different from the need to make things right for his family. He wondered if Karim or Ahmed understood that.

"No, I am not included. I'll call you as soon as I get back," said Bob. "We can go grab a bite and a drink." The man was humming an old Creedence Clearwater song as he walked away. Farid wouldn't have known that except CCR was one of Sarah's favorite bands.

Ahmed's housekeeper showed Nancy and her two traveling companions into the ornate sitting room of a small mansion near the embassies in Tbilisi.

The woman spoke only Georgian and Farsi, which was being interpreted by Jana's one American agent who specialized in Georgia. "Ahmed says he will be right down. May I bring you some tea?"

"How may I help you?" came from the doorway as the housekeeper left the room.

"I'm a American reporter," said Nancy. She handed Ahmed a card from *THE NEW YORK TIMES*. "Paula here is my interpreter, and this is Gregor who is helping me with research. I'm working on an historical piece of how Iran and the United States got themselves into a situation where war could break out at any time."

Ahmed took a minute to study Nancy and her companions. "It does seem almost inevitable, does it not?" he replied.

"I have a source that tells me you and your family have been caught up in conflicts in the region for decades. I was hoping you could offer some background."

"My family left Iran during the revolution. I chose to live here where the culture is similar to the old country. My brother lives in France where he has taken on the responsibility of managing what wealth we brought with us for the benefit of the entire family. I have almost nothing to do with Iran anymore."

"That same source told me that you lost another brother in Iraq."

"That is true. He and I were in a car accident. I survived, but he did not."

"What would take two men with successful lives back

to a part of the world where conflict and death are all too normal?"

Nancy waited in silence, not sure if Ahmed was going to answer.

"My brother and I were doing something similar to your mission, as you describe it. We were trying to understand why people fight and kill one another. My brother dedicated his life to bringing peace. And he might have been successful had I not been such a terrible driver."

"Have you or others in your family followed in his footsteps?"

"No, we pray that someday the entire region can find peace, but as I said, we have almost nothing to do with Iran. Like so many in the region, we wonder about America's interest in the region. It was once oil, but that is not so important anymore. I read that many in your own country have similar questions."

Nancy felt she was prepared for the interview, but it wasn't going as planned. Maybe a more direct approach would work.

"I'm sure you have heard of the attacks on America?"

"I have and hate to believe that any such attack would seem necessary to anyone."

"As an expat, who do you think could do such a thing?'

'Your guess is as good as mine," said Ahmed. "If they did originate in Iran, then only the Revolutionary Guard would have the power and intelligence to succeed against a powerful intelligence organization such as exists in America. Even a small country like Israel has shielded itself from this kind of attack."

"If you were us, where would you start your search for what started all of this?"

Ahmed's face twisted as he fought to control a smile. "You represent one of the most powerful newspapers in the world," He paused to look at the card in his hand, "Ms. Omfir, your archives must be immense. Many in Iran resented your close relationship with the Shah. America was right to be outraged by the attack on your embassy. In thirty years of conflict in the region, forces supported by Iran have clashed with Americans. You could pick any one of those as your starting point." Ahmed walked to the windows, turning his back on his guests.

"And how will this all end? Again, I don't know. Perhaps when every culture respects every other; or when groups whose purpose is only to fuel hate no longer exist. I should be so lucky to live that long." Ahmed turned and then smiled. "I am not much help am I. Perhaps when you have moved forward with your research and have more specific questions I can offer more."

"Well, what do you think?" asked Nancy as the three drove away.

That man either truly knows nothing," said Paula, "or he figured out who we are and did a good job of deflecting us. He offered a perfect mix of 'I'm concerned, with I hope you figure it out." Paula leaned over from the from the front seat and stared at Nancy. "I got the message that he isn't going to put any energy into figuring this out, or if he does, we will never know."

"What we got for sure was that his brother died in Iraq in a car," said Nancy. She took out her encrypted phone from her purse and called Walker.

"Thad, we have confirmed that Ahmed's brother died in a car in Iraq but got nothing more we can work with. Can you track down whoever was flying the Predator drones that day in Iraq and confirm that they actually hit a fifth target?"

"I'm on it, Nancy. Where are you off to next?"

"Honestly, we need a few hours of sleep, and then we'll work with our local people to try to confirm that Soviet Georgia once actually had RA-115 weapons and see if we can pull a string or two to see where they went. At the time when the Soviet Union collapsed, the kind of money that it would take to buy a nuclear weapon should have stood out like a sore thumb."

"Good," answered |Thad. "And get the local agency people to set up a phone and data intercept for this Ahmed guy and arrange to have him shadowed. We might get lucky with an intercept, or he might lead us somewhere interesting. You can sleep later."

"Anything else, boss?" laughed Nancy.

"Yeah, and I hope this helps when you start interviewing locals. The Israeli's confirm that they did in fact track down several portable Russian built portable nuclear devices. They gave us nothing more than a simple 'yes' when asked. The weapons existed."

For TWO, his first stop after picking up a rental car was at a small motel along highway 94, only an hour northwest of the Minneapolis airport. He slept for six hours before continuing his drive toward North Dakota. He finally pulled up to the storage yard gate where he'd left the truck a little after three that afternoon. He entered the secured area and parked his rented Toyota next to the truck. He took a few minutes standing and stretching and then jogging in place, the kinds of exercises someone who had just driven a long distance might use to loosen up. He needed the exercise, but his primary reason for the pause was to confirm that none of the security cameras around the yard pointed toward where he'd parked.

Thankful that he'd placed the bomb in the largest of the truck's locked boxes, he carefully opened the case. Using a battery powered drill, he pulled the screws covering the battery compartment and examined the battery. The LED lamps installed by ONE feathered a stoplight array, and while the red-light indicating battery failure was not illuminated, the yellow indicating low battery was on.

He carefully drilled a small hole through the cover and then another through the aluminum lid of the bomb case. He ripped open the cardboard box of the five-amp solar charger he'd purchased in Bismarck earlier and laid the charger on top of the truck next to the tiny charger he'd already installed for the cell phone. Threading the power cable through the hole he drilled, he stripped off an inch of insulation before securing the wires to the positive and negative battery connectors.

He checked to make sure that the two plastic tabs that kept the detonation circuit from being accidently activated were in place. He would need one more trip here to arm the bomb. With the battery box re-secured, he closed the aluminum lid. Replacing the Master lock, he was back in the Toyota and on his way back to Bismarck by four.

After a steak dinner, he checked into a motel and slept. The next morning, he laid his cell phone on top of a map of the Midwest and then asked Siri about the drive to Malmstrom Air Force Base in Montana and then to Ellsworth Air Force Base in South Dakota. 'No fucking way,' he said to himself after Siri told him that he'd need to spend three more days in the area to survey the two alternate targets he'd identified. Minot Air Force base would be the target, if one was necessary. It was perhaps America's most important base, with both interceptor aircraft and most of the country's nuclear capable bomber fleet. TWO smiled. He'd always planned on three bombs.

The encrypted teleconference began a little after seven. Farid wasn't sure that his exhaustion was from a horrendous day at work trying to reschedule one airplane on the runway in Denver, or dread at the coming call.

"Farid," started Karim, "the family thanks you for helping ten years of planning become reality."

"That's all this call is about?"

"No, nephew. When I called you there was no movement from the most powerful antagonist. Since then, the news is full of stories. As a businessman, you need to anticipate that air transportation will be interrupted for some time."

Farid knew that his uncle was reluctant to say something or struggling to put it into words that did not incriminate if somehow the call was being monitored. A call originating overseas was not privacy protected under U.S. law. "Uncle, I spent the day on rescheduling the one plane in the country and trying to get the second plane to someplace where it could be inspected. We will have to cancel our foreign contracts for now. We can really use that second plane in the states. I need to brief Dorsey tomorrow."

There was a pause as a third party entered the call. "Stay really focused on your work," said Salam. "Our best international customer Bob is in America now. He may need help moving the inventory we already carried for him to wherever it is needed."

"About Bob," started Farid, "I talked with him yesterday. He seemed a little off balance, you know, not a care in the world. How did we make contact with that man?"

"I tracked him down in Saudi Arabia. There was a news story about him which included personal comments. He was available and had similar interests to us, so I helped him get a new job. That was several years ago. When you see him, ask him about it."

"You know how slammed I am now," said Farid. "I've given Bob about all the time I committed to."

"Perhaps he will need no more help." said Salam. "But if he does, I would be grateful if you could find the time."

"I have done my part," replied Farid.

"As we all have," replied Karim. "But none of us are finished until we are successful."

"Say hello to my mother," said Farid as the call wrapped up.

He turned on the television, needing a distraction. The 24-hour news channel had a journalist reporting from Iran.

"There are sirens screeching all over the country," he said. "Iranian authorities are reporting more than two hundred American aircraft have penetrated Iranian airspace in the last two hours. But I've heard no reports of actual bombing. There are also reports of a fourth American aircraft carrier in route to the region. The authorities are warning people to stay safe and assuring them that the Guard is prepared to protect the nation. Here in Tehran, it is deathly still."

❧

Olga had been on duty for twenty-six hours, but she knew that the adrenalin pulsing through her veins would keep her from sleeping. She found Sarah on the back porch, her face in her hands.

"We are still on a security alert," she said, "but there is no launch alert at the base. I guess the powers at the Pentagon decided that there was no role for B-52 bombers in whatever they have planned."

"I guess that's good," replied Sarah. She used a Kleenex to wipe a tear from her eye.

"What's going on?" asked Olga, pulling a chair next to her friend. "And after more than a day without sleep, I'm in no mood for that traditional woman's answer."

Sarah looked up. "What answer is that?"

"Oh, nothing.'"

Sarah smiled. "I need some coffee. We can talk while I make some."

Coffee in hand, she settled onto a stool at the kitchen counter. "It's Farid. He blew out of here yesterday morning; said he had to be back in New York for a conference."

"Sarah, there is holly-hell breaking out in transportation all over the country."

"But the attack in Reno seemed to really shake him up," said Sarah. "He refused to watch it with me. And after he got some kind of message, he was even more shaken. He almost demanded that I come back to bed and once there, we didn't make love or anything. He just wanted to hold me. When I drove him to the airport all he said was I love you over and over. When we got to the airport, for the second time he said he hoped this was all over, without explaining. It was all he could do to walk through the front doors."

"Sarah, the guy is from a part of the world where he never actually knew peace. It might be a little PTSD or something."

"Maybe," said Sarah, "and I'm here to support him, but I've watched him go from one of the most confident, joyous people I've ever known to this in a year. Even his dream of being a global businessman like his uncle has disappeared. We spent two hours just sitting on a fucking rock watching a river flow. Then he said he might actually like to move here."

"Give him a day. He'll call. Now I need to try to get some sleep."

⁂

Gritt was at his desk in the work room while Thadius was finally getting a little sleep. It amazed Gritt that the man in his seventies was managing the pace. Chad was monitoring a data feed that had been refined to only share information about what was going on in the Persian Gulf region. He already knew that the U.S. was demonstrating a massive show of force and wasn't really surprised that the Iranians had not launched any aircraft or fired any anti-aircraft missiles. Faced with overwhelming force, it was prudent for them to conserve every possible tool they had to defend themselves until they were actually attacked. At a press conference, the president of The United States had stated unequivocally that every option was on the table. "Iran will never become a nuclear power." Gritt took that as good news. It meant that the president wasn't convinced that Iran was directly responsible for the two bombings.

More than fifty senators and congressmen on the other hand were demanding that the president unleash the power he had massed in the region and 'blast the Ayatollah and his government off the face of the earth.'

"Hey, Chad," called Winston. "I've got something."

Chad clicked off his computer and hurried to where Winston was holding down the data research fort while Pinky got some rest. "Okay."

"Customs did not get any pictures when they cleared that air-freighter in Greensboro. But the plane had not only two pilots, but a passenger. That's very unusual. The two pilots each have more than twenty-five years of experience. Both came out of retirement to help a new carrier, WILTON, get into the business. They look clean. Not even a parking ticket on their record and they've cleared customs literally hundreds of times."

"So, they are not interesting," replied Gritt.

"Right. But the other guy, a Robert Thompson, is a lot sketchier.

Gritt slipped into Pinky's chair and rolled it over next to Winston. "Oh?"

"The passport for this guy was renewed three years ago, in New York. But the original was issued to a man in Oklahoma. Here's a picture." Winston skipped to a new screen. "The guy is an ex-Marine, and I found a note from the State Department that he went to Ukraine years ago to fight as a mercenary. Then there isn't a trace of him until this passport renewal."

"Anything more?" asked Gritt.

"There are records of him traveling in and out of the country more than twenty times since he renewed. All of the incoming flights originated in Italy or France. But the last two were both on a WILTON freighter, the one that we know about in Greensboro, and three weeks later he cleared customs again in Atlanta."

"Do we have an address for him?"

"He no longer lives at the address in the passport. His former landlord told me that he believes that Robert moved to Europe."

Gritt looked around the room. "Where's Tony Gerano?"

"He's taking a nap."

"See if you can get him here. I want him in New York as soon as he can get there. In the interim, see what more you can find on this Robert guy. Maybe you can find another New York address."

"I'll call Tony," replied Winston. "I've already started a search for Robert Thompson in the New York area. There are about three hundred."

"Figures," replied Gritt. "There's nothing about this fucking mess that is easy." He stood, looking down at Winston. "I'm sorry about the language. I know you're a very spiritual man, but sometimes my Navy jargon comes out."

"No apology necessary, because the next piece might best be described by what you just said."

Gritt nodded, "Oh?"

"Yeah. Immigration is refusing to send me a picture of this guy, not a passport photo or what they collected in Atlanta. They claim there is some law or something. They want a warrant and even when we get them one, they say it may take a few days to comply."

"I'll start work on that. In the interim, get on the phone with anyone you can think of and see if you can get a description. Have Pinky help when she gets back. Maybe get her on a call to this air freight company. If they can't give us a description, maybe they can get us the pilot's phone numbers. Those guys are usually great at remembering details. Also, see if you can find anyone in Oklahoma who can help."

Chapter 38

General Ashraf knew that Mohamed had access to at least three old Russian nuclear weapons. The replacements for the stolen Iranian enriched uranium proved that. He wasn't surprised when Mohamed indicated that he might be able to get his hands on a fourth weapon. Right now, there was no way to get into or out of Iran. America's NATO ally, Turkey had shut down the border; even the Russians had closed their border.

"The weapon, if I can source one," said Mohamed, "will not have a nuclear core in it."

"That's fine," said Ashraf. "My chief scientist just wants to study the detonation mechanism."

"Do we really want to help the Guard develop this weapon?" asked Mohamed. "Our whole mission is to reduce or eliminate their influence."

"I hope it is not needed," said Ashraf, "but can you even imagine the Americans not destroying the Guard if they fully believe they have such weapons?"

"You do not believe the two explosions in America have convinced them?"

"Probably. Unlike the Russians and a lot of other countries, the Americans like to fight wars with few casualties. They may just be taking their time to fully develop a plan."

"A little delay may work in our favor," said Mohamed. "Right now, the borders are shut tight, but if there is no war for a couple of days, some of the old smuggling routes will reopen and I can get you what you need."

"Do you really believe that you can get one of the old Russian weapons?"

Mohamed laughed. "You are not that naive, my friend. Give me three days and then we can talk about how to get it across the border. We are close now my friend. We cannot back away, and we cannot run up any red flags with the Guard."

Ashraf clicked off the secure encryption application on his phone and pocketed it. He walked across the garden and into the building. "Would you please call Nader's room and ask him to meet me here?" The middle-aged woman at the reception desk picked up the phone.

He wandered over to where a television was playing martial music interspersed with visual messages from the Iranian leadership. All targeted the populous with announcements of how the country, led by the Guard, were defiantly preparing to teach the Americans a lesson."

Nader tapped him on the shoulder. "You wanted to see me?"

"Yes, Nader, it is a beautiful evening. Let's go for a short walk.

The two men walked silently until they were a hundred meters from the compound. Ashraf turned to Nader.

"I have a source who told me earlier that the device you need, the one where you want to study the mechanism is available and the only challenge will be getting it across the border. He asked for three days or so."

"You realize that with that help, we can probably finish our work within a month?" asked Nader.

"I do," replied Ashraf.

"Allow me to observe," started Nader, "that I suspect that does not make you happy."

"What do you mean my friend?"

"I am not a stupid man," said Nader. "I am an old man who learned only today that my wife is dying. She did not tell me, but the clues are in what she says and does not say. That is just like the clues I have observed over the last couple of months. Someone has stolen enriched uranium cores from the vault and replaced them with other cores. I am probably the only one here who could tell the difference. Someone is using the stolen cores to attack America and leaving footprints that lead to my country. Someone is making sure that those footprints walk directly to the Guard and at the same time, someone is poking the Guard a little harder all the time. You are probably the only one I know who could have orchestrated the core exchange and you have quietly spoken more than once about where the Guard is leading the country."

Ashraf stopped; his face ashen.

"Do not worry my friend," continued Nader. "I share your concerns. I will say nothing. But I do have a great fear that men like General Hussein are just arrogant enough to actually test a nuclear weapon or even launch one against an American ship. He believes that the Americans will back down. I do not share that belief."

"I am not the only one trying to change the country's direction," said Ashraf.

"That is also obvious from the clues. There must be a large group of you to orchestrate such a complex plan and make it work up to this point," said Nader. "Is the goal to goad the Americans into destroying the guard?"

"I cannot comment. It would take only one slip of the lips to get a lot of very good people killed. In the interim, it is critical that we humor General Hussein and buy time." Ashraf tapped a cigarette from a pack and slipped it between his lips. He lit it and then puffed a cloud of smoke up toward a star filled sky. "We are a nation with a remarkable history. We gave the world so much in mathematics and science and even poetry. We must return to our culture; not the dark ages or forward into the insanity of the west with few rules and little respect for history or even faith."

"I agree, my friend," said Nader. "I will slow the process as much as I can without appearing to be sabotaging our work. Our nation does not need massive weapons. I fear that possessing them may end our history. I will also think of alternatives if your plan fails."

⁂

Bob called Farid on his way from JFK. "I think we are all set. Are you up for a drink tonight?"

"I can come by your place after work," replied Farid. "My uncle suggested that we talk. He said I might understand what motivates you more after we do."

"I sensed a little discomfort in Minneapolis," replied Bob.

The two men settled into chairs overlooking the lights

of Manhattan. "I kind of like this rye whisky," said Farid. "It's new to me."

"I acquired a taste for it in the service," replied Bob. "I spent three years in the Air Force, working my way into a posting in Saudi Arabia. I flew F-16s. If I'd been able to continue as a career, I'd probably still be in. I liked it."

"It takes a lot to become a pilot," said Farid, sipping his drink.

"Yeah, I let my hatred get out of check," said Bob. "I talked too much about what had happened to my parents. One of the guys in my squadron got worried and talked to my C.O. Nobody said anything, but one day, after months of planning I was about to fly a practice bombing mission out to a target range only a hundred miles from the base. My mistake was asking for three times as much fuel as I needed for the mission."

"I don't understand," said Farid.

"I wasn't headed for the practice range. Hell, I had four thousand pounds of bombs, and I was only a couple of hundred miles from Iran. I was going to go blow the shit out of some stuff."

"What happened?"

"Like I said, someone had tipped them off. They parked a truck in front of the plane and five minutes later a squad of military policemen hauled me away. I told them exactly what I was planning, in fact I'd already sent a letter to the media. It hit all the Arab papers." Bob sighed.

"They threw me in jail and fully planned on convicting me and sending me to Leavenworth for twenty years. Instead, they decided they didn't want any more publicity, so they just let me rot in a jail in Saudi Arabia while they played like they were going to prosecute. I spent two years in that shithole before they quietly kicked me out of the Air Force and left me penniless in Rediya."

"Is that where you met my uncle?" asked Farid.

"It is. The Saudi papers picked up on the story and some Saudi prince decided that wanting to go bomb Iran was enough to get me a place to stay and a little spending money. I don't know how Ahmed learned about me, but I was only out of jail two weeks when he roared in on the family jet and offered me a ride to Europe and a job. On the way, I guess he figured he could trust me. I've been working for him since."

"So, this is your revenge against Iran for what happened to your parents and the U.S. for doing nothing about it?" said Farid.

"And against the Air Force for two years in jail. Greensboro was your family's first shot at revenge. Reno was mine. I've still got a shot at all three."

"You may have to give up on that third shot," said Farid.

"Why? Your uncles think the plan is working well," replied Bob.

"Because the government is starting to poke around. I got a call from someone today. He wants to meet me tomorrow or the next day. He wants to talk about our flights from Georgia and he asked if I could describe the passenger who cleared customs in Greensboro and again in Atlanta."

"I've still got a passport in another name," said Bob. "As long as they don't have a good description, I can finish the job. I'm not done yet. You can't give them a description."

Farid took a deep breath. "As far as they know, I've

never met you. You're good for now. I'll keep you posted on what they say. But you need to know that I've already told my uncles that I hope we don't have to use that third bomb. My part in this is about over."

"I'm not done my friend. I may still have a job to do. I still have to arm that third bomb if I'm told to use it. Once its armed, I can detonate it from anywhere. There won't be many casualties, but it will really rattle the Air Force."

Bob stood and grabbed his jacket. "How about some Italian food, I'm buying."

ᘚ

The top leadership of the Guard gathered at an underground bunker only ten minutes from their headquarters in Tehran. Over the previous two days, they had quietly emptied most of headquarters, which was an obvious target for the Americans. The six top officers were all studying an intelligence report from their allies in Russia. It reported that the Americans were preparing for a major strike on Iran, with almost three hundred planes poised at sea and on American bases.

The problem with the Russian report was that it could be Russian disinformation. The Guard's own intelligence organization warned them that the Russians were good at stirring up trouble around the world for the Americans.

"We are within a month of producing the weapons the council ordered," offered Hussein. "The scientists at EAGLE are perfecting the detonation system. The warhead can be fitted to existing short and medium range rockets."

He referred to his notes. "Our scientists and engineers believe that they can deliver as many as six weapons. The army general who commands EAGLE believes that it would be a mistake to use one of the weapons as a test; that it would only provoke the Americans into using their nuclear arsenal. I agree with him. If we use any of the weapons, we need to strike two or three sites at once so that the Americans think we have enough weapons to really hurt them."

"Does the army general know who is already using such weapons against the Americans?" asked one of the aides to Guard commander. "We are not responsible, and we have stated that again and again. But somehow the Americans still think it is us."

"I do not discuss things like that with General Ashraf," said Hussein. "I do not wish to distract him from supervising his nuclear development team."

"General Hussein, we are all counting on you. Perhaps the French or some other nation will step up and try to open a dialog between us and the Americans. But if that does not happen, we will be at war with them within weeks. Our only chance of holding them off will be if they believe that we can hurt them so bad that continuing conflict against Iran is not worth it," offered the Guard Commander.

"I am told that the scientists will be ready to show us finished weapons within thirty days. Without actually exploding a weapon, I believe that it is critical that we all understand exactly what that weapon can do and how we can use it," said Hussein. "Until then, it is prudent for us to all travel at night and to disrupt our normal schedules and locations. If we have learned nothing more about how the Americans operate, it is that they will first try to take down our leadership."

Chapter 39

"NANCY CONFIRMS THAT two Georgian born former KGB operatives probably did market the bombs immediately after the Soviet Union broke up. They have a lot of money and use it to tell the Georgian people that independence from Russia was a mistake."

"Can she find them to confirm any of this?" asked Chad, staring at his computer screen as Walker stood next to him.

"Not possible," said Walker. "The two men were instigators of the brief war between Russia and Georgia, where the South Ossetia region declared its independence from Georgia. They are now part of that break-away region and are protected by Russian troops." Chad continued to study his screen.

"So, what we really have boils down to a possible group headquartered in Tbilisi, led by a former security officer for a man killed by an American aid strike in 2020. The group, backed by a lot of family money, has somehow managed to bomb two American cities," said Chad. "This is really thin."

"The family appears to have fled Iran during the Iranian revolution," replied Walker, "so they may have a beef with both sides." Chad continued to study what was on his screen.

"If that's true," added Walker, "the group may have been plotting this a long time. They may have opposed the new regime from the beginning. The dream to overthrow the Iranian regime became a passion with the death of the senior brother. That would be consistent with family politics in Iran. In Italy they call it a vendetta."

"Or," offered Pinky who had just walked over to where the men were talking, "the Guard might actually be responsible for this. Our counterparts in Britain just received a memorandum that appears to be authentic. It lays out a strategy for the guard to plant a few bombs in the U.S. and then blackmail us to leave Iran alone by threatening to detonate a dozen more."

"The nightly news had a similar story last night," said Walker. "It was attributed to some unknown source."

"Seems a little to cut and dried," said Chad.

"Possibly," said Pinky, "but the Brits claim it was smuggled out of Iran by a reliable source, someone they know who has close contacts with both the Iranian Army and the Guard."

Chad looked up. "We started with two possibilities, either the Guard or some terrorist organization. We've made no progress."

"We need to keep digging," said Walker. "Since the U.S. decoded the Japanese naval codes in World War II, the ones that said they were going to attack Midway Island,

I've never heard of any intercept that actually spelled out what our enemy was doing. It always takes humans to put together the pieces of the puzzle." He turned to Pinky, "get me a copy of that memo; I'll take it to the director. But we need to keep digging."

"Maybe this will help," said Chad. "The FAA found that WILTON airplane at the Denver Airport. They are preparing to depart for Dallas with a load of freight."

"Have the airport cancel their clearance and hold that plane," said Walker. "Have the airport give the pilots your cell phone number. Find out what they know and get a description of this shadowy passenger." Walker, his cane still hanging from his chair turned to shuffle back to his desk.

"You know that airlines have multiple crews for their planes," said Chad. "This crew might not have been flying when the plane came in from Georgia."

"Or, we could finally get lucky," said Walker. "Call me after you talk to them. I'm going up to brief the director."

It took less than a minute for Chad to reach the airport control tower in Denver. 'It's amazing how fast people respond when you are calling in the name of the president,' he thought. He was still on his secure land line when his cell began to ring.

"This better be legit," came a voice with a southern drawl. "Mick and me haven't been home in ten days and I already promised my wife a night of dancing when I get home."

"My name is Chad Gritt, and I am deputy director of a special task force that is investigating the bombings. I need to know if you were piloting the flight that landed at Greensboro or the one that cleared customs in Atlanta last month."

"Mr. Gritt, we were the crew on both flights. The name is Stan Stephens. How can I help you?"

Gritt and Stephens talked for ten minutes, the last few minutes included a detailed description of Robert Thompson. Gritt released the flight with the agreement that if the pilots remembered anything out of the ordinary, they would call from Dallas.

Gritt waived at Winston. He handed him a handwritten description of Thompson. "Get this out to all of the law enforcement agencies and to the media. Send it to Tony in New York. I want to know if anyone has seen a man by the name of Robert Thompson matching this description. I want this everywhere within a couple of hours. We need to find this guy."

Winston started to walk away. "Hold it," said Chad. "Before you start, can you message me with the address on the original passport for this Thompson guy? I want to confirm the description."

While Winston prepared the kind of message that no police force or media could ignore, Chad called the number.

"Oh my God," echoed through the room as he hung up. You could hear a pin drop as he called Walker's phone. "Thad, we got it, confirmation that something here is really wrong. This Thompson guy is a fake. The original passport was issued to a Robert Thompson of Oklahoma. The guy was six three and two-hundred-thirty pounds, with black hair and brown eyes. The description I got from the pilots who flew him from Tbilisi was for a guy about five-eight and not more than a hundred and seventy pounds, and light sandy hair. They said he had blue eyes." There was a pause, before he added, "the description came directly from Thompson's wife. She was told that he was in a hospital in occupied Ukraine several years ago. She's recently filed paperwork to have him declared legally dead. He never came back from volunteering in Ukraine."

ꟹ

Farid walked into his apartment a little after eight that evening. He put his order of Italian take out into the microwave and poured himself a Scotch. It had been a pretty good day, in that the only thing on his calendar was work for WILTON, including news that the second plane would be clearing customs in Newark the next day. The first plane was finally in Dallas.

He carried his drink to the couch and clicked the remote to turn on the television.

"The government has asked every American who may know the whereabouts of a Robert Thompson to call them at the 800 number at the bottom of the screen. Mr. Thompson is described as a man about five feet eight inches tall with a medium build, light sandy hair, and blue eyes. He has small scar on his chin and usually wears casual business attire. Again, the government is asking the public for their assistance in finding Robert Thompson."

Farid froze but only for a moment. He picked up his phone and called Bob. "I need to see you right now."

It took thirty minutes by cab to reach Bob's neighborhood and another five to find the hideaway bar where he wanted to meet. "Have you seen the news?" blurted Farid as he slid into a chair opposite Bob.

"Keep your voice down. This place is empty, and your voice carries." Bob sipped his drink as he pushed some soggy nachos around with a fork. Finally, he answered, "no, why?"

"Robert Thompson and your description are all over the news. The government has a bulletin out with a good description of you and are asking the public to call if they know where you are."

Bob walked over and stared at the television above the bar. He watched for five minutes before turning back to Farid. "Man, that fucking sucks. I'm almost done here. I only need to make one more trip and I'm out of the country." Bob seemed almost unconcerned.

Farid stood, his face quivering with nerves. "How in the hell are you going to do that now?"

"Sit down. I'll use my other passport and credit cards," said Bob. "I'll need to die my hair back to its normal color and let my beard grow to cover up the scar." He pointed at his eyes; "colored contacts, but I may need a little of your help."

"I promised Salam that I would help," said Farid, "but you need to get out of here and by that, I mean out of the country. If they find you, it will lead them back to me."

"The way my beard grows, it will cover my scar in four or five days. I'll make two reservations for us using the backup credit card and I.D. that Salam gave me." He paused, starring at the bartender who was busy reading the paper. "We'll travel together. It will be less conspicuous."

"Where will you get hair dyed?" asked Farid.

"Bob laughed. It's in the apartment bathroom right now. "FIVE insisted on it. It's part of his contingency security plan. That man is more than a little paranoid; never trusts anyone."

"I'll need to make arrangements to be gone a day or two," said Farid. "Where are we going? I'm going to need to make up something that justifies the trip. He pulled his phone out and tapped the memo feature.

"Bismarck," said Bob. "I'd originally planned on driving to and from Minneapolis, but I think the fewer stops we make, the better."

Without thinking, Farid tapped in Bismarck. "Bismarck, like in North Dakota?" asked Farid.

"Yup, that's the place. I'm not supposed to disclose the target, but under the circumstances, you're going to figure it out anyway. I'll want you to drive me from Bismarck to Minot. I've got the bomb in a truck in a storage place near the Air Force base, but we'll need to move it closer and then get back to Bismarck. You fly home, and I'll fly to someplace where I can get a direct flight to France."

Farid sat totally immobilized. He said nothing. His heart was pounding.

"What's wrong?"

"You can't really mean Minot, North Dakota," said Farid.

"That's the target. There isn't an Air Force Base in the country that will shake up the military like hitting a base where they store nuclear weapons."

"You will have to find an alternative target," said Farid. "My girlfriend lives only a few miles from the airbase. We need to move the truck somewhere else. We are not detonating a bomb where it might kill Sarah."

"Farid, with my description all over, moving to either of the other bases in the region will increase our risk of getting caught. It's an eight-hour drive to either Malmstrom in Montana or Ellsworth in South Dakota." He could tell that Farid was about to come unglued.

"I'll call Sarah and get her to leave. She travels a lot

for work, maybe she won't be there. I need to find out. Oh hell, we don't know when it might blow. Maybe we won't need it. But I need to get Sarah out of the area." Farid was literally shaking.

Salam could veto the use of another bomb, but Minot had always been Bob's first target.

It was clear that Bob needed to get Farid out of the bar. Farid's fears could sink the entire plan. Farid, walk with me back to my place. We can work out a plan. Maybe we will never need the third bomb."

They left the bar and turned down a back alley that led to Bob's building. "You know," said Bob, "that if you make that call to your girl and she puts two and two together, she will get us both arrested. You tip her off and all of this will have been for nothing."

"Hell, it's not Sarah that will figure it out," mumbled Farid. "Her roommate is an Air Force officer who works at the base in security. I need to find a way of getting Sarah out of there or call Salam and either call this off or get him to postpone a third bombing until we can figure this out. I'm not going to help do anything that could hurt Sarah. You aren't going to blow up Minot while she is there."

Farid never felt the pistol press against his back, but the first shot shattered his spine spilling him onto the pavement next to a dumpster. He looked up just in time to see Bob's pistol barrel between his eyes and then he saw nothing.

The owner of the deli arrived at five the next morning. His first customers would be there a little after six for muffins and coffee. The fry cook would get there just before that to start making breakfast burritos. The owner warmed the oven up and opened the display case next to the cash register and removed yesterday's muffins. He tossed them into a trash bin at the end of the counter and then carried the bin to the back door. He lifted the lid of the dumpster and froze. Staring up at him was the face of a dark complected man with two clouded eyes and a hole in his forehead.

❧

It didn't take long for the homicide unit to join the NYPD officers on the scene.

"Maybe a robbery," said the homicide detective as he carefully searched Farid's body. "No cash and no wallet, but the guy is well dressed. And they missed his phone, but it's secured." He lifted Farid's arm and slipped off an expensive watch. "They missed this," he said as he turned it over in his hands. "Hey, there's two phone numbers etched on the back. Maybe we can at least get an I.D. from one of them."

Chapter 40

OLGA LOOKED AT her watch as she made coffee. Maybe she could finally get Sarah calmed down and figure out what happened. She needed to make the mandatory security meeting at eight.

"For God's sake, Sarah, you need to calm down and tell me what is wrong."

Sarah sat at the kitchen counter, her face in her hands, tears running down her arms. "It's Farid."

"What about Farid?" asked Olga.

"I just got a call from my dad. He's dead." Sarah's head slipped from her hands and banged on the counter.

Olga lifted Sarah's shoulders and walked her over to the couch. "Sarah, who is dead? Your father? You said Farid."

"When Farid graduated last year, my dad gave him a watch with his phone number etched on the back in case Farid ever needed help. Some cop in New York just called him to confirm a description. Farid is dead. They found him this morning, shot." Sarah fought to control her sobbing. "I knew that something was wrong, I just knew it. It had to be something with his family. He hasn't been the same since his family gave him a big graduation party in Paris."

"Sarah, it could have been anything, he was in New York City, maybe is was a robbery that went badly."

"My mom and dad are flying in this morning," said Sarah. "My dad said it will take an hour or two to get his pilots to the company jet. He talked to the detective for several minutes."

Olga called in a favor and within an hour the base chaplain along with a medic and a base social worker were sitting with Sarah, who refused the medic's offer of a sedative. Without a shower or makeup, and wearing a crumpled uniform, Olga pulled up to the front gate at the base.

"You look like you must have had one hell of a night, Ma'am," said the guard as she waited for her I.D. to be confirmed.

"You have no idea," replied Olga as she rolled her Dodge Charger toward her office. She was almost there when her head finally began to function. Rushing upstairs to her office, she grabbed the lieutenant in the next room. "John, I need to make an emergency call. You have the morning meeting. Tell the colonel I will explain later. She opened her computer and downloaded the morning security bulletins and handed them to the lanky lieutenant.

She called Chad's cell.

"Well, this is a pleasant surprise on a morning that I could really use one," answered Chad.

"Not for me," replied Olga. "Remember when you and I were talking about what you learned from Thadius

Walker? You mentioned that most mysteries were solved by someone hearing something, someone who isn't involved in the case."

"Yeah, that's about all we have on this bombing thing right now," he replied. "Why?"

"My roommate's boyfriend was just found shot to death in New York."

"That's terrible."

"Don't talk, listen," said Olga. "According to Sarah, the guy has been an emotional mess. It started about a year ago when he graduated from college in London, and it seems worse every time they are together. He was here, and Sarah's description is pretty accurate. When that bomb went off in Reno, he got some kind of message or call and rushed out of here like his pants were on fire, and according to Sarah, he was so shaken that he could barely walk."

"A lot of people around the country are still so shaken that they are taking sedatives," said Chad.

"I'm not finished. His name is Farid Hakimi, and he is originally from Iran. His dad was murdered there, which he carried like a lead weight around his neck. He grew up in Lebanon. His family are all Iranian refugees from the revolution, but wealthy ones. After his dad died, his mom and Farid moved to Paris where his uncle put him through college at Cambridge. The family arranged for him to get a great job as director of a small international air freight company."

Olga paused a moment. "Weren't you working on alternative means of an enemy launching a nuclear attack on the U.S?"

"I was, and the team has concluded that whoever is

responsible for the Greensboro and the Reno bombings smuggled the weapons in by air."

"Like Walker told you, this may be nothing, but to my security-trained head, there is something here that needs to be investigated."

"Anything more?" asked Chad.

"Nothing critical."

"Olga, I've got to go. I need to see how this might fit with the other tiny pieces we have. We're racing. You have access to our briefings; we think there is another bomb out there. I'll keep you posted if anything clicks." He hung up.

"Hey," he boomed across the room. "Does the name Farid Hakimi mean anything to any of you?'

"Not Farid, but the guy that Nancy interviewed in Tbilisi was named Ahmed Hakimi," said Marjorie. She began tapping on her keyboard. "And the brother that we suspect was killed in the drone strike was also a Hakimi." She continued tapping. "And he had a son, by the name of Farid."

"Well, someone in New York just killed a Farid Hakimi. And Farid was the director of a small international air freight company."

Thad Walker used his cane to get out of his chair. "I think this is the break we have been looking for. Unless anyone has something better right now, drop everything and concentrate on the Hakimi family for a day. All except for you Chad, I want you to stay focused on any leads we get on this Thompson guy."

The same team that had launched the missiles at the American destroyer in the Strait of Hormuz sat quietly studying the headquarters of the Revolutionary Guard in Tehran. They were aware that the Guard had quietly moved most of their people out of the facility, all except for a security group and handful of people who continued to send nonsensical encrypted messages and make phone calls to assure that American intelligence still believed that the facility was operating normally. They knew that the Americans could not break the encryption protocols but were confident that they continued to try. If a war broke out, the team wanted the enemy to think they could take out the Guard leadership with one blow to headquarters.

The team's job that night was to destroy as much of the building as possible and make it look like an American air strike. Dressed as Guard senior intelligence officers, they presented I.D.'s and documents at the check station in front of the building. "We're here for just an hour," said the head of the team. "We need access to some achieved files. We need access to the old paper archives on what the Americans did during the embassy takeover. Command thinks that they might be helpful in figuring out what they will do next."

The guards pointed toward two security men sitting at a sandbagged desk just inside the front doors. "You will need to take one of the interior guards with you while in the building. They need to make sure that you don't interrupt any of the messaging that is set up to fool the Americans into believing the building is operational."

The four men carried only briefcases as they descended toward the basement where they spread out across the huge storage and archive area. The internal guard, bored to death after six hours of doing nothing, found a desk where he tapped into a game app on his phone and began to play.

The two men on the far side of the archive used a pick

to open the locked door to the building's massive room where the utilities that kept the operation running were located. There they clamped a brass bracket around the incoming natural gas feed and then slowly twisted the valve into the pipe until they could hear gas escaping. They opened the valve two turns, just enough not to disrupt the flow of gas to the water heaters and furnace in the next room, but enough to flood the utility room with gas. On their way out, they sent two of the elevators to the top floor and locked them there.

Confident that the gas would fill the room within four hours, they hid a tiny timed explosive device and then returned to the archive area. Twenty minutes later the team, carrying two boxes of nonsense files from the building, stopped to chat with the internal guards as they left. "We will be back if the files we are taking aren't what we need," they said to the outside guards who waived them through the checkpoint.

As they drove away, the leader called General Reza. "Sir, I ate something that didn't agree with me. It gave me gas. I'm headed home to see if I can find something that will take care of the problem. I'll check back with you in four hours."

In minutes, the message was relayed to General Ashraf who sent it on to Mohamed. The next phase of the plan was in motion. In Tbilisi, FOUR began to draft news announcements. Somehow, the Americans had flown one of their stealth bombers right over Tehran and dropped bombs on the Guard Headquarters. The details indicated that the bombs had penetrated all the way to the basement where they exploded, crumbling the building. *Luckily*, the announcement read, *the Guard had vacated the building just before the bombing which saved hundreds of lives.* FOUR would use virtual routing through five different hubs to send the untraceable messages. He switched on a television next to his desk and waited until the news channel reported the explosion in Tehran.

Salam sat quietly at his desk. He wanted to share the news with Ahmed, but after the Americans had visited his home, he assumed that they could be monitoring his calls. Ahmed would have to learn of the attack in Tehran from the news like most of the world. If the Americans didn't launch an attack on the Guard in the next couple of days, the destruction of the Guard headquarters would be used as an excuse for the guard mounting a revenge attack in the U.S. Putting one of America's most important bases out of commission had to trigger a response.

The video of the building on news stations around the world was beyond his wildest dreams. The room where the gas was released was over 100,000 cubic meters and that volume explosive gas had turned the building into a twisted mass of beams and wiring. Almost all the walls and windows were reduced to shards. It didn't matter that only a handful of people had died. The image would convince the world that the Guard was justified in retaliating.

❧

It took two days for Sarah to pull herself together enough to realize that Farid's family did not know of his death. She picked up her phone and called Laila in Paris. "Please find a place to sit, ma'am," she started. "I have some terrible news to share."

Within minutes a shrieking Leila stormed into Karim's private study. "What have you done?" she screamed.

"What are you talking about?"

"You have killed Farid," screamed Laila.

"I have done no such thing. What are you talking about?'

"Farid is dead. He was murdered in New York two days ago."

"Laila, Farid was like my own son. His part in our plan was almost over. He did everything we expected of him and more. Ahmed and I would never allow any of our people to harm Farid."

"Well, he is dead. Someone shot him in the head." Laila stood shocked until her brother- in-law wrapped an arm around her and guided her to a chair.

"We are in the last phase of our plan," said Karim. "It will be over in a few days. When it is, I promise that I will leave no stone unturned until I find out what happened. We have one other partner in New York, he was mugged just weeks ago. This was probably a robbery. If it is possible, I will avenge Farid's death personally."

Most of the members of Team Walker had worked through the night, and several had finally succumbed to the need for rest. Thad, who's discipline included rest every six hours sat with Chad, Margaret, and Pinky around a conference table.

"All right, we think we know how the bombs were smuggled into the country, said Chad. "The pilots of that WILTON plane called this morning and mentioned that while they were on the ground in New Jersey, the inspectors were upset by a special lead-lined compartment in the instrument bay of the jet. It was there for a good purpose but was the perfect place to smuggle a small nuclear device into the country. Those guys are really rattled, shocked that they might be part of this. I've asked the Dallas FBI office to interview them."

"There is no connection between the Hakimi family and WILTON that I can find," said Pinky, but we have confirmed with the company that Farid was running their new airfreight division, and that he hasn't reported for work in two days."

"The connection between Farid and Ahmed Hakimi in Tbilisi is solid," said Margaret. "But these guys are good at covering their tracks. There is not a shred of evidence that either was part of a plot to smuggle bombs."

Walker turned to Pinky. "Do you or Winston have anything more?

"Not solid," she replied, "but we are running down the company that received the first shipment in Greensboro. The two pilots say the shipment was almost all wines and liquor. The second shipment from Tbilisi was also wine and liquor as well as a bunch of gourmet foods including caviar from the black sea."

"When you get a solid company name and better yet a human contact, I need to know immediately," said Chad. "The pilots told me that their manifests went to this Farid guy in New York, but the WILTON office there can't find them. They may have been mailed to London."

"So, we can't link any of this to the Hakimi family, other than Farid was managing the planes. But we will nail it, given enough time," said Walker. "But that doesn't matter right now. We know that there was not a third WILTON flight from Tbilisi, but if I were running this operation, after the first explosion, I would have moved any other bombs immediately before security got so tight that it was impossible. If a third bomb came in on the same plane that delivered the Reno bomb, it was moved somewhere else using surface transport. We need to focus on that possibility."

"I'll get the local media in the Reno area to flood the airwaves with our description of Robert Thompson," said Chad. "We will include that we believe that this Thompson arranged transport for a small package or that he rented a car and drove it himself."

"I'll have the director contact his counterpart in the FBI and have them canvass the car rentals in the Reno area," said Walker.

"That makes sense," said Chad, "but any paper records from the airport disappeared in the blast, so they need to focus on electronic records. The pilots told me that nothing was moved off from the airplane when they cleared customs in Atlanta and that the plane was empty when the ferried it out of Reno. If there is a trail, it starts in Reno."

Chad was back at his desk only minutes when his cell rang. "Hi," said Olga, "it's me. I was just wondering how you are holding up and if anything came of the information I called with?"

"The information was gold," replied Chad. "We know how the bombs got into the country and that this Farid guy is involved. His extended family has plenty of reason for attacking both Iran and us, but we can't prove anything…yet."

He paused and leaned back in his chair, trying to slip out of his work mood for a minute. "How are you doing, and even more importantly, how is Sarah?"

"I'm fine, just jittery. Every military base in the country

could be a juicy target. Sarah left with her parents this morning. Her dad is a big wig with his own plane, and they thought some time at the family home might help her. I've got this big house to myself if you ever get the urge to come visit."

"When we track down this third bomb, I'm on the next plane. Love you, see you soon, gotta go."

Chapter 41

AFTER FIVE DAYS, Bob couldn't have been more ready to get out of his apartment. He wore a sweater-vest under his dress shirt and a vest over the sweater under his jacket. He'd played with various clothing options for days, figuring out what might make him look pudgy. He'd traded his business slacks for a pair of faded jeans and his dress shoes for running shoes. His hair was dyed dark brown, matching his natural seven-day beard. He'd spent three days getting used to the brown tinted contact lenses that he'd been fitted for two years ago.

He'd talked to Salam over his secure laptop twice. First was to tell Salam about the media blitz trying to find Robert Thompson and that he was shifting to the new persona created by FIVE. The second call was from Salam, asking if he had any information on the death of Farid. Salam was really wound up, not sure that the Hakimi brothers were prepared to finish the project after news of Farid's death reached them.

It didn't matter to Bob. His job was to arm the bomb and be prepared to detonate it. He had to go to Minot to arm the weapon and for best results, move it closer to the Air Force base. But he couldn't leave it somewhere that it might draw attention, so it might have to stay in the storage facility only two miles away. If that was the case, he would monitor the winds in the area and detonate it when the prevailing winds would cover the base with fallout. But most important to Bob was the need to arm the weapon and then get out of the country.

Changing planes in Minneapolis would get him to Bismarck at just after seven that evening. He was traveling light, only one suitcase. He'd packed two boxes of personal things. FedEx had picked up the packages the day before. They would be waiting in Paris when he got there.

He reserved a rental car in Bismarck and had a reservation for a return trip to New York. But he wasn't coming back to New York. He'd ignore his connecting American Airlines flight from Minneapolis and instead board a non-stop flight on Delta to Amsterdam where he would catch a train to Paris. He hadn't figured out where home was going to be, but he still had over half of the first million dollars he'd been paid at a branch of Deutsche Bank, and when he called Salam to notify him that the third bomb had been armed, he'd be given the account number of the French bank where the last four million dollars was deposited in his name.

When he called Salam, he planned on giving him the phone number of the cell phone detonator on the Minot bomb. He wanted to be the one who set it off, but if Salam decided it was needed before he was in Europe, he could live with that.

He sailed through security at JFK and a little after twelve his flight for Minneapolis lifted off from the runway. He was sixty hours away from a new life, one where he was no longer haunted by what had happened to him or his parents. Ahmed had given him an opportunity to clean that slate.

ꝏ

In Tbilisi, Nancy had made little progress finding the bombs or their source. The taps on Ahmed's phone and internet yielded a picture of a quite the boring existence. The only call of note was from Ahmed's brother announcing Farid's death. But she already knew about that, and Ahmed's response had been exactly what one would have expected when informed of the death of a relative. The only odd phrase was when Ahmed told his brother that he would pass on the news when he could. But he'd given no idea of who else might be interested.

ꝏ

Chad's computer beeped. Pinky sent him a bare-bones message, just a company name and phone number. He used his personal cell to call.

"Exotic Liquors, how may I direct your call?"

"My name's Chad, and WILTON AIR gave me your name as a reference. Is there someone there I can talk to?"

"Let me see if the local manager is available." There was a click and then soft country music over the phone. The hold seemed to go on forever.

"This is Ted, how can I help you?"

"Ted, I'm Chad Gritt, deputy director of the president's bombing investigation team. What can you tell me about the WILTON Flight that came through Greensboro?"

There was the sound of a deep breath and a long silence. "I was there when it arrived and met Mr. Thompson. I was tied up the next day, so I'll have to talk to my warehouse people about unloading the plane."

"Let's stay on Thompson," said Gritt. "What can you tell me about the man?"

"I didn't get much time with him. He stayed on the plane except for arranging a gate pass with the airport manager's office so that he could visit some old friends. We couldn't unload until the next morning."

"Would you please describe Mr. Thompson?"

"I can do better than that. I took his picture to give to my crew. Thompson's company just invested in Exotic Liquors. I wanted to make sure that if the crew had any questions, they would recognize him."

It was Chad's turn to pause. "Please listen very carefully. I need for you to add my phone number to your phone and then send me that picture immediately. I'll have to call you back in a couple of hours after I have my people analyze the photo."

Less than two minutes later Chad stood next to Pinky's desk. He handed her his phone. "This is a photo of Robert Thompson. We need to get it out immediately. Couple it with the previous notices so all of the information goes out to the media again. Start with the Reno area."

"Can do," replied Pinky."

Make sure that we emphasize that time is critical and anyone recognizing Bob Thompson needs to call us immediately. Add a new 800 number and arrange to have all calls routed to my phone or Thad's."

~

The Navy had pulled most of their ships away from the Strait of Hormuz as had their allies. All tanker traffic was being held in port or outside the Gulf of Oman. Navy intelligence flights made passes from Oman to the Persian Gulf every half hour. They were utilizing the data gathered by the damaged destroyer *Walter*, comparing that data to what they registered coming from the Iranian side. What they saw was troublesome. Virtually every anti-ship and anti-air site on the north side was now active.

At the four airbases where the Americans were massing planes and on the four carriers now within striking distance of Iran, armorers were busy hanging bombs and rockets on planes. Aboard four submarines and sixteen surface ships in the region, targeting techs were loading the latitude and longitude of targets into more than 200 cruise missiles. Final targets for the aircraft would be defined using the latest information from the command center. The cruise missiles were only viable for identified fixed targets.

Less than a hundred miles inland of the Navy patrol planes, two Air Force command and control intelligence planes were tracking activity on the ground behind the Iranian missile shield. That data went to the emergency command center set up in Kuwait as the Saudi's, which for some reason, had denied the U.S. access to the command center both countries had used since the Iraq war. At the Kuwait center the data provided by the planes was matched with other surveillance and satellite images. The U.S. and Iran were not at war, but the Iranians were dispersing as much of their military as possible, moving much of it closer to tidewater.

⁂

Hundreds of miles to the north, General Ashraf sat in the back of a helicopter parked on top of a hill near the Turkish border.

"General, two men with a donkey just appeared in the valley below. They waited until they saw our helicopter land before they broke cover. They will be on the trail just below us in less than ten minutes."

The man reporting was the same Captain that had been on duty when Mohamed had made the uranium switch in the vault. "Captain Reza, take one of your men and meet them." Ashraf handed the captain an envelope. "Here is a little bonus for their work this morning. Bring me the package they are carrying as quickly as possible. I've promised it to Nader this afternoon before he leaves for the hospital to visit his wife."

Three hours later, Ashraf and Hussein watched as Nader carefully opened the old aluminum case on his lab bench. "It looks completely intact," said Nader. He carefully separated the pieces of an octagon shaped assembly with wires connected to each piece. "That surprises me," said Nader. "I would have thought that the Russians would have simplified the detonator, but this one is more complex than our design. I'll have to have one of our electronic engineers look into the detonator circuits. They obviously have overcome any possibility of delays in the circuits."

He lifted one of the explosive blocks. "No uranium. But unless I miss my guess, the ones we have in the vault will fit almost perfectly."

"Maybe, but the Russians also have a propensity for

over engineering things," said Ashraf. "Many of our new Russian weapons systems are actually more complex than the thirty-year-old American systems we are replacing." He watched Hussein's face turn ugly.

"They are more complex," added Ashraf, "but they are also more powerful and a lot less expensive. He really didn't care if his second statement mollified Hussein.

He turned to Nader. "Thank you for taking time away from your wife to help us with this today."

"I too am sorry about your wife," said Hussein, "but I must insist that you be back at work the day after tomorrow. We need to finish your project."

"And if my wife hangs on a few days more than expected?" replied Nader.

"You yourself said her cancer is inoperable, that she only has days to live. I'm sorry that she didn't tell you earlier so that you could have spent more time together at the end."

"You didn't answer my question," said Nader.

"I am sending two of my security men with you. I'll order the helicopter to land at the hospital. They will make sure that you get an uninterrupted day with your wife before they escort you back to EAGLE."

"Give me a few minutes with my staff and then I'm ready."

It took fifteen minutes for all three of Nader's deputies to get to his lab. "I will be back in two days. While I am gone, I need you to analyze the detonating circuits and figure out how the Russians designed a circuit with no delays to any of the wires. If there are delays, figure out how they compensated. Finally, find replacement batteries and figure out how we can disconnect each of the circuits and then simulate an actual firing. Make sure that whatever you do, the mechanism can be reconnected exactly as it was designed. We need to demonstrate our design versus this design to the leadership and get their approval on finishing this project."

❧

Chad was at his desk when the special phone linked to the 800 number rang. "You the guy looking for that Thompson guy?" asked a voice.

"I am. Do you have something to report.?"

"The name's Mike. I sold that guy my truck a few weeks ago."

"I'm listening," said Gritt. He shifted in his chair and slid a pen and pad closer.

"He said he was a contractor with a new project down by Vegas. He needed a truck with locking compartments that he could leave at a job site. I sold him my truck and he paid me in cash."

"Can you give me a description of your truck?"

Three-quarter ton Ram truck, dark blue in color with a big aluminum work bed on the back. You know, one of those with multiple locking compartments for parts and tools. The truck's got a pipe rack on top."

"What's the year made and the license plate number?"

"I bought it used, I think it was a 2017 or so. The license is CALMIK9, you know like in

Call Mike and the number 9. I had some of those magnetic signs on the side and thought that the license would generate some calls, but I don't think it did. I took the signs off when I sold the truck."

"Mike, this is really helpful. Is there anything else I should know?'

"Well, one thing seemed funny," said Mike. "When this Bob guy was fixin' to leave he asked for directions to highway 80. I live west of Reno, and he wanted to go through Sparks and then head out on 80. That's a damned funny way to head toward Las Vegas."

"I hope you and your family are not affected by the contamination from that blast in Reno," said Chad.

"The wind was just right, took it on past us, but thanks for asking."

"Mike I've got to run but call me if you think of anything else."

Chad hung up just as Winston wandered into the room, rubbing sleep from his eyes.

"Winston, we have a description of the vehicle that Thompson is driving. The guy who called it in thinks he headed east out of Reno. We need to get a bulletin out to look for that truck. My guess is that it's parked somewhere close to the next target." He handed the man the data on the truck before chugging his third Dr Pepper in the last two hours in a bid to stay awake.

The Bismarck airport was virtually shut down when Bob arrived after delays in Minneapolis. There was nobody at any of the rental car desks and the emergency numbers for the company with his reservation rang five times before a voice announced, "we will open at eight tomorrow morning."

He would have preferred to finish his work that night, but he'd already reserved two nights at a small motel near the airport and there was a good chance that there would be no cabs or Uber available in Minot that late. He'd need one to drive him back to his rental car after he repositioned the truck from the storage yard."

He called the number of the motel and offered the night clerk a twenty-dollar tip if he could arrange to pick him up.

It felt good to get the contacts out of his eyes after four days of wearing them. He was exhausted and the irritation of the lenses in eyes that had never needed them had been interrupting his sleep. He set is phone for a 6 a.m. wakeup and collapsed into a lumpy bed. He would be at the car rental when the attendant arrived and, on his way north a little after seven.

Chapter 42

By midnight, Team Walker had fielded eighteen Thompson sighting calls. None of the callers could offer a precise date or time of the sighting, but all emphatically claimed to have seen him. Some of the calls came from as far as Southern California and Florida and they'd even received one from Alaska.

Pinky sat with Winston plotting the call locations on a computer-generated map. "Is that a pattern or am I just tired goofy?" asked Pinky.

"You're always a little goofy," replied Winston, "but not on this. If you throw out the outlier reports, the remaining twelve are all on a line that runs from Minneapolis west and Reno east. The two from Minnesota are only an hour apart by car, moving kind of northwest. We have a report from the Salt Lake area and then right up by Yellowstone and Butte and Billings, Montana. There are six from North Dakota and South Dakota."

Pinky waived at Walker and motioned him over. "We just wanted to show you a data plot on the leads that have come in since we posted the pictures. There are some stray reports, probably people who are really anxious to help, but there is a pattern emerging."

Thad leaned on his cane as he peered at the map. "There's nothing worth attacking in northern Minnesota, nothing east of Sheridan Wyoming, little in eastern Montana but Billings could be a target." He paused. "Can you narrow the map scope to just the central states?"

Winston refocused the map.

"You have nothing plotted in Iowa or in Nebraska," said Walker. "If this is right, and I recognize that we are working with only a few hours of data, we need to concentrate on Billings and Sheridan and all across North and South Dakota."

I'm going to roust Chad. Hell, he's had three hours of sleep; plenty for a guy in the prime of his life," said Walker. "I want him to develop some specific targets before we issue another bulletin. Grab some coffee while you wait, if you can stand another cup."

Chad sat in a chair next to the data team. His tired eyes felt like they were filled with sand. "So far, they have hit commercial airports, in smaller cities. In Reno, the airport included an Air National Guard base. If that is important, then we need to look at small commercial airports with military close."

"Man, if you look at northern Nebraska, Northwestern Wyoming, Eastern Montana and the Dakotas, that only leaves about a dozen targets," said Winston. "The furthest west is Malmstrom in Montana, north of the sighting in Billings. Then there's Ellsworth in South Dakota and Minot in North Dakota. Beyond that there are eight national guard facilities. Most of them are just local armories."

"We have a Montana sighting well east of Billings," said Pinky.

"I see that," said Chad, "and there's not much around Glendive, but we need to alert the authorities around Great Falls and at Malmstrom anyway. Bob might have double back. As major targets, that leaves Ellsworth in South Dakota and Minot in North Dakota. Get warnings out to all three major bases and to the commands of the National Guard in all four states that track. It will be light in a few hours, tell them to get everything they can out on the ground and as much air surveillance as they can. Make sure your bulletin includes everything we've got."

Chad waked back to his desk and just stood staring.

"What's going on in that brain of yours?" asked Thad.

"Remember Olga's call about that Farid guy and how freaked out he seemed?"

"Yes."

"Well, if he really was part of this and someone targeted a base close to where his girlfriend was living, that might explain Olga's description of a man coming unglued. If he threatened to go to the police, that would explain a bullet in the brain."

"Good pickup," replied Thad. "Call Olga."

"I'll do that, but can you get us a plane?"

"Who's us?" asked Thad.

"Tony Gerano got back from New York last night. There was nothing more he could do in a city teaming with cops and surveillance cameras. He needed some sleep. I'd like to head to Minot, and then have the plane drop Tony at Ellsworth. We're closer to this case than any of the local people, maybe we can pick up a clue they'd miss."

"I can get both of you on a helicopter to Andrews

immediately. From there it would be faster to put you on separate jets. You can brief Tony on the helicopter. How fast can you be ready?"

"I'll go wake Tony. Give us fifteen minutes."

"I'll roust the pilots of the standby copter and then build a fire under the folks at Andrews. The director is about to get a wake up." Walker smiled at the younger man. "Again, I'll be here to kick loose anything you need. Good hunting."

"We're due for a pheasant hunt when I get back," said Chad. "That is if your dog even recognizes you anymore."

"All will be forgiven when the first bird flushes," replied Walker.

Gritt and Gerano's helicopter touched down only fifty yards from Air Force One. A one-star general met them in a hummer which five minutes later dropped them next to two Air Force Gulfstream executive jets with the engines running.

"How long to Minot?" asked Chad as he bounded up the stairs and stuck his head into the cockpit.

"Three hours wheels up to touchdown," answered the copilot.

Chad glanced at his watch. It was already four in the morning. That would put him on the ground in Minot at about seven. He struggled with trying to figure out what was wrong in his tired brain. *That's 6 a.m. with the time change*, he finally figured out.

"I need a couple of hours of sleep," he said to the steward who handed him a blanket and a pillow. Wake me in two hours, I need to make a call about an hour out."

Team Walker continued to field phone calls on the 800 number, most of them scattered across the country. Three were from New York. Pinky carried the updated map on her laptop over to Walker's desk. "Look at New York; three reports all over a week old. What do you think?"

Walker looked at his watch. "That Farid guy was shot in New York, so these might be solid," replied Thad.

"But there are no new sightings in a week," said Pinky.

"If he knew we had a description out, he might have gone to ground. Maybe we should have left Gerano in the city. He won't be on the ground at Ellsworth in South Dakota for a half hour. Maybe we should turn him around."

"A bombing in New York runs against what little pattern we have," said Pinky. She stood plucking at a diamond stud in her nose. "Maybe he changed his appearance and waltzed right out of town."

Walker called up the photo from Exotic Liquors. "It's easier to go from fair to dark when you are in disguise."

"I have an idea," said Pinky. "Let me run this photo up to the lab. I'll have them run an AI pass on the photo. They can generate some solid pictures of what he would look like in disguise."

"How long will that take?" asked Thad.

"Maybe a half hour. If they have to call someone in, then an hour or two."

"If you need to roust someone, make it someone who lives nearby and give them a police escort. Use the presidential authority if you need to."

❧

The clerk at the motel offered a cab driver, a friend, half of a fifty-dollar bribe to pull out of the cab line at the airport and take a short fare to the rental car office. The doors were still locked when Bob arrived, but he waited only about five minutes before a balding middle-aged man who had probably never missed a meal arrived.

"You waiting for me?"

"If you're the guy who can get me a car, I am. My flight was delayed last night. You were closed. The name's Peterson."

The attendant opened the door, pointing at a couple of chairs across from the counter. "It will just be a minute," he said. "I'll get the coffee going and be right with you." The man disappeared into a back room. He didn't come back for more than five minutes and when he did, he had a ceramic coffee cup in one hand and a paper cup in the other. "Here, it's early for you too. I'll bet you haven't had your coffee. What was the name again?

"Rob Peterson, let me get my phone out and I can get you a reservation number." *Be patient. You don't want to be memorable,* he thought.

"That won't be necessary Mr. Peterson," said the clerk. "It's right on top of the schedule. You're lucky, it's flagged as a no-show, but the car hasn't been reassigned. Driver's license and Credit card please and we will get you on your way."

Bob handed the man a driver's license and credit card. The license hadn't been used in a year and reflected his original appearance with a persona generated by FIVE as a backup. The credit card was on file in New York and covered the rent for his apartment.

Bob drove a dark green Chevy Impala from the fenced lot he asked Siri to map out the fastest route to Minot. It took twenty minutes to get through Bismarck. It would have been faster if he hadn't stopped at the drive through for an Egg McMuffin meal and a large coffee. Highway 80 ran straight to Minot and then on to the airport and Minot Air Force Base just to the north. He checked his watch. He'd be at the storage lot about 9 o'clock, and with any luck back at the motel before three. If he could pull that off, he'd try to get an afternoon flight back to Minneapolis. His flight to Amsterdam didn't leave until eleven the next morning, but he'd feel more invisible in a larger city.

❧

Chad's plane landed just after seven. The steward somehow found two stale packaged cinnamon rolls from a previous flight and had spent the last hour before touchdown refilling Chad's coffee cup. As he descended the stairs, the pilot leaned out the door and yelled.

"Commander, there will be an airman inside the transit lounge waiting for you. He will drive you over to the security offices."

Chad looked nothing like a Naval Officer. He hadn't shaved in two days and wore jeans and a burgundy sweatshirt under a leather jacket. He noticed the confused look on an airman's face near the front door. He pointed at himself and then at the men's room. Four cups of coffee in the last hour needed to go somewhere before he started a day that might go fifty hours.

"I guess I was expecting someone in uniform," said the driver.

"I've been hitting it pretty hard for several days. I didn't even know that I was making this trip until five hours ago."

Chad's phone buzzed. It was a message from Thad, giving him an update including the discussion he and Pinky had about Thompson being in disguise." He checked for other messages, finding none.

"Is this place always this quiet?" he asked.

"The base is pretty much locked down. I guess that's why you are here. Security is going through the base with a fine-tooth comb, looking for some truck."

Chad was a little disappointed that Olga was not there as he was led into a large conference room. A full colonel sat next to three marker boards. "You Gritt?"

"I am, Sir, and I'm not here to interfere with what you are already doing. I've been chasing this issue for a month now and have a deep understanding of what we are dealing with. I'm just a new set of eyes and someone to bounce ideas off from."

"Hell Commander, if this is real, we will take all the help we can get."

"Sir, I've been on this since before the bombing in Greensboro. The threat is real. As of last night, the team I'm part of believes that Minot, Malmstrom and Ellsworth are the most logical targets for a third bomb we think is in play."

"I've read the bulletins. Right now, we are combing the base itself. There are a thousand places a truck like that can be hidden. There is some ground cover just north of the base that will be next. Your friend Olga will be back in an hour. Right now, she's in town briefing the local police. They are organizing a search, but it will take a few hours to really get them in motion."

After a rush to Andrews and a flight across half of the country, it felt odd to Chad to be doing nothing.

He walked over to a huge coffee urn and filled a cup,

and then found a seat. Studying the boards behind the colonel, Chad recognized a well-disciplined search was underway. The base had been broken into two pieces, each represented by search teams assigned to sections. The third board was blank. Two men and two women sat at desks monitoring radios and staring at computer monitors. Off to the side, a television was tuned to cable news.

Just before nine, Olga rushed into the room. "The local police will have a search underway by ten," she said to the colonel. "Their read is that any attack will be at or adjacent to the airport like what happened in Greensboro and Reno. They will start there."

She turned to Chad. "This is not what I had in mind when I told you I had that big old house to myself."

"I'm happy to see you too," replied Chad. "I'm here to help."

"Turning to the colonel, he asked, "are you deploying any air assets, Sir?"

"Not right now, the state boys will have all three of their helicopters airborne in the next couple of hours. We don't have the ability to control both them and us right now. Nobody wants an accident."

"So now, we wait?" asked Chad.

"We'll wrap up the base search before ten. If we find nothing, we move to the next phase."

Turning to Olga, he offered, "take Commander Gritt here over and get him some breakfast. Be back in a half hour and we can plot out what's next."

❧

Bob arrived at the storage yard at nine. Instead of driving in, he drove the rented Chevy north toward the base. The main gate was blocked by two Humvees and at least six Air Force Guards with M-16's stood at parade rest behind them. The level of security surprised him.

A quarter mile further he found what he was looking for. There was an abandoned old gas station with bordered up windows. He pulled in next to where there used to be gas pumps. A sign on the building simply read, COMING NEXT SPRING, SIX NEW ZERO LOT LINE HOMES. Below the sign was one for a real estate office and a phone number. Next to the building was an old Ford truck covered in dust. The site was close enough to register blast damage at the base. It would do. Bob slid out of the seat and tried the door to the old garage. It was locked. He looked around, there were no cameras and for some reason no traffic on the road.

He picked up a piece of concrete that had broken off from the gas island and slammed it against the door handle of the office. The handle shattered. He hit the door next to the handle and it popped open. Inside he unlocked the garage door and used the chain to open it an inch. Satisfied, he drove the rental back to the storage yard, let himself in and parked the Chevy next to the truck.

Five minutes later he drove the truck from the yard and headed north. Pulling up to the abandoned building, he jumped out of the truck and forced the garage door open, bracing it with an old two-by-four that probably had been used for that purpose forever. With the truck parked inside, Bob checked to make sure nobody had stopped nearby, then he closed the door.

He unlocked the truck compartment. Opening the bomb case, he looked through the hole he'd drilled into the battery box. The green LED was illuminated. He unlatched the old buckle latch over the control assembly cover and carefully removed the two tabs blocking the ignition circuit. He closed the cover and then the lid. It had taken less than one minute to arm the bomb.

Bob relocked the truck storage compartment, then the truck, dropping the keys into his coat. He called for an Uber and waited inside for a several minutes and then left through the office using a splinter of wood from the frame to jam the door closed. He walked around to the old Ford and opened the side door just as a Prius with an Uber sign pulled up.

He slammed the truck door and made a big deal of studying his keys before pocketing them. "A buddy dropped me off a half hour ago. He wanted me to move this old truck to a storage yard, but it won't start." He slid into the back seat, studying the older woman driver. "I need a ride back to my car."

"I'd kick my buddy's ass for dropping you like that," she said. "That truck probably hasn't been started for years. You'll be lucky if it will start with a jump."

Bob looked at a placard next to the driver. "Thanks for the ride, Angie."

"Happy to do it, Rob. I only drive in the mornings. Retired from the state corrections department and use Uber to make a little extra."

Bob clicked on the 20% tip button as they pulled up to the storage yard. There was a Ward County Sheriff's car sitting inside the fence. A deputy was standing next to a full-sized storage unit.

"You know, Angie," started Bob, "I haven't had breakfast yet. Is there any place within walking distance of here that puts out a decent meal?"

Angie pointed toward a small bar and restaurant only fifty yards down the road. "The bar isn't open yet, but the restaurant is. They make a damned good omelet."

Bob handed Angie a ten-dollar bill. "I already closed out your bill, how about dropping me off at that restaurant?"

"No need for the additional tip," said Angie.

"I insist. Thanks for the help."

He walked into the restaurant and found a seat at the window where he could watch the gate of the storage yard. "Just coffee and a cinnamon roll or something like that," he called to the waitress coming around the counter.

Chapter 43

THAD WALKER STARED at the three faces on Pinky's computer. If he tried, he could find Bob Thompson in the photos, but each of the computer-generated images changed his appearance so much that they no longer were even close to the description of the man they were looking for.

"Get these out to the media. Make sure that you send them to Gritt and Gerano. Send them directly to all the media you can locate in the Midwest cities we are focused on. Use the same 800 number we are already using."

Gritt's phone beeped. He opened the message to find a note from Pinky and the three pictures. He handed the phone to Olga. "Look at these. Hardly looks like the same guy."

Olga took Chad's phone and stared at the pictures. If this is the guy we are looking for, all the descriptions and pictures already in circulation are all wrong."

"But it makes sense," replied Chad, "if this Thompson guy knows we are looking for him, he would change his appearance.

Olga jumped up from her chair, a fork full of eggs still in her hand. "Come on," she said. "We need to get back to the command center." She headed for the door.

"Colonel," she blurted, "look at these new doctored pictures. The just came in on Gritt's phone." She handed him the phone.

"I see the differences," replied the colonel.

"Sir, it will take an hour or two to get these out to the media and for them to get them on the air."

"I'm no media expert," he replied, "but that sounds about right."

She stepped to the side where she could address the colonel and Chad. "Almost every place in the country now has an AMBER Alert system. What if we could get a message and these pictures out on that medium. Every cell phone in the area would get these instantly."

"I wouldn't even know how to do that," replied the colonel.

"I was at the emergency command center this morning. It's where I briefed the police. If we can get them these pictures someone will know how to get them out."

The colonel handed Olga the phone. "Start with 911 and tell them what you are trying to do."

"Have them use the same 800 numbers we are already using. Team Walker can sort the calls and forward any leads to whoever is closest," said Chad.

"Angie had just pulled into her driveway when her phone beeped. She was ready to sign out of service with Uber, but if it was something really good, she would consider it. Instead, an AMBER Alert popped up. It took her less than a minute to dial the number on the alert.

"My name's Thadius Walker. How can I help you?" came over her phone's speaker.

"My name is Angie. I am an Uber driver in Minot, North Dakota, and I just dropped off a man who looks almost exactly like one of the pictures that just came out on a local AMBER Alert. The name on the alert is Bob Thompson."

"Angie, I need for you to tell me which of the three photos, and where you dropped off Mr. Thompson, and then stay on the line in case we need more information.

Chad's phone rang. "Chad, it's Walker, I am on the phone with an Uber driver who swears she just dropped our guy off at a restaurant in Minot."

"Thad, let me put you on speaker."

"Our caller says he wanted to go to a storage yard a short distance from the restaurant, but he got hungry when he saw a sheriff's car in the lot."

"Give me the addresses, Olga is right here. She's been working with the local police all morning."

"One more thing," said Walker, "the photo she referred to is the first one of the computer-generated pictures; the one with really dark hair."

"That restaurant is only a few hundred yards from our house, said Olga. "There is a storage yard between the house and the restaurant. It's less than ten minutes from here." She made a quick call to police headquarters.

"The police are all on the other side of town. They are working with the sheriff's office on a search near the airport."

"Where's your car?" asked Chad.

"Right outside, why?"

`"I want to see this guy for myself. It's critical that

nobody kills the bastard and that he not use a cell phone. We think that's the most logical trigger for the bombs."

"Major," snapped the Colonel, "go. Stay on the line with the emergency center while you drive. I'll have one of the security units at the front gate follow you."

Olga tossed her keys to Chad as she opened the passenger door. She covered the mouthpiece of her phone. "Drive, I'll give you directions."

It took only two minutes to reach the front gate. There was a gap where one of the Humvees had been parked. It was running and waiting just outside the gate as Chad pulled out onto Highway 83. The Humvee fell behind quickly as Chad ran the engine to redline between each shift.

"The sheriff says he has no patrol cars on this end of town," said Olga. "It must have been an off-duty officer checking on his own storage. The sheriff has someone dialing for dollars trying to find the car." She said something over the phone before turning back to Chad. "Turn left in two miles, before you see the airport exit."

Bob stuffed the last of a cinnamon roll in his mouth and dropped a five-dollar bill on the table. He watched from the front door as the sheriff's car pulled out of the storage yard after closing the gate. He started the five-minute walk to the yard.

Opening the gate, he looked up at the surveillance cameras and smiled. His rental was parked at the rear of the yard. Running across the yard might look funny. He left the gate open; he'd be leaving in minutes. He had taken only a few steps when a black Dodge Charger screamed off from the freeway and toward him.

"That's the restaurant in front of us," said Olga. "There's a state cop and local sheriffs' car on the way."

Chad caught movement in the storage yard. He slowed without locking up the brakes. "Our target is in the storage yard. Pass that on in case he gets past us." Chad did a U-turn and slowly reversed course. "Across the yard, near the green car. The guy just tossed his coat into the back seat and slammed the door. My guess is that his cell phone is in the coat."

Olga reached into the console of her car and produced a 9mm Barretta. "I've been so busy this morning, I never strapped this on."

"I'm going to try to get to that guy before he can reach for his coat," said Chad, flooring the Charger.

Bob turned as he heard the tires squeal behind him. He stood open mouthed as the car roared toward him, but only for a moment. He reached into the car, trying to find something under the front seat, as Chad slid to a stop only twenty yards away.

Chad threw open the door and yelled. He launched himself out of the car, sprinting. Bob backed out of the open front door, a pistol in his hand. He said nothing as he began shooting wildly toward Chad.

Chad felt something slam his left leg and then he was tumbling into the dirt. He looked up, shocked as the man next to the green car continued to fire. Behind him, Chad heard one shot and watched as the man with the gun folded in the middle and dropped to his knees. Chad watched Olga walk calmly by him, her gun pointed forward. The man tipped slowly forward, his head resting on the ground.

Chad could hear sirens in the distance.

Olga walked back from where she had checked the shooter for a pulse. "Damn," she said, "I didn't want to kill him, I just reacted when I saw you go down." She knelt next to Chad, pulling off her jacket and pressing it against the blood pouring from his leg.

"I didn't hear a bomb go off," mumbled Chad and then he closed his eyes.

✧

He awoke in a bed with crisp sheets and two monitors clicking away above his head. Olga sat in a chair next to him, holding his hand.

"Welcome back, my dear," she said. "I wasn't worried, your too tough to let a flesh wound take you away from me."

The two talked for a few minutes before it occurred to Chad to ask about Bob and the bomb.

"I've never had to shoot at a live target before," said Olga. "Center mass. I didn't want to kill him."

"I served with a couple of Texans," said Chad. "They would have said, he needed killin'."

"The woman who called in the sighting gave us an address where she originally picked up that guy. It was an abandoned gas station. They found the truck. A state bomb squad flew in and defused the bomb. It seems to be identical to the other two. It would have done a lot of damage at the base if it had gone off."

"You know that I love you," said Chad.

"Yes, I know, and I know you know I feel the same."

"The doctor says he can release you tomorrow. No permanent damage. I talked to Thad, and he has no objection to you staying here for a few days before they want you back in DC."

"I'm not in the shape to be much of a romantic," said Chad.

"Some things are worth waiting for."

Chapter 44

THE PRESS WENT crazy reporting that a third bombing had been averted, and even more when the American government announced that they were investigating a shadowy Middle East group who might have been responsible for the bombings. The government spokeswoman also said that the enriched uranium used had come from Iran and that the U.S. and its allies were working on a plan to assure that Iran would not be a nuclear threat, even if that took direct military action.

Ahmed got a secure call from his brother, who was monitoring the story on French television. “Brother, we have failed. The Americans may still use force in Iran, but they are not going to destroy the Guard leadership as we had planned. The Americans are also reporting that the man placing the bombs was an American with an axe to grind with both the U.S. and Iran. He was killed in a shootout, and the gun he was using was linked to the murder of Farid.

"News reports here in Tbilisi indicate that the Revolutionary Guard are threatening atomic war if the Americans attack," said Ahmed.

"Maybe that would be good, it might finish the job we started," said Karim.

"Perhaps," replied Ahmed. "But for now, we need to make sure this doesn't lead back to us."

"I agree, brother. Meet with Salam and have him take care of it. There is enough money in the bank in Tbilisi to meet all of our promises to those who were critical to our mission. FIVE has a plan to assure those who we cannot trust with our lives are taken care of."

Two hours later Salam and Ahmed met at a park only a mile from Ahmed's home. Both were dressed in hats and raincoats as they walked and talked in a driving storm.

"I will shut down the lab. I'll call Mohamed. We sent the last Russian suitcase to Iran, but we still have one enriched uranium core. It was wise not to keep it in the lab. Everything else can be explained," said Salam.

"Better yet, my friend, the ownership of the building is untraceable, just clear out anything that ties us to the bombs and go home," said Ahmed. Get ONE out of there immediately. We don't want a man with a doctorate in nuclear physics picked up, even if he would never talk. Have him pick up the nuclear core from the other facility and find a way to drop it in the ocean."

Salam paused before getting into his car. He made a coded call to Mohamed. Then he drove straight to the lab where he informed the staff that they would be working late destroying any evidence that tied them to the bombing. It would have worked had Ahmed not missed the two local CIA operatives who trailed him to the meeting and then, knowing where to find Ahmed if they needed to, trailed Salam to the building. While one continued to observe, the other raced to headquarters to organize a response team.

It was almost seven in the evening when Georgian security forces and the small team of Americans entered the building. The lower floors and all the classrooms were empty. On the top floor they used explosives to penetrate a heavy steel door. Inside they found two ceramic furnaces still blazing next to a dozen empty file boxes. There were eight computers. All were missing the hard drives.

"What in the hell is this place?" asked Nancy.

"Two decades ago, it was the headquarters of Soviet intelligence in Georgia," answered the commander of the Georgian security team.

Inside a locked conference room, they found four dead men. There wasn't a mark on them. All were laid out shoulder to shoulder. A door in the back of the conference room led to a narrow shaft with a fireman's type pole in the center. One of the Georgian officers slid down the pole and reported that it led to a hidden door in the back of the building and a walkway surrounded by bushes. At the end of the walkway was a small empty parking lot.

"About a quarter after five, the institute let out," said the agent who had been observing the building. "About thirty people left the building, mostly young student types. I took a dozen pictures with my phone, but I don't know how good they will be. From where I was hiding, every picture was from the side, and most of those who left were covering up in this rain."

"Thad," said Nancy shielding her phone from the rain outside the building, "there is a case here, but it's going to take a lot of police work to nail these guys. The two or three that were identified from their pictures are all just archeological students. Just like how they ran their operation, they are very good at covering their tracks."

Thad fumbled with the phone cord. With the third bomb accounted for, most of the rest of Team Walker were gone. "Nancy, I'm headed back to Montana tomorrow. Someone needs to ramrod this. These people killed at least a thousand Americans. If you and Gerano would like the job, I can assure you that the agency will work with the FBI and justice department to pay you well for the effort and give you whatever resources you need."

"We are confident that this is the nerve center of the plotters," said Nancy. "Somewhere we will find the thread to unravel this, or someone will break. I'd like to work this. Besides, I'm a single woman with nothing but a cat to go home to and I kind of like Tbilisi."

"I'll start greasing the wheels tonight. I'm having dinner with the director and the president." He paused a minute. "But, Nancy, remember, this is an international problem in a part of the world where the legal system isn't the same as ours. You may have to take whatever win you can put together, not what you want. If, and when you need me, I'm only a phone call away.

Chapter 45

Mohamed, Nader and Ashraf were seated on a hillside bench overlooking snowcapped mountains only a few miles away. Mohamed had arrived at EAGLE only an hour before. The metal fencing behind the men would interrupt any distant listening devices.

"The Americans may still be coming," said Mohamed, "but it will be to destroy our nuclear capability. That would mean hitting six locations with deep penetrating weapons, probably over and over. They are not going to decapitate the Guard as we hoped."

"Then it is up to us," said Nader. "We must show the Americans that we are not a nuclear threat and that we can clean up our own messes. If we can destroy the Guard Leadership at the same time, I can go to my grave in peace."

"Nader, my old friend, you have done enough. It is unconscionable that you are here today instead of with your wife," said Ashraf.

"I was told this morning that she is in a coma. She will not reawaken. But if you are asking me about how I feel about the Guard holding me here like a prisoner, then I will tell you. I am angry."

"How would we do what you suggest?" asked Ashraf.

"You will meet with Hussein and tell him that we have reached an impasse. The future of the Guard, maybe even the nation requires decisions. We have three different designs for weapons and delivery, but to produce weapons quickly they must choose one. The choice will be based on the Guard's political and military needs. I will take care of the rest."

Mohamed stood, staring at the fading evening light. "Even if the leadership of the guard disappears, that still leaves the other nuclear sites. The Americans will not stop until they are confident that Iranian made weapons are no longer a threat."

"Those issues must be dealt with by Ashraf here and his friends," said Nader. "I can only do my part. Can you arrange with Hussein for such an executive presentation?" he asked Ashraf.

EAGLE was deserted except for thirty trusted Guard security personnel. All of the scientists had been sent home and only General Ashraf and one aide were allowed to remain as four helicopters arrived. They landed next to Ashraf's personal helicopter. Sixteen men, the entire senior staff of the Revolutionary Guard and the two liaisons between the Guard and the leadership of the government walked through the empty lobby of EAGLE to the doors to the tram. The ride to the lab below the adjoining mountain would take six minutes.

An hour later they were all seated in the conference

room as Nader fiddled with several prototypes in the front of the room.

"I must object to this meeting," said Ashraf. "On decisions as important as this, the Army, Air Force, and Navy should be represented. I thought you would be inviting them?"

"General Ashraf," said Hussein, "before any final decisions are made, we will of course consult with all of you. If you are uncomfortable with your role here today, maybe it would be better if you go back to your office on the surface and wait for us."

Ashraf rose and stuffed his laptop into his briefcase and without a word left.

"Now, Nader, you promised this would take only a couple of hours, so let's get started. It is unwise for all of us to be away from our units for very long."

"General Hussein, is it not pleasant for all of you to be together again, even if it is only for a short period? You've been scattered all over the country since your headquarters were blown up."

"The scientist is right," offered a man with no rank on his uniform. "I have not had my entire staff together for many weeks." He turned to Nader, who checked his watch. "But Hussein is also right, we should get on with what brought us all together. Show us the three prototypes."

"I will, but first let me give you a little background. It will take about fifteen minutes, but it will make the rest of my presentation more meaningful."

❧

Ashraf arrived at the surface and summoned his aide. "Prepare our helicopter. We have been dismissed from the meeting. The aide rushed away as Ashraf picked up a small package from the receptionist's desk. Then he made his way past the Guard's security team and boarded his helicopter. The blades started to turn. Moments later they were airborne.

"I want you to land on the top of the hill across the valley, overlooking the facility," ordered Ashraf.

"What is in the package, Sir? asked his aide, as they landed only four miles from EAGLE.

"It is a quilt that Nader's wife made for him the first year they were married. He asked me to take it to her bed and spread it over her as if he was there to protect her."

Below, Nader began his presentation. Before I show you our designs, I want to show you a Russian weapon that we have been studying. It is the same weapon that reportedly was used to bomb two cities in America. Nader placed the aluminum case on a table in front of him.

"This weapon is of about the same yield as the weapons that Hussein has us working on. The device itself will not work on a rocket, but only because of its shape and the controls needed to detonate a hand delivered weapon versus one launched toward an enemy on a rocket or flying bomb."

Nader opened the lid. This weapon can be detonated by using a remote device like a cell phone. An alternative would be to detonate it as it was originally designed, that is with a timer. Obviously neither of those methods would work for a weapon on a missile." He paused and smiled. "The only other method of detonating this weapon would not work either. That would be if the person controlling the weapon were to push this red button.

⁂

From the hilltop, all eyes were drawn to the rumble below and the shaking of the ground under the helicopter. Four miles away the entire EAGLE campus rose into the air and then collapsed into a large hole where it had once stood.

Ashraf stepped from the helicopter and called a number on his phone. "It is done," was all he said. Then he climbed back into the aircraft and ordered it to the hospital where Nader's widow lay unmoving.

⁂

"Get both Chad Gritt and Thad Walker on a conference call said CIA director Mat Chang. While he waited, he reached into the bottom drawer of his desk for a bottle of Gentleman Jack and poured himself a short drink.

"They are both on the phone director."

"I just wanted you two to know that I am breaking my own rules and I'm having a drink in the office. The Iranian army is apparently taking control over all of the nuclear sites in the country and have announced that they will be destroying those sites and all of the weapons grade uranium they find there. They just blew up a site that we didn't even know existed. They report it was being used by the entire senior staff of the Revolutionary Guard."

Walker just laughed. "So, the bastards who were trying to use us won in the end. Well, that's just dandy. Mat, Chad and Olga are coming out to do a little bird hunting with me next week. Would you like to join us.?"

"I could use a few days off. When do you want me there?"

"We're going to be there Tuesday," said Chad. "Olga's

been shooting some clay pigeons on the base while I got my leg back under me. But nothing will keep me from this hunt."

When they hung up, Walker reached down and rubbed the ears of his Gordon Setter, Winchester. "I know I've been gone a lot but were about to make it up to you."

He used his cane to get out of his chair and then headed out the open front door. The dog followed him down the gravel path to the dock on Flathead Lake picking up his favorite ball on the way.

Acknowledgements

THE SHADOW GAME

THE TEAM WALKER SERIES are stories of everyday people who were prepared. By that I mean, they are skilled in their professions and most importantly they are aware that they don't have the answers. Each team member contributes one piece to a group challenged with finding answers. From the tattooed, gay, data genius of Pinky to the ultimate traditional conservative Thad, they need, trust, and respect each other. I miss that in today's world.

For years, my family lived in Iran. Even after they left following the fall of the Shah, those years were filled with my dad and stepmom's most cherished memories. A deep respect for the people, their culture and especially how they blended tradition with their dreams of a modern society became part of our family. Iranian exiles never lost that dream and recent events in that ancient civilization indicate that those same emotions are still shared widely by their citizens.

Authoritarian governments, especially those based on faith or dogma, seek to suppress all thought that differs from the official narrative. But history has proven again and again, that suppressing free thought and liberty does not make it go away. On the contrary, it just lights a fire and it is only a matter of time until the people rise up.

The Persians gave us algebra, the guitar, modern agriculture, the postal system, and a road system along with a system of routes that expanded three continents. Ibn Sina is widely recognized as the founder of modern medicine. Along with a functioning governmental system, the Persians published the first charter of human rights, one that included respect for the beliefs and faith of others and that there was strength in diversity and multiculturalism. Unfortunately, in Iran today, the government and especially the Revolutionary Guard that protects it, learned little from that country's rich heritage.

Thanks to the Iranian exiles I've known over the years, and to my late father for his insights on that nation and its people. Thanks to my friends who shared their experiences in intelligence work and military operations. Thanks to Damonza for their expert help in cover design and formatting. And as always, special thanks to my wife, Carmen, for her support and the days she spent coordinating the editing and finish work on THE SHADOW GAME.

If you liked THE SHADOW GAME, please consider posting a review on Amazon or Goodreads so other readers can find my stories. Thank you for reading my story!

www.rodgercarlyle.com
Goodreads Author Rodger Carlyle
Amazon Author Rodger Carlyle